COME
NOVEMBER

A NOVEL

NOVEMBER

SCOTT LORD

GREENLEAF
BOOK GROUP PRESS

This is a work of fiction. Although most of the characters, organizations, and events portrayed in the novel are based on actual historical counterparts, the dialogue and thoughts of these characters are products of the author's imagination.

Published by Greenleaf Book Group Press
Austin, Texas
www.gbgpress.com

Distributed by Greenleaf Book Group

For ordering information or special discounts for bulk purchases, please contact Greenleaf Book Group at PO Box 91869, Austin, TX 78709, 512.891.6100.

Design and composition by Greenleaf Book Group
Cover design by Greenleaf Book Group
Cover image © Shutterstock/Jonathan Weiss, Shutterstock/ pisaphotography, Shutterstock/Ka-TeRina14, Shutterstock/Here

Publisher's Cataloging-in-Publication data is available.

Print ISBN: 979-8-88645-052-1

eBook ISBN: 979-8-88645-053-8

To offset the number of trees consumed in the printing of our books, Greenleaf donates a portion of the proceeds from each printing to the Arbor Day Foundation. Greenleaf Book Group has replaced over 50,000 trees since 2007.

Printed in the United States of America on acid-free paper

23 24 25 26 27 28   10 9 8 7 6 5 4 3 2 1

First Edition

For my mother, Gloria Jeanne. Her stories about her trip to the UN in November 1947 with a group of Chicago high school newspaper editors gave me the idea for this novel. Her lifelong love and encouragement made me believe I could write it.

CONTENTS

PART I

2003

1

The study was her favorite room in the house. It was where she spent most of her time teaching English composition online to junior college students, talking on the phone, and writing poems and short stories for obscure literary magazines. She and Jim had decorated the room together—built-in bookshelves of dark California walnut, a Persian rug shot with red and gold, a black leather couch. The shelves were littered with their family's books, photos, and accumulated objects. They had worked across from each other at the big partners desk until he was too sick to sit up.

Jeanne gazed over the desk through the sliding glass door as she waited for her computer to boot up. The spring sun was climbing and there was a sliver of Santa Monica Bay a half mile away. Her view was unobstructed now that she'd finally moved Jim's computer and monitor into a closet. She supposed she should give them away. Maybe her granddaughter could use them. What would it cost to ship them to New York?

Even after a year, it hurt to see his empty chair across from her. Would she ever stop missing him? The desk was really too big for one person. She had tried spreading her things across the Maginot Line only they knew existed, first inching a small brass clock, then a wire pencil holder, and finally a stapler into territory she could now sadly claim was hers alone.

The first few months after he died, she had spent most of her days crying and sleeping. Friends had said the pain would recede. They didn't

say that about the loneliness though. It snaked its way through her and
wrapped itself around her heart. It was there waiting when she went to
sleep on her side of the bed; it was in the kitchen where she had cooked
for him; it was there when she returned to the empty house after a visit
or shopping or, last night, from two days in the hospital.

She had been spring-cleaning on Sunday—furiously scrubbing,
dusting, vacuuming, and polishing every surface in her house—when
suddenly she couldn't catch her breath. Her heart was skipping, then
pausing, then speeding, then thumping like a wobbly globe spinning
eccentrically on its axis. She had gone to the hospital because there was
no one to tell her it was nothing. "You'll be fine, just put your feet up for
a few minutes," Jim would have said.

"Definitely not a heart attack," Dr. Dahlberg, her cardiologist at St.
John's Hospital, had said last evening. "But I don't like the fluid buildup
in your legs. Given your age, uh—"

"Seventy-two," she had said impatiently.

"Right. Just a kid."

"Don't patronize me."

"I'm not, Jeanne," he had answered crisply. "I'm seventy-four. To me,
you're a kid. But I want to keep you on the monitor another night. We'll
do a cardiac catheterization first thing in the morning. That should give us
the answer." He snapped her chart shut as though the matter were decided.

"I'm going home," she said. "If you need to run more tests, I can do
them as an outpatient."

"Jeanne—"

"I want to go home," she said. "I spent enough time here last year,
when Jim was sick."

Dahlberg relented. "All right. But no caffeine and you have to promise to take the medicine I give you if your heart acts up again. Call first
thing to schedule the procedure."

Michael, her son, had been less understanding. "Mom, you're not
okay," he'd argued when she told him she was going home. "Two days
ago, you could barely breathe."

"You're exaggerating. But now we know it wasn't a heart attack,
thank goodness."

"Sure, but there are other kinds of heart problems. I checked your symptoms online. You could have congestive or constrictive heart failure."

"I *could* have a lot of things, but I don't." She sighed. He had always been a little panicky, especially after her divorce from his father long ago. He'd grown even more jittery since his wife, Kerry, and daughter, Alice, had moved to New York seven months before.

"I just couldn't catch my breath, so I got scared. For goodness' sake, I took a cab here. I didn't even call an ambulance," she said.

"Mom, what if something's really wrong?"

"I know you're worried. But I'm going to be okay. I just need to take care of myself. Believe me, I'm not going anywhere yet." Naturally the thought of her death was upsetting for Michael, who wasn't quite forty; at seventy-two, she was used to the idea.

"Okay," he grumbled, "I'll come get you."

"I took a taxi here and I can take one home."

"Mom—"

"It's fine." She put a smile in her voice. "I'm not being a martyr."

A lime-green Prius with *Taxi! Taxi! Taxi!* stenciled in white on the doors and roof was waiting for her at the hospital entrance. Despite her brave words to Michael, she grew anxious when it dropped her off in the semicircular drive of her dark house.

She had walked slowly through the empty rooms, switching on lights, first in the wood-beamed living room, then in the white-plastered halls, in the small formal dining room, and finally in the kitchen. The air was still filled with the smells of furniture wax and ammonia from her spring-cleaning.

Jeanne's house was in a development built for working-class families in the 1920s, when Santa Monica was just a sleepy beachfront town on the edge of Los Angeles. She bought it thirty years earlier, just before housing prices skyrocketed. The first time she'd walked through the door, she had felt at peace and that feeling had never left. There was a small lawn in front and a larger backyard cut into a slope where she now kept a vegetable garden.

It had been a desperate financial stretch for her. She had bargained the price down ruthlessly, borrowed money from everyone she knew, applied to dozens of banks to find the best mortgage, even tried to find a co-owner. Just this year, she had made her last payment and now, in that lovely legal phrase, owned her home free and clear.

She picked up the boxlike train case she had owned since high school and nervously mounted the stairs to her bedroom. Eight steps, then a landing, then nine more. Her heart and lungs protested the strain.

Once in her bedroom, she undressed and went into the tiled bathroom. She pinned up her hair, a stylist's artful mix of her natural gray and an approximation of her original silvery blond, and stepped into the shower. She made the water as hot as she could stand it and soaped away the astringent smell and contagious fear of two days in the hospital.

When she was finished, she wrapped herself in a bath towel and opened the door to let out the steam. She stood in front of the mirror, listening to the sounds the house seemed to make only when she was alone. She began applying moisturizer. The planes of her face had softened over the years and the large orbits of her blue-green eyes had deepened. As the mist on the mirror cleared, she saw the dread she had managed to keep at bay for the last two days and burst into tears, her shoulders shaking. She leaned against the counter and waited for the fit to pass. When it was over, she splashed her face with cool water and patted it dry.

She put on her favorite nightgown. It smelled fresh, because she had hung it outside to dry in the sea air rather than put it through the dryer with a chemical freshener. She slid into bed, but before putting her legs under the covers, she contemplated her ankles. Were they a bit less swollen than yesterday?

She switched off the lamp and pulled the duvet up to her chin. A motorcycle engine crackled and throbbed in the distance. Now that she was in bed at last, she couldn't fall asleep. She wondered if she would always feel this way, anxiously wondering if she would make it through the night. She lay awake for an hour, listening to her heart, her breathing, and the familiar night sounds of her house.

• • •

When she awoke in the morning, the anxiety had vanished. The disturbing sensation that her heart was bumping and straining against her chest was gone too. She put on her robe and went downstairs to the kitchen. Remembering the doctor's warning about caffeine, she reluctantly ignored her beloved espresso machine and made a cup of chamomile tea. *Because that's what old people do*, she grumped. *They drink calming cups of tea instead of hot jolts of fragrant coffee.*

For the first time in days, she was hungry. She took a cast-iron skillet from the hanging rack and set it on the stove over a low flame. She added a few drops of olive oil and, while the pan was heating, scrambled two large eggs in a bowl with a fork, adding a dash of salt and pepper and a spoonful of milk. When the oil was hot, she poured in the mixture and stirred it gently. While the eggs were cooking, she sent a couple slices of wheat bread down the toaster and retrieved a crock of butter and a jar of strawberry jam from the refrigerator.

She checked the clock as she took out two blue-and-white ceramic plates and set them on the stone counter by the stove. She needed to call the doctor to schedule the catheter procedure. When the food was ready, she put a piece of toast on each plate and carefully scooped half of the eggs by their side. Was she supposed to call his office or the hospital?

She carried the two dishes to the kitchen table and set them down, then stood staring dumbly at the needless second plate. She picked it up and briskly walked it to the sink.

Her appetite had vanished, but she forced down a few bites, then quickly washed the dishes. She shuffled to her office and sank into the chair at her desk. She switched on her computer to check the email that had accumulated over the last two days.

She saw his name, John McGrath, immediately amid the jumble of other emails. Her heart began to knock and clatter as though she had mainlined a forbidden double espresso. She'd felt the same way the first time they met when she was seventeen. Should she take one of her pills? The tip of her right forefinger quivered over her mouse as she debated whether to open the message or delete it unread. Was he dying? Was this a farewell, a last attempt at an overdue apology?

"Just read it, Jeanne. What could it hurt?" she imagined him saying.

She hated the way emails created the illusion they required immedi-ate action when there was really no need to hurry. She had all the time in the world. She slowly sifted through the dozen other emails in her inbox and worked for a while responding to and then deleting them.

Only the one remained.

She straightened her back, holstered her trigger finger in her bathrobe pocket, and looked out the window of her study. She forced herself to wait another minute. Finally, she returned her gaze from the window to her screen, drew her finger out of her pocket, and, as though she were unlock-ing Pandora's Inbox, tapped twice on the mouse. The email flowered open.

Hello Jeanne,

I know it's been a long time and I hope you don't mind me emailing you out of the blue, but something came up tonight that kind of involves you.

You remember I've always wanted to write about that earth-shattering week we shared in New York in '47—the unbe-lievable story they didn't want me to tell. Well, it's finally going to happen. A publisher asked me to write a memoir of my time there. With the war going on now in the Middle East, he thinks it might sell.

His time? It was her time, too.

So naturally I thought of you. There'll be a lot of research and it would be a big help if we could talk about those days. Except for Mrs. Eban, I think we're the only ones still around who know the whole story. I would love to pick your brain and compare notes. Maybe write some of it together?

I live in Todi, Italy, in an old farmhouse I'm turning into a B&B. I could always come to you, of course, but I remembered how much you love Italy. Would you consider coming here for a couple of weeks? I think I could talk my publisher into picking up your expenses and it would be wonderful to see you. I still remember our time together very fondly.

If you're able to open the picture I've attached, that's me in
front of my farmhouse. Haven't changed a bit, right? You could
stay here, there's plenty of room. Or there are some wonderful
places in town.

Needless to say, I know we didn't end well. Either time. Has it
really been thirty years? Anyway, I hope you'll say yes. Hey, what
could it hurt?

Love,
John

"What could it hurt?" She let out a derisive laugh that ended in a
slight snort—something that had been happening more frequently in
the last few years, to her undying shame.

He must be seventy-six now. No, the email was dated April 1, 2003.
April Fool's. His birthday. He was seventy-seven.

She tapped the attachment, and her screen was filled by a picture so
glossily perfect it could have served as an advertisement. The sky was an
oversaturated blue, the clouds ostentatiously fluffy, and the grass was dotted with red and yellow wildflowers. An exterior stone staircase led to the
second floor of the house, which had a perfectly weathered terra cotta roof.
There was a vine-laced pergola shading a long trestle table. John stood in
front of the house, looking directly into the camera.

He was dressed in faded jeans, a white shirt, and black lace-up work
boots. Although the photo was taken from a distance, she could see that
his once-black hair, which had begun to go gray thirty years ago, was now
completely white. He looked like a slimmer version of Robert Frost in
his later years—the same white hair, the same intimation of an inquisi-
tive and humorous intelligence. He didn't seem old. Would she to him?
She squinted through her reading glasses. She tried enlarging the picture,
but it smeared and blurred.

They were in shiveringly joyous, stingingly painful love when she was
seventeen. That was the story she liked to remember. They tried again
when she was forty-three and he shattered her heart. That was the story
she had tried to forget. But what did it matter? She was seventy-two. It

was too late for anything but memories. There were no love stories for people their age.

She thought of a phrase in his email, opened her browser, and typed in a name. There it was—last November in Tel Aviv, of complications from Alzheimer's. She should send a condolence note to Mrs. Eban who, along with her brilliant husband, had been so kind to her on that epic day. Jeanne would never forget the stifling crush of desperate people in the great hall and the dramatic roll call of all the countries of the world. She still sometimes dreamed of seeing the killer's malevolent face as he crouched in shadows like a predator high above the crowd—locked, loaded, and ready to murder the hope of millions.

Why write a book about it? The attack on 9/11 was still a searing wound in the soul of the Western world. Did anyone want to be reminded of where it all began?

Jeanne had never heard of Todi, but John was right about Italy. She had spent a glorious two weeks there in her twenties and had fallen hard for the country—the unencumbered emotions of its people, the passion that seeped from the city walls and village streets, the mesmerizing brightness of its sun, and the monuments to beauty everywhere. She still dreamed of returning one day.

Something inside her jolted back to earth. That was all this was, a silly dream. She had a sudden, unreasoning stab of rancor and her grip on the mouse tightened. She moved the cursor over the delete button, hammered her finger twice, and, with sour satisfaction, watched him disappear.

Her inbox was empty; not even hope remained behind.

2

Michael Hanson, phone in hand, stood looking out the window of his second-story office on Montana and Twelfth Street in Santa Monica. It was an inexpensive suite on an expensive street—just one small room and a secretarial station—but it was a prestigious address and that was important to him.

Diane, his secretary, went home early because of a childcare emergency. Ordinarily, Michael would have been annoyed, but somehow aiding Diane in her childcare efforts worked to assuage his considerable guilt regarding his daughter, Alice, who now lived on the other side of the country. His lawyer had told him that since she was sixteen, most judges would let her choose which parent she wanted to live with and, to no one's surprise but Michael's, she chose to live in New York City with her mother, Kerry.

With Diane gone, he had to answer his own phone, which was why he was now stuck talking to one of his disgruntled investors, Emily Poverstein. He held the receiver an inch or two away from his ear.

"Michael, you said I'd have my fifty-thousand-dollar investment back by January, but it's almost June," she said.

Mrs. Poverstein was one of ten investors he had sold on the Casa Palacios project, at fifty thousand each, which he had to personally guarantee. That had been the only way to convince them to trust him with their money. Real estate was booming then and it hadn't seemed like much of a gamble. Then all the trouble in the Middle East started. Weapons of mass destruction were everywhere, they said, and no one wanted to buy the expensive condominiums he and his partners were building.

"Well, it's actually April, but I know, it's absolutely wrong that they haven't paid you your money yet," he said in the low, comforting tones of a professional mourner.

"You told me I'd double my money!"

"Now, Mrs. Poverstein, I might have said that was *possible*, but if you look back at the materials you signed, you'll see that we were giving you our best projections, not making any promises."

"You know, I've been very patient, but I have half a mind to report you to—"

"Mrs. Poverstein," Michael interjected, his patience exhausted, "please don't say something we'll both regret."

"Sorry."

Michael drew a deep audible breath, an indulgent parent reluctantly preparing to reason with an unruly child. "I think you are being unfair. But," he said, holding up his hand as if she could see him taking a pledge, "I won't have an unhappy client. If you want me to take you out of your position, say the word. I'll write you my own check for your fifty thousand." Not that he actually had that much. "But if you wait, the projections as they stand now lead me to believe you won't be doubling your money—you'll be *tripling* it."

Mrs. Poverstein gulped. "Tripling?"

"Just be patient a little while longer. Remember, Emily, I'm in this with you." That, at least, was true. Michael had invested every penny he had in the project.

"If you really think so."

"I do."

"Tripling, you think?"

Michael did something he hadn't done since he was twelve. He crossed his fingers. "Tripling."

"All right then, I guess I'll stick with it."

"You won't regret it. Goodbye, Emily."

Michael was trembling. This was the third such call this week. His investors were nervous. Construction was six months behind schedule for no discernible reason and pre-sales were slow.

He walked from the window to the antique oak bar that stood in the corner near the window. It had belonged to his father. "My inheritance," he'd tell people. He poured an inch of Irish whiskey into a low tumbler and drank it off in one swallow. It had been a two-drink minimum kind of day, so he poured another, this time mixing in soda and ice. He took the fresh drink back to his desk, sank into the high-backed leather chair, and stared out the window into the gathering dusk. He looked around his modest office. He was turning forty this summer. If success was going to happen, shouldn't it have happened by now?

It was nearly five thirty. Damn! He'd meant to check on his mother. She picked up on the first ring.

"Hello?"

"Mom, it's me."

"Michael." The way she said his name always made him feel she was enormously glad to hear his voice. "How are you, honey?"

He smiled. "No, how are you?"

"I asked first."

"Come on," he said, "tell me."

"I'm fine, really. I spent most of the day reading. Went in the garden for a bit and took a walk around the block. I don't have classes because of spring break."

"You timed your hospital visit for spring break?"

"Of course. I didn't want to put anyone out." Her considerate nature had always been a joke between them. "It was wonderful just to be out in the sun. There was a little breeze coming from the ocean. Makes me feel like taking a trip."

"I know. I wish I could have gotten out of the office."

"How is work?"

Michael thought about confiding in her but rejected the idea. He trusted her to be sympathetic no matter what the problem, but this was different. The money he'd invested belonged to people like her, older folks who had trusted him with their retirement savings.

"Oh, you know, same old, same old. Real estate development isn't for sissies."

"You're not a sissy, Michael."

"I was just joking."

"I know," she said, forcing a chuckle. "Anything really wrong?"

"No, not at all."

"You'd tell me?"

"You'd be the first one I'd tell. You know I'm a momma's boy." They both laughed. It was a story from his childhood. It started when his parents told him they were separating. Their words were hardly out of their mouths when eight-year-old Michael blurted out, "I'm gonna live with Momma." It was one of his father's rare sober days. He had nodded grimly and, as he was leaving, Michael heard him say, "What do you expect? He always was a momma's boy. Kid's a sissy."

At first, Michael had seen his father every other Saturday. But soon he began to cancel their visits. Weeks, then months, would pass between them until eventually they ceased altogether. His mother gently explained to Michael that his father, while a good man in many ways, had a viciously intractable addiction to alcohol. He died when Michael was in college.

"You sure you're okay, Mom?"

"I'm sure. And I see the doctor again tomorrow. He's going to run a couple of tests in the office. I'll drive myself."

Michael didn't respond. He knew it irritated her to feel dependent. "Something else on your mind?"

"Well, yes. If you have a minute."

"I'm all ears."

"I got a funny email today."

Michael couldn't help laughing.

"Stop it," she said, a smile in her voice.

"It still cracks me up. Five years ago, you didn't own a computer—now you email like an old pro and teach classes online."

"You're exaggerating. Anyway, I got an email."

Michael, still laughing a little, said, "From an old lover, right?"

"Yes, as a matter of fact."

Michael stopped laughing.

"I . . . It's hard to talk about." She seemed to change her mind. "Actually, it's a long story. I'll tell you tomorrow. If you're really interested, that is."

"I am. You should get some rest, anyway, and I have a few calls to make." *A few more investors to soothe.* Maybe he should just tell her he needed her help.

"By the way," she said, "that lawyer you referred me to says the insurance company will pay off soon."

"Yeah?" he said quietly, struggling to sound casual at the mention of money. "He thinks they'll cave?"

"That's what he says."

Although it had been a year since his death, Jim's life insurance company still hadn't paid Jeanne the proceeds of his policy—one million dollars. The adjuster assigned to the case had raised questions about the pain medications Jim had been taking—implying he'd taken his own life, which would allow them to reject the claim. Jim's medical team had managed to douse that suspicion. Undeterred, the company then asserted there were technical deficiencies in Jim's original application and they were investigating the "possible concealment of a serious medical condition." It was then that Jeanne hired Michael's lawyer.

A million dollars. To a woman who owned her pricey home free and clear and had six figures in stocks and bonds. The thought of that much money made Michael almost physically ill. She could easily afford to help him out of his present difficulty.

"Mom?"

"Mm-hmm?"

No, not yet. "Nothing." It was too soon to ask for her help and to confess his failure. He said instead, "I'm just glad you're okay. Take it easy."

"Okay, honey, thanks for calling."

"Of course. Bye."

"Bye."

Michael hung up. He had planned to call his other investors but decided tomorrow would do. He grabbed his jacket, locked the door, and walked the mile to his two-bedroom apartment on Ocean at the end of Montana. Normally, he would have driven his Porsche 911 to the office, but it was ten years old and not as reliable as it once had been. Like a lot of things.

3

At six the next morning, Jeanne was in a taxi heading south. It was still dark as the car ascended the long upward curve of the road toward San Vicente Boulevard and stopped at a red light. While they waited, Jeanne watched the joggers who, despite the early hour, were using the broad median strip of the boulevard for their daily exercise. She was envious of their rude health. They were all ages, the boys without shirts despite the cold; the girls in ponytails and skin-tight exercise outfits; young mothers pushing bundled-up babies in jogging strollers; middle-aged business types getting in a workout before they headed to the office. And a fair sprinkling of seniors whose hearts were probably in tip-top condition and were no doubt training for a marathon.

The light turned green and her taxi continued along Seventh, turned east at Santa Monica Boulevard, and entered the parking circle of St. John's. The eastern sky was beginning to lighten over downtown Los Angeles.

"If I could get your date of birth?" said the hospital receptionist.

"June 14, 1930." Jeanne smiled. "Flag Day. Sounds more ancient every time I say it."

"Mrs. Carpenter, if you could just fill out these forms," the receptionist said, handing her a clipboard. Jeanne found a seat, then glanced around the room. The low lights and muted color palette were strangely depressing, although they were meant, she supposed, to be soothing.

Jeanne worked steadily, filling out the forms until she reached the line for next of kin. She started to write Michael's name, then stopped.

She scratched out what she had written and wrote in Kerry's name. For "Relationship" she wrote "Daughter." Kerry was the only family member she'd told about today's test. The forms finished, Jeanne stood up and returned them to the receptionist, who was on the telephone. She held up her hand. Jeanne waited obediently while she finished her call.

"Okay," she said, "let me check through these." She flipped through the pages, then asked, "Is your daughter, uh, Kerry, here with you?"

"No," Jeanne said.

"Is there someone to take you home?"

"I'll take a taxi."

"Okay, if you'd have a seat, someone will be out to get you in a few minutes for your procedure." The procedure was a catheterization.

"But you already did an EKG and an echocardiogram," she had protested to Dr. Dahlberg on the phone.

"I need it to confirm my diagnosis. I suspect there's an issue with the lining of your heart but can't be sure without this test."

"Does the test hurt?" Jeanne asked.

"Hurt?" She imagined Dr. Dahlberg's wrinkled face wrinkling a little more. "I'd say no. A little pressure at the neck where we make the insertion, but we numb the area. We give you light antianxiety medication to help you keep calm. But when I take the samples from your heart, it makes your heart jump."

"Jump?"

"That's right. Tends to freak people out." It was odd to hear him use the modern phrase. "I don't blame 'em. It can be scary if you haven't felt it before. But it's perfectly safe. I could knock you out if you really want me to—some people prefer that. But then you'll have to stay in the hospital for several hours after the procedure."

"Have you done many of these?"

"About five thousand, give or take."

"Well, you certainly sound like the right man for the job."

An hour later, Jeanne was lying on a metal table, wearing a drafty hospital gown, in a very chilly operating room. A camera-type device hovered over her chest. She could see the pictures it was taking of her heart on a nearby monitor. Dr. Dahlberg spoke in a low voice.

"Okay, here's the pressure . . ." She felt a hard pressure on her neck. "And that's it. I'm going to thread the electric lead through. In a moment, you'll feel your heart jump. Remember, that's perfectly normal."

She was completely unprepared when her heart suddenly gave a knock and a rattle, then seemed to stop. Jeanne panicked and tried to raise her head, but it was completely immobilized. "Um, is my heart still beating?"

"Your heart's still beating," the doctor chuckled.

"Wow."

"Bet you've never felt anything like that before."

But I have felt that before, a long time ago when I was seventeen.

Waiting in the recovery room made her think of Jim. How many times had she taken him to the hospital? If he were alive, he'd be with her today, holding her hand and reassuring her. It was one of the things she loved most about him: his reliability.

What if she had married John? He had never seemed like the hand-holding, calmly reassuring type.

The television in the room was tuned to CNN at low volume. Its anchor quietly repeated the day's stories about the fighting in Iraq, millions of protesters in the streets of the world's capitals, and the spread of a respiratory illness called SARS you could get if you traveled to Asia. The endless drone of the anchor made her sleepy. She closed her eyes.

"Sorry," Dr. Dahlberg said as he entered the room and plopped down on a chair. "I had three other procedures." He was tall, stoop-shouldered, with wispy gray hair. Liver spots dotted the backs of his hands, one of which grasped a large, ceramic coffee cup. He took a sip while he looked at the notepad in his lap. Jeanne imagined that forty years ago he would have had a cigarette going. He looked like a smoker.

"Ready?" he asked.

She nodded tightly. He wrinkled his brow and began to speak.

"Jeanne, as I suspected, you have what's called constrictive pericarditis. The lining around your heart, which is normally very flexible, has thickened and stiffened and is literally stuck to the muscle of your heart. It's like there is a cage around it that prevents the rest of the heart from beating as efficiently as it should. It's a form of heart failure."

Heart failure. She thought she had fainted but realized she hadn't because she could still hear Dr. Dahlberg speaking.

"Not to despair, though. We can treat this."

"With what? How?"

"We use anti-inflammatories to try to unstick the pericardium from the heart muscle."

Now it was Jeanne's turn to wrinkle her brow. "Anti-inflammatories?"

"Yes, like Advil and steroids. We'll also put you on a couple of other drugs. Since those have side effects, we have medicine you'll have to take to counteract them." Dr. Dahlberg pointed a finger in her direction. "Now, there's no assurance that the drugs will cure you. But they can sometimes slow the progress of the condition."

"Progress?"

"Yes, the lining can become stiffer and stiffer until . . ."

"Until my heart can't beat?" Now she was sure she was going to faint.

"Well, let's say until your heart becomes so inefficient your life would be in danger."

"What do you do then?"

He looked surprised, as though he thought she already understood this. "We have to operate, of course."

"And do what?"

"We remove the pericardium. Usually peels right off. Sometimes it's more difficult, kind of like taking bits of shell off a hard-boiled egg. People can live completely normal lives without the pericardium."

That didn't sound so bad. "So why not operate now?"

"Jeanne. It . . . it's open-heart surgery. We would have to stop your heart."

"Oh." Her stomach sank. "And at my age, who knows if you could start it again," she whispered.

"Well, maybe." They were both silent for a while.

"I know this is a cliché, but how long do I have?"

"To live?" he asked with a smile.

She nodded, tears in the corners of her eyes.

"Jeanne, my father practiced medicine until he was ninety-four. I plan to do the same." He took both of her slender hands in his large strong ones and looked in her eyes. "When the time comes for me to hang up my stethoscope, you'll still be around. You and I are going to grow old together. Well, older," he laughed. "You'll die with this, not of this."

"Can I do normal activities? What about my diet?"

"Jeanne, you should live your life. It'd be nice if you were on some sort of low-fat, low-sodium diet. Exercise all you want. The better shape you're in, the better you'll feel. If something makes you tired or breathless, rest. But you have the arteries of a teenager. That's something else I checked when we were in there. You're not going to have a heart attack or stroke. Any questions?"

"No, I guess not."

He waited another moment, then shrugged and started to leave.

"What about traveling?" she blurted out to his departing back.

He turned around. "Where to?"

Italy.

"Oh, I'm not really sure."

"Not mountain climbing or deep-sea diving?"

"No." She managed a weak smile.

"Best thing for you. No reason to sit around worrying all day. Like I said, you should live your life."

"Okay."

"Younger people don't understand," he said. "We look different than we used to, but nothing's really changed, has it? We still feel as passionately, desire as deeply, and hurt as bad as the silliest teenager."

She nodded but didn't—couldn't—reply.

• • •

That evening, sitting quietly in her study, she thought of what the doctor had said. She opened her email's "Deleted" folder, found John's email, and moved it back to her inbox. She read it once, then read it again. *Still remember our time together very fondly . . . I hope you'll say yes . . . What could it hurt?* What indeed? She opened the picture and sat staring at it for a long time.

4

Kerry looked at her name printed on the slick paper of the program from her performance the night before and wondered if it was the reason she wasn't more successful. "Kerry Hanson" didn't sound like the name of a famous opera singer. It sounded like the name of a clerk at the Jewel grocery store in her hometown of Evanston, Illinois.

Her character, Suzuki, was the maid for the tragic heroine in Puccini's *Madama Butterfly*. It would be Kerry's third Suzuki this season, in this instance for the Paragon Opera Company in Lower Manhattan. There was nothing intrinsically wrong with singing the same part over and over again. Her lyric mezzo-soprano voice was well suited for it and mezzo-sopranos everywhere made a good living singing all those friend-of-the-heroine roles. But she hadn't endured tens of thousands of hours of practice to spend her career singing best-friend roles in small houses. No, she wanted glorious, life-altering success. She dreamed of thousands screaming "*Brava!*" as she bowed and smiled from the massive stage of the Metropolitan Opera in New York City, of singing notes so clear and pure that the crowd's admiration would approach worship.

So far, the closest she had come to singing at the Met was when she took the subway uptown to her voice teacher's apartment around the corner from Lincoln Center.

She knew that she had to make a major move if she was going to have a real career, and it hadn't been hard to make the decision to put her dull, safe marriage on hold and move to New York. The make-or-break age for sopranos was thirty-five. If your career was not on a sharp upward trajectory by then, it was time to look into teaching music at high schools and giving voice lessons to overprivileged ten-year-olds. She was thirty-seven, although people always told her she looked years younger. Looks counted in these days of filmed performances, far more than in times past when opera fans would willingly accept a forty-five-year-old, two-hundred-fifty-pound woman playing a teenage Japanese geisha as long as she could hit the money notes.

Kerry was tall, gently curved, and blond, her complexion creamy and her large blue eyes clear. She'd managed to avoid the weight gain that dogged so many singers.

Spoleto could—had to—change everything.

She was up for the lead part of Dorabella in *Così Fan Tutte*, Mozart's evergreen comedy of love and infidelity. It was being performed this summer at the Festival of Two Worlds in Spoleto, Italy, with one of the world's great conductors, James Nelson. It could make her career. It was that kind of part and that important a venue. Her audition had gone well. She hoped to hear good news at any moment.

She cleared the remains of her lunch from their tiny, round kitchen table. When she and her daughter moved to New York last summer, they had found a small two-bedroom apartment in a decidedly down-market part of Manhattan. The ad had said it was in the smugly hip East Village, but it was actually in the one-day-hope-to-be-dope-dealer-free Bowery, just off Delancey. And the rent was *still* thirty-two hundred dollars a month for six hundred square feet, in a building whose stairwells smelled of garbage. At least she and Alice each had their own bedroom and there was enough space in the larger of the two for a desk, where Alice could do her homework. The living room was the size of an elevator; the doorway to the bathroom was so narrow they had to turn sideways to enter.

Alice would be home in an hour. She usually slumped through the door in bruised silence. She was acutely unhappy about moving to New York and made Kerry suffer for it.

"It's so unfair," she had screamed at her parents when told of the need for her to make a choice. Since then, Alice played on Kerry's guilt with the untutored genius every teenager possesses. Kerry responded with the occasional bribe. Her latest was a pair of tickets to a concert at Madison Square Garden featuring the rapper 50 Cent. When she'd given her the tickets at breakfast, Alice had allowed a trace of a smile to cross her lips before frowning.

"These aren't very good seats."

Kerry kept her temper. "It's sold out, but Curtis, our corner dope dealer, moonlights as a scalper. These are the best I could do without raffling off a body part."

She couldn't understand Alice's love for rap. There was a time when she shared Kerry's love for classical music—opera in particular.

"I'd rather do three hours of homework than sit through another opera," she had said. When Kerry responded with a disparaging comment about 50 Cent, Alice had said, "I listened to your music all my life. Why can't you let me enjoy mine?" But how could anyone seriously contend there was any comparison between the soaring glory of "Un Bel Di" and the mindless thumping of "In Da Club"? What were they teaching her at the fancy private girls' school in which Kerry had managed to get her enrolled?

Which reminded her, she needed to call Jeanne about her test results and she would have to bring up the monthly tuition payment. Michael's check was two weeks overdue.

She picked up her new phone and hit the speed-dial button.

"Hi, Mom." Kerry had started calling Jeanne "Mom" when she and Michael were married. "I always wanted a daughter," Jeanne had said.

"How did it go with the doctor?"

"Well, it's sort of good news, bad news. I have this very minor inflammation in the lining of my heart. But they can handle it with medication."

"What kind?"

"That's the good news part. Advil."

"Advil? How bad could it be, then?"

"I know," Jeanne said. "Doctors like to scare you to death. So how are you, honey? And how's my granddaughter?"

"We're fine. Alice is doing okay in school. Which reminds me," she said, as though the thought had just occurred to her, "the school said they didn't get this month's tuition. I'm really sorry to bring it up, but I can't get Michael to answer me."

"No, you *should* bring it up. I know he's been busy, but, tell you what, you email me the information and I'll take care of it. Michael can pay me back later."

"That'd be great. I hate to bug him." She laughed. "I don't want to be that kind of ex-wife."

"You're not an ex-wife."

"I know, I didn't mean—"

"Don't give up like that. You're married."

"I know I'm married, Mom." Kerry had been separated for months, but she hadn't gone on dates and laughed off occasional flirtations. That wasn't why she'd come to New York.

"I could use some advice," Jeanne said.

"Sure. What's up?"

"Well, I got an email." Jeanne told her about the invitation from John.

"So," Kerry said, "do you want to see him?"

"I don't know, maybe."

"That would be totally adorable!"

"You make it sound silly."

"I didn't mean—"

"You wouldn't say that if I was your age. Whatever it might be, it isn't 'adorable.'"

"Sorry."

"Oh, I don't know," Jeanne burst out. "Maybe it is silly. I mean, I'm almost seventy-three and suddenly I'm going to fly six thousand miles and see an old boyfriend. Who does something like that?"

"I guess it depends on how you feel about the old boyfriend. It doesn't sound like it ended well." She could tell that Jeanne wanted to go and she just wanted a little push.

"Uh, no."

"So tell me, was he good-looking?"

"Oh, yes," Jeanne said.

"How's he look now?"

"Well, older. But you know, good."

"What was he like?" Kerry asked.

"Really something special. Whip-smart, brave, full of Irish charm.

His parents were from County Cork. He could talk about anything—history, literature, politics, you name it. And he wrote like a dream. He had a way of making me feel like I was the most important person in the world. You know, I was a tomboy as a kid, kind of gangly. I always thought the only thing special about me was my intelligence. If someone didn't see that, they didn't see me. John saw. He was three years older—which matters at that age—and was in the war. He swept me off my feet without hardly trying."

"I bet he's interested in more than your memory, Mom."

"Oh, come on. I'm sure it's just about his book. He was always ambitious. Anyway, I'm so much older now."

"You look amazing."

"For my age, you mean."

Kerry heard a ping and the message symbol appeared on her phone. Was it Nelson? Why oh why hadn't she paid for call waiting? *Damn, damn, damn!*

"I have to check a message."

"Sure, go ahead."

"In a minute. But if you want my advice, I think you should do it. It'll be an adventure. What's the worst case? You have an awkward lunch and it doesn't work out. But you still get to have a nice vacation in—hey, do you know where he lives in Italy?"

"In a town called Todi. I looked it up. It's in Umbria."

"That's so weird! The job I'm waiting to hear about is in Spoleto. Also in Umbria."

"I might go if you were there," Jeanne said.

"You could ask Michael to go."

"I doubt he would."

"He'd do it if you ask him. I was going to take Alice. How about instead she travels with you and Michael? You know how much she loves being with you."

"She did until she found out I'd never heard of 50 Cent," Jeanne said.

"Oh, baloney. She's going through her teenage years, which are just like her terrible twos except she sasses back. Look, this way you keep it casual. Say you'd be happy to chat about his book. You're coming to see your daughter-in-law perform and you'll be in the area. See where it goes."

"He'll think I'm making it up."

"So what? It's true. Mostly. And it would be good for Michael and Alice to spend some time together."

"That would be good," Jeanne said. "I can't stand seeing them so mad at each other. Just makes me want to shake them."

"Uh, well, I wouldn't force it," Kerry said. "She's just being a teenager."

"You make it sound like a disease."

"Something like that. But at least she'll grow out of it," Kerry said.

"And then get old—I'm not sure which is worse."

"Mom, are you sure you're okay?"

"Yes, I'm just feeling a little sorry for myself. I'll be fine. Now go. And good luck!"

Kerry's trembling fingers dialed voicemail and at once she heard a cool, female voice saying, "This message is for Kerry Hanson. Maestro Nelson will discuss your audition with you today at four thirty. Please be prompt." She gave an address in the West Seventies.

Kerry looked at her watch. Three thirty! Only an hour to change and get uptown in the middle of rush hour. She went to her bedroom and pulled one of her two audition outfits out of the closet, a wine-red silk dress with cap sleeves and a modest décolletage. It was wrinkled, but her other good dress was at the cleaners. She picked out a pair of flats so she wouldn't tower over the diminutive conductor.

Quick, quick, quick! Grabbing her purse, she found a Post-it, scribbled a quick message to Alice, slapped it on the fridge, and raced out the door. She ran down the four flights of stairs, crashed through the lobby door, and stopped a passing cab. *He wouldn't see me in person just to give me bad news, would he?*

Distracted by her thoughts, she forgot to tell the driver to take Seventy-Second Street through the park instead of Sixty-Fifth because of construction and now they were stopped dead. *Shit, shit, shit!* She contemplated running the last half mile, but the signalman waved them through, and the taxi rocketed forward. She made it to her destination, a plain brownstone, with a minute to spare. Taking a deep breath, she forced herself to walk slowly up the stoop into the lobby. She gave her name to the doorman and he gestured to the elevator.

On the fourth floor, the elevator opened and James Nelson answered the door at her first knock. He had light brown hair just going gray. His head seemed a trifle large for his narrow shoulders.

"Thanks so much for coming," he said with an easy smile on his boyish face, reaching out his hand. She could hear remnants of his Bronx childhood in his voice. They walked through a dark hall into an aggressively elegant room. Even in her flats, she was taller.

"I don't want to keep you in suspense, Kerry," he said, going to a sideboard. "I want to offer you Dorabella. I hope you're still available. Can I get you anything to—?" He stopped and turned because she had emitted a decidedly unmusical sound that was somewhere between a sob and a sharp gasp.

"Kerry, are you okay?"

She took a deep breath and nodded, smiling brightly, too overwhelmed to speak.

"Maybe you should sit down. I was going to offer you water, but maybe you could use a drink?"

She shook her head and at last was able to say, "Water, please," then added, "Um, I think I would like to sit down." She moved to a low chair, heavily upholstered in expensive fabric, and sat.

Nelson handed her a glass of water. "You're sure you're okay?"

Kerry snapped to—she didn't want him to think she was "trouble." Only the famous could afford to be trouble and still get hired.

"I'm fine. It was just such a . . . it's just such good news. I'm sorry."

"Don't be sorry. I know where you are in your career. I know what this means to you. One of the great parts of my job is to be able to give good news." He went on, "You gave a great audition. You know you have the technical chops, but, just as important, your voice will blend perfectly with the other leads."

"Thank you."

"Can you stay awhile? I'd like to talk to you about what happens next."

"Sure, as long as you need me."

"Let's go to the piano. There are things I'd like you to start working on right away."

She stood up—steadier now—and noticed for the first time that there was a Steinway grand in a corner of the room. Where had that materialized from? She felt dizzy again.

Nelson sat at the piano and turned to her. "I know you've sung this before. But let's go through it like it's your first time, all right?"

Kerry nodded enthusiastically. They worked through her character's first solo slowly while her voice warmed up, Nelson making technical comments as she sang. When they were finished, he nodded with approval.

"Very nice. There are some marvelous solo pieces in the opera, of course. But the difference between a good *Così* and a great one is in how well the ensembles are performed, those transcendent harmonies Mozart wrote. The principals have to blend exactly. If they do, you really have something special. If not, well, it's just another night at the opera. I don't do those." He was saying that if she couldn't deliver at the highest level, it would have been better not to have gotten the part at all.

The maestro began to play again and for the next hour, they worked meticulously through each of Dorabella's scenes in his heavily marked copy of Mozart's miraculous score. She could feel her throat warm and her body vibrate and, as sometimes happened, a part of her seemed to rise to a higher plane, where she imagined her gleaming voice shooting silvered streaks of sound across a sapphire sky. It was a feeling like no other, which could not help but make the rest of life seem disappointing.

5

Alice stood at the dingy entrance to the subway station at Eighty-Sixth and Lexington. She was wearing the light sweater and skirt of her school's spring uniform. She wiggled her feet and swung her arms to stay warm in the biting April wind.

She didn't look like her mother. Kerry was tall and slender; Alice was stubby. Kerry's hair was blond and flowing; Alice's short, dark-brown hair was a tangled mess.

Geoffrey had said he'd meet her at three thirty, but it was almost four. She was freezing. *Screw it—it's not as if I really like him.* But almost anything was better than going home to her tiny apartment and fending off her mother's questions about how her day had been, was she making friends, did she like her teachers. She decided to wait a little longer.

Jesus, it was unbearable. How could they expect her to live in a room no bigger than a closet? In a building that didn't even have an elevator? How, she wanted to scream, could she have any of those stuffy girls visit her when it stunk of garbage and there was literally no room to sit down? Assuming their drivers would risk their Lincoln Navigators in the Bowery.

And a motherfucking girls' school. Her mother had announced that she would be going to Curtis, a fashionable school on Manhattan's Upper East Side, like she was giving her a new car. Alice had rebelled, committing every angry, rebellious, guilt-inducing act in her arsenal. It was bad enough they had to move to New York because her parents had separated, but to have to go to a goddam girls' school, wear a shitty uniform, and sit around with a bunch of trust fund skanks and no boys was totally insane.

All of which could have been avoided if her mother had just done what her father had wanted her to do and taken the teaching job at USC. If she had, they could've all stayed together. They argued about it for months until her mother abruptly announced she was moving to New York and told Alice she had to decide whom she wanted to live with.

"Why can't I stay with Grandma?" she had asked, then stood trembling in a dark hall and listened to her parents argue about it through their closed bedroom door. Their pacing shadows flitted across the strip of light at the bottom of the door.

"For chrissakes, Kerry, she's seventy-two. The last thing she needs is to babysit a difficult teenager."

Difficult? It was like he'd hit her.

"You could ask her, Michael."

"I don't want to put her in that position."

"Oh, bullshit—what you don't want is for her to think your daughter would rather live with her than with you. Forty years old and you're still scared to death of what your mother thinks."

"I'm not forty."

"That's the least important part of what I just said."

"Goddam it, Kerry, if you'd just realize you're never going to be some world-famous opera diva. Don't get me wrong, I think you're a wonderful singer—I always have. But if it was going to happen, it would have by now. Even your teachers say that. Be a grown-up and take the job at USC."

"Is that what grown-ups do, Michael—settle?"

"Yes. They do what they have to do for the good of their families."

"Well, I'm not going to settle. I have three good job offers in New York this season and I'm going to accept them." And so it went.

In the end, Alice didn't really have a choice, although it might have been a different story if she had known about the girls' school. Even after eight months, she couldn't get used to a school where the only guys were a gym teacher and the janitor. No boys. Unbelievable. No guys to flirt with, to dress up and makeup for, to talk about with her friends, to go on dates with. Not that she'd been a big hit with the boys at the progressive school in LA she'd attended. But at least there'd been the possibility. Now, nothing, which explained why she had been willing to go to Starbucks last week with Lydia Wadleigh's unappealing brother, Geoffrey. By the time she found out that, in addition to his other deficiencies, he was a sophomore, they were already on their second mocha and it was too late to bail. But he was okay to talk to. He didn't make her feel self-conscious, not like some of the guys at her old school, who walked around in T-shirts and baggy shorts halfway down their ass and acted like they were doing her a favor if they spoke to her.

She checked the pretty watch with the colored band Grandma had given her last Christmas. If she didn't go now, she'd have to wait another twenty minutes for the next train. She had started down the dirty chipped steps when she heard Geoffrey's deep voice bark her name, loud enough to be heard above the car horns, delivery trucks, and gunning engines.

"Alice! Alice, wait, please wait." *God, he's so lame.* She pretended she hadn't heard him, but he bounded up to her like a big puppy, his long, red hair and khaki-colored jacket flapping around him.

"So sorry," he said breathlessly. "We got kept after. There was a bomb threat and they wouldn't let us go until the cops said it was okay. Everybody's still so paranoid." Since 9/11, he meant. "We couldn't use our phones or anything or I woulda called you." He took a deep breath. "Sorry."

"It's okay," Alice said, shaking her head dismissively. She put a hand to her face as though she were scratching her chin but really to cover up a tiny pimple.

"Hey, you're shivering—take my coat." He stripped it off and put it around her shoulders. Its musky scent enveloped her.

"Do you still want to go to Starbucks?"

"Yeah, but let's get it, then walk to the park or something," she said.

"I thought you were cold."

"Not now. I got your jacket."

He gave a honking laugh. "Let's do it, then. We could smoke."

God, he's so childish. Like smoking is such a big deal.

They got their drinks and walked toward the park. She was never sure about how to move. Were her arms swinging too much? Should she put them through the sleeves of his jacket or wear it like a cape? But it didn't matter—it was just Geoffrey. Twenty minutes later, they were sitting on a bench on a path near Central Park's Great Lawn. She was warmer now, thanks to her mocha and his jacket. "So," Geoffrey said, "do you want to smoke?"

"I don't smoke. It's stupid."

"Not cigarettes," he said.

"Oh, yes, absolutely," she said, trying to sound casual, although she'd only tried pot once at a party and hadn't liked it. "Is it cool in the open like this?"

"Oh, yeah. I do it here all the time. The cops don't care. I hear that some of the park police light up. Here, let me just—" He reached into a pocket of his jacket she still wore. She felt his hand root around near her thigh but acted like she didn't notice. He pulled out a plastic lighter and a joint. He fired it up and they passed it back and forth. Geoffrey watched her and said, "No, no, you're blowing it out too quick. Like this." He took a deep lungful of smoke and held it. As he reached the end of his endurance, he comically expanded his cheeks and crossed his eyes. She laughed. When he could hold it in no longer, he blew out the smoke and passed her the joint. She did as instructed and held the smoke until she felt dizzy. Just as she handed the joint back to Geoffrey, she saw a police officer walking toward them.

"Oh, come on, guys. We can smell that from the house." He pointed to the park precinct building not a hundred feet away through the trees. "I gotta take you in."

He shook his head in bored irritation, took the joint from Geoffrey's hand, put it out, and carelessly dropped it into a plastic bag. He found the lighter in the coat pocket and put that in the bag as well.

• • •

After two and a half agonizing hours at the precinct house, Alice and her mom were in the back of a taxi heading home. The cop had treated everything as routine. There were forms to fill out and appearances to arrange. Geoffrey was under sixteen and so would appear in Family Court in two weeks. Since Alice was over sixteen, her case would be reviewed by the district attorney, who would then decide whether to prosecute her for possession.

As they were leaving the precinct, Geoffrey had pulled her aside and said, "I told them it was mine, that I was the only one smoking it, that you didn't have any. Okay?"

"Oh, yes, you're my hero," she'd replied, rolling her eyes, "considering the cop saw me hand you the joint."

Traffic was heavy and it took forty-five tense, silent minutes to go the relatively short distance to their building. While her mother paid the driver, Alice jumped out and ran up the stairs. As she passed the kitchen, she saw a yellow Post-it note on the fridge. "Got a callback! Wish me luck!!!"

She stared at the yellow square of paper for what felt like a very long time. Her mother came into the kitchen, took the note, crumpled it up, and dropped it into the wastebasket without a word.

Alice went to her room and softly closed her door. She could hear her mother in her bedroom crying, which made her feel even worse. She started crying too. She took out the slick new Sidekick PDA her mother had given her and dialed.

"Hello?"

"Grandma, I'm in trouble."

"Big trouble?"

Alice sniffled and said, "Medium, I'd say."

"Why don't you tell me all about it?" Alice could hear her grandmother clattering around her kitchen and settling herself in for a long chat. With an inexpressible sense of comfort and relief, she poured her troubles into the ear of the one person in her life who had never let her down. Alice had once asked her why grandparents and grandchildren get along so well. She had smiled and said, "A long time ago, I saw a comedian named Sam Levenson at a nightclub in New York. He told a joke: 'The reason grandparents and grandchildren get along so well is that they have a common enemy.' Maybe that's it."

"Is that all?" her grandmother asked when Alice finished telling her story. "You took a couple of puffs on a joint?"

"Yeah," Alice said.

"Well, I'll tell you, I can't believe they even bother with pot anymore. I think it's ridiculous to waste everyone's time. I'm sure it'll be all right."

"You think?"

"Of course, honey. A lot of people think it should be legalized anyway."

Alice was silent a moment, then said, "I guess I feel worst about making my mom upset. She was at some big audition when I called her. It must've been embarrassing to get called 'cuz your kid's in jail."

"I'm sure it was. Look, Alice, you can't change what happened. But you can make sure your mom knows you're sorry. That's the grown-up way to handle this."

"You're right, Grandma. I'll apologize in the morning."

"Now, Alice. It won't get any easier if you wait. I guarantee it will make you both feel better." If one of her parents had given her an order like that, she would have shut them down with a rude comment. But it was different coming from her grandmother.

"Okay, Grandma. 'Night."

"Good night, honey."

Alice crept to her mother's door, gave a tiny knock, and called softly, "You still awake?"

"Yes," her mom answered softly.

Alice walked in. The room was dark. "Can I come in with you?"

"Sure." Her mother scooted over and Alice climbed under the covers. Lying there felt strange but familiar. When she was little, she'd come into her parents' bedroom and beg her mom to sing to her, one song after another, until she fell asleep. As she got older, she came less and less and then one day stopped altogether.

Alice snuggled closer in the dark and her mom began to gently stroke her tangled hair.

"Mom?"

"Yes?"

"I miss Dad."

"Of course you do."

"Do you think he misses me? I think he's glad I'm gone."

"Not at all. He loves you—he misses you, too."

"Do you miss him?"

Her mother paused for what seemed like a long time. "Sometimes."

Alice began to cry. "Do you think I'll have to go to jail? Or they'll kick me out of school?"

"No, no, of course not."

"I'm so, so sorry," Alice sobbed.

Her mom put her arms around her and hugged her close. "I know you are. Everything is going to be okay," she said, but Alice only cried harder.

6

"Jack! Signore! *Attenzione!*"

Jack McGrath—only his few remaining Chicago friends still called him John—looked up and saw the huge wood beam teeter for a moment on the edge of the scaffolding, then slip out of the rope looped around one end. With a clumsy back step, he tripped and tumbled out of the way just before the beam smashed the tile floor where he had been working. Riccardo Capotosti, the man who had shouted the warning, rushed to him and cried, "Jack, Jack, *stai bene?*"

"*Sí, sí, sto bene,*" Jack answered in functional Italian. He slowly rose to his feet and brushed the dust off his shirt. His elbow ached where it had cracked against the floor. "What the hell happened, Ricci?"

Riccardo was his *geometra*, a combination architect, engineer, surveyor, and project boss essential to any building project in Italy. Only a *geometra* could steer you through the Byzantine Italian bureaucracy, knew the appropriate bribes to secure building permits from the venal local planning authority, and keep nosy tax officials at bay. He would also prepare building plans in the proper form, hire the workers, and oversee the project to completion. Riccardo was in his midfifties, a square truck of a man, bald and red-faced. He was seldom at the house more than a few hours a day. The rest of his time was spent holding court in his favorite bar in Todi.

The accident was probably Riccardo's fault, but he assumed a stern expression and said, "Let me talk to these *stronzi*." He fired a stream of incomprehensible Sicilian at the four Calabrian laborers who, without so much as a glance at Jack, had descended the scaffolding and were matter-of-factly reattaching the huge beam to the lifts and pulleys that differed little from the tools and devices used by the *lavoratori* who had built the farmhouse five hundred years ago. Jack was certain Riccardo spoke Sicilian so that he wouldn't understand their conversation. After a few minutes of loud back-and-forth accompanied by much crude gesturing, Riccardo shook his head and motioned him outside.

They walked out the newly installed entry door and Riccardo stopped to light another in an endless chain of Marlboro Reds.

"They've smashed up two days' tile work," Jack said. "Not to mention almost killing me. Is there any point asking who's going to make reparations?" The word in Italian, *riparazione*, was so much more musical than the English word.

Riccardo shrugged. "Jack, they're poor workers; where they gonna get the money? It's just part—"

"I know, it's part of the cost of the work." Jack had moved to Todi from Milan upon his retirement from full-time journalism ten years earlier. Two years ago, he decided to sink his entire life savings, including his pension, into the purchase and renovation of the farmhouse, known as *Casale Leonardo*, with the idea he would run it as a fancy inn for well-to-do tourists to support himself. But now his money had all but run out. Whenever he asked Riccardo when the work would be done, all he got was a shrug.

"Signor Jack, why you want this kind of worry?" Riccardo had said to him three months ago when he told him his money was almost gone. "Let me arrange a loan. Very standard. They give you half a million, I supervise it all, you pay them back out of earnings. No paperwork, no mortgage—a handshake only!" Jack had declined, knowing that only one kind of lender would make that sort of loan. They were no different here than the loan sharks he'd known when he was a young crime reporter in Chicago.

But what a relief it would be to have the money. He could finish the work properly and buy the endless list of furnishings, fixtures, and supplies he still needed. And the place was sure to do well. There were many other small inns in Tuscany and Umbria that were making money hand over fist from American and English tourists. Staring down at his dusty work boots, he made a decision. "Ricci, I think maybe it's time I talk to your friends."

Ricci exhaled a lungful of smoke and smiled, showing teeth stained from wine, coffee, and tobacco. "*Bene, bene.* Now you're talking. You won't regret it, I swear to you."

"That doesn't mean I'll do it," he said, but they both knew he would.

Jack walked down the gravel drive. When he reached his car, a battered, black Alfa Romeo sedan, he turned to look at the house. Its beauty thrilled him every time.

It had been his idea to complete the renovations to the exterior first so he could use pictures of it in online advertisements. "Jack, you're crazy," Ricci had said. "Finish inside. Then rent it out while we finish the outside." The house looked perfect—the thick stone walls, the new windows, and the restored wood trim were finely crafted. The grounds were filled with roses, lilac, lavender, lemon trees, and sunflowers. A stone fence ringed the property, covered with wisteria and blackberry vines. Ancient oak trees stood guard. It was a place to live and write and think, one that could sustain him financially and allow him to live out what remained of his life in quiet beauty, a refuge from the violent world that seemed ever more determined to destroy itself.

He ached at the thought of having come this far only to fail. He would do whatever he had to do to complete it, even if it meant borrowing money from Ricci's friends. Opening the car door, he yelled to Riccardo, "I have a meeting in town. I'll be back in a couple of hours."

Jack drove the winding road toward the medieval town of Todi, which sat on a tall, two-crested hill overlooking the Tiber River. Todi was in Umbria, the so-called green heart of Italy, one hundred miles north of Rome. As he negotiated curve after curve, he put the house out of his mind. This morning, he had received Jeanne's reply to his email.

He still didn't know what to make of it.

He was surprised to have had any answer at all. He'd written her after a birthday dinner given for him by some friends in the expatriate literary community. The meal had been lubricated with wine and brandy. Talk of the current war in the Middle East had naturally led to a discussion of his coverage of the creation of Israel in the early days of the United Nations, about which he had broadly hinted he had a great untold story.

One of the guests, Roland Schafnitz, was a semiretired editor for an American publisher. He had thinning, sandy-gray hair and freckled, paper-dry skin. Schafnitz cornered him after dinner and led him outside to the elegant garden. He offered Jack a Montecristo from a leather case and took one for himself. He ignited them both with a gold Dunhill lighter and, when they were going, said, "I've always been an admirer of yours, Jack, going way back. Never forget your stories on the first Gulf War. They were brilliant."

"Thanks." He sent a plume of cigar smoke into the pine-scented air and waited for the editor to get to the point.

"You ever think of doing a book on the UN thing you mentioned?"

"Sure. Always seemed like it might make a good one," Jack said.

"Can you tell me the big secret?"

"Well, Roland, I could tell you, but then I'd hafta—" He laughed and drew a finger across his throat.

"You tell me and, if it's any good, we might publish you."

"Thought you were retired."

"Mostly, but I can still pull the trigger on a project."

"It's a long story."

"I got time. Let me get us a couple more brandies."

When Roland returned with their drinks, they sat on a wrought iron bench in the warm night air and Jack told him the whole story.

"Is that all true?"

Jack nodded. "Every word."

"You coulda been killed."

"Almost was."

"Then they asked you to bury the story?"

"Yeah, just the part about the assassin. It was the right thing to do, but man, it hurt! I was the only reporter who knew what happened."

"And that's the only thing that kept you from telling the whole story before now, your promise to them?"

"More or less."

Roland nodded thoughtfully. "It's good, really good. Tell me more about the girl. Not the Syrian one—the girl from Chicago."

"Jeanne? Really special. She was editor in chief of her school paper, straight A student, smart, pretty, and a heart of gold."

Roland looked amused. "Sounds like she got under your skin. The one that got away?"

He forced a laugh. "Maybe."

"So a seventeen-year-old girl visits the UN for a civics lesson and gets involved in one of the biggest stories of the century. Jesus." Roland looked off in the distance. "That'll sell it."

"What do you mean?"

"Jack, like I said, you got a good story. But what you need for a breakthrough book is all those women of a certain age who still buy books. With the girl front and center, you'd have a shot at getting them. Would she cooperate in writing it?"

"Maybe. We haven't exactly kept in touch."

The editor stood up. "Talk to her, Jack. Get her involved and we have a deal. An eyewitness memoir about a week in New York that shook the world."

"Lake Success."

"What?"

"Most of it happened in Lake Success and Queens. If we do make a deal, I'd need an advance."

"How much you thinking?"

"A hundred?"

Roland laughed. "Woodward gets a hundred. How about twenty?"

"Fifty."

"I'll see what I can do," Roland said, putting out his hand. Before he allowed Jack to take it, he said, "But you'll get the girl, right?"

Jack smiled. "It's done." They shook.

When he returned home after dinner, full of wine and remembrance, he wrote his email to Jeanne. He woke the next morning with a bad hangover sharpened by embarrassment and regret. Had he said too much? Too little? He realized, with a shock, he was afraid. Afraid of trying to write a book but even more afraid of seeing Jeanne again, that he wouldn't measure up to the man she remembered.

It's done, Jack, forget it. She won't even answer.

He was wrong. Her response had come last night. He was confused. If she hadn't answered, he would have understood. If she had been dismissive or rude, he would have cringed but moved on. What he was not prepared for was her blithe acceptance of his invitation and her downright jolly tone. He ran through her email in his head as he drove the winding road. His bruised elbow hurt every time he twisted the wheel through a tight turn.

"Dear John," it began. "I was delighted to hear from you and about your good news. We always said that would make an exciting book!" *Why the exclamation point?*

"I would love to see you again and talk about those days in New York although I'm sure you don't really need any help from me!"

And another!

"You won't believe this but as luck would have it, my family and I are traveling to Spoleto in June to attend the music festival. My daughter-in-law is performing in—" Here his memory failed him, some damn opera or other. "Spoleto is only an hour away from Todi. Could we meet for lunch? I so look forward to seeing you. Thanks for writing!"

Yet another! She may as well have ended her email with a smiley face.

He hadn't known what to expect, but it certainly wasn't this relentless friendliness. He tried to harmonize the kaleidoscope of his recollections of her—the bright, serious young woman; the lively, passionate adult— with the cheerful dowager she'd apparently become. She'd even attached a photograph and a maddeningly casual postscript. "Sending a recent picture taken in front of my house. Ciao!"

He barely remembered the house but would have recognized her any-where—older yes, but still slender, her fine-boned face lined and pale, her light-colored hair just touching her shoulders, the large ovals of her deep-set, aqua-colored eyes looking hopefully at the camera, the start of a slight smile.

I give up, I'm stumped.

Then, as he took the last turn before Todi, it hit him. It was the "ciao" that gave it away. *Jeanne, you almost had me fooled.* He could hear her cool intelligent voice in his ear. "Really, John, would I ever seriously say 'ciao'?"

It was a time long ago in Los Angeles, when their year-long second try at a relationship was skidding to an end. As a distraction, they went to a party given by one of his friends in the entertainment industry. They spent a painful half hour cornered by a curvy blond actress, whose name-dropping and intellectual pretensions were insufferable. As she was saying goodbye, the actress kissed them on both cheeks, gave a backhand wave, and said in a baby's breath voice, "Ciao!" After they left the party, Jeanne performed a dead-on imitation that made him laugh so hard his driving was impaired. "Jesus, John," she'd said, "no one who's not a native Italian should ever be allowed to say 'ciao.'"

They went to his hotel in West Los Angeles and spent what remained of the night talking, arguing about their future, making love, and then arguing some more. They didn't fall asleep until just before dawn. It was their last night together. When he left her that morning, she said she wouldn't see him again.

And here she was now, ending her cheerful message with that inane ciao. It was her semaphore signal to him, in case he was too dim to understand, that the only part of her message that mattered was that she wanted to see him. The rest of the email was just her way of reminding him that there were secrets and hidden places in each of them only they knew existed. He suddenly realized how much he wanted to see her again.

He parked in a lot at the base of the hill leading to Todi. From there, you could walk the kilometer up to town or you could ride the *ascensore*, a cog rail funicular, since there was almost no parking in town for non-residents. When he began living in the area, at a youngish sixty-seven, he would generally park and walk. Ten years had taken their depressing toll on him, though.

He bought a round-trip ticket from the pretty young woman at the *biglietteria*. Their hands touched as she counted his change and slipped him his ticket. They smiled—his full of cool appraisal, hers having only that sweet, condescending friendliness women reserve for small children and men who had aged out of sexual relevance.

In town, he shopped in several stores, then stopped by his bank. By the time he was finished, it was nearly three. He walked to the café on the ancient piazza, to keep his appointment.

She already was at the café waiting for him. He walked up to her and set his packages on a chair. She was tall with thick, dark hair done up in a loose bun, and wore a brightly colored silk print dress with gold jewelry at her throat and wrists.

"Benedetta?" She nodded nervously but didn't say anything. "Thank you for taking the time to meet me." "Benedetta" was Professoressa Benedetta Giambattisti, who taught art history at the university in nearby Perugia. Shortly after he bought the house, Jack had heard a rumor that its name, Casale Leonardo—*casale* means farmhouse—referred to Leonardo da Vinci and that it was so named because he had lived and worked there briefly. Far-fetched though it seemed, he was intrigued. What better way to bring in tourists than to associate his house with the greatest artist of all time? The recent publication of the wildly popular novel *The Da Vinci Code*, whatever its literary merit, had stirred even greater interest in the man. Who wouldn't want to stay in a house he had visited centuries before? Jack needed more than a rumor, though—he needed proof.

He called the university and was connected with Benedetta. When she heard what he wanted, she was encouraging. "It is certainly possible that Leonardo stayed there. It's old enough, and he was known to have spent time in the area. I could research the matter for you."

Jack was frank. "If you could establish a connection between my house and Leonardo, that would mean a lot to me."

"I don't want to mislead you. It would be difficult to say such a thing with certainty."

Disappointed and more than a little desperate, he talked it over with Riccardo the next day. Riccardo nodded and said with a chilly smile, "Don't worry, boss. I'll talk to her."

Two days later, Benedetta called Jack and in a strained voice made this appointment. Neither of them referred to their earlier conversation or to Riccardo.

As soon as he sat down, she handed Jack a bound document. "This is the research you requested." Jack awkwardly handed her an envelope filled with cash.

"The paper will be published next quarter in the university journal."

"Does it—?"

"Yes, I added the sentence you asked for," she answered, not looking him in the eye. What had Ricci done? He had a flush of guilt. Should he tell her to forget it? She waited for him to speak. When he didn't, she shook her head with disgust, got up, and walked away, her high heels tapping on the large, gray paving stones of the square. Jack opened the document at the place she had marked with a blue paperclip. The first sentence read, "The weight of scholarly evidence suggests that Leonardo stayed in the Casale Leonardo in 1513 while traveling to Rome." There were no supporting citations for the assertion, but Ricci had said Benedetta's reputation as a scholar would be proof enough. The rest of the article discussed Leonardo's design of Todi's cathedral, Il Tempio di Santa Maria della Consolazione, which was well documented in Leonardo's famous notebooks. Jack put the article in one of his shopping bags and walked back to the *ascensore*.

He felt queasy and foolish. Was this incipient senility? What the hell was he doing getting involved with loan sharks and creative history? As he descended from the ancient city, he had a hallucinogenic flash he was being drawn into Italy's violent history. The effect was heightened by the medieval towers, scarred walls, and stone fortresses spread before him. He shook his head to dispel the illusion, but he couldn't escape the sense that the cog railway was plunging him inexorably into the past.

PART II

1947

7

CHICAGO SUN, NOVEMBER 14, 1947

NOV. 25: BIG DAY IN THE LIVES OF 4 PRETTY GIRLS

By John McGrath

"November 25 is a red-letter day on our calendars." That's how four very pretty girls felt when told that they would be among the 75 high school newspaper editors invited by THE CHICAGO SUN to go to Lake Success, N.Y., on Nov. 25 to see the General Assembly of the United Nations in action. "Mom dropped her knitting when I told her about it. She was as excited as I was," said Jeanne Cooper, 17, of 6656 Diversey Ave., editor in chief of the Steinmetz Star of Steinmetz High School.

Jeanne Cooper turned to Caroline and smiled. "I know. Mom couldn't knit to save her life. It just came out."

"Oh, it's just an expression. Keep reading," Caroline said. "This is so exciting."

"It *is* exciting," Jeanne said.

CONGRATULATIONS FLOW IN

"I've never got so many congratulations in my life." Jeanne is a member of the National Honor Society and of Quill and Scroll, a national honorary high school journalism society, and wants to write stories, plays, and take a fling at reporting. Caroline Pearson, 17, features editor of the Steinmetz Star said: "I've wanted to go to Lake Success for a long time. I think it's a fine thing for the SUN to sponsor this trip. It will be very exciting to visit New York!"

The students will travel in style on the Pennsylvania General, leaving at 3:30 p.m. and arriving in New York the next morning. They will be accompanied by chaperones and this reporter.

The two friends sat on Jeanne's bed in her small home on Diversey Avenue in Montclare. Ten miles west of downtown Chicago, Montclare was a small town with tree-lined streets, modest houses, shops, churches, and a tavern on every block.

They had taken their shoes off so as not to soil the white cotton quilt sprigged with tiny green flowers. The windows rattled every time an electric trolley bus or a large truck rolled by. It was late fall and although it wasn't quite four o'clock, the sky was nearly dark. Freezing rain rocketed against the storm window. It smelled like snow.

"We do look pretty," said Caroline, looking at the photograph accompanying the article. She gave a sideways glance at the large, rounded mirror on Jeanne's Art Deco vanity table. Her green eyes were just barely visible beneath the dark fringe of her bangs. She twisted her petite figure back and forth and flipped her hair, which hung in waves around her head and shoulders. Caroline's exuberant vanity was part of her charm.

Jeanne had been told many times that she was pretty, but she still thought of herself as the studious and awkward girl she had been. Now, at seventeen and a half, she was five-seven with a light complexion and silvery blond hair. Her face was fine-boned, almost sharp, with deep-set, blue-green eyes. She couldn't help but wish her figure was more womanly, even though other girls asked her for dieting advice. She would usually make something up based on a magazine article she'd read to conceal the annoying truth that, no matter how much she ate, she never gained a pound.

The two friends had met as freshmen in high school and quickly bonded over a shared dislike of the required physical education, Jeanne because of its regimentation, Caroline because of its impact on her carefully arranged appearance. The friendship was cemented when they both joined the school paper.

"I wonder why John McGrath didn't interview us for his article instead of that Terry woman we talked to," Caroline said. "And what a silly headline, '4 pretty girls.' Do you think he wrote it?"

"I doubt it—probably the editor. Maybe McGrath was too busy," Jeanne replied. "He usually writes crime stories. I think I've got one of his articles here."

"I've never met anyone who reads as many newspapers and magazines as you," Caroline said, eyeing the huge pile next to the bed. "The *Tribune*, the *Sun*, the *New York Times*, *Life*, *Time* . . ."

"I like to keep up."

"I wonder what's so important that he couldn't find time for us?" Caroline asked.

"Well, he wrote an article a couple of days ago about a guy he was investigating who was blown up in a phone booth," Jeanne said. "They found him all over the place."

"That's disgusting."

"They think he was killed to shut him up." She found the paper she wanted and spread it on the bed. "Here it is. Listen."

BLAST IN BOOTH KILLS MAN WITH BAG

By John McGrath

Robert "Bob the Mole" Bailey picked up a small black bag and walked from his table into a phone booth right outside Stu Polska's downtown diner last night. The Mole had just finished his dinner of Polish sausage washed down with a couple of pints of Milwaukee's finest.

When he left the diner, he told his boss, James "Big Jim" Winter, he'd
be back in a minute. Moments later, there was an explosion that shat-
tered windows of the restaurant. When Big Jim saw what remained
of the Mole, Big Jim's dinner came up and added to the mess. When
he was done upchucking, he jumped into a taxi and hasn't been seen
in public since.

Sgt. Albert L. Embry of the police homicide squad confirmed
the identity of the victim by his prints, even though what remained of
the corpse was a few fingers short of the usual ten. There is speculation
that the Mole had turned stool pigeon and was killed to silence him. This
reporter will keep investigating until his killers are brought to justice.

"I love how he writes," Jeanne said. "Personal, like he's part of the
story. I can see him there, his overcoat flapping in the wind, walking
through swirling smoke and debris. And he's funny."

"What's funny about that poor man being blown to bits?"

"I wouldn't feel too sorry for the Mole."

"You make him sound like a Mickey Spillane character," Caroline
teased. Jeanne had gone on about how much she loved Spillane's *I, the
Jury* when it came out earlier in the year.

"That's what I want to do after college, make my living writing."

"Detective novels?"

"Why not? Books, journalism, anything. I could even write a musical.
Eight years of piano must be good for something."

"Ugh, why work if you don't have to?"

"I want a career, not just marriage and children. I want to do something important. Why else are we working so hard in school and on
the paper?"

Caroline shrugged. "First of all, I don't work nearly as hard at school
as you. Just enough to squeeze through." Her grades were resolutely
mediocre. "You get along so well with all our teachers. They just think I'm
a chatterbox like most girls." She paused. "Except you, maybe. Anyway, as
for the paper, I do it because it's fun. All I want's a good-looking husband
who'll give me a couple of fat babies and a big house in Highland Park.

But not until I've had plenty of fun first." They both laughed. "So, do you think your Mr. McGrath is handsome?"

"Oh, who knows."

"Mm-hmm. Hey, have you decided what clothes you're bringing?"

"No, and it's less than two weeks away. How about you?"

Caroline shook her head.

"Let's look at some magazines. Maybe we'll get some ideas." Jeanne fished around in the pile on the floor and pulled out a couple of *Seventeen* magazines. She plopped them on the bed and they began to thumb through them.

Caroline pointed to one of the advertisements in the July issue and said, "Do you think your mom'll let you wear platform heels like those?"

"It's not Mom I have to worry about," Jeanne answered, thinking of her father. He was still of the opinion that nice high school girls wore long skirts, baggy sweaters, and sensible shoes. "My dad gave me a new set of luggage for the trip. Want to see?"

"Of course."

Jeanne went to her closet and pulled out a set of salmon-colored "Globetrotter" Samsonite suitcases—one big, one small, and a matching train case with a mirror inside its lid.

"Aw, that's sweet."

"Hey, do you want to stay for dinner? Dad said he was bringing home steak."

"Steak! You don't have to ask me twice." Steak was a rare treat because wartime rationing—meatless Mondays, eggless Wednesdays, and poultry-less Thursdays—was still in effect to support the post-war relief effort.

Jeanne looked dreamily at the model frolicking in the turquoise water of Nassau on the cover of the magazine Caroline was reading. "I love that bathing suit." It was a daring two-piece in cool green with a fringed skirt. She had a swift vision of splashing in the warm Bahamian waters.

Caroline laughed. "I don't think we'll be needing bathing suits in New York in late November."

The trip had been scheduled for Thanksgiving week, after much consultation among the *Sun*, the superintendent of schools, and various parent groups. Parents' desire to spend the holiday with their children had given way to the superintendent's insistence that the students miss as little class time as possible.

"Anyway," Caroline said, checking the price, "it costs eight dollars. For a bathing suit! Listen, we have to get organized about this." Caroline began counting on her fingers. "The trip will be a total of seven days, one day traveling each way and five in the city. We can wear the same thing both ways on the train. Then, at least two days at the General Assembly, sightseeing, maybe a fancy lunch and nights out."

Jeanne began listing the items they'd need. "We'll want warm coats. I love the tan wool one we saw in the window of Marshall Field's. We'll need sweaters, skirts, nylons, two or three dresses, as well as hats, scarves, gloves, and matching shoes." Caroline's face grew longer as though she was mentally adding up the cost. Caroline's father had been killed in the Ardennes Forest in late 1944. Her mother worked as a secretary. There wasn't any extra money.

"You know, we don't really need all those new things. I have oodles of clothes you can borrow," Jeanne said. "Of course, I'm so much taller than you."

Caroline rolled her eyes.

"But anything that doesn't fit, we can alter."

Caroline grew serious. "Thanks. I just couldn't go to Mom and ask her to buy lots of new things for me."

Jeanne took Caroline's hand. "Don't worry, this is going to be the best trip ever. It doesn't matter what we're wearing."

"You're right. But she might get me a coat. What do you think of this one?" Caroline turned a page in the magazine and showed her an inexpensive rayon reversible coat, white on one side, leopard print on the other. It was hideous. "See, it says you can wear it one way during the day like sportswear and then you reverse it and it's a fancy evening coat. Perfect for El Morocco and the Stork Club."

"It's cute. Tell you what, let's take the bus downtown tomorrow right after school. We'll go to Marshall Field's, Spiegel's, Stevens—all the stores. They might have things on sale. Afterward, we can see a movie. My treat. I've been dying to see *Forever Amber*."

"Me too."

"Now, we've got half an hour 'til dinner. Let's go through my things and see what I have that you can borrow."

• • •

On Tuesday afternoon almost two weeks later, Jeanne's mother was driving the girls to Union Station. Jeanne used her coat sleeve to wipe the mist off the car's side window and peered out at the station's mottled limestone. A hat-snatching wind blew the snow sideways. Jeanne was wearing a houndstooth jacket and skirt and her tan overcoat. Caroline wore a dark green dress and the reversible leopard print coat she had inveigled her mother to buy. They held their hats on their heads while Mrs. Cooper recruited a porter to bring their luggage into the crowded station.

Inside the Great Hall, Jeanne's mother hugged them both. "Girls, I know you'll have a wonderful time. I only wish I could go with you." She hugged Jeanne again. "Be good and call if you need anything, okay?"

Jeanne was surprised to find herself wet-eyed. She'd never been away from home before. "I'll tell you all about it when we get back," she said.

"Here, maybe this will help." Her mom handed her a small package wrapped in red tissue paper.

"What is it?"

"Just a little present."

Jeanne peeled off the paper. "Oh, Mom. Look, Caroline—it's a reporter's notebook in a leather case."

"Take good notes. I want to hear about everything. Bye, honey."

Jeanne felt anxious and lost in the huge hall. She held tight to the hard rubber handle of her suitcase as she looked for the group from the *Chicago Sun*. The station was overrun with people moving in every direction, many of them in military uniforms. She was overwhelmed by the smell of dead cigars, wet wool, and warm bodies. The marble floor rolled out hundreds of feet in each direction and was surrounded by massive Corinthian columns. The arched ceiling stretched 120 feet high. The danger of air raids was long past, but the skylights were still blacked out as though the city remained in mourning two years after the war had ended. "Do you remember where we're supposed to meet?" she asked Caroline.

Caroline shook her head. "Check the letter."

Jeanne took the *Sun*'s invitation letter from her coat pocket. "It doesn't say. Do you see anyone who looks like a nun?" To reassure nervous parents that their teenagers would return at the end of the trip as immaculate as they were at its inception, the *Sun* had recruited a waddle of nuns and religious brothers, captained by a priest, as chaperones. She put out her lower lip and blew upward in frustration. "Where is everyone?"

Caroline shook her head. "Let's try over there." She pointed to a room just visible through the columns. They half carried and half pushed their suitcases across the floor toward what was known as the Union Gallery.

Seventy-five student editors, half a dozen chaperones, a photographer, and representatives from the *Sun* were seated at round tables. A man was speaking from a raised dais at the front. Behind the dais was a banner that read—

CHICAGO AREA HIGH SCHOOL EDITORS
UNITED NATIONS SPECIAL
SPONSORED BY THE CHICAGO SUN

The clatter caused by the two girls sliding their suitcases along the waxed marble floor caused some of the students to look at them. Caroline smiled and waved, but Jeanne ducked her head and felt her face turn bright crimson. She plucked at Caroline's sleeve and motioned her to an almost empty table at the back of the room. They stumbled and bumped their way there and sat down.

They nodded at the other two occupants at the table. One was a heavyset man in a rumpled suit without a tie and a gray wool newsboy hat stuck square on his head. He gripped a large glass containing a dark brown liquid. A smoldering cigar pulled down the side of his mouth. Seated next to Jeanne was a man in his early twenties. He was neatly dressed in a wide-lapelled navy-blue suit, a blindingly white shirt, and a red-and-black-striped silk tie. She could see the dull glow of gold cufflinks. His hair was black, cut short and combed back, his pale, cleanshaven face slightly pocked. A dark fedora and a bottle of Coca-Cola sat on the table in front of him. There was a fresh scent of soap mixed with an aftershave that seemed to be a combination of cinnamon and cedar.

She fixed her eyes forward. She was humming, something she did when she was embarrassed. Marshall Field Jr., the assistant to the publisher of the *Sun*, was in mid-oration.

"This is but a prelude to the privilege of seeing in action the significant and colorful congress of all the people of the world, brought into focus for you, the youthful American editors of tomorrow. The United Nations, in spite of its defects, is the last best chance for peace that we have."

The young man whispered, "The 'Battle Hymn of the Republic'?" It was the song she was humming. "Very patriotic."

She turned and whispered back, "I thought it was just the right accompaniment to the speech."

The young man's sardonic smile turned to one of approval. His deep dimples sent a tingle of tension down her back. "So it is," he said.

Their eyes met. Her heart began to pound and she looked away as she felt her face color again.

"I hope we didn't miss too much," she said, turning to Caroline, who stopped flirting for a minute with a boy at a nearby table and leaned forward to get a better look at the young man next to Jeanne.

Field plodded to his peroration. "We on the *Sun* consider it a great privilege to introduce you to the United Nations, the living parliament of man. I hope you'll get a great deal out of it as we make this pilgrimage dedicated to future peace. Before I finish, I want you to meet some of the people you'll get to know better over the next several days. First, to my right, is Father Bernard of St. George High School—he's in charge of the chaperones accompanying you."

A silver-haired man wearing a dark overcoat buttoned to his chin and rimless spectacles stood and nodded at the speaker and the assembled students.

"In charge of the girls will be Sister Mary Camilus and Sister Rose Catherine, both of Trinity High School." Field chuckled fatly. "You know, nuns always travel in pairs."

Two severe-looking ladies in full habit rose slightly in their chairs and nodded. Neither appeared amused at the gentle jibe.

A man near Field leaned in and whispered in his ear.

"What?" Field's face lit up with amusement as he turned back to the room. "I was forgetting. Some of you may have already met him. You've certainly seen his name if you've been reading the *Sun*"—here he laughed and wagged a finger—"as I know you all do regularly." A polite titter came from the students.

Field looked around the room and his eyes seemed to light on Jeanne. For a nauseating moment, she was sure he was going to ask whether she read his paper regularly and why she was late. She was formulating a reply when Field said, "John, could you stand up?"

The young man sitting next to Jeanne pushed back his chair and stood. He was tall, a couple of inches over six feet. "*Sun* reporter John McGrath, ladies and gentlemen." There was a smattering of applause. "And with him, the *Sun*'s city desk editor Henry Hershon. John specially asked for the privilege of covering your journey for the *Sun*. He's our youngest reporter, but, if you've followed his last two series for us on corruption in the Office of Price Administration, you'll agree he's one of our best." John gave a slight bow and sat down.

"Jeez, Henry, he makes it sound like I'm doing something noble, not babysitting a children's tea party," John said.

His words deflated some of Jeanne's excitement. Hershon laughed, put his glass to his mouth, and tossed down the last of his drink. "Relax, John, it could be worse. You could be covering Miss Photo Flash of 1947," he said, referring to the winner of the annual beauty contest sponsored by the paper.

"That's an assignment?"

"Yep. Full bio, interview—you know, get her views on world affairs and such—the works. Now that you're going on this trip, Terry's gonna cover it."

"Lucky me."

"Hey, you asked for it and I agreed. You're always begging to cover stories outside of Chicago. UN's a good place to start."

"Once," he said, holding up a finger. "One time before I asked if I could travel."

"You wanted to go to Hollywood, for crissakes."

"I wanted to go to Los Angeles last June when Bugsy Siegel got hit. I know it was connected to Capone's death in January and if you'd let me go, I could have proved it."

"Sure, Johnny, you coulda solved it when nobody else could."

"Maybe I could have."

"You're crazy. Your dad was the cop, not you. And he ain't around."

John stared at Hershon.

"Sorry I said that." Hershon looked embarrassed. "Listen, kid, nobody knows who iced Siegel. Nobody ever will. Anyway, water under the bridge." He lowered his voice. "Tell you the truth, you're smart to go. Good idea to get out of town for a while after that source of yours, the Mole, got turned into marinara sauce. And you'll get a plush train ride with a bunch of nice kids, collect a little expense money, see the big city. Might even be a good story at the UN. If we can get the fucking paper out at all."

The powerful printer's union had voted to strike all of the Chicago papers the night before. All of its members—pressmen, typesetters, lino-type operators, ink boys—had walked off the job.

"Anyway, it'll be good experience. What are you, twenty-one?"

"Yep."

"Shit, I got underwear older than you. You still gotta lot to learn."

"Maybe. But if you really thought there was a good story at the UN, you'd send somebody else."

"Nah, we usually leave the hoity-toity foreign policy crap to the *Tribune* or buy coverage from the *New York Herald*. Believe me, the UN angle could be something."

With a quick glance at Jeanne, John lowered his voice. "Really? Not just a bunch of diplomats jerking each other off?"

Hershon laughed. "Maybe not. UN's supposed to vote on whether to give the Jews their own piece of Palestine. After what happened during the war, everybody feels so shitty guilty. They want to give 'em some land they can call their own. Only hitch, there's like a million Arabs who live there already and they don't want any more Jews. There's already been a lot of trouble about it."

"Heard about that," John said.

"People blowing up hotels and buses, shooting each other in the street." Hershon looked at John. "Actually, it's your kinda trouble." He stood to leave. "But remember, your first job is to cover the kids." Hershon grabbed John's Coke, drained it, then smacked it down on the wood table and left.

John stood as well and said, "Ladies, hope we didn't disturb you. Have a pleasant journey."

Caroline and Jeanne murmured a goodbye as he walked away. Field had finished his speech and the assembly was over. They headed to the concourse.

• • •

Two hours later, Caroline and Jeanne were busy unpacking in their Pullman sleeper Master Room.

"I thought we'd be sitting up all night," Caroline said excitedly. "Did you see the ladies' dressing room down the corridor? It's huge, and there's a maid."

"I know. Mr. Field said they're sparing no expense. They have a full day of activities lined up tomorrow. He wants us to arrive fresh."

Caroline squeezed past Jeanne into the tiny washroom and began unpacking her pins, curlers, cotton wool, bottles, and tubes. "What time did they say for dinner?"

Jeanne picked up the itinerary they'd been given for the trip. "Seven thirty. Then social time in the observation car. Oh, I didn't see this. We're supposed to be in our rooms by ten."

"Ten? Do they think we're kids? I have plans tonight." One of the things Jeanne admired about Caroline was her complete confidence with the opposite sex.

"Uh, Caroline, did you see who's in the room next to us?"

"Boys?" she asked hopefully.

"No, sweetie, the sisters."

"Whose sisters?"

"*The* sisters, as in Sister Mary and Sister Rose. Our chaperones?"

"No problem. I bet they're in bed by ten fifteen. We just wait 'til they're asleep and slip out. They'll never know a thing."

"We?"

"Yes, we. You don't mean to tell me you're going to just sit in the room with a glass of warm milk?"

"Caroline, do you have a date tonight?"

"I have two dates tonight."

"You're incredible. How are you going to pull that off?"

Caroline explained as though she were talking to a small child. "Easy. One's at nine; one's at midnight. I like the one at midnight best so I saved him for last. And"—she pointed her finger—"you're coming with me."

"Oh no I am not."

"What am I supposed to do with their roommates if you don't come?"

"What am I supposed to do with their roommates?"

"Whatever you want." Caroline waggled her eyebrows. "I'm just kidding. Talk to them, have a few laughs. I mean, come on. Don't make such a big deal about it."

"I'm not going on two blind dates on my first night on this trip. And it sounds to me like you better take the bottom berth. Easier to sneak in and out."

Caroline looked stymied for a moment, then said quickly, "You're right. I don't mean to be selfish. It's your trip, too, and you should do whatever you want. Anyway, you're taller than me. Easier for you to get into the top bunk. You're feeling all right, aren't you?"

Jeanne took Caroline's hands in an effort to restrain her flow of words. "I'm fine. I just don't want to get sent home the first day for breaking the rules."

"It's 'cuz of him, isn't it?"

Jeanne was all innocence. "Who?"

"You know who I mean. 'Mr. Wonderful,' that John McGrath. You like him."

"Caroline."

"I saw the way he looked at you this afternoon. And, what's more, I saw how you looked at him."

"You're seeing things."

"Am not."

"Are so," she said and then they were both laughing.

8

John McGrath resigned himself to sitting up all night in the club car. He was still smarting from his discovery that the students were in Pullman sleepers while he was stuck in the coach-chair car for the eighteen-hour trip. He was supposed to eat dinner with them but had declined with bubbling anger. *Plush train ride.* It would be just like Hershon to have lied about that. At least Hershon didn't know that the real reason he'd suddenly asked for this assignment was because the biggest crime story of his young career—a story about a crime that hadn't been committed yet—had dropped in his lap two weeks earlier. And he had almost missed it.

Two weeks ago, a man had been waiting to see him when he arrived at the tall, gray Art Deco building on the Chicago River that housed the *Chicago Sun*. It was Armistice Day—November 11. John had begged Hershon for the day off. "Nope. You're a kid. Kids work holidays." Feeling rebellious, John had slept in and then walked to work along the river from his rooming house rather than catching his usual bus. He dawdled at a café over a donut and coffee, and then took his time crossing the La Salle Street Bridge and watched the river traffic until he was shivering from the icy wind coming off the lake. When he finally arrived in the building lobby two hours late, the security guard pointed toward a man and said, "This guy's been waiting to see you since dawn. He was just about to take his story to the *Trib*."

The man marched over to him. "Mr. McGrath?" He had an accent

John couldn't identify. He was almost six feet tall and heavy, with brown skin, thinning black hair, and a closely trimmed mustache going gray. A silver watch chain hung from the vest pocket of his dark wool suit.

"Yes?"

"I am Mahmoud Haleem." He clamped two hands around John's extended hand and shook it vigorously.

"What can I do for you, Mr. Haleem?"

"I have a story to tell you," he'd said in a hoarse whisper. "Can we talk in private?"

"Sure, let's go upstairs. Want some coffee?" Haleem nodded. John turned to the watchman. "Larry, can you send out for coffee? One for you, too. We'll be upstairs." He handed him a quarter.

"You don't want to drink the newsroom stuff—trust me," John said.

They rode the elevator in silence to the newsroom floor. He led Haleem to a glassed-in office, unoccupied because of the holiday, and closed the door. Haleem sat in a chair in front of a large, wood desk and John sat behind it. Haleem fumbled out a pack of cigarettes and offered it to John with a slight tremor in his hand. John shook his head. Haleem lit one for himself with a silver lighter. He snapped the lid of the lighter up and down several times as he inhaled deeply.

John waited patiently. This wasn't the first time a story found him rather than the other way around. He received tips by phone, letter, and, occasionally, in person. Most of the people he spoke with were nervous.

"You live around here, Mr. Haleem?" John finally said.

"Eighteenth Street near Michigan Avenue," Haleem had answered, breathing out smoke. "By the coffee shop."

Eighteenth and Michigan was the center of Chicago's nascent Arab Quarter, a small group of Syrian and Palestinian immigrants who had moved there in the first decades of the century. The coffee shop was a neighborhood meeting place—it doubled as a mosque.

"I come here in 1924 with nothing," Haleem began. "Now I have a store. You know, dry goods, tapestries, rugs, jewelry. My wife, just before the war, she wants to start a restaurant. I say sure, why not, we have empty place next door. Palestinian food, like from home. It is called after my wife—Fatima's. You should come sometime. Be my guest."

"Maybe I will."

"I read the *Sun*," Haleem went on, "you know, every day. *Tribune*, also," he said, holding up his hand with a gold ring on his pinkie, "but I like the *Sun* best. Read your stories about all the crooks in this city. You are very good, I think."

"Thanks."

A boy knocked on the glass door and brought in their coffee. He set two cardboard cups on the desk along with sugar packets and wooden stir sticks. He tossed a dime to John who caught it midair and flipped it back to him. The boy nodded and left. John peeled the lids off the cups and handed one to Haleem.

"If I tell you something, do you have to put my name in the paper?"

"No."

"It would be very bad to get mixed up in something like this."

"I'm not the police, Mr. Haleem. What you tell me is unofficial. Unless you say it's okay, I don't use your name."

Haleem looked relieved. "I think I come to the right guy." He stirred three packets of sugar into his cup and took a swallow. He grimaced, then tried to hide his expression.

"Something wrong?"

"No, no, it's . . . it's just American coffee is weak."

Haleem looked through the glass at a man walking by and waited until he had passed, then seemed to make a decision.

"I sold a gun. I worry this was very wrong."

"What kind of gun?"

"Japanese rifle. War souvenir."

Although imports of captured weapons were technically restricted by military rules, most GIs ignored regulations and returned home with souvenir knives, swords, handguns, rifles, and, in one arson case John had reported, a fully functional flamethrower.

"That's not against the law, Mr. Haleem."

"Sure, I don't think so. People bring them in. I buy some, sell some. A nice business, you know."

"Were you in the war?"

Haleem sat straighter. "You bet. US Army. Thirty-seven when I join up. They say I am too old to fight so I do radio communications at ETO headquarters in London, some translations. You too, sir?"

"Yep."

"You are very young."

"There were plenty younger. Fighting or no fighting, you served. That's what counts."

"This is what I think also."

"Why are you worried, Mr. Haleem?"

Haleem looked shamefaced. "The man who bought it, I think now he is dangerous."

"Why?"

"A few nights ago, some people come to the restaurant. The woman that bring them is friend of my wife; they both from Syria."

"You're Syrian?"

"No, Palestinian. Lot of us here in Chicago. So these guys are part of the Syrian delegation to the United Nations. They visit Arab people in this country. We eat dinner. I show them my store and this big guy, very serious fellow, right away he's interested in the guns."

"What's his name?"

"Mohammed Alfagari."

John asked him to spell it and made a note.

"Anyway, this Alfagari, ask lotsa questions. 'How much for this one, how much for that one?' So I tell him. Finally he says, 'How about that gun on your wall?' Mr. McGrath, it is the best, you know, a Japanese sniper rifle I buy from a Navy guy a year ago. Beautiful. Engraved flower on the barrel. Army buddy of mine shoots it in the woods. Says it's dead quiet, no flash, shoots straight, range over half a kilometer. Japanese musta kill a whole lot of our guys with that rifle."

"So you sold it to him?"

Haleem's lips tightened and he nodded. "I think maybe it's not for a souvenir."

"Why?"

"Later, Fatima tells me about him. She and her friend, Liliane, after dinner, they talk in our back room. She tells this to Fatima about that man fighting. Before war, he kills the French and British for the Mufti of Jerusalem who leads the fight against the Jews. During war, he kills them for the Germans."

"For the Nazis?"

"Lotsa Arabs do this because the Germans fight the French and British like us. Not so unusual."

"And since?"

"Since the war, Liliane tells Fatima, he kills again Jews for the Mufti." Haleem looked at his hands where his cigarette had burned down and gave a deep sigh. "Mr. McGrath, this Liliane says he is a sniper."

"So he's gonna kill Jews in Palestine. How does that—?"

"I sell a sniper rifle to a sniper, sir," Haleem broke in, stubbing out his cigarette in an overflowing ashtray on the desk. "He kills somebody, maybe I'm in trouble too."

"Palestine's pretty far from Chicago."

"Liliane, she tells Fatima maybe he use it here."

"In Chicago?"

"Fatima don't ask her." His voice dropped. "You heard of this Mufti of Jerusalem?"

"No."

"Or the big vote in New York about Palestine in a couple of weeks? Kick Palestinians out of their homes, give the Jews that land?"

"I heard about it."

"Lotsa my people want to stop the vote. Guys like the Mufti. He hates the Jews. Would kill anybody if it stops the vote. Maybe they do that in New York."

"Why not go to the police?"

Haleem gave a sour laugh. "Police in Chicago?" He paused to drink some more coffee. "They don't help a guy like me. Only if you pay."

"My dad was a Chicago cop."

Haleem looked embarrassed. "I'm sorry, Mr. McGrath. I'm not talking about your father, but, please, sir, you know some of them—"

"Yeah, yeah, I know." He wasn't going to debate the legendary corruption of the Chicago police.

Haleem hurried on. "So, Mr. McGrath, I like it better if you look into this, not police. You know, like you do about the Mole guy exploded his guts all over that phone booth. That musta been something, huh?" He took a deep inhale of smoke, then expelled it. "You say in the paper you keep after those guys until you find out the truth. If this Alfagari's gonna do something bad, you find out, then maybe you tell the police. But not where he got the gun."

"Can I talk to this Liliane woman by herself?"

"That one is tough, Mr. McGrath. You are not *mahram*. These guys are very old-fashioned. They make her dress in full robe and niqab. I totally condemn this, but they won't let her see a strange man alone."

"Mr. Haleem, I have to talk to her."

Haleem nodded. "Maybe Fatima can help. You come to the restaurant for dinner, maybe a week from tonight. Say eight o'clock?" He smiled, showing a gold-capped incisor. "The food is very good. And the coffee better than this. And maybe Liliane visit Fatima that same time. You make a new friend."

"Will she meet me?"

Haleem waggled his head back and forth. "I think maybe she's more modern than she look. They're traveling now. St. Louis, Kansas City. But back next week."

"Okay, I'll be there. Week from tonight."

"Unofficial?" The Palestinian American man had stared meaningfully at John.

"Right, Mr. Haleem. Unofficial."

Now, John was waiting for his first close look at Alfagari and the men he worked for. He'd checked the passenger list with the conductor and confirmed they were on the train. Three men entered the club car. John shifted on his barstool. The first two were slender and slightly under medium height. They wore similar dark pinstripe suits. Bright white shirts contrasted with their light brown skin. They took seats in large club chairs near a low cocktail table at the other end of the car.

The elder of the two men wore horn-rimmed glasses, had a salt-and-pepper beard and a well-trimmed mustache. His black shoes gleamed with polish. The younger man had a full beard and he too wore glasses.

The third man was much taller than his companions and matched Haleem's description of Alfagari. His thick shoulders stretched the jacket of the metal-gray suit he wore. His clean-shaven face was broad and hard, with a large nose and a wide, muscular neck that bulged the top button of his shirt and the knot of his tie. Dark silvered hair, cut close, clung to his head. The man approached the bar and said to the bartender in French-accented English, "Two whiskeys and soda. You have cigarettes?"

The bartender nodded.

"Two packages."

With quick, practiced gestures, the bartender mixed the drinks and placed them with cigarettes and matches on a silver tray.

As the man stretched for the tray, there was the flash of a leather shoulder holster and the butt of a gun under his left arm. He carried the tray to the other two and set it on the low table. The younger man handed one of the drinks to the elder, said something, and laughed. They each took a deep drink and relaxed back in their chairs. He slit the cellophane on one of the cigarette packs with his thumbnail and tapped out two cigarettes, handed one to the older man, and put one in his mouth. He lit both cigarettes from a single match.

"Give me another," John said. "Less sugar this time." The bartender nodded. More quietly he asked, "Know those guys?"

"Yeah, Arabs, diplomats. I rode out from New York with them a few weeks ago."

"What kind of Arabs?"

"Syrians, I heard." The bartender seemed glad to have someone to talk to. "You know their religion is teetotal." He shook his head. "Guess they think no one will know if they break the rules so far from home."

"Guess so."

"Seems like God would know," the bartender said.

"Seems like He would," said John. "Know their names?"

"Nope."

"The big guy doesn't look too diplomatic."

"Nope. I think he's security. Seen guys like him during the war." He looked carefully at John. "You were in it." It wasn't a question.

"Sure. Third Army, '44 and '45."

"Patton, huh?" The bartender looked impressed. "Kinda young, no?"

"Seventeen when I joined up. Where'd you serve?"

"Italy, '43 and '44."

"Lots of action," John said.

"You, too." The bartender smiled and reached out his hand. "Bernie White."

"John McGrath."

"McGrath, huh?"

"Yeah."

"Got something for you." White handed him a small cream-colored envelope. "Passenger gave it to one of the porters, said to hold it for you here."

The envelope was addressed in delicate cursive, "John McGrath, Chicago Sun." He tore it open. There was a note on a sheet of heavy paper in the same hand. "I have your proof." There was no signature, but he knew it was from Liliane. Where was she?

"So, Bernie, can you help a fellow GI?"

"If I can."

"I'm a reporter, *Chicago Sun*. I'm doing a story on those guys." He nodded at the Syrians. "Like to find out as much as I can about them. Do you know which compartment they're in?"

"Well, they don't have a compartment. They have a whole car to themselves. Private, at the end of the train. Never been in it, but I've seen pictures. Special made by Pullman. It's the fanciest thing on wheels."

"Any way to see it?"

"You could ask them," the bartender said, indicating the Syrians. He picked up a glass and started polishing it.

"Wouldn't want to interrupt them. They gonna make a night of it?" he asked.

"Probably. They did on the way out. In here 'til dawn."

"Any other staff, anyone staying with them? A woman?"

"Not that I've seen."

"Think I'm gonna stretch my legs," John said. He threw back the last of his drink.

"You do that, Mac," Bernie said. He lowered his voice even further. "But be careful."

"Thanks."

John walked out of the club car toward the rear of the train, glancing at the Syrians, who didn't look up as he passed. The bodyguard—it had to be Alfagari—wasn't drinking or smoking. He had taken a stool from the bar and placed it in a corner. He was facing the door, his back to the wall, giving him a wide field of view and a clear field of fire. *He's a soldier, all right.*

As John made his way to the rear of the train, he thought about the meeting he'd had with Liliane the week before. The day after his conversation with Haleem, John had asked Hershon for the New York assignment with the student editors. Hershon had seemed suspicious but gave in. He had liked the article John wrote about the "Four Pretty Girls" going on a visit to the United Nations. A few days after the article appeared, John had walked into Fatima's at eight o'clock. Mahmoud Haleem greeted him as though they were old friends, pumping his hand, seating him at a corner table, introducing him to his wife as the "best reporter in Chicago," and then had buried him with an avalanche of food John had never heard of. After coffee, Haleem asked him if he would like to have a look around. He led John out the back door and opened the door to his store in the next building. "Turn left, then follow down the hall."

Suddenly nervous, John had asked, "You're not coming?"

Haleem shook his head. "You are the one she came to see."

John walked through the dim corridor until he came to a door that was ajar. He pushed it open and stepped inside. It was a large room filled with Persian rugs piled high against three walls. Against the fourth wall, there was a divan with cushions covered in thick, patterned cotton. There was the faint smell of wool and cardamom. A heavily shaded floor lamp cast a dim yellow light. Seated on the divan's edge was a small, solitary figure draped in a flowing black robe that covered her head and body. Narrow wrists and slender fingers rested on her lap. A black veil covered her face except for a narrow opening around the eyes.

"Mr. McGrath?"

He took a step closer, caught a faint floral scent.

"Yes?"

"I am Liliane al-Haffar." She spoke quietly, with a slight tremble. Her English was accented, a mix of French and Arabic.

"I'm John."

"John." She pronounced his name with a soft "J" as though it were French. It excited him for reasons he couldn't explain.

He cleared his throat. "Well, Miss—"

"Liliane."

"Is it all right if I sit?" he asked, gesturing to a place near her on the divan.

She nodded and moved away as he sat, and the slight opening around her eyes seemed to widen. She had dark, beautifully shaped eyebrows and long lashes over large black eyes.

"Mr. Haleem says you're from Syria. You're with the delegation?"

"I am with Houman al-Hafiz. I am unofficial. He has his wife; he has his children. And he has me. Mahmoud says you can be trusted and I have no one to trust."

"Why not the police?"

"The police cannot keep secrets."

"So why me?"

"Are you not the right man?"

He was suddenly afraid he would lose the story—if there were a story. "No, no. I just wanted to know."

"Mahmoud has read your work. We see you are an honorable man and have courage. When we read in your paper this week about the trip to Lake Success, we know for sure."

"Know what?"

"That it was meant to be. 'We will tell John McGrath,' we said. 'He will go to Lake Success. He will know what to do.'"

Again, the frisson of pleasure at the way she said his name. "It wasn't exactly my first choice, babysitting a bunch of school kids. But after I spoke with Haleem, I kinda volunteered."

"You must stop this great evil."

"Well, I'll do what I can."

"What do you know of Palestine?"

"I can find it on a map."

"And the vote for the Zionist state?"

"Nothing."

"I will tell you."

"Sure." *How old was she?* he wondered. *Thirty? Older?*

"Listen to me. The Jews have been coming to Palestine since the last century, more each year. Since the end of the war, many more are pressing at the gate and soon they will be allowed in. This cannot be stopped."

"They say it's their land, that God gave it to them," he said.

She gave a bitter laugh. "And what do we tell the Palestinians who have lived there for thousands of years? God says you must move along now?"

"I don't know."

"You have heard of the Mufti of Jerusalem?"

"A little."

"He is a bad man. There are many reasons I say this, but it is enough to know he worked in Berlin during the war with his man, this Alfagari. He tells Arabs on the radio to fight against the Allies. He meets with Hitler, is friends with Eichmann. You know of Eichmann?"

John froze for a moment, then said, "Yeah, I've seen his work up close."

Her eyes were liquid brown, not black. And she wasn't thirty; she was younger. What rules were they violating by being alone? What was *mahram?*

"This Alfagari came to work with the delegation only recently. Houman was made to hire him."

"Made how?"

"Blackmail."

"How do you know?"

"I know." He was about to press, but a flash of shame in her eyes stopped him. She went on. "Alfagari is the Mufti's man. He trained at the French military academy in Homs and served in the Syrian army as a sniper. He worked for the Mufti in the Arab rebellion in the 1930s, killing Jewish terrorists."

"Jewish terrorists?"

"Of course. You do not know of the Irgun? Or their Stern gang?"

"No."

"But they have killed so many Palestinians and British, John." She sounded puzzled at his ignorance.

"I didn't know."

Her eyebrows arched.

"And now?"

"The Mufti uses Alfagari in his war to stop the partition of Palestine."

"Uses how?"

"To kill. In Jerusalem before. Now, in Rome and London before we came here. You read what happened?"

He shook his head.

"Three weeks ago. A bomb in the British embassy in Rome."

"That was him?"

"I am sure of it. He was away from us that night. Then, two weeks ago in London, a British envoy for Palestine was shot dead in the street by a large man who was seen but escaped."

"Alfagari?"

She nodded.

"Why are you so sure it was him?"

"Houman tells me. Now I think they will do something in New York."

"At the UN? That's crazy!"

"No, John. It's the Middle East." She leaned toward him and looked him in the eye. He caught the floral scent again. "I must tell you a story. One day not long ago, an Arab boy, fifteen, goes swimming in a quarry in Jerusalem. He has trouble, yells for help. People hear him, but no one saves him. He drowns."

"Why didn't they help him?"

"Police were angry; they ask people later, 'Why do not you save this boy?' 'Because the boy was Muslim,' say the Jews. 'Because the boy was a Jew,' say the Muslims. 'Because he wasn't a Christian,' say the Christians."

John shook his head in disgust.

"For you, safe in America, John, this sounds crazy. But the Zionists and the Arabs are willing to kill. They have in Palestine and Rome and London. Why not in Lake Success?"

"Miss Haffar—Liliane. If I'm going to report this, I'll need proof."

"But Haleem told you, Alfagari bought the sniper rifle."

"Yes, but—"

"Why does he need this rifle if not to kill?" Her eyes were angry. "Must you wait for him to use it?"

Was she telling the truth? It was hard to know when you couldn't see a person's face. John tried to imagine what Hershon would say. What was her angle? A grudge against her boyfriend, Houman? Sympathy for the Jews? Some wrong done to her by Alfagari?

"Tell me about yourself."

There was a slight shrug underneath her robes. "I am with Houman."

"You said, but—" He was embarrassed to ask his question.

She asked it for him. "Why?"

"Yes."

She told him her story. She was born in 1922 in the Arab Mountain area of Syria to a Syrian father and French mother. Her parents divorced when she was ten and she was sent to live with an aunt and uncle. They were rabidly opposed to the French occupation. They fled Syria for Egypt to avoid persecution and lived in Cairo for a time.

"There were few choices for girls. My English wasn't good, but I was pretty. So when I was eighteen, I began singing in nightclubs. I met Houman at the club. We had an affair. My family was scandalized. They forced me to give him up. We returned to Damascus, but my family disowned me. I had to work and had many jobs. Then came the war. The Vichy government controlled Syria and I was recruited to work as a courier for the Allies. For three years, I carried messages between the British and the Druze military. But near the end of the war, I was arrested. Houman heard of this and stepped in."

"Why?"

"He remembered me from Cairo." She looked down and her voice became a monotone. "When war broke out, Houman collaborated with the Vichy government informing on Arab rebels. He visited me in jail. He told me I would be freed on the condition I become his mistress. If not, I would be executed. I said yes."

They were silent for a moment.

"So why are you doing this?" John asked.

"The Mufti dreams of a great war of Arabs against the Jews, driving them into the sea. After six years of war and sixty million dead across the world, he wishes for more bloodshed. This killing must end. The Jewish state will come. John, I love my country, my people. If Syria is to have any hope for the future, we must find a way to live with the Zionists and the West. Or be destroyed."

"What's Alfagari's job with the delegation?"

"He provides security. And keeps them out of trouble."

"What kind of trouble?"

"Mostly women and whiskey."

"Does Houman know what the Mufti and Alfagari plan to do?"

"They tell him some things, yes. But they would not trust him with something as important as this."

"Liliane, can you get me proof of who he's going to kill?"

"I can try. There is not much time. The vote is very soon."

He wanted to tell her not to run the risk of being shot. Or blown up in a telephone booth. But he didn't.

"How can I get in touch with you again?"

"You cannot. I will touch you."

He smiled at the solecism. "When?"

"Soon."

"Which train to New York will you be on?" he asked.

"I don't know. I will tell Houman we must take the one you and the children take. He will do what I ask."

"Yes, I'll get them tucked in and have a drink in the club car with the grown-ups."

"That is where Houman spends much of his time too, drinking. I am not allowed."

"Where will you stay in New York?"

"I do not know."

"We'll be at the Paramount Hotel," he said.

"Paramount," she repeated, quizzically. "This means 'supreme'?"

"More or less. Why?"

"It is auspicious. It is one of the ninety-nine attributes of Allah."

"Oh, yes?"

"I must go."

They stood. She was smaller than he had thought, a couple of inches over five feet. He held out his hand. She hesitated, then reached both hands out and grasped his. Her long, cool fingers curled softly around his hand. He fought the urge to put his arms around her and instead nodded once and left. As he walked out of the building and into the night, he looked around, afraid they were being watched. No one was there.

• • •

Now they were all on the same train. John studied the entrance to the private car. The upper half of the door was amber leaded glass. A thick, golden rope was strung across the door and a sign hung from it that read, "Private Car, No Admittance."

He turned the doorknob and went inside. The sitting room was as luxurious as the bartender had described—lots of red velvet, satin, and polished brass. No one was there. He carefully closed the door.

At the far end of the room was a connecting door. He knocked gently. No answer. He knocked again. Taking a deep breath, he grasped the doorknob and pushed. It didn't move. The door was locked, but there was a thumb turn on his side. *Odd.*

He turned the bolt, slowly pushed the door open, and stepped inside a large ornate chamber decorated like a Hollywood set designer's idea of *Arabian Nights*. Sitting up on a large bed was one of the most beautiful women he had ever seen. She was reading a book by the light of a table lamp with a red-fringed shade. She wore a cream-colored nightgown of heavy silk, cut low. Her hair was thick and black and hung down past her breasts. She looked up and smiled. He recognized her eyes.

"Liliane?"

"Yes, John. You had my message?"

"Yes."

"They are drinking, Houman and his son, Adnan?" she said.

"Yes."

"Then we have until Houman passes out. Alfagari will carry him to this bed."

He glanced nervously at the door. "Should I lock it?"

She shook her head. "It locks only from the outside. It is to keep me in. Before Alfagari enters, he will call to me to move into the next room."

"He's already had a lot to drink," he said. "We probably don't have too long. Your message said there is more proof?"

"Yes. John, the Mufti has issued a call to all Muslims to stop the vote by any means necessary."

He tried to hide his disappointment. In a speech that received substantial press attention, the Mufti had called on all Arabs to liberate Palestine from the "filth of the Jews." "Count them one by one," he had said, "and annihilate them down to the very last one."

"That was in the paper two days ago. That's your proof?"

"No. That was for the public. In private, the Mufti has threatened some of the most important UN delegations. If they don't withdraw their support for the Zionists, he says there will be fatal consequences."

"How do you know?"

"The head of our delegation told Houman. He told me."

"But we need more than . . ."

"The word of a woman like me?"

He flushed. "I didn't mean that. I meant one of those delegates going on record or something in writing."

"There might be a writing. I will find out if I can. But I know the names of some of the diplomats. Maybe you can talk to them?"

He took out his pad and wrote as she dictated half a dozen names.

He shook his head in disbelief. "They would kill all of them?"

"You are surprised? The Arabs have death lists; the Jews have death lists. If men like the Mufti have their way, Syria and Palestine will become a stinking pit of death."

The image of emaciated gray-green bodies stacked like firewood went through John's mind.

"Come, let me see if you have written the names correctly." She swiveled and sprang off the bed. There was a flash of her thigh. She landed lightly on her bare feet and the hem of her nightgown floated to the floor. He handed her his notepad. Their fingers touched; her scent drifted to him.

She studied the names, nodded, and returned the pad to him. They didn't speak for a moment. Then she said, "It is correct. Now you can stop these crimes."

"It'll help if there's something in writing."

"I said I will try. You must go now, John."

He made no move to leave. She smiled as though she were familiar with her effect on men. She touched him lightly on the arm to start him moving.

"Haleem told me seeing you like this is against your rules because I'm not *mahram* or something."

Her face tightened. "They are not my rules. *Mahram* are male relatives, father, brothers, uncles. All mine are dead."

He touched her arm. "I'm sorry." He lost himself in her eyes for a moment. "Right, okay." He cleared his throat. "I will find you in New York."

"Good. Now you must go. They will kill you if you are with me like this." Her hands gestured at her face and her body.

As he was about to leave, he turned back and said, "I can help you leave him." Wasn't that really what she wanted? He suddenly wanted it too.

"Goodbye, John."

"Goodbye, Liliane." He closed the door behind him.

"John!"

He opened it again quickly.

She smiled. "Remember to lock the door."

He didn't return her smile. He lifted his hand in a wave, closed the door, and locked it. At the same moment, the front door of the car opened. Adnan, the son, walked in. Alfagari was behind him, carrying the inert bulk of Houman in his arms.

John stumbled forward and fell to his knees. He struggled to stand, leaning on a chair, and weaved drunkenly.

"Where's the damn bar?" he said, deliberately slurring his words. "Was in the can for two minutes and can't find the bar."

"This isn't the bar, sir," Adnan said stiffly. "You must leave immediately."

Alfagari laid Houman on the couch.

"Not leavin' without a goddam drink. Where the hell's the bar?" John kept weaving, stumbling toward another chair. Alfagari unbuttoned his jacket. He eyed John without expression.

"You must go," Adnan said with finality. He said something to Alfagari in Arabic.

Taking two quick steps, Alfagari grabbed John's right arm, jerked him to his feet. He twisted the arm behind him and marched him to the door.

"Ow! What the hell?" he whinged. Alfagari shoved him through the door. John tripped on the jamb and fell to his knees. Sloppily, he pushed himself to his feet and, in one clumsy motion, turned, and threw a long, looping punch purposely missing by a wide margin. Alfagari didn't bother to block it. He smashed a short jolting right to John's jaw, using the heel of his palm. The blow knocked him flat on his back. As he tried to rise, Alfagari took his revolver from his shoulder holster and whipped it across his face. He then pointed the gun at him and thumbed back the hammer. The cylinder turned. There was a sharp click. John froze. Alfagari gave a thin smile, then slowly let the hammer down. He motioned with the pistol for John to leave and slammed the door after him, rattling the leaded glass.

Gasping from pain and exertion, John looked at his reflection in a window. There was blood coming from a cut under his left eye. He took out a handkerchief and wiped his cheek. He worked his jaw. It was sore but not broken. His head was ringing. The night-shadowed landscape of Indiana—or was it Ohio?—raced by at fifty-seven miles per hour. Maybe a drink would dull the pain.

He pulled the handle of the electro-pneumatic door to the next car. It hissed open. He was dazed—from alcohol, from the beating, from what he had learned of the Mufti's plans—but most of all from the achingly lovely image of Liliane, now chased and blazoned in his brain.

9

Two men half carrying a third were leaving the club car just as Jeanne had entered from the other end. A sign propped on the bar said, "Closed." She had explained to the bartender that she just wanted a place to read and he had nodded his approval. He turned the lights off except for a table lamp at the far end of the car and she sat there in its yellow glow. She had changed from her traveling outfit and was wearing a patterned burgundy cashmere sweater and a gray pleated skirt.

"Aren't you a little young to be closing down a bar?" a voice called from the entrance.

John McGrath! She sat up straighter. "There were some men here, but they left a while ago," she called back, squinting to see him in the dim light. "The bartender said I could stay."

"Three Syrian gentlemen?" he said, walking to her table.

"I don't know, but one of them was pretty scary. He carried one of the other men out."

"I'm John McGrath," he said, extending his hand.

"Of course, I know. Jeanne Cooper." She took his hand briefly and felt her face grow warm. "What happened to you?" she said, hoping he wouldn't notice she was blushing.

"Long story."

"Do I look like I'm going anywhere?" There was strain in her voice.

"You okay?"

"I should ask you that. You're the one that looks like you went a couple of rounds with Joe Louis."

"I got in a beef with a guy—some fat salesman from Missouri."

"What about?"

"Baseball. Cardinals and Cubs, never fails."

"Really? Do you want to sit for a minute?"

"Sure. How about a drink?"

"Thought I was too young."

He appeared to study her closely. "You're old enough."

"Do you think the bartender will mind?"

"I'll square it with him. What can I get you?"

"I don't know. I've had champagne at weddings, but I didn't really like the taste."

"Most people don't—they like the way it makes them feel." He thought for a second, then said, "I know the perfect thing; it doesn't even taste like a drink. Trust me."

"I don't know why I should."

"Hey, we sat through those speeches together."

"I heard what you said about our trip."

"I was afraid you did. I hope I didn't offend you."

"I know we must seem like a lot of—what did you call us, schoolchildren?"

"Uh, yeah, sorry for that. Come on, let me make it up to you." He went behind the bar and checked the bottles and the small refrigerator. "Everything we need." Jeanne walked over to the bar and sat on one of the stools.

As he busied himself behind the bar, he said, "You probably don't know this, but you are legally required to tell your bartender your troubles."

"I am?"

"Sure. You seemed upset when I came in."

"I was, but you'll think it's juvenile. My friend, Caroline—you saw her this afternoon—we just had different ideas on how to spend the evening."

"She wanted to have a party—"

"That's right."

"—and you wanted a quieter night."

"Right again."

"And she wanted to use your room for a while, so you either had to fight off her date's friend in his room or find refuge here."

She shook her head in wonder. "Are all bartenders as good as you?"

He shrugged. "I went to high school too, not that long ago. Anybody can see that Caroline is a, uh, fun-loving girl. You seem . . . more the serious type." He mixed heavy cream and crushed ice in a large silver cocktail shaker, then took two bottles, held them high above the shaker, and poured in a liberal amount of each. He put the cover on the shaker. "This is the important part." He did a fast shimmy shake—behind his back, under his leg, over his head—that had her laughing. He poured the creamy mixture into two stemmed cocktail glasses and handed her one. "Let's sit at the table." He brought the shaker with him.

"What is this?" she asked as they sat down.

"It's called a Brandy Alexander. Named after a Russian czar."

She started to take a sip.

"Whoa! Can't drink until we toast. What should we drink to?"

"You say."

"Okay." He raised his glass. "To love and joy."

"Ugh, that's the corniest thing I've ever heard."

"I thought—"

"You thought it's what a high school girl would like."

He laughed. "I guess so. Sorry." He began to take a sip.

"Wait, we still need a toast, don't we?"

"You're so smart, you think of one."

"Sheesh, simple." She raised her glass again. "May our week in New York be one to remember."

"Hmph. Well, it doesn't stink."

"John . . ."

"I'm kidding." He smiled. "I'll drink to that."

They clinked glasses and drank. "It's delicious, like a chocolate malted," Jeanne said.

"That's the crème de cacao," he said.

She finished her drink and licked a dot of foam from her upper lip.

He refilled her glass and raised his. "To New York."

Half an hour and several refills later, Jeanne suddenly realized that she had never ever found anyone so attractive. His intelligent smile and the adorable way he laughed and told story after fascinating story. And his eyes, oh, his eyes. They shined like they had their own source of shimmering blue radiance. She wished she could find the words to express what she was feeling, a warmth she had never felt before—perhaps, she thought excitedly, a warmth no one had ever felt for anyone before!

I have to tell him. My heart is so full, so full of boundless admiration.

"My bounty is as boundless as the ocean!" she blurted out.

John paused mid-anecdote. "What?"

"As boundless as the ocean. My bounty. Is," she said.

He brightened. "You mean 'the sea'? It's 'as boundless as the sea'? That's the line, isn't it? From *Romeo and Juliet*?"

She nodded happily. *He knows Shakespeare, too? He is perfect. I will swoon 'ere long.*

John resumed the story he had been telling of his experiences serving with Patton. She sat back, so relieved to have told him how she felt. She supposed she should have acted less familiar, pretended not to like him, that was how everyone said you should act, but she just couldn't. She was surprised to find she was free of the self-consciousness that always unnerved her when she was talking to a boy she liked.

But that's just it. She leaned forward again. *That's just it, I'm not talking to a boy. For the first time in my life, I'm with a man, not a boy!*

Her excitement at this revelation was quickly followed by panic when she realized she'd lost the thread of his story. *I can't let him know—he'll think I'm a silly high school girl.* She narrowed her eyes, leaned forward even further, and nodded wisely. She stared at him intently and tried to listen harder. As he continued talking, however, watching his lips move distracted her. She blinked, then concentrated harder on each word he said. Something bubbled up inside her stomach. *I feel like I'm floating. I'm going to burp. No, I'm gonna be sick.*

She had a sudden, brilliant epiphany.

I'm drunk as . . . as a skunk.

What would her mother think? Her father? What would Caroline, who called her "Miss Primrose Proper," say?

She giggled. John stopped talking again.

She burped and, a long moment later, covered her mouth with her hand. Which made her giggle again, then burst out laughing.

"Oh, dear," he said.

"What? What is it?" she asked in a whisper.

"You're a little drunk."

"No—" *Oh goodness, I've forgotten his name.* "Um, I am not a little drunk."

"Jeanne . . ."

"I'm a really big drunk." She giggled. "Maybe just a little more?" she said, holding out her empty cocktail glass.

"Uh, no." He took her glass from her hand, and she reached across the table for his glass, which was still half full. "And that one, too, yes," he said, taking both glasses and the cocktail shaker to the bar. "What am I going to do with you?" he said as he returned to their table, shaking his head.

"What *are* you going to do with me?" she said flirtatiously, then felt herself blush furiously.

"Jeanne." He looked exasperated, nervous, and not a little guilty.

"What should we do with me?" she whispered as though she really wanted an answer and they were talking about someone else.

He took a deep breath, blew it out, and shook his head.

She had an inspiration. "Coffee. You must bring me a good deal of black coffee," she sputtered, remembering a line from a movie.

"Good God, no. Then you'll just be drunk and wide awake." The train rocked around a long curve.

She held her head. "Oh, John. I feel like everything is rolling and swaying."

"Everything is rolling and swaying. We're on a train."

"Right, right, that's right. Oh my goodness, it's past curfew. I have to go," she said. "The nuns, they'll send me home." She struggled to her feet, but a swerve of the train almost sent her backward over the chair. John steadied her and she threw her arms around his neck and collapsed against him.

"Here, here, come sit in one of these." He half dragged her to one of the armchairs, then gently disengaged her arms. "Now, don't move."

She lifted an arm, then let it flop down and giggled. "Look, I moved."

"Stay."

He went to the bar and returned with a large carafe of water, a sandwich wrapped in wax paper, a large bottle of Pepto-Bismol, and a spoon.

"Now, listen. Jeanne, you're drunk and no matter what people say, the only thing that can make you un-drunk is time. But that time goes easier if you eat something solid, drink lots of water, and have a couple of spoonfuls of this." He poured a large dose of thick sickly sweet pink liquid into the tablespoon.

She grimaced. "Aw, John, that stuff's for kids."

"You are a kid."

"Am not." Jeanne shook her head, screwed up her face, but swallowed the Pepto-Bismol. Bristling with resentment, she drank an entire glass of water without taking a breath.

"Hey, hey, slow down. We don't want it all coming up again."

"Upchucking like Big Jim Winter." She burped.

"What?"

"Like you wrote." She lowered her voice to a whisper. "You know, about the Mole."

"You read that?"

"'Course."

"Peachy. Now, eat something."

She looked at the sandwich. "It'll make me sick," she said, but grumpily took a large bite.

"There's a good girl." He watched as she chewed. "Now another. You'll be good as new in no time."

He went to the bar and opened two bottles of Coca-Cola, tilting back his head and drinking an entire bottle in one go, then pouring the contents of the second bottle into a glass over ice. He pulled two singles from his wallet and left them on the bar. He sat down next to her and took a sip of the iced cola and gave a long exhale. He picked up a copy of *Time* with Charles de Gaulle on the cover from a rack nearby and began reading, occasionally glancing at her. He poured her another glass of water from the carafe. "Keep drinking." She frowned but took another long drink.

Over the next half hour, Jeanne managed to eat most of the sandwich and submitted to another dose of the Pepto-Bismol.

"You sleepy?" John said.

"Nope."

"Well, try closing your eyes for a bit."

She shut her eyes, which made her feel dizzy. She opened them again. "Close 'em," he snapped.

She settled deeper into the seat and eventually drifted off. When she awoke, the world had stopped spinning and her stomach had settled. The train seemed to be rocking less. Her eyes snapped open like a marionette's. "John."

"Yes?"

"I'm feeling better."

"Dandy."

"So tell me about all this." She gestured with her hand at his face and, still uninhibited, leaned over and lightly touched his injured cheek. "There wasn't any Cardinals fan."

He grinned. "No, there wasn't. I got in a little scrap with one of those Syrian gentlemen."

"Which one?"

"The big one."

"He's pretty scary. What was it about?"

He hesitated, then said, "Well, I was in their compartment asking his boss's girlfriend, Liliane, some questions. They're pretty protective of their women. He saw me leaving and it got kinda physical."

She wanted to ask for more details but stopped herself. "Excuse me for a minute," she said. As she was walking away, she called over her shoulder, "Oh, could I have a Coke, too?"

Jeanne went into the ladies' dressing room at the end of the corridor. It was well stocked with a full array of fancy soaps, lotions, and perfumes. She looked in the mirror and was surprised to find she didn't look nearly as bad as she felt. She unwrapped one of the soaps and washed her face, scrubbing off what remained of her makeup. She retrieved her hairbrush from her purse and brushed her hair. There was a small basket containing disposable toothbrushes and tiny tubes of toothpaste. She took one

of each and brushed her teeth. She wondered about "dousing" herself
with perfume as the ads in magazines suggested but decided against it,
instinctively understanding that being clean and seventeen was far more
attractive than any makeup or store-bought scent. She smoothed her
clothes and went back to the club car. She didn't feel normal, but she
wasn't drunk anymore. As she entered, her eyes met his and they were
both still for a moment.

"Better?" he asked, his voice barely above a whisper. He cleared his
throat and said hoarsely, "Are you feeling better?"

"Much. Thanks." She sat down in the chair next to him instead of the
one across from him.

"Here's your Coke."

"Thanks."

"I'm so sorry, Jeanne. I never should have let you drink so much."

"It's not your fault. I'm a big girl."

"I know, but I'm supposed to be looking after you."

"You were, you did. I want to hear more about those Syrians. What I
don't understand is how you got the nerve to talk to her in the first place."

"I'm a reporter. One thing I learned in the war is that being scared
doesn't have to stop you from doing what you need to do. And to tell the
truth, I was really hoping I'd get out of there before he came back."

"I feel like I'm scared all the time. Not like in a war or anything. But,
you know, scared of what people think, of disappointing my parents or
teachers, afraid of the future."

"That's how most people feel."

"How come no one ever says so?"

"Pride, maybe? Not wanting to seem weak? Seems like half our lives
are spent trying to act different than we really are, to hide how we really
feel. The important thing's not to let fear keep you from achieving what
you want." He smiled sheepishly. "You don't need another speech."

"No, I like what you said." She put her hand lightly on his arm. She
saw him register the contact and let her hand linger a moment. Caroline
had told her once, "You have to be so careful what you do around guys.
Every part of their body is an erogenous zone. Not just their thing." Caroline could be so . . . explicit.

"How long have you worked for the *Sun*?"

"On and off, about six years. I started as a copyboy when I was fifteen, then worked as a stringer while I was in high school. They hired me as a reporter right after I was discharged from the Army."

"Do you like the police beat?"

"Sure, I asked for it. I get to be a reporter and kinda of a cop, too, you know, investigating things."

"I heard what Mr. Hershon said about your father. He was a police officer?"

John nodded. "For twenty years. He was killed in the line of duty. I joined the Army the week after it happened."

"Do they know . . . ?"

"They never figured out who did it."

"Must have been hard on you and your mom."

He shrugged. "My mom died when I was a kid."

"You're all alone?"

He laughed. "Nah. In the Army, I had my sergeant, and now I have Hershon."

"What?"

"I'm kidding."

She could tell he wanted to stop talking about himself. "What did you ask her, that Liliane, about?"

"About the vote coming up on Palestine."

"Why should she know about that?"

"Just a hunch," he said quickly, glancing at his watch. "Hey, it's late."

"But that sounds really interesting."

"Yeah? You follow international politics?"

"Sure, I do. I read the papers, and *Life* and *Time* and *The New Yorker*. That's what I want to do when I get out of school—be a writer and work as a journalist."

"Sounds like a fine idea."

"I bet I know more about the UN than you do."

"That wouldn't be hard," he laughed.

Her voice was small but clear. "Maybe I could help you? You know . . . with your reporting."

He laughed. "Sure, that'd be swell." He stood to leave.

"I'm serious, John. I take great notes and I'm a really good researcher. If not on the UN stuff, just on our trip."

"Jeanne, come on."

"It would give you more time to report on the vote. I could take notes for your articles about us. Please? I've written lots for the school paper. I know what you'll need."

"This is the *Chicago Sun*, Jeanne, not the *Steinmetz Weekly Shopper*."

"It's the *Steinmetz Star*, you're really close. Come on, you said yourself this is just a 'children's tea party.' How good a reporter do I need to be?"

"Hey," he laughed, "I'm sorry for that crack."

"Just give me a chance. Please."

He was shaking his head but seemed to be thinking about it.

"Of course," she said, drawing out the words, "I suppose I could just tell Sister Rose that you spent the evening plying a young woman with booze and cigarettes."

"I didn't give you any cigarettes."

"That is the least important part of what I just said."

He didn't answer.

"If you let me help you, it'll be like tonight never happened."

He blew out a breath. "So, blackmail, right?"

She nodded.

"Now you're thinking like a reporter. Okay, you got a deal. You take notes for my article on the trip tomorrow, show me what you've got, and we agree tonight never happened. Deal?"

"Deal." She put out her hand and he held it gently for a moment longer than necessary.

He cleared his throat. "Let's get you back to your room now that you can pass a sobriety test."

John took her elbow, although she was quite steady. When they reached her compartment door, she turned to face him. They stood a few inches apart, swaying. The next door over was unlatched, opening and closing with the movement of the train. He brushed her arm as he reached past her and pulled it closed with a click. She smelled the remembered aroma of his aftershave. It was fainter now and mixed with a dark scent that was his alone. She put her hands on the crook of each of his arms, stood on tiptoe, and kissed him lightly on his cheek, near where he had been injured. She drew back slightly and looked in his eyes. He hesitated, then put his hands on her shoulders. She kissed him on the mouth. She moved closer and their bodies pressed together. His tongue touched her lips. She opened her mouth and put her arms around his neck. His right hand slipped down to the small of her back and pulled her firmly against him. When at last they broke their kiss, there was the sound of rapid breathing and she was surprised to find it was her own. He drew back and put his hands on her shoulders.

"Jeanne, I'm sorry, I shouldn't—" he whispered.

She leaned in and they kissed again. "Okay," he said firmly, breaking it off. "Time for bed."

"Really?" *I sound like Caroline.*

"Jeanne—"

"I know." She squeezed his hands and let them go. "Good night, John." He turned and she watched as he walked down the lurching corridor. Despite the train's movement, his broad shoulders never touched the walls. She felt a rush of affection for this man she had known less than twelve hours.

When he was out of sight, she carefully opened her compartment door, undressed, and slipped on her nightgown. Just as she was boosting herself into bed, Caroline's hand snaked out and grabbed her ankle. "Got you, sneaky," she hissed and began laughing. "Guess you should have taken the bottom bunk."

Jeanne wriggled free. "Stop it, the sisters will hear."

"Oh, they'll hear all right. They did a bed check a couple of hours ago."

"What?"

"They're worse than cops."

"Oh my god, oh my god, oh my god," she recited as rapidly as a rosary.

"It's no good praying now."

"What did they say?"

"Relax. I told them you were in our little washroom puking from motion sickness. They have no idea what a wild woman you really are, Miss Primrose Proper."

"And they believed you?"

"Of course they believed me. You know what a good liar I am."

"Thank you so much."

"So give. What have you been up to?"

"Nothing."

"Don't give me 'nothing.' Maybe I'll wake Sister Rose."

"You wouldn't."

"No, but come on, I covered for you. Don't I deserve something? My night was a disaster."

"Oh, I'm sorry."

"So?"

"I'll tell you everything in the morning."

"Is Mr. Wonderful a good kisser?"

Jeanne was silent.

"Well?"

"Really wonderful. Now, that's all you're going to get. Go to sleep."

Her body was still glowing from excitement. She replayed the whirl of events of the evening. *I'll never be able to sleep. Whatever we said, tonight really did happen.*

10

Jeanne's eyes snapped open at seven, her stomach filled with untethered dread. She squeezed her eyes shut in panic. Random pictures chased through her mind. The empty club car. John looking like he'd been in a brawl. The phantom memory of that drink, its smell, its taste still in the back of her throat. *I was so stupid.*

She turned on her side and stared at the shadows flashing at the edge of the window shade as the train rattled and lurched. More memories trickled in. John's indulgent smile when he realized she was tipsy. And then, later, something different. Fondness? Desire? He must like her or he wouldn't have kissed her like that, would he? She arched and stretched and rolled to her other side, bringing her knees up and holding her pillow in her arms.

Was I too forward? Her stomach fluttered. *Did I act like that because I was drunk or was that just an excuse to act like . . . like I'm 'easy'?* What a stupid expression. Sexual desire could be fun and exciting and bewildering; nothing about it seemed easy. She turned again and the sheet twisted around her legs. After struggling for a moment, she finally threw off her covers and swung down from her bunk.

She gave a whispered shout. "Rise and shine. Let's get breakfast."

Caroline lifted her pillow off her head, half opened one eye, and stared menacingly. She said hoarsely, "You have got to be kidding."

"Come on. We'll be the first ones there."

"Who cares? Let me sleep." She rolled over and jammed the pillow on her head.

"I'm hungry." She picked up the menu that had been left in their room. "They have kippered herring."

"Yecchh," Caroline's muffled voice said from under the pillow.

"Fried ham? I know you like that."

"Double yecch."

"Browned corned beef hash."

There was a pause. "Will they have ketchup?"

"Bottles and bottles. And there's sausages and wheat cakes."

Caroline peeked out from under the pillow. "Give me ten—" She checked the wall mirror. "—uh . . . fifteen minutes." She locked herself in the bathroom while Jeanne dressed; then they traded places.

They made their way to the restaurant car. Its walls were lined with dark wood paneling, the floor covered by thick, blue carpet. Each window was framed by gold curtains held back with braided cords, allowing the morning sun to warm the room. A dozen tables for four lined one side of the car and an equal number of tables for two lined the other. They were covered with white linen tablecloths and carefully set with china, silver, and glasses that tinkled cheerfully with the movement of the train.

It was empty.

"Where is everyone?" Caroline said.

"Breakfast isn't for another half hour, ladies," a voice answered from behind them. They turned to see a steward carrying a tray of water glasses. He was thin and dark and dressed entirely in white.

"I thought breakfast was at seven thirty?" Jeanne said.

"No, miss, eight o'clock."

"Uh-oh," she said, glancing at her friend. Caroline crossed her arms resentfully.

"But I can start you off on juice or coffee, or," he said, "I could get you cold stuff, uh, cereal, rolls, or the stewed prunes."

"Thank you. May I have coffee and orange juice, please?"

"Sure thing, miss. And for you?" he said, turning to Caroline.

She shook her head grumpily, but said, "The same, thanks."

"Coming right up." He set glasses on each table and went to the kitchen.

"Do you think we're still in Pennsylvania?" Jeanne said.

Caroline stared out the window at the lightening sky.

The steward returned with their juice and coffee. "Cook says you can order hot food now, if you like."

Jeanne looked at him gratefully. "Ham and scrambled eggs, please."

"I'll have the hash and a fried egg, please," Caroline said. "Can I get extra hash?"

"Double hash. You got it."

Caroline gave her first smile of the day.

Taking advantage of this thaw, Jeanne said, "Tell me about your dates."

It had not gone as planned. Caroline's nine o'clock date was a good-looking bore whose idea of fun was quizzing her about the United Nations as a way of demonstrating he could name all fifty-seven member countries and their capitals. She told him she felt ill and sent him on his way. Her midnight, Tony, was a jumpy junior she'd talent-spotted at the table next to them at Union Station as he took careful notes on Marshall Field's speech with a much-bitten yellow pencil.

"Once he relaxed, he was a lot of fun. He's really smart, but he doesn't have to show off. He came into our room, but he left after only ten minutes. Just said 'good night' and left. Said some of the boys were having a late-night Monopoly game. He deserted me for Monopoly. What did I do wrong?"

"You mean besides having a boy in your room?"

"You sound like my mom. Anyway, look who's talking."

"Right. Um, did you kiss him?"

"Of course, but I thought a boy alone in a bedroom with me would try for more. Why didn't he?"

"Any boy would jump at the chance to go too far with you."

"Not Tony," Caroline said mournfully.

"He didn't want to take advantage. He must like you—he's a gentleman."

"That's so corny."

"There are good guys, you know."

Caroline groaned. "Oh, god, stop!"

"Stop what?"

"Being so moony about your new boyfriend."

"He's not my boyfriend."

"So, this Mr. Wonderful. Is he a 'gentleman'?"

She was saved from answering by the arrival of their food. As they ate, she wondered about John. He must have been with girls before. Her heart twisted at the thought. Although Jeanne wasn't the obedient Catholic girl she'd once been, neither was she one of the free-spirited women she so admired in life and in literature who slept with men as and when they pleased without regard for convention. Her parents would be shocked if they knew her thoughts.

"Sure he is," Jeanne said, glancing around.

"You can stop. He's not here," Caroline said. "You really like him, huh?"

She bit her lip. "I really do."

The restaurant car was now full of their fellow students. The two nuns were headed in their direction. Jeanne was worried, as though they might somehow have read her thoughts. She looked carefully at her plate, waiting for them to pass by.

"Jeanne Cooper?" said Sister Rose, the elder of the two.

"Yes, Sister?" She couldn't look her in the eye.

"We would like to speak with you in our room. Right away." They walked quickly out of the restaurant car.

Jeanne rose to follow them.

"Remember, you were in the bathroom!" Caroline whispered.

Jeanne gave her a panicked look and followed the nuns. When she arrived at their compartment, Sister Mary was holding the door open.

"Well, come in. Don't loiter in the hall."

"Yes, Sister; I'm sorry, Sister."

Jeanne stepped inside. Their room had already been made up. Sister Mary sat down on a small chair near the window. Sister Rose stood stiffly and gestured to the low Pullman couch. "Sit."

Jeanne felt as though she were a fifth grader again at Our Lady of Angels. "Well," rasped Sister Rose, "what have you to say for yourself?"

Like any prisoner about to undergo torture and interrogation, Jeanne had, in the few minutes it took to walk from the restaurant car, rehearsed her attitude and her story.

"Sister?" she asked, eyes wide.

"Don't play innocent with me. You were out of your room until all hours with a boy. Unless you want to be sent home, you'll be honest and tell us the boy's name."

"Sister, I'm sorry—you're mistaken. I was in my compartment. There was no boy."

"Young lady, that might work with your teachers at that institution you attend they are pleased to call a school. It won't work with us. We heard you in the corridor."

Jeanne remembered their door was ajar when she returned with John.

"I was in the corridor for a moment, just to get some fresh air. One of the stewards walked by and said good night."

"I think you are lying," Sister Rose said, "and unless you tell us the boy's name, you will be sent home on the next train."

"I've told you what happened. I can't tell you something that isn't true."

"Very well. Father Bernard will deal with you. It is his decision, but we will recommend that your parents be notified immediately and you be sent home. You may go."

Jeanne rushed out of their room and into her own. She threw herself on the lower bunk and began to cry. She would never be able to face her parents, her friends, or her teachers. She had never felt more like a grown-up than she had last night—and she had never felt more like a child than she did now.

11

Jeanne's face was pressed to the window as the train trotted the last few miles into New York City. They pulled into Penn Station at nine thirty, exactly on time. Porters hustled their luggage into the waiting buses. The student editors were herded through the station for the short ride to the Paramount Hotel on West Forty-Sixth Street, a block from Times Square.

She was walking with Caroline and Tony and a group of other students when John passed them. She tried to catch up with him, the small train case she was carrying bumping against her leg, her heels clicking on the marbleized concrete floor. He must have seen her. Why didn't he say hello?

"John?" He didn't turn, so she said his name again louder. "John, hello. Good morning."

He turned. There was a look of irritation on his face, which he changed to a polite smile a moment too late. "Good morning."

"Do you think we're on the same bus?" she said, trying to keep the hurt out of her voice.

"No idea."

Not a hint he even knew her. "Well, I just wanted to say hello," she said. He nodded and cantered ahead. She was burning with embarrassment.

"He could get fired for being involved with a student," Caroline said quietly from behind. She put her arm through Jeanne's and they walked through the enormous concourse of Penn Station, with its walls of faux travertine and decorative ceiling high over their heads. They made their way past hundreds of travelers getting an early start on their Thanksgiving journeys, nearly tripping over a weary mother sitting on her suitcase. Her small daughter, a white bow in her hair, was squeezed next to her facing the opposite direction.

They climbed the famous triple staircase sweeping up and out to Seventh Avenue and went through the heavy brass doors. Jeanne's excited recollections of countless scenes in books and movies were slapped away by the raucous reality of Manhattan.

The clichés were all there in the cold, dirty air, but they were frightening, not romantic. The buildings that towered over them in every direction looked ugly and menacing; yellow cabs big as tanks swerved through dark puddles of water; hard-faced pedestrians pinballed along the jammed sidewalks. The *Sun*'s double-parked buses, brown exhaust spewing from vibrating tailpipes, blocked traffic.

"Oh, look, it's Macy's, like in *Miracle on 34th Street*," Caroline said. The "World's Largest Store" didn't look like it had on the screen. Its stone walls were dark and scarred, its display windows shiny with greed, not glistening with generosity.

Sister Rose stood by the door of the second bus with a clipboard. She waved an arm stiffly as they approached. "Hurry, ladies, you're holding up traffic," she scolded.

Most of the seats were already taken. John was halfway back. Jeanne walked toward him, trying to exude nonchalance. He poked the man next to him, who swung into action.

"Hey, girls, look this way," the man said, holding up a large camera with a flash attachment. Jeanne stopped and looked at him uncertainly, but Caroline struck a pose and gave a dazzling smile as his flashbulb exploded.

While the photographer wrote down their names, John winked at Jeanne.

Her heart squeezed, then bloomed. Maybe it was the flash, but it seemed to her that the forbidding city had suddenly become bright with sunlight.

"Oh, shoot, Jeanne. You've got it bad," Caroline said.

"Mm-hmm," she murmured. "And that ain't good." They made their way to an empty seat near the back and sat down as the bus began to move.

"It's the Empire State Building," called out Caroline. The others craned their necks as the bus lumbered up Seventh Avenue, thrilled when they were able to see a bit of the Chrysler Building or some other landmark.

"Times Square," one student exclaimed.

"Look at all the theaters," said another. There were signs for shows that were already legendary, such as *Oklahoma!*, *Annie Get Your Gun*, *Born Yesterday*, and *Brigadoon*, and billboards advertising new productions such as *Crime and Punishment* and *A Streetcar Named Desire*.

The bus turned west into the narrows of West Forty-Sixth Street and stopped just short of Eighth Avenue. The students poured onto the sidewalk and into the two-story lobby of the Paramount Hotel. A *Sun* representative stood behind a long table. "Everyone, this way, please. Get your room assignments. Find your name on the list and pick up your keys. There's a printed itinerary for each of you and a brochure on 'Control Procedures.' Please take one of each. Remember, there's to be no wandering around the hotel or city on your own. We'll meet in the restaurant for lunch at twelve thirty and leave directly after for our sightseeing tour. It's chilly today and we'll be out on the water, so dress accordingly."

Caroline pushed forward to the table and returned with two keys and copies of their itinerary. "Tenth floor."

Their window looked out on West Forty-Sixth Street. They could see the top of the theater marquees, their lights glimmering shyly in the daylight. Their suitcases had been placed at the foot of the twin beds and they quickly unpacked.

"Mind if I take the first shower?" Caroline asked. Jeanne shook her head. Caroline went in the bathroom and Jeanne sank onto her bed, exhausted. She propped a pillow against the headboard, laid back, and tried to read the itinerary, but the paper slowly dropped to her chest. The telephone rang, but she could not move to answer it. "No, I'm sorry, she's not available," Caroline said in a chilly distant voice. "Yes, I'll give her that message."

Someone was shaking her.

"Honey, you have to wake up if you want to shower before lunch." Jeanne finally managed to open her eyes. "Oh, thank goodness, I thought

I was going to have to set off a bomb," Caroline said. "I let you sleep as long as I could, but it's ten after." Jeanne nodded and blinked. To keep from falling asleep again, she swung her feet onto the floor.

"Who was on the phone?"

Caroline was silent.

"Caroline?"

"What?" She looked at the floor.

"Caroline, it was him. Why didn't you wake me?"

"You needed your sleep! Besides, I don't like him."

"But I like him. What did he want?"

Caroline set her face stubbornly.

"Caroline."

"He said to meet him at twelve fifteen in the arcade off the main lobby."

"That's in five minutes. I don't have time for a shower." She rushed to the bathroom, washed her face and hands, then ran to the closet and pulled out a fresh sweater and skirt.

"You just changed your clothes this morning."

"But he's seen me in these already." As she wriggled out of the old outfit and into the new, she added, "Save me a seat at lunch."

"Jeanne," Caroline cried as Jeanne was running out the door.

"What?"

"You forgot your coat."

Jeanne dashed back, grabbed her coat, scarf, hat, and gloves, and ran out. "Thanks."

"Lobby, please," she said to the elevator operator. She tried to compose herself.

The operator was Black. His right sleeve was empty and pinned to his chest at the elbow. There were so many men like him since the war, with wounds visible and invisible. What was it like knowing that people were staring and wondering? She shifted her gaze to the floor numbers over the door.

"Left it in Bastogne, Christmas '44."

"Pardon me?" she said, although she knew what he meant.

"The other one," he said, pointing to his empty sleeve. "People generally want to ask."

"I'm sorry, I didn't mean to stare." Her face grew warm.

"That's all right."

"I didn't think . . . I mean—"

"I know," he said. "We were the first Black troops to fight on the front lines. Thought all of us, White and Black, were goners till Patton showed up day after Christmas. Best present I ever got."

"I have a friend who was with Patton."

"That so? Well, you tell him thanks from me. Where you from?"

"Chicago."

"Cubs fan? You ever see Jackie play?"

She nodded vigorously. "Twice. The whole South Side came out to see him. They beat us both times. He scored most of their runs. My dad said to cheer for him, even though he's a Dodger, to make him feel welcome after the way they treated him in St. Louis."

"Just voted rookie of the year."

"He deserved it." Jeanne felt she should say something more. "It must have been hard for him, being the first." There weren't any Black students at Steinmetz.

"That's a fact."

The elevator bounced to a stop. "Here we are. Enjoy your stay, now."

"Can you tell me, please, which way is the arcade?"

"To the left, miss."

"Thanks for the ride," she said and proffered a quarter tip to him instead of the dime she had planned.

He raised his hand and said, "No need."

She felt a rush of warmth. "I have to. My dad said you're supposed to tip everybody in New York and gave me extra for it. Please?"

"Sure," he said, slipping the coin in a vest pocket.

She couldn't rid herself of the feeling it meant far more to her to give him the money than it did to him to accept it. She stepped out of the elevator, looked carefully around the lobby, then set out for the arcade. There were dozens of people walking in the long dark hall. She went toward the shops, thinking perhaps John was inside one of them. There was a bank of telephone booths with wooden doors on her left. The doors had small opaque windows instead of the usual clear glass. As she walked by the last phone booth, the door swung open and John stepped out and touched her arm.

"Jeanne. You got my message."

"I was so glad you called. I was afraid—"

"Afraid?"

"You were sorry for last night."

He looked surprised. "No, not at all. Are you?"

"No. But when you saw me in the station this morning, you acted—"

"I know, I figured you were upset. There's something I want to talk to you about."

"Should we step into the phone booth?" She smiled.

"Too cloak-and-dagger?" He looked up and down the arcade. "Okay, no nuns in sight. Let's sit for a minute." He took her hand and led her to a nearby bench. Their hands dropped to their sides, but they sat only inches away from each other as though it would pain them to be farther apart.

"Listen, I thought more about what you said about helping out, more than just taking notes. Do you still want to?"

"Really?" Her voice squeaked like a six-year-old's and she forced herself to calm down. "Absolutely," she said in a near whisper. "Anything I can do. What made you change your mind?"

"I'm going to be a lot busier than I thought reporting on the UN. I have an appointment downtown with a police detective in an hour. That's who I was on the phone with."

"The police. Why?"

"Something Liliane told me. I called my paper early this morning from the train. I told Hershon there might be some violence involving the delegates with this vote coming up. He gave me the okay to look into it."

"I know there's been a lot," Jeanne said excitedly. "I've read articles about the fighting in Palestine."

"Not just Palestine. Someone bombed the British embassy in Rome a few weeks ago."

"Right," she said. "The British papers say that the Zionists are threatening to kill people."

"Where?"

"Uh, in the *Daily Mail*, I think."

"No, what city?"

"In London."

"The Zionists, not the Arabs?" He looked confused.

"That's what the papers said."

"Did they kill a diplomat there?" he asked.

"Not that I've read. Why?"

"Nothing, there was a rumor they had."

"She told you that?"

"It's not important. Anyway, Hershon wants me to check with the local law enforcement, see if they have any information on trouble here in New York."

"Are you going to write an article about it?"

"Nothing to write about yet." He paused a moment. "You might be able to help me gather info on that, too."

"Really?" Her voice moved into a higher register again.

"Relax, sweetheart. You won't be running around in a trench coat, packing a .38."

God, I must have told him how much I love Mickey Spillane last night.
"No, right, of course not."

"But first, I need you to cover the sightseeing tour today for me. Can you do it?"

She was disappointed. The tour of New York she had been so looking forward to now seemed a dull thing compared to international intrigue.

"You can count on me, John."

"Then, if you have time, you could contact the UN press office. See if you can get some background on the members of the Syrian delegation."

"Really? What kind of background?"

"Whatever they have—bios, press releases, pictures."

"But . . . but what should I say? Who should I say I am? Why am I asking?"

He chuckled. "We have a saying at the paper. 'As a very last resort, tell the truth.'"

She shook her head, not understanding.

"Tell them you're a reporter for a Chicago paper, the *Steinmetz Post-Picayune*."

She tsked. "It's the *Star*."

"Sure. No need to say you're in high school, but don't lie, either. You're in New York City to learn more about the United Nations. You understand that these men are important diplomats and you'd like to know more about them."

"I'm on it, John. I won't let you down."

"I'm sure you won't." He seemed to be suppressing a smile.

"I'll get you my notes on our tour as soon as it's over."

He looked momentarily confused. "Uh, sorry, I guess I wasn't clear. When I said 'cover,' I meant I want you to write the article for tomorrow's paper."

"Really?"

"You know, kiddo, it'd save us a lot of time if you just assume I mean everything I say to you."

"Everything, John?" She scooted closer until they were touching. She was surprised at herself, how free he made her feel.

"Knock it off."

"Fine." She scooted an inch away. "I'll stick to business." He cocked his head and looked at her skeptically.

"You sure you can do this?"

She tried not to let her irritation show. "Didn't you say you were seventeen when you joined the Army?"

"Yeah, so?"

"Well, so am I. And if you could beat Hitler when you were seventeen, it's just possible I can write an article for a second-tier Chicago daily about some high schoolers sightseeing in New York."

"Second-tier daily? Ouch."

"Well, the *Sun*'s not exactly the *New York Times*, is it?"

He laughed and stood up. "All right, fine. Have your draft at the hotel reception desk by six. I'm off. I may make it for part of the tour this afternoon. Don't be upset if I, you know—"

"Come on, what do you think I am?" she said, standing. "Maybe we can meet tonight?"

He thought for a minute. "There's probably some outing for your group after dinner. I don't think we'll have time to meet beforehand, but—"

"But what?"

"Do you like jazz?"

"I love jazz," she lied.

"That's great because the best jazz band in the world's playing a few blocks away."

"Who is it, Bennie Goodman? That would be wonderful."

"Oh, please."

"Glen Miller?" He shook his head in mock disgust. "Tommy Dorsey? Frank Sinatra? I love him and I saw he's in town. But I think he's at the Capitol."

"Nope, better," he said. "Bird himself, Charlie Parker, with Miles Davis and Max Roach." He spoke their names as if they were the Founding Fathers. "After tonight, you'll never want to hear anyone else."

"Wait. Oh, no. I can't. Shoot! I just remembered. We do have something tonight. We're going to Radio City."

"It won't be a problem," he chuckled. "That'll be over by eleven. These guys don't even start warming up 'til 'round midnight."

"Around midnight?"

"Like the song 'Round Midnight'? Come on, you don't know Thelonious Monk, either?"

"That is not a real name."

"So much to learn."

"But what about—?"

"The Sisters of No Mercy? There are fire stairs at the back of the hotel. After you get back from Radio City, go up to your floor, then right down those stairs. I'll meet you at the rear exit. You game?"

"You bet, but it's better if we meet at the club."

"Okay. It's called The 3 Deuces on West Fifty-Second. Hey, it doesn't look like we're going to get much sleep on this trip."

"I don't mind."

"Me either. We can snooze in the sun when we're old and gray." They both laughed. "I gotta go."

"I can't wait to hear what you find out," she said, hoping he would kiss her goodbye.

He patted her shoulder and walked away. Disappointed, she watched until he was around the corner. He never looked back.

I've got it bad, all right.

PART III

2003

12

Early Sunday morning, June 22, 2003, Jeanne tottered off the shuttle at London Heathrow Airport carrying an oversized bag whose strap dug a crease in her shoulder. It didn't help that her heart was still beating overtime from watching, terrified, as the seemingly suicidal shuttle driver, a Sikh wearing a bright orange turban, drove at hypersonic speed through the airport on what her brain bellowed was the wrong side of the road.

She waited impatiently in front of the soaring glass curtain wall of Terminal Four as Michael got off the bus. Persuading him to come had been easy. His token show of resistance evaporated when she said, "It'll give us a chance to talk about what's going on with your business." His eyes had lit up and he accepted her offer of a two-week deluxe vacation to Italy. She knew he wanted her to rescue him from his latest difficulty and she hadn't decided what to do. Saying no to your children, whatever their age, was hard, but saying yes brought complications too.

Kerry and Alice's flight from New York had landed a few minutes ago and she wanted to be in the terminal when they arrived. Kerry would spend a few days in London rehearsing before traveling on to Spoleto, where they would all meet later in the week. Jeanne hoped that some enforced togetherness in Italy would ameliorate the bitterness that now infested their little family. She hadn't yet told Michael that Alice would be traveling with them instead of with Kerry and she worried about his reaction given how hurt he'd been by Alice's choice to live with her mother instead of with him.

"Michael, come on. The travel agent said security here takes forever," she said.

"So why didn't she book us a flight to Rome on the same airline so we didn't have to change terminals?"

"Because it was two thousand dollars more."

"Sometimes it's worth paying for convenience."

She bit her lip.

Once inside the terminal, they stopped at Caffè Nero. They stood at a small table while he had coffee and a croissant.

"Michael?" she finally said.

"Mm-hmm."

"I meant to tell you, Alice will be traveling with us instead of her mom."

"What?"

"Kerry is going to be so busy the first week, I thought it made more sense."

The cup in his hand tremored and he opened his mouth to respond.

"Smile," she said. "They're here."

Michael smacked his cup down on the small round table and turned around. When Alice saw Jeanne, she brightened, ran the few remaining yards between them, and wrapped her tightly in her arms. Jeanne nearly lost her balance.

"Oh, god, sorry," Alice said. "Did I hurt you?"

Jeanne smiled. "No, not at all."

"I'm so glad you're here," Alice said. As if noticing him for the first time, she half turned and said, "Oh, hi, Dad."

"Hey, honey," he said.

Michael and Kerry hadn't looked at each other.

"Kerry," Jeanne said, embracing her. "It's so good to see you. We have a few minutes. Have a cup of coffee."

"Okay," Kerry said, setting her bag on the floor. "But before I forget—I wanted to thank you for paying the school fees."

"Yes," Michael said, "thanks. I'll write you a check when we get home." His voice was stiff with resentment.

"Alice, come on, let's get you and your mom something to eat," Jeanne said. "You can set your things under the table." She linked arms with Alice and they went to order. Kerry and Michael were left standing together in chilly silence.

"How are you, Grandma? Did the flight tire you out?" Alice asked.

"Not at all, sweetie. My heart doesn't bother me a bit. It's just I couldn't sleep very well. Your dad snored the whole way. How about you?"

"We had the greatest seats. I've never flown in business class. The best was when you made the seat lie flat, most of your body went into this pod and you were all covered and snug. I want to get one to sleep in at home."

"I hoped it'd be nice," she said.

"It was. I'm totally spoiled now."

"Then I've done my job."

It was their turn to order. Jeanne had forgotten what Kerry wanted. Alice remembered and ordered. Jeanne paid and they walked over to the pickup point.

"So, did everything work out with . . . the pot thing?"

"Mm-hmm. The DA was really nice; she said she wouldn't file charges if I attended a drug class. If I don't get in trouble for a year, it all gets wiped off my record."

"How was the class?"

"Not as bad as I thought. The best part was I saw one of the snotty girls from my school there. You better believe that got around pretty fast."

"Have you been making friends?" Jeanne asked.

"You sound like my mom."

"Well?"

"Not really, though there's this goofy kid I hang with. Geoffrey."

"You have a boyfriend?"

"God, no. Just friends. He's a sophomore and sorta weird looking, but we hang out sometimes, go to the movies or to the galleries. He's the kid I got in trouble with. But he's nice, really smart. He wants to be an artist."

"Being smart can make someone attractive."

"Not him."

"What's he doing this summer?"

"His parents are dragging him and his sister all over Europe to 'further their education.' You know, museums and that kind of stuff."

"I suppose if he wants to be an artist, it's possible they're not dragging him."

"I guess."

"Here's our drinks. Help me take them to the table. Look at your folks together." *It's working already!*

When they arrived at the table, though, it was clear that nothing was working. Kerry and Michael were wrapped in frozen bubbles of silence, evidently praying for the moment they would be able to go their separate ways. Alice sat as far away as possible and put her earbuds in.

"So what should we talk about?" Jeanne asked.

"Logistics," Kerry finally said. "Opening night for the opera is next Saturday the twenty-eighth. I was hoping you could bring Alice."

"She hates opera," Michael said. "I don't want to spend the week fighting with her."

"It's not your fight, Michael—it's mine," Kerry said, staring at him. "I don't need your help."

"That's enough," Jeanne said. "Where are you staying?"

"The Stafford by Green Park. I can walk to the rehearsal rooms near Covent Garden. Nelson must have a lot of pull. Singers don't usually stay in places that fancy." Kerry looked at her cardboard cup for a moment. She turned to Michael and put her hand on his arm. "I'm sorry, I shouldn't have said that; I don't want to fight."

"Then maybe you could think before you speak for once." He jerked his arm away.

"Michael," Jeanne began.

He turned on her. "Stay out of it, Mom. This isn't your business."

Jeanne thought of a variety of richly satisfying but incredibly unhelpful retorts. She kept them to herself and sat down.

Michael's face was rigid. "Maybe somebody should have asked me before dragging her on this trip."

Kerry inhaled deeply, then nodded. "You're right."

"And, Mom," he continued. "I know you think you can fix anything. But you can't fix us."

"You can't be sure of that," Jeanne said. "I don't mean to interfere, but I just want you both to be happy. I guess this was all a bad idea." She lowered her head.

"No, it wasn't," Kerry said.

"It was," she said. "Everything. Italy, seeing John, you guys, bringing Alice. I don't know what I was thinking." She began to cry quietly.

Kerry and Michael looked at each other, stricken. Kerry said, "It's going to be fine."

Michael said, "We're really sorry—it won't happen again. Okay?" He bent his head and tried to look into her eyes.

Kerry put a hand on Jeanne's shoulder and gently rubbed. "Really, Mom," she said, "it won't."

Alice noticed Jeanne's tears and tore off her earbuds. "What did you guys do to her?"

Jeanne looked up and dabbed her eyes with a tissue. "Nothing. I'm just jet-lagged. Hey, there's a bookstore. Let's get you something to read on the flight to Rome."

"And I need to get going, I have a rehearsal this afternoon," Kerry said, standing. "Mom, Alice has her passport and some money in her backpack and two books she's supposed to read over the summer." She picked up her shoulder bag. "Do you know where I can get a taxi?"

"Oh, good lord, don't take a taxi. That will cost you an arm and a leg," Jeanne said. She whipped out a London guidebook and checked the Tube map.

"You have a guidebook for London?" Michael asked, shaking his head.

"We're in London, aren't we?"

"For like two hours, Mom."

"Take the Heathrow Express, Kerry. It gets you to Paddington and from there you can catch the Tube for the Green Park station. It'll let you out right next to your hotel."

"Thanks. Bye, guys," Kerry said, hugging Alice, then Jeanne. "Can't wait to see you in Spoleto." She began to walk away but turned back to Michael. "See you, too, I guess."

He moved toward her, but she was already walking away.

13

"I don't want to sit there," Alice said loudly, stopping stiff-legged in the middle of the airplane aisle like a recalcitrant horse.

"Well, that's your seat, Alice." Michael's voice was edged with malice. "If you don't like it, talk to your grandmother. She arranged everything."

Jeanne had had enough. "Oh, for goodness' sake. You're holding everyone up. Sit down," she commanded. She felt as though she were speaking to two small children. "It won't kill you to sit together."

Alice huffed as she sat, her face a perfect picture of misery. She pushed up against the window, as far away from Michael as possible, put her dangling earpiece in her ear, and closed her eyes.

"Sorry about her, Mom," Michael mumbled and snatched a magazine from the seat pocket in front of him and stared at it until he realized it was the safety briefing card.

This was another in a series of tantrums Alice had thrown since Kerry had left them. The first occurred while standing in the middle of one of the long and pointless security lines in which Heathrow seemed to specialize. Alice announced she was hungry. Michael nodded an acknowledgment but didn't act as though this called for any action on his part.

"I have a protein bar," Jeanne said, digging in her bag. "Here."

Alice looked at the bar. "Cranberry raisin, yecch! Are you kidding?"

Jeanne dug further, keeping her temper. "Here's an oatmeal."

"That's worse!"

"Sorry, that's all I have."

"But I have a headache and I feel like I'm going to faint."

"Try to hang on," Jeanne said.

"I'm literally going to be sick if I don't get something to eat right now."

"I don't know what you expect me to do," Jeanne said with rising frustration. This was new to her. Michael, whatever his faults as an adult, had been a remarkably easy child. "Stop acting like this is the Bataan death march."

Alice stared into space, her face scrunched in anger, arms tightly crossed.

Ten minutes later, the death march was at an end. Alice laced up the stylish combat boots the unyielding security officer had forced her to remove.

"There's a restaurant," Michael said, pointing to a sign that said, "Giraffe."

"Let's go," Jeanne said.

Alice exploded again. "That looks gross! I want to eat at Wagamama."

"At what?" Jeanne asked.

"Wagamama."

"But it's on the other side of the terminal," Michael said, reading a directory. "It'll take twenty minutes to walk there."

"But it's so good," Alice pleaded.

"How do you know?" Michael asked.

"A friend told me we have to eat there."

"No, Alice, no." Jeanne rounded on her, finally ready to confront her unreasonable granddaughter. "Five minutes ago, you were so hungry—" But something in Alice's eyes beyond reason stopped her. She took a deep breath and swallowed some pretty choice words she had ready to go. "Okay. It's all right, Michael—I'll take her. You eat here. Have a beer, take it easy. We'll meet you at the gate."

His face relaxed in guilty gratitude and he walked off as fast as he decently could.

"Grandma, we could get there quicker if we get one of those golf carts to give us a ride," Alice said cheerily as though the entire storm hadn't occurred.

"That's for the handicapped."

"It is not. It's for anyone who needs help. You have a heart thing. You're over seventy. You need a little help. Come on, I'll ask."

"I'll show you who needs help." She began walking through the crowd at a fast clip, her heavy bag bumping against her side, its strap burning a rut in her shoulder. She immediately regretted her decision but refused to slow down. It was her turn to feel faint.

• • •

Jeanne tried to shake off the bickering of her prickly progeny as she settled into the aisle seat behind them. She placed her large handbag in the middle area between the seats and pulled out their tour itinerary for Rome, a thick, plastic-bound document filled with pages of pictures and descriptions of each monument and museum. As she read, she circled things she wanted Alice to see, becoming so engrossed she barely looked up when a stout man squeezed over her legs, mumbled an apology, and plopped down in the window seat. He immediately opened a small laptop and began tapping away, not stopping even during takeoff, despite the flight attendant's remonstrances.

She put the itinerary aside and opened a *New Yorker*. She flipped through it, searching for something—anything—that didn't mention the war in Iraq. She settled on an article about the Three Gorges Dam in China, which had been under construction for nearly ten years. She dutifully slogged through page after expertly edited page for half an hour until she finally admitted she had no interest in the childhood struggles and humble origins of the engineer who had designed the dam. She let the magazine fall to her lap and looked out the window across the aisle. They had passed over France already and the white peaks of the Alps were outlined against the steel-blue sky. Her seatmate stirred and spoke.

"I'm sorry," she said, turning.

"What? Oh, no, I wasn't . . ." His voice trailed off. He looked at her shyly. "It was nothing."

"No, tell me, please," she said, eager to talk to someone who wasn't a relative.

"Well, if you insist. It concerned the Ultramontanists. I'm writing a journal article on them." His English had the curled vowels and clipped diction of a BBC World Service announcer. "Of course, you wouldn't know who they were," he hurried on. His broad pale face grew red. "Sorry to disturb." He looked at his computer screen.

She said quietly, "It so happens I do. They were Europeans who looked to the Pope 'beyond the mountains' for political authority, right?"

"Quite right. Extraordinary."

"Why 'extraordinary'?"

"I wouldn't expect—"

"An American to know of them?"

"No, no, of course not," he mumbled. "I must sound dreadfully pedantic."

"A little. Are you an historian?"

"I'm a professor of European history, Renaissance and Reformation."

"Are you at Cambridge or Oxford?"

He shook his head, his pedanticism punctured, which pleased her. "No, nothing so grand. University of Sussex. Sorry to disappoint. It has no history to speak of, but it's quite near the sea as it happens, lovely beaches and so forth."

"I'm not disappointed. But, tell me what you said."

"Stupid, really. We were heading toward the Alps and we're on our way to Rome. I said, 'The Ultramontanists return on high.' To Rome, you know, from 'beyond the mountains'? Well, I was concerned you heard me and consequently felt foolish. Not unusual for me, by the way." He smiled, which suggested a warmth at odds with his donnish manner.

"I'm Ernest Holmes," he said, extending his hand.

"Jeanne Carpenter," she said, taking and holding his hand a moment longer than necessary. It was warm and comfortable if perhaps a bit moist. "Do your friends call you Ernie?" She was teasing. No one she had ever met seemed less like an "Ernie."

"Good lord, no."

"I teach as well. Literature and composition for junior college students."

"Oh, well done. That sounds splendid."

"Does it? I guess I feel about it the way you feel about Sussex. When I say I'm a college teacher, people are impressed, but when they learn it's only online courses, they quickly lose their enthusiasm."

"Nonsense, it's impressive."

"Not really," she said.

"At least you've mastered the computer skills. Not many in our age range have."

"And what do you imagine our age range to be, Professor?"

He looked embarrassed again. "I don't seem to be able to keep my foot out of my mouth. I'm sixty-four. Of course, you're far younger. Not that I'm asking." He blew out a breath and wiped his perspiring brow with a clean white handkerchief, then ran his hand through his thinning gray-brown hair.

"Don't worry. You're safe—we're in the same range." *More or less.* If he doubted her, it didn't show.

The flight attendant came with a tray of beverages. Jeanne asked for water; Holmes, a glass of champagne. They sipped their drinks; then he cleared his throat and said, "Are you staying in Rome?"

"For a few days. I'm traveling with my son and granddaughter." She indicated the seats in front of them. "They've never been and I want them to see the sights."

"And after Rome, the grand tour, I expect?"

Why did everything he said carry with it a wisp of condescension? "No. We're staying in Umbria for a couple of weeks."

"Very wise. Most people try to do too much in too little time. The main tourist haunts, you know, Rome, Florence, Naples, and Venice. Like checking them off a list."

"We're going to visit an old friend and see my daughter-in-law sing at Spoleto."

"She's an opera singer?"

"Yes. They're doing *Così Fan Tutte.*"

"One of my favorites. And visiting an old chum, you said?"

Was that what John was? "Yes," she said. "Are you staying in Rome?"

"Just the night. Journeying onward in the morning. I have a summer teaching post, in Umbria as well, as it happens."

"Really?"

"Yes, the university in Perugia. I'm co-teaching a survey course in art history with a professor there, Renaissance art from Giotto to Michelangelo."

"You speak Italian?"

"I do, not too badly. However, the course is for English-speakers who have some Italian and Italians who have some English. My colleague and I will lecture on 'till truth make all things plain.'" He looked at her expectantly.

"*A Midsummer Night's Dream*, Professor?" She wasn't sure why she was playing along.

He smiled, pleased.

"Is your wife joining you?" she said, glancing at his wedding band.

His face froze. "No, uh, no, she's, she—" He looked at the ring. "Didn't feel right to take it off."

"I'm so sorry."

"Cancer, you know. Bloody awful."

"I do know. I went through the same thing last year. My husband."

"My condolences." They looked at each other for a moment as though they wanted to go on but couldn't think of what to say. Holmes resumed looking at his computer screen. Jeanne turned a page in her magazine, skimming a snarky review of a book she would never read. The revelation of their common loss had leapfrogged them to an intimacy that left them unable to return to the small talk of strangers on a plane. Her shyness would normally have kept her silent, but somehow the fund of courage she had drawn on to get her to Italy had enough remaining to enable a step further.

"Um, Professor Holmes." His head turned slightly. "Are you busy tonight?"

"No, nothing." A hopeful look appeared on his face. He cleared his throat. "You're free as well? No plans with your family?"

She leaned toward him and lowered her voice. "Frankly, I think we can use a bit of a break from each other. I know I could."

He brightened. "Then, would you care to have coffee or an after-dinner drink with me, Mrs. Carpenter? Perhaps an evening stroll."

"That sounds perfect. And please call me Jeanne."

"Shall we say nine o'clock? Perhaps we can meet at the foot of the Spanish Steps?"

"Wonderful."

She wanted to say more but was stopped by a burst of excruciatingly loud announcements in English and Italian from speakers positioned directly over their heads informing them that they were beginning their descent into Rome.

14

Jack fingered the note from Ricci and stared at the young messenger who had brought it.

They were standing in the *soggiorno* of Casale Leonardo, the main living room. The Calabrian workers whose negligence nearly killed him a couple of months ago had, in the end, done fine work restoring the room. The ceiling beams were securely in place, the stone fireplace finished, and the handmade terra cotta floor tiles installed. The plaster walls were colored a delicate yellow orange. Rather than simply painting them, Ricci had bought raw pigments, mixed them with the wet plaster, and then applied them in a final coat.

The messenger was a slender young man of perhaps twenty. He had arrived on an ancient green Vespa that trailed a poisonous dark cloud.

"So you're Ricci's nephew?" he asked in Italian.

The lanky youth nodded, brushed a thick strand of long black hair away from his olive-skinned cheek, and looked at Jack with placid hazel eyes.

Jack looked at the note. Ricci had written to remind him that the first payment on the loan they had finally agreed to last April was due in July, less than a month away.

When he had accepted the loan, it had been with a tremendous sense of relief. "You got half a million to finish the house, boss," Ricci had told him, slapping him on the back. "Your worries are over."

Now it appeared he had only succeeded in replacing one problem with a much greater one.

Ricci's message also asked if Jack could find work for "my poor dead sister's son, Antonio."

Jack understood he was not free to refuse. It was *una piccola gentilezza*, a small favor, to show his gratitude for the financing. Good manners, not to mention good sense, required him to acknowledge his debt by granting such favors. It was not the first. At least this one was legal.

Since the loan, Ricci began taking a proprietary interest in the project. He worked longer hours, pushed the laborers harder, drove sharper bargains with suppliers, and took almost an artist's pleasure in the work.

Antonio coughed respectfully. Jack realized he'd been staring at him. "What can you do?"

"Well, signore," Antonio said, looking at the ground as Ricci walked up, "I can paint a little."

Jack nodded. "*Va bene*. Painting it is. Ricci, tell Antonio here what needs painting, maybe start on the rooms upstairs."

"He ain't that kind of painter, boss. He's an artist," Ricci said, clapping both his large paws on Antonio's shoulders.

"What the hell do we need with an artist?" Jack said.

"You ask me that when you talking about a house that Leonardo once stayed in?" Ricci said with a hard bark of a laugh. "This house has to be special, not just another farmhouse renovated by a rich American. You gotta have art."

"He's gonna give me art?"

"Let him try on that wall," Ricci said, pointing near the stairs leading to the upper floor. "Antonio," Ricci went on, "can you do one of those trees, the Etruscan designs like the ones they found in the ruins by Lake Trasimeno?"

"*Sì, mio zio.*"

"Wait'll you see what this kid can do, boss. There won't be nothing like it in all Umbria."

Jack held his hands palms up in surrender. "Okay, okay. Make some art."

When Antonio was out of earshot, Ricci said, "You got my note?"

"Yeah, but if we don't open soon, I won't have the money." Unless the publisher's advance came through, but that depended on Jeanne.

"Don't say that. You have to have it." Ricci's mouth became a firm line and he crossed his thick arms over his huge belly.

"And if I need a little more time?"

"Aw, boss, that's a problem. It's a point a week or make some other arrangement." Meaning get a mortgage from the bank—which in Italy could take forever—or sell the house to the lenders.

"Then let's make sure we open."

"Fine, we got work to do." Jack followed Ricci outside to an unfinished pinewood worktable in front of the house. Ricci plopped his sizable bulk down on a dirty white plastic folding chair. He looked up at Jack and said, "Sit down, let's go through things."

Jack sat down in the other chair at the table. He had the feeling that their situations had reversed, that he was now working for Ricci.

"All right, we got fourteen sets of antique doors. Should come in today. The crew can have them sanded, stained, and hung this week. They also got a couple of mantelpieces from old farmhouses, for the upstairs guest rooms. They'll finish by Friday. I got an idea for the floor in the master."

Jack was looking away in the distance.

"Jack?"

Jack snapped back. "Sure."

"Okay, instead of tile floors like everywhere else, we do a wood floor."

"Wood? It's not authentic."

"Hear me out, okay? You ever smell Italian cypress?"

Jack shook his head.

"Ah, it's wonderful, so fragrant, almost like cedar. I got a friend, he got a yard full of seasoned cypress trees. We get it sawn into planks—it'll scent the house for years."

Jack shrugged. "Okay, fine."

Ricci heaved his bulk out of the chair and went in the house. Jack was relieved to see him go. In the field next door, sunflowers were blooming, their bright yellow blinding in the late morning sunlight. Ricci's pack of cigarettes was on the worktable and for the first time in many years, Jack had the urge to smoke.

One wouldn't kill him. He extracted a cigarette and lit it. He inhaled, blew out the smoke, and thought about all the things he had to do.

His online advertisements, full of gorgeous pictures of the outside of the house, had worked. Five of the six rooms were booked starting early July if they could finish on time. Only three weeks to go, though. There was an endless list of things to buy: furniture, linens, china, crystal, silver, and kitchen supplies. It would be more efficient to buy all those things in Rome. He had to go soon. He still needed a staff, someone to cook, someone to clean.

It was all starting to seem foolish and, to compound his sense of ridiculousness, there was Jeanne. Seventy-seven years old and he's meeting an old girlfriend? It was silly, a midnight fantasy, the two of them in their golden years finding each other again, writing a book, maybe running Casale Leonardo together. Absurd.

Time to put 1947 back in the memory box where it belonged, 1973 too. What a year that was. A war worse than the one going on now. Why was the Middle East such a perpetual thorn in the side of the world? The one in '73 had threatened to go nuclear. This one could too. Problems at work and at home and then Jeanne had come back into his life.

His mind wearily plodded around in circles: the house, Ricci, money, to-do lists—and Jeanne.

"*Padrone*, I brought you something to drink," Antonio said.

He didn't know how long he'd been daydreaming. The cigarette had burned down to the filter and left a black spot on the table where it lay.

"Aren't you supposed to be painting?" he asked, his voice hoarse.

"Here, try this." Antonio had an ice-cold half bottle of *prosecco frizzante* and a crystal champagne flute that glinted in the sun. "From a winery here in the valley. My uncle brought it for you to taste."

"Ricci did?" he asked, squinting in the harsh light.

"Yeah, try some." Antonio uncorked the bottle and poured the sparkling white wine into the glass, careful not to let the white foam rise above the lip. He watched like a sommelier while Jack tasted the wine and nodded his satisfaction. Antonio poured a little more into the glass and slipped the bottle into a terra cotta wine cooler.

"You have a beautiful place here, *padrone*."

"Thanks." Jack took another sip of the delicious ice-cold wine and let the cheerful bubbling liquid trickle down his throat.

"You like something to eat? How 'bout some pappardelle with sum-mer truffle, first of the season. With a little cheese and fruit. What do you say?" Pasta with truffles was an Umbrian specialty.

"You can cook?"

"Maybe better than I paint. My *nonna* taught me," he said with an embarrassed smile. "You want I make it?"

"Sure, sounds good. *Grazie*, Antonio."

Jack expected him to leave, but he remained, taking in the sunflowers, the trees, the mountains in the distance, and, past them all, the startling blue sky. There was a soft unfocused look in his eyes.

"You gonna clean up, boss. Five guest rooms, five or six hundred euro a night. You'll be a happy man, boss."

15

"**E**arly!"

The piano stopped.

"Again," James Nelson snapped. He signaled the downbeat. Kerry sang her first note.

"Early!" He glared, then waved his hand at the repetiteur.

She sang her entrance again, and again he barked, "Early!"

Kerry looked pleadingly at the conductor and started to speak but stopped when he held up a warning finger. How had the kind man from the audition morphed into this martinet?

They were rehearsing her first-act duet. Her singing partner smirked behind the maestro's back. He was a startlingly handsome young Latvian tenor named Anatoljis Bumbulis. The opera fanzines and blogs referred to him by his cloying childhood nickname, "Toljy." They ran story after story, breathlessly linking him with every soprano under sixty. She was so annoyed at him she overcame her fear of the maestro.

"Could I just say, I'm having trouble with the tempo?"

Toljy gave a theatrical gasp. Nelson looked at her icily. The repetiteur lowered his gaze to the piano keys in front of him in mock horror and played a downward minor cadence.

"Knock it off," Nelson said to them.

"It's just that it's so much slower than I practiced it," she went on. "I mean, usually it's a little, you know, faster?" Her voice rose on the last syllable in a vain hope that framing her comment as a question might lessen its offense. It didn't.

After a seeming eternity, Nelson said, "Kerry, I thought I made it clear that I'm not interested in opera as usual."

"You did, absolutely, yes, but—"

"You must trust me. We have far less rehearsal time than I would like. I don't have time to debate."

"I know. I do trust you, I really do."

"Ready to try again?"

She bit her lip and nodded.

"Toljy?"

"*Sì, sono pronto, Maestro.*"

The little kiss-ass. Sì, Maestro. No, Maestro. Can I wipe your ass, Maestro?

Nelson, with a nod to the repetiteur, indicated a stately, measured tempo with his hands. This time Kerry hit her entrance exactly.

Despite Nelson's scolding, her mind wandered as they rehearsed. Toljy sang a difficult solo passage with easy grace, gorgeous tone, and unerring accuracy. He was one of the finest tenors she had worked with, not to mention one of the best-looking men she had ever seen. He was also conceited, shallow, nakedly ambitious, and a ruthless womanizer. Almost everything he did irritated her, but she was honest enough to admit that some of her irritation sprang from the fact he had never given her a second look. Nearly ten years her junior and he made her feel every one of those years. The gossips said his current love was the surly young Romanian singer playing Despina, which didn't stop him from aggressively flirting with every other woman in the theater. Except her.

A grimace flitted across the maestro's face.

Oh, shit, I was flat. Pay attention, dammit.

She couldn't afford another mistake. Singers could be replaced, even during rehearsals. If Nelson became sufficiently unhappy with her, he'd do it. There were plenty of mezzos to take her place. *This is your last chance. Don't screw it up.*

It was midafternoon when they broke for the day. After the previous days' rehearsals, she had chatted with the other singers or with the pianist, sometimes even with the maestro himself, but everyone seemed to have dis-appeared. She stepped outside. It was raining and there was a chilly wind. She buttoned her raincoat and wrapped her scarf close around her neck. Where to? The prospect of spending the rest of the afternoon and evening in her room wondering if she was about to be fired depressed her. Being without her husband and daughter left her far lonelier than she had antic-ipated. She decided to stroll through Covent Garden. Despite the weather, it was crowded. Street performers—musicians, acrobats, puppeteers—were everywhere and she paused to watch. Everyone in the crowd seemed to be part of a group—a family, a gaggle of students, a hand-holding couple.

She saw the Flower Market Grill and decided to go in. She'd heard it mentioned as a hangout for some of the creative types who worked in the area. Inside, there was an elaborately decorated bar whose wood-paneled elegance looked comfortable and warm. They had a fire going and Kerry took a small booth near it.

A waiter stopped at her table almost immediately. "What may I bring you on this wet and windy day, ma'am? A cup of mulled wine perhaps?" He was in his early twenties with a sharp, plain face.

Ma'am. Do I really look that old?

She resisted the temptation to drink alone. It occurred to her it was teatime and she was in England.

"No, thanks. May I have tea?"

"Yes, brilliant."

She couldn't help but smile. "With those little sandwiches and scones and clotted cream?"

"Certainly, a full tea it is."

"In the States, we'd say with all the fixins." *Why not?* She thought defensively. She had an inner dieting coach who ruthlessly monitored her intake of food in the weeks before she appeared in a show and savagely criticized her for eating a calorie more than that required for bare survival.

Two busboys in livery swiftly set the table. First, a glowing white linen tablecloth, then a cup and saucer patterned in blue and gold, a matching sugar bowl and creamer on the right, then plates, white nap-kins, and sterling silver in the center. The waiter brought two pots in the same pattern, one for the tea and one with extra hot water.

"Milk or lemon?"

"Milk, please," Kerry said.

He placed a silver strainer over the cup and poured her tea. "I'll be back in a flash."

She added milk and took a sip. It was far too hot. Moments later, he returned with a three-tiered sterling-silver serving tray loaded with pastries, crustless finger sandwiches, and warm scones. He began to describe the various items on the tray but stopped when she pulled the tray closer and grabbed one of the fresh-baked scones.

"I'll leave you to it, then. Give a shout if you need anything else."

She split the scone in half and loaded it with clotted cream and strawberry jam. It was gone in seconds. She spread even more cream and jam on the second half of the scone and finished it almost as quickly. She reached for a second scone while her eyes tallied the assortment of cakes and sandwiches that covered the other tiers of the tray. She would never be able to eat them all.

But I can try.

As she was finishing the second scone, the heavily accented voice of her singing partner, Toljy, said, "A moment on the lips, always on your hips."

She looked up and said with her mouth full, "Where in the world did you learn that?"

"It's true, no? You must be careful. Sopranos can't afford to get fat these days."

"Oh, screw you, Toljy."

He laughed. "That is what you want, no?"

She rolled her eyes and stuffed an entire finger sandwich in her mouth.

"Here, my dear, let me save you from yourself." He sat down opposite her and helped himself to sandwiches from the tray.

"Hey, I was going to eat those. I'm hungry."

"Not for food. You are clearly substituting."

Her brow wrinkled. "What?"

"This isn't correct? Substituting for what you truly want?"

"Sublimating?"

"Yes, as you say, sublimating."

"For what?"

"For sex, of course."

"Oh, of course. With you, I suppose?"

"I see how you look at me as we sing today."

To cover her blush, she took a swallow of the too-hot tea and burned her tongue. She was put off by his cocky assurance, but at the same time she noted with self-disgust she was undeniably pleased by his attention.

"I thought you and Despina were an item?"

"She is a silly girl."

"I see."

"And she had another engagement this evening. Maybe you and I, we could be an item?"

"I don't think so."

"But why not?" He seemed confused. Women probably didn't say no to him very often.

"Any number of reasons." She began ticking them off on her fingers. "One, we work together. Two, I barely know you." She stopped, stumped.

"Only two." He shrugged as though these were not very convincing objections.

"And, wait," she said like a dim student suddenly remembering the right answer. "I'm married."

"Ah, but you live without your husband. He is many miles away, true?"

Damn those backstage gossips.

"Well, yes."

"So, there is a great separation?"

"No, well, yes. I mean, we're apart for a while. It—it's hard to explain." The longer she was away from Michael, the less she understood her reasons for leaving him.

He finished the cakes and made a move for the last sandwich, but Kerry was quicker.

"Let me save you from yourself. You don't want to become one of those fat, sweaty tenors, do you?"

He laughed. "This could never happen."

"That's what Pavarotti thought."

He looked concerned. "Is this true?" His face cleared. "No, you are joking." He placed his hand over hers. "Come, my dear. You are alone.

I am alone. Why not be together? I am staying at the Savoy. We will have a party."

She withdrew her hand. "No, Toljy, we cannot have a party," she said more kindly than she meant to. "But I'm flattered."

"Then we go to a movie? Like two old friends?"

"Have you ever been friends with a woman?"

"No," he said with a frown as he contemplated this undeniable truth. "Didn't think so."

"Like brother and sister? I have sister."

"I wouldn't mind seeing a movie," she said, giving in. She really didn't want to be alone.

It wasn't a date. Just two colleagues. Who could object? It wasn't her fault that anyone seeing her with him—like her husband—would assume they were lovers just because he was so good-looking.

Toljy stood up. He had paid the bill while she was daydreaming.

"You shouldn't have done that. I'll pay for the movie. What is 'thank you' in Latvian?"

"*Paldies.*"

"Pull-deeyehs?"

"Very good. And I say to you, *lūdzu*," he said, giving her a brief but lascivious kiss on the mouth.

"Toljy!" She should stop this now, send him on his way.

"It is how we say 'you're welcome.'"

"I'll bet."

"Shall we go to my hotel?"

"Stop it!"

"A joke only." He smiled and held up his hands in surrender.

He helped her on with her raincoat. As she buckled the belt, he rested his hands on her shoulders and then let them run down her arms. Her back arched involuntarily. Toljy smiled and they walked outside. It was still raining, but the wind had slackened. As they strolled toward Leicester Square, most of the women and some of the men stared at Toljy, then shifted their glance to her as if assessing whether she was worthy of him. She had to admit, she enjoyed their attention.

16

"This doesn't look like a five-star hotel," Michael grumbled as their taxi rolled to a stop in front of the Casa di Santa Brigida on a narrow street near Rome's Piazza Farnese. Jeanne climbed out of the taxi on the passenger side, hoping to avoid an argument. Michael looked doubtfully at the soot-stained stone walls and weathered wooden doors and didn't move. "You said the Hassler or St. Regis."

She had her answer ready. "I know. But it's June, Michael. The fancy hotels were booked. It should be very interesting," she added. "It's part of a convent run by the sisters of the Brigittine order."

"A convent?" Alice said, an earbud dangling. "First you stick me in a girls' school, now I have to stay with a bunch of nuns?"

"Just come on, unless you want to spend the night on the street." Michael and Alice crept out of the car, then stood blinking in the searing afternoon sun. The driver, whose duties did not apparently extend to helping with luggage, sat placidly while the three of them wrestled their bags out of the trunk and pulled and pushed them across the cobbled pavement and through the convent's ancient doors.

The small lobby was tranquil and cool after the chaos and heat of their drive through the city. The sunlight was filtered to a pale glow by four tall windows covered with thick glass and iron bars. The noise of the street was reduced to a dull and distant hum.

A tiny woman in a dark habit behind a small desk stood and greeted them. Her brown, wrinkled face was framed by a white collar and a dark veil, topped with the Brigittines' trademark headgear of two bell-curved, white, metal strips crossed at the top like a crucifix.

"I am Sister Gertrude. Welcome to the Casa di Santa Brigida," she said in Indian-accented English.

"Jeanne Carpenter."

"Of course, welcome. Let me show you to your rooms. Do you need help with your luggage?"

Michael opened his mouth, but Jeanne cut him off. "We can manage, thank you."

"There are refreshments in your rooms and dinner will be served at eight thirty. If you would follow me, please?" Her pleasant welcome and the hush that permeated the building seemed to soothe Michael and Alice. They followed her to the elevator.

"All three rooms are on the third floor," Sister Gertrude said as they entered the elevator.

"I get my own room?" Alice said, perking up.

"Yes," Jeanne said. "If it's okay with your father."

"Sure," he said. "I think it's a good idea."

They stepped out of the elevator.

"If you wish, come to our roof garden terrace before dinner to enjoy the evening and something to drink," the sister said as she showed them to their rooms. "Now, unless there's anything else, I'll leave you to get settled."

Jeanne closed the door to her room and breathed a sigh of relief at being away from the pressured pleasure of her family. The room wasn't large, but it was spotless and painted a light yellow. There was a pretty walnut writing desk and a leather-backed chair. Above the desk was a gilt-framed portrait. A small brass plate read, "Santa Brigida." The saint's head and accompanying halo were tilted and she had a disapproving look on her face. On a table near the window, there were flowers in a terra cotta jug along with bottled water and a glass bowl filled with fruit.

Jeanne switched off the air-conditioning and opened the white-framed window. A breeze carried in the sounds of the street and the scent of the city. What had been an oppressive heat outside registered in her room as a pleasant warmth. For the first time, she allowed herself to be excited at returning to Italy.

She opened her suitcase and pulled out a midlength cotton jersey dress with a subtle floral print. It had survived the journey unwrinkled. She hung it in the wooden armoire. She slipped off her shoes and lay down on the comfortable bed. Her eyes closed and her face relaxed into tired lines. She was almost asleep when there was a knock. Without waiting for an answer, Alice opened the unlocked door and poked her head in.

"Grandma?"

"Come in," Jeanne said hoarsely. Alice pushed through the door. It banged noisily against the wall and bounced almost closed.

"How's your room?"

"Really nice," Alice said, walking to the window and looking out. "It's bigger than my room at home, not like that's saying much. But not like I thought a convent would be. I was wondering if you wanted to take a walk after dinner. You know, see Rome by night?" She looked at Jeanne. "Oh, shoot, were you sleeping?"

"Just resting. And a walk would be lovely, but I'm afraid I have plans."

"How can you already have plans?"

"Ernest Holmes, the nice man I sat next to on the plane? He asked to meet me after dinner."

"But you barely know him."

"You sound like my mother."

Alice gave her all-purpose shrug and said, "Fine, okay. So go on your date."

Jeanne sat up on the bed and settled a pillow behind her back. "It's not a date."

"I didn't mean anything, jeez." She turned to leave, but Michael walked in, rapping on the door as he entered. It banged against the wall again. Alice retreated to the writing table, bumping it so that it scraped on the floor. Jeanne winced.

"Mean anything about what?" he said, picking a strawberry from the bowl of fruit, plucking off the stem, and popping it into his mouth.

"Grandma's got a date," Alice said.

"The old boyfriend?" Michael asked, now crunching on a cracker.

"No, of course not. It's Ernest."

"The guy on the plane?"

Jeanne nodded, surprised he had noticed. "It's just coffee. We're meeting at the Spanish Steps."

"Very romantic," Alice said.

"Stop that."

"Well, I was going to ask if you wanted to take a walk after dinner," Michael said. "Rome's supposed to be better at night."

"Alice was just saying the same thing," Jeanne said. "Now you two can go together." She turned toward the wall. "I'm going to rest for a bit." As they shuffled out of her room, a smile crossed her face.

17

Michael watched Alice fidget over her food as they had dinner at the hotel. She put down her fork and twirled her iPod. He considered telling her to finish the expensive dessert she'd had insisted on ordering yet barely touched, but he didn't want to risk a tantrum. He studied the city map he'd found in his room, still angry at his mother for maneuvering him into this excursion.

His mother had left for her rendezvous with Ernest. Michael felt guilty over what he had heard of her conversation with Ernest on the plane. He hadn't helped much when Jim was sick. Kerry had shouldered the load for both of them—calling Jeanne and Jim frequently, visiting, sending cards and flowers, and holding Jeanne's hand at the hospital during Jim's procedures. Kerry had always been like that, actively kind and caring. His mother had never said if she resented him for not being there for her. Her love had always seemed like such an elastic thing—no matter how poorly he behaved, it seemed to stretch to accommodate whatever new defect of character he revealed. If she knew that the reason he'd agreed to come on this trip was to ask her for money, would her affection stretch to cover that as well? He didn't have a choice, though. Unless she helped him, he was ruined.

He glanced at his watch. "Well, when in Rome," he said, "we might as well see it."

Alice grunted. "This won't take long, will it? I'm really tired from the flight and the time change."

He was determined not to react to any provocation. "We'll keep it short," he said. "Finish your dessert."

She pulled the plate nearer, shoulders hunched. What was it that transformed children from tiny beings who couldn't get enough of you into discontented houseguests who couldn't wait to get away?

He sipped his double espresso and sought for something to say.

"How 'bout your grandma, huh? Comes to Italy to meet an old boyfriend and one day in she goes on a date with another guy."

Alice shrugged.

"Like a midlife crisis, I guess."

Alice shrugged again.

Or was it something more serious, like dementia or Alzheimer's?

"Maybe the guy's after her money," he said.

"Is money all you think about?" she said, looking up from the table.

"No, but I mean, she's got plenty with the insurance coming and the house and investments." It was supposed to come to him one day, wasn't it?

Alice was still looking at him. He was suddenly afraid she knew what he was thinking and he felt a stab of shame.

"Let's go," he said and without looking to see if she was following, he walked out of the dining room and down the stairs. He pushed through the doors and headed out.

Michael aimed for the Colosseum but was stymied by dead ends and streets that weren't on the map. Alice poked along behind him. After half an hour, he stopped on yet another nameless street and pointed. "Look." It was the jagged outline of the Colosseum just visible over a nearby church.

"Mm-hmm."

"Alice, for crissake, you're in Rome. Try to enjoy it. Why do you always have to be so down?"

She didn't even shrug.

I'm the last person she wants to be with. This is hopeless. I don't even know where I am.

He pointed to the small church. The door was open and shadowy figures moved in candlelight. Alice stared in the opposite direction, music buzzing from her earbuds.

"Should we go in?"

Alice didn't bother to reply and he struggled to keep his temper. "Why don't we look around, then call it a night?" *Maybe someone speaks English and I can find out where the hell I am.*

Silence.

"Do you have to listen to that damn music every second?"

"Look—" she began, then stopped. "Never mind. If you want to go in, let's do it."

"Forget it. Let's just keep going," he said.

They resumed their grim march. A few minutes later, they found themselves in a huge square. Michael was mildly excited because he finally knew where they were. "This is the Piazza Venezia. There's a picture of it on the map."

"Can I see?" Looking quickly, she said, "We've gone in a circle. We could be back at the hotel in like ten minutes."

"You know what this reminds me of?" he said. "All those times we went to the zoo at Griffith Park. Do you remember?"

Alice's forehead wrinkled. "Maybe."

"Sure you do. You always wanted to hold the map and lead the way to the different animals. Remember? It had the pictures of the lions and elephants and monkeys."

She shook her head.

"Oh, you have to. We were there practically every weekend."

"I remember going there like twice."

"Twice? Are you nuts?"

"I hated the way it smelled."

"You're crazy."

"I'm not crazy."

"Sorry, sorry, I just meant—" He stopped as she handed him the map and turned away. "That big white building with the steps," he pointed out, "that's the, uh, Altare della Patria, the Victor Emmanuel monument." He began walking to the steps of the imposing neoclassical structure. She trailed behind.

"Come on," he said, looking back over his shoulder. "Let's climb the stairs. It's supposed to be a great view." He increased his pace, trotting up the stone stairs of the huge monument. Alice halted partway. He looked back. She was standing near a group of teenagers dressed in jeans and T-shirts.

With a sigh, Michael walked down to her and said, "A hangout for the local losers, no doubt."

"Like me?"

"You're not a loser. Now come on."

"Oh, bullshit. I know that's what you think."

Michael was flabbergasted. "Alice, that's crazy. I mean—"

"All you ever do is criticize me—that is, whenever you happen to notice me."

Michael's stomach was churning. "That is so untrue."

"Bullshit!"

"Alice, shh. People are looking." He glanced at four carabinieri standing at the bottom of the stairs.

"So what?"

"Okay, okay. I'm sorry. Whatever you think, I love you."

"That is such a meaningless thing to say." She teared up and leaned back against a marble column at the side of the staircase. "You were thrilled when I moved to New York so I wouldn't be around to embarrass you anymore." She slid down the column and sat, crying now.

Michael took a step toward her with the thought of comforting her, then realized he didn't have any idea how to do that. When she was little, it seemed like there was no upset a cookie or a scoop of ice cream couldn't magic away. That gave him an idea.

Just past the group of teenagers, near the bottom of the steps, there was an old man with a battered ice chest and a cardboard box full of candy and cigarettes. Michael trotted down to him. He was about to choose two Cokes but changed his mind and asked for two Peronis and a couple of chocolate bars. He scrabbled in his pocket for money and found a ten-euro note. He handed the bill to the old man, waving off any change. He took the cold beers and candy and bounded up the stairs. Alice sat with her knees pulled up to her face and her arms around her legs.

"Hey, I've got supplies."

Her tears had stopped, but she didn't move.

"Come on," he said, holding up one of the icy green bottles covered with moisture. She lifted her head slightly. He added casually, "You drink beer, right?"

Alice eyed him suspiciously, as if this were a clever ploy designed to trick her into a damaging admission. Michael twisted the top off the bottle and handed it to her along with a candy bar. He opened his beer and took a long, blissful swallow.

"God, that's good," he said, wiping his mouth on his sleeve.

Alice took a furtive sip of her beer and then a longer one. She wiped her mouth with the back of her hand.

"I do like a beer now and then," he said, looking down onto the piazza. "I never drank much when I was your age. Not"—he held up his hand to fend off an imagined protest—"because I think it's wrong. But you know your grandfather—my dad—was an alcoholic."

Alice nodded a fraction.

"I didn't want to end up like him. He left us, you know."

She nodded again and whispered, "Yeah."

"I didn't see him much after that. Then he died."

She peeled the wrapper off her candy bar and took a bite.

He sat down on the step she was sitting on, careful to leave a yard-wide neutral zone between them. "I mean, I know I'm not like him with drinking. I can take it or leave it. But I made up my mind I would never neglect my kids like he neglected me." Turning to her, he said, "So, whatever you think, honey, I'm not happy to be three thousand miles away from you. I always want to be there for you."

He knew he sounded stiff. He took a sip of beer to cover his embarrassment. Alice took one, too.

"Look, I know it wasn't your idea to come to Italy and to spend time with me," he said. "But we're here. And we have at least one thing in common. Neither one of us wants to make your grandma unhappy. Especially with her heart."

"Do you think it's bad?" Alice said. "She won't talk about it."

He shook his head slowly, tightening his mouth. "I don't know—she acts like it's nothing. But maybe that's where this thing with the old boyfriend is coming from. She's feeling her mortality."

"I don't think it's that."

He was surprised to see a slight smile appear on her face. Were the beer and candy working?

"It's not?"

"I think she still loves him. And I bet he still loves her, too."

"Well, it's pretty to think so."

"Hemingway," she said in a whisper.

"You know Hemingway?"

"Don't get too excited. I literally just finished reading it in school. Do you know where the title is from?"

He knew but shook his head.

"The Bible. Ecclesiastes," she said. "'The sun also ariseth, and the sun goeth down, and hasteth to his place where he arose.'"

"Wow. You have a great memory. Just like your grandma."

She looked pleased. "I like the old King James version." She looked down self-consciously. "The other ones sound . . . they're just not as poetic."

"Did you read it in American lit?"

"Yeah. Our teacher called it 'a shocking example of the patriarchal testosteronic *Weltanschauung* that dominated early twentieth-century literature.'"

"Jesus, that's a mouthful."

"I know. I feel like they're trying to brainwash us."

"Yeah?"

They fell silent.

This was the longest conversation he'd had with his daughter in months. He sought for something to say. "Is that even a word?"

"*Weltanschauung*? It's German—it means 'worldview.'"

"No, the other one."

"Testosteronic? I don't think so; I think they invented it just for Hemingway." She gave a little laugh.

The conversation lagged again. Alice looked at him expectantly. He racked his brain. "Um, you like it?"

"The class?"

"The school."

"It's not that bad. I tell Mom it's like a reform school filled with mean girls from the Hitler youth, but it's actually pretty much like any other high school, except no boys. But so fancy. Jeez, the bathrooms have gold faucets. Well, maybe they're brass. But the cafeteria has real silverware, so when they eat soup, they literally have silver spoons in their mouths."

"So that's what we're paying all that money for." He paused awkwardly, wondering if she knew about the delinquent tuition payment. "That bother you, the no boys?"

"At first, yeah, but not really. I mean, it's school and it's pretty much going to suck either way, right?"

Michael nodded and finished his beer. He didn't want their rapport to end. He walked down to the vendor and returned with two more bottles and sat again. He saw Alice was only half finished with hers, although her candy bar was gone. He opened his new beer and took another long drink.

"So how do we keep Grandma happy?" Alice said.

He thought for a moment. "Did your mom ever tell you about our vacation rules?"

"No."

"When we were first married, we went on our honeymoon. We had a pretty good time. But we also had a lot of arguments. We didn't want that to happen again so we invented what we called 'vacation rules.'"

"What are they?" Alice asked, seemingly delighted at this insight into her parents' life.

"Simple. When in doubt, you do what'll make the person you're with the happiest. If the other person wants to go on a hike, you go, even if your leg is broken. Let them pick the restaurant even if you hate the food. Things like that. We figured that if we spent our time trying to make the other one happy, we'd both end up having a good time. Damned if it didn't work. Which is why we always had such nice vacations. I hope you remember that?"

"I guess."

"So, let's make a pact. We do whatever it takes to make your grandma happy. If you and I need to have it out about something, we do it when she's not around. Think you can do it?"

"Do you?" she said with a trace of truculence.

"Yeah," he said, smiling, "but I've had a lot of practice biting my tongue around you and your mom."

"Dad! Jesus—"

"Whoa," he said, holding up his palms. "I didn't *mean* that. I just said it as an *example* of the kind of thing we won't say around Grandma."

"You're such an asshole," she said.

"Hey!"

"Just an *example*. Getting it out of my system, you know, for Grandma's sake." Her face had a taut smile.

"Touché."

She burst out laughing and he remembered how much he loved the sound of her laughter when she was a little girl, a staccato rat-a-tat-tat forced out of her tiny body by pure joy.

"So . . . deal?"

"Deal," she said. They clinked beer bottles.

"You gonna want this one?" he asked, pointing to the unopened beer.

"Nah, I'm good. But I'll take the rest of your candy bar," she said. He handed it over. "I've got an idea," she said suddenly.

She took the unopened beer and walked down to the group of teenagers they'd seen earlier. She handed it to one of the boys. He smiled and spoke to her. They talked for a few minutes; then he grabbed her wrist. Michael rose to intervene but stopped when he saw they were laughing. The boy took a pen out of his pocket and wrote something on her arm. When she returned, she was smiling.

"They're Americans, Dad. High school kids, here for a summer course."

"Really?"

"And you thought they were a bunch of losers."

"Looks like I was wrong." *What kid doesn't like to hear that from their father?*

"Justin, the boy I talked to, told me there's a concert tomorrow night. He wrote down where it is."

"I saw," he said dryly.

"Do you think I could go?"

He didn't want to say no. Playing for time, he said, "Let's see what Grandma has planned."

"Okay."

He yawned elaborately. "Listen, it's getting late."

"But I'm not tired," she said.

"Even with all the travel and the time change?"

She looked embarrassed. "I just was saying that. I slept on the plane." She paused, then said in a small voice, "Maybe we could walk a little more?"

She wanted to spend time with him? He forced himself to sound casual. "Sure, I guess."

They walked down the steps and tossed their beer bottles in the trash. The old man tut-tutted, picked the bottles out of the trash can, and rattled them into a wooden rack with his other empties.

"I think the good stuff is that way," Michael said, pointing in the direction of the Colosseum. They began walking. He tried to damp down the septal bounce of his resurgent heart. His sole task for the next hour was to not say anything monumentally stupid. It was deceptively simple sounding to anyone who wasn't the father of a teenage girl.

Awash though he was in the pleasant glow that a moment of passable parenting can produce, Michael wasn't fool enough to believe that the weeds of anxiety and distrust grown rough and wild between him and his daughter could be plowed under and replaced in an instant with the verdant lawns of gentle understanding. There was a limit, after all, to the magic contained in a bottle of beer. But he was dreamer enough to hope they had made a start.

Michael and Alice walked side by side through ancient streets alive with people. The dark moonless night hid the city's blighted present from their view; the spotlit treasures of Rome's beguiling past were all that they could see.

18

Jeanne and Ernest strolled past the stores of the Via del Corso, one of the main shopping streets of Rome, not far from the Altare della Patria. Although most of the shops were closed, they paused now and then to look in the windows. Jeanne was cool and fresh in her cotton dress. Ernest was uncomfortable in the early evening heat. He was wearing a dark wool blazer and charcoal slacks, more suited to an English autumn than an Italian summer.

"I don't get it. What's so special?" Jeanne asked as they stopped to look at a window display of enormously expensive purses. "It's the same things you could buy in any big city—LA, London, New York—even the same stores."

She watched their shadowy reflections move together in the window. No one seeing them would know whether they had just met or been married forty years, although a cynic would say the fact they were smiling and talking made the latter less likely.

"I'm sure you're right. Not much of a shopper myself, though my wife enjoyed it," he said.

Still watching herself out of the corner of her eye, she asked, "What else did she like to do?"

"You want to talk about my wife?"

"Sure, why not? I like talking about Jim. It's a way to keep him alive."

"It is, isn't it? Well, to answer your question, nothing extraordinary, I don't think. Read, cook, work in the garden a bit. She was a musicologist.

She always had music playing on the hi-fi, some of it quite awful, if I have to be honest."

"Did she play an instrument?"

"Yes, she was adept on the clavichord, if you know what that is."

Jeanne shook her head.

"It's a small, fourteenth-century keyboard instrument set in a wooden box. Fairly quixotic because while it's difficult to master, it can't be heard more than ten or fifteen feet away. So one works very hard to produce music few can enjoy. She would perform marvelous concerts in our home on Sunday afternoons for our friends."

"Sounds wonderful, like a kind of Zen poetry."

"Oh, yes, it was. She was wonderful." He made a sound that was meant to be a laugh but came out harshly. "Hard to get used to, isn't it?"

"Talking about them in the past tense?"

He nodded, and they began to walk again.

"You know, this is a first for me," he said. "Being out with a woman."

"Me too. With a man, I mean. My granddaughter teased me about going on a date."

"Are we?"

"On a date? Good god, no. It's just two people taking a walk," she continued. "Why do people have to put labels on everything?"

"I'm sorry, I'm not . . ."

"Oh, not you, Ernest. But ever since I decided to take this trip, everyone in my family thinks they have the right to offer their opinion. It's a part of getting old I hate, the way everyone treats you like you're a child again."

"They didn't think you should come to Italy?"

"It wasn't Italy they minded so much. It was, well, the reason I wanted to take the trip."

"How could they possibly object to you wanting to hear your daughter-in-law sing or see an old friend?"

Jeanne sighed. "It's kind of a long story."

"I like long stories."

"Then I better buy you a coffee. You'll need it."

"Coffee sounds wonderful, but I'm buying."

They retraced their steps to a small café called I Condottieri. "You know who they were, of course, the condottieri?" he asked, rolling the R.

"Are you testing me, Professor?"

"Sorry, I'm just awful."

"Oh, it's all right." She laid her hand on his forearm. "They were soldiers, no?"

"We have a winner, ladies and gentlemen." He took her hand and held it up in triumph. "Precisely, they were mercenaries who fought for whatever Italian city paid them the most."

"It's a funny name for a coffee shop," she said, gently disengaging from his grasp, although she liked his touch. His hands were soft and warm, different than Jim's, which were slender and sensitive, or from John's, whose hands were skilled and strong.

"No stranger than calling one after a fictional Nantucket sailor with a fanciful name, I suppose."

Jeanne laughed. "You have me there." They took seats at a marble-topped, wrought iron table outside the café. Just a block away was the tall, horsed figure of Vittorio Emanuele and his brightly lit monument. People dotted its steps. She wondered if Michael and Alice had gone there on their walk.

A waiter scurried up and took their order for coffee. "And a small liqueur, perhaps?" Ernest asked.

"I'm really not supposed to."

"But you must. Perhaps a tiny Frangelico?"

"Why not? After all, we are in Italy."

He nodded at the waiter, who left to fill their order. "Now," he said, "you promised me a story."

She sat back in her chair and looked at his broad face, wondering if he could possibly understand. "You're sure?"

He smiled. "Quite sure."

"I tried to write it all down a little while ago, a kind of memoir. Even gave it a title. Do you remember the Shelley poem, 'A Gentle Story of Two Lovers Young'?"

"Tell it to me." Perhaps professors from England weren't supposed to admit they were unfamiliar with the works of famous English poets.

"It kind of describes us, except of course we didn't die in sorrow. But we certainly ended in it." Her spirit drew inward and her face grew solemn.

"Once upon a time . . ." he prompted.

"Yes," she said distantly, deep in memories she had visited often. "That's exactly how it begins.

"Two young lovers met in late autumn a long and complicated time ago in a world weary of destruction. She was seventeen. He was twenty-one. Although he'd been to war, he was as innocent as she. They fell in love on that first day. Their time together was brief, but it seemed to them they lived a lifetime in a few short weeks. Sadly, it ended and in sorrow too. Love betrayed them and they were condemned to live their lives apart."

"Was there no pardon or reprieve?" he asked, entering into the spirit and language of her story.

"There was, a short one. Many years later, in another town, they tried to recapture the joy and light of that first dream, but it slipped from their grasp. They were helpless, like two swimmers, exhausted, drowning, who couldn't find dry land."

She paused and looked at him.

"You're a wonderful poet."

"I'm not a poet, Ernie. Ernest. I teach online English to kids struggling to make something of their lives. I scribble things in my spare time. But it does feel like a poem . . . about something that happened to someone else. I hoped it would help me understand, I guess."

"And did it?"

"Yes, but not in the way I thought it would."

"Will you tell me the rest?"

"Well, the rest is far more prosaic." She laughed, pleased by his reaction. She felt enormous relief at the chance to reveal the private thoughts that had lived so long near her heart. "His name is John McGrath. He lives in a town called Todi."

"Todi? I once . . ." he began, but something in her aspect and her eyes stopped him.

She told him everything. Ernest suggested ordering something more and they settled on a large bottle of sparkling water.

"*Acqua frizzante,*" Ernest said quietly to the waiter who returned a few moments later with two frosted tumblers, lemon slices, and a large bottle of Sanfaustino. Ernest poured the bubbling liquid into the glasses and added the lemon slices.

All the while, she kept talking, a smile on her face and a faraway look of remembrance in her eyes. When she was finished, she picked up her water glass and drained it. A few drops of moisture dripped and fell where the bodice of her dress formed a V and slipped between her breasts. She felt a chill despite the warmth of the evening.

"God, that's good." She dabbed at a spot on her dress with a cloth napkin. "Thank you." She touched his hand briefly. "I don't remember ever telling someone the whole story at one sitting. Just bits and pieces. My family usually roll their eyes."

"So that's the last time you saw him? Thirty years ago?"

"Yes."

"Might I ask a question?"

"I think you're entitled."

"Is the story finished?"

"I think so," she lied smoothly. "I would just like to see if he's happy and healthy, remember old times—to say a real goodbye. It's too late for anything else."

"Could it be he has any, well, ulterior motive?"

The stiffening of his English voice made her laugh. "That's what my son thinks. Look, I'm not naïve, but really, Ernest, what ulterior motive could he have?" She gave a little laugh. "Sex?"

Could they still want each other that way? Was such a thing possible at her age? "It's not out of the question, but let's be realistic—I'm no one's idea of a sex object."

"I respectfully disagree," he said.

"Are you flirting with me, Professor?"

"Not in the least, madam. Just stating the obvious."

"You're very kind. What else? Money? I'm sure he's comfortable. Do you think I'm making a mistake?"

He looked off in the distance for a moment, then returned his attention to her. "Not at all. It's something you want to do, and you've earned the right." He poured the last of the sparkling water into their glasses.

She began to respond but stifled a yawn behind the back of her hand. "I've so enjoyed this, but I'm sorry to say I'm a little tired."

"Ah. So our evening and, I suppose, our time together comes to an end." He signaled for the check. When it came, he asked the waiter to call a taxi.

"Will you be very busy in Perugia?" she said.

"Not unreasonably. Perhaps we could meet again?"

"That would be lovely."

"As a matter of fact, I don't really need to be there for a few more days. If I were able to extend my hotel reservation here, could I hope to see anything of you?"

"Well, I've arranged an all-day tour for tomorrow. I left our evening open, though."

"Then let me suggest the following—I know a wonderful little restaurant in Trastevere, a sort of Bohemian quarter, on the other side of the river. There's a clear view of the Castel Sant'Angelo if you remember your *Tosca*. If you're tired after your day, we can sit outside and relax or, if you're up to it, we can walk a bit after dinner and see how the non–*La Dolce Vita* crowd lives."

"That sounds marvelous."

"Then it's a date."

She shot him a look. He returned it steadily.

She smiled. "It's a date."

"Your taxi is at the corner, *signori*," the waiter said.

"Shall we go?" Ernest asked. She nodded and Ernest ushered her into the taxi and closed the door gently.

"The Casa di Santa Brigida," he said to the driver and handed him some bills.

Jeanne rolled down the window. "That's not necessary."

"Please? I'd like to. Tonight has been such a pleasure for me. *Permesso, signora?*"

She nodded and extended her hand. "All right. *A domani*," she said, remembering the phrase for "see you tomorrow" from her Rome guidebook.

He took and held her hand for a moment. "*Bravissima, ci vediamo domani.*"

The taxi rattled off through the warm Roman night.

• • •

When she returned to the hotel, the entry door was locked. She knocked and the night porter let her in. One of the sisters was asleep behind the reception counter, her veil with its metal cruciform crown askew.

Once in her room, she used the phone on the desk to call Michael's room to remind him that their tour would be leaving at nine. There was no answer. She tried Alice—no answer there, either. What could have happened? She tried texting. "Just a reminder, we need to leave the hotel by 8:45 tomorrow for the tour."

She had just slipped on her nightgown when her phone dinged.

"Sounds good," Michael wrote.

At least he wasn't lying dead in a Roman aqueduct.

"Can you let Alice know?" she texted back.

"Just did."

"Everything okay?"

While waiting for his response, she took out a blue plastic double-sided day-of-the-week pill case and swallowed six of the pills Dr. Dahlberg had prescribed. Six in the morning, six at night, three at noon. "I can't promise these'll work, but they're worth a try," he had said. "Check your legs every so often, too."

She gently pressed her thumb against her legs in several places. They felt soft and spongy. The indentations she made remained. The water pills must not be working. She felt a sudden ache in her chest, not due to her malfunctioning heart but from fear.

She sat down at the writing desk facing the portrait of Santa Brigida on the wall. The saint was wearing a white wimple that stood out from the golden halo painted behind her. Her cheeks were red and roughened, her eyes cast downward. Jeanne realized she had been wrong earlier. The saint's expression wasn't one of disapproval—it was one of injured expectation. She knew the feeling.

There was a printed history of her life on the desk. Born exactly seven hundred years ago, on June 14. *Same birthday as mine!* She was married at thirteen and had eight children before she became a nun. During her life, she was always seen to be smiling.

She wasn't smiling in the picture. Perhaps the artist had caught her on an off day or thought smiling wasn't saintly.

Ding.

"Yep," Michael replied. "Walked all over the city. Eating gelato. See you at 8:45."

Evidently, he and Alice had managed to spend an entire evening together without emotional bloodshed. A minor miracle? Just in case, she gave a prudent nod of thanks to Santa Brigida.

• • •

The next day was filled with the exhausting "Treasures of Rome" tour. Their guide was determined that no sight be left unseen. They rushed from the Colosseum to the Forum, to the Vatican and the Pantheon, the Villa Borghese, several museums, piazzas large and small, and more churches than they could count or remember. At the Trevi Fountain, they were allowed four minutes to toss a coin and have their picture taken. Jeanne was out of breath several times during the tour, especially climbing stairs, but she did her best to conceal it from Michael and Alice. She didn't want to be coddled.

On the bus ride home, Alice asked if she could go out with her new American friends, but Michael was reluctant to give his permission.

"She wants to be with other kids," Jeanne said. "I understand that. I remember when I was in New York at her age—don't roll your eyes, Michael—we were stuck with guides and chaperones most of the time. But the best part was when we went off on our own. I've told you how I snuck out at midnight to go to a jazz club. Alice knows to stay with her group, right?"

Alice, seated by the bus window, had leaned forward to look at Michael across the aisle. "Of course. Dad, Rome can't be any more dangerous than New York. I promise I'll be careful."

He shrugged. "Fine, you explain it to Kerry if anything happens to her."

"That's what you're worried about, what Kerry will think?" Jeanne said. Michael tensed and turned to face her. "Now, listen, Mom—"

Alice coughed meaningfully.

Michael sat back and took a deep breath. "I just meant Kerry might have a different view."

A tiny smile flashed across Alice's face.

•••

Although Jeanne was tired after the day-long tour, she revived in the evening for her date with Ernest. After dinner, they walked the narrow cobblestone streets and alleyways of Trastevere, going into some of the small shops. He was easy to be with—undemanding, intelligent, humorous, perhaps occasionally dry. He had an English modesty, and his obvious admiration for her was extraordinarily pleasant. He insisted on walking her back to her hotel.

Early the next morning, Jeanne's phone rang and she answered on the first ring.

"Hi, Mom!"

Jeanne turned gently in bed. She knocked her reading glasses off the bed table with a bare elbow. She squinted to see the clock, but the room's thick curtains were closed and the room was dark.

"Kerry?" she said softly, propping herself up on an elbow.

"Did I call too early?"

"No, not at all."

"You're so quiet. Is someone there?"

"Don't be silly. How's it going?"

"Better now. But today's rehearsal was canceled, so I decided to fly to Rome. I was hoping to see everyone tonight before I head up to Spoleto."

"Tonight? Um, sure, that would be great, but, uh, the thing is . . . I have plans for tonight."

"What are you doing?"

"Going to the opera at the Baths of Caracalla."

"You got Alice and Michael to go to an opera?" Kerry laughed. "You are good."

"No, they're not. I mean . . . I'm the one going."

"By yourself?"

"Uh, no, with a . . . a friend."

"Really?"

"Yes, really."

"Who?"

"Just a man I met on the plane. He's from England."

"Hmm, an Englishman." Then, in a stage whisper, "Does he know about your other lover?"

"Kerry, please, I get enough of that nonsense from Michael and Alice. We're all having an early dinner. Join us. I'm sure they can squeeze in one more."

"I'll be there. How about Alice? Do you know if she has plans?"

"She's coming to dinner but then going out with some kids she met."

"Michael's letting her go out by herself? I'm not sure that's a good idea."

"It was my idea, though Michael thought we should ask you first. She went out with them the night before and there was no problem. She texted us several times and came home when we said to. They stay in the tourist areas where there are plenty of people and carabinieri. It's a nice group of American students. Alice said their program sounded neat—she might want to do it next summer."

"Really?"

"Yes. It's so nice to see her make friends."

"Well, I won't be the wet blanket, then. That's usually hard for her."

"And she and Michael seem to be getting along better."

"That's good to hear. Oh, do you think they might have a room for me at your hotel? Just for the night. Or maybe they could put a roller bed in Alice's room?"

"I'm sure."

"Thanks. Well, I better get going. Can't wait to see you. Love you."

"Love you too."

Jeanne lay back down, pulled the covers up to her chin against the chill of the air-conditioning, and turned to Ernest, who was lying in bed beside her. "Kerry is going to join us for dinner."

"Your daughter-in-law?"

"Yes. Hope you didn't mind the 'friend' comment."

"Not at all. We are friends . . . with advantages, I think they say."

"Benefits, Ernest. Friends with benefits is what they say."

"Sorry."

"Don't apologize. You're even less cool than I am."

"In any event, I quite understand. This is probably best kept our little secret."

"It's not that I regret anything."

"I don't either. Far from it," Ernest said. "So, whatever your reasons—"

"Well, I didn't want you to think I was a tease."

"No danger of that. And may I just say a belated 'hurrah!' You are wonderful."

"You're not so bad yourself, Professor."

"We academics are a passionate lot."

She gave him a light kiss. Their eyes met. Her hand went to the side of his face and they kissed once more, longer this time. Then, to their mutual surprise, they made love again. It was more relaxed than the night before—more about the moment and less about the end, although they achieved a very satisfactory end.

When they were finished, she turned and lay with her back snuggled up against him. His substantial body seemed to cushion and envelop her. He rested one of his heavy arms on her hip. He was still breathing rapidly and her own heart was thumping against her chest. Dr. Dahlberg had said she couldn't hurt it by exercising. She wondered if he had sex in mind.

They lay silent for a while. Finally, Jeanne said, "I don't want to move, but I have to. Would you mind getting my robe from the bathroom? I don't seem to have any clothes on."

"Of course. That is if you don't mind seeing my flabby old arse."

Jeanne watched as he rolled out of bed and disappeared into the bathroom. She hadn't seen many men naked. He was different than Jim, who had been slender, or the taller, sturdier John. Ernest was much heavier but in a round, comfortable way that was oddly attractive. He didn't seem self-conscious about his body, but when he returned with her robe, he had a towel wrapped around his ample middle, so perhaps he was.

While she got out of bed and put it on, he courteously moved to the writing table and studied the printed history of Santa Brigida.

"Would you mind terribly if I took a quick shower?" he said.

"Of course not," she said, grateful for his sensitivity. She wasn't quite ready to parade around naked in front of him. "Just give me a minute."

She went into the bathroom and closed the door. She stood in front of the mirror and allowed her robe to fall open. The dim light coming through a small translucent window sponged away some of the imperfections of her face and body. She could not help but be pleased by the illusion. "Well, well," she whispered. "Not so bad."

Skin can be scarred by injury. It can be damaged by hardship, childbirth, or disease, and it is eventually left in ruins by the thoughtless violence of time. Why is it that the good things—a loving touch, a gentle kiss, or a passionate caress—leave their signs only in memory?

The first night she was with a man, she had looked at herself in a hotel bathroom mirror afterward. She had felt scared then, yet safe, nervous and excited, full of hope and riven by fear. Her world had tilted and changed and she was shocked there was no outward sign or inward shame. She had wondered what God must think of her. She wasn't worried about that now. She retied her robe, opened the bathroom door, and burst into laughter.

Ernest had opened the curtains and the room was full of light. He was on his hands and knees next to the bed. His substantial rear end was in the air and was too large to be entirely covered by the towel. His face was on the floor and he was fishing around under the bed with an extended arm.

"Lost something?"

"Oops, so sorry," he said breathlessly. His free hand plucked at the towel in a fruitless effort to twitch it into place. "Can't seem to find my drawers. You wouldn't by any chance—?"

"Let me see." She picked up the comforter and snapped it. A large pair of multicolored boxers fluttered out. Dropping the comforter, she snatched them in midair before they landed.

"Aha!"

He stood up laboriously, his knees cracking. The towel around his middle had loosened and was threatening to fall off in full view of the window.

"Um, Ernest."

"Yes?"

"You'll shock the sisters."

"What?" He looked down. "Egad, that won't do."

"Did you say 'egad'?"

"I may be the only Englishman to still use that word."

"I thought you were being extra English for my entertainment."

"Sadly, no. I'll quite probably say 'cheerio' when I leave."

"Your turn for the bathroom. I'll order breakfast. Tea? Pastries? Fruit?" How easy it was to slip into the comforting routines of domesticity.

"Actually, a cappuccino for me rather than tea. They don't seem to know how to make it here. Otherwise, perfect, thank you." He grabbed his clothes and started for the bathroom. "I won't be a moment."

"Take your time," she said. "With any luck, you'll still be in there when they bring our food. It's bad enough having a saint looking at me. If I have to face Sister Gertrude with you here, I know I'll be going to hell for my sin."

He smiled. "If that was sin, then, as Romeo says, 'Give me my sin again.'"

"Again?" She raised an eyebrow. "You're not that young, Professor. Off to your shower!"

He went in the bathroom and closed the door. A moment later she heard the water running. She called for breakfast. After ordering, she asked to speak to someone about getting a room for Kerry.

"Yes," a voice said. She recognized the sweet accented tones of Sister Gertrude immediately. "One of our guests has requested a change to a double room for tonight," Sister Gertrude said, "so we'll have a single available on your floor."

"Perfect, please reserve it."

"Certainly. I'll be up with your breakfast in fifteen minutes. For two, you said?" Was there a hint of amusement in her voice?

"Yes, Sister, it's for two," Jeanne said, feeling like she was seventeen, not seventy-three.

An hour later, Jeanne had dressed and was sitting at the writing desk looking out the window as Ernest turned the corner at the end of the street and vanished from view. She nibbled on the remains of a chocolate croissant. She had shaken and smoothed the bed cover before

Sister Gertrude had arrived. It no more told the story of the night than did her skin.

Was it possible at her age to be . . . whatever you call a woman these days who sleeps with a man she barely knows? There probably wasn't a politically correct term for it anymore. She smiled, thinking about the night. It had all been so easy.

Easy! That was the word the nuns used when she was a girl. Because girls were supposed to make it difficult.

When Ernest took her arm as he walked her home last night, she felt a deep sense of warmth and pleasure. She knew he wanted her and she was extraordinarily complimented by his interest. She invited him to her room —not for a drink, not to discuss medieval theology, not for a good night kiss. Just, "Would you like to come up?"

In the darkened room, they had moved to the bed in a relaxed fashion, undressed, and climbed under the covers without fumbling. She had been eager to kiss him, for him to hold her, to feel the skin of their bodies touch and the solid weight of another person. It had been pleasurable, not only physically, though it was certainly that, but in the joy their chance discovery of each other brought them. The warmth of their connection had worked to melt away the hard shell of loneliness that had encased her since Jim's death. Yet she was feeling anxious and confused. Was she going to continue seeing Ernest? What would be the point?

She needed to move. She grabbed her purse and walked out of the hotel toward the piazza. She passed the Church of Santa Brigida and decided to go in. She walked through the ancient doors and sat in one of the wooden pews near the altar. The ceiling was covered by a large fresco, but she had seen so many paintings on the tour she didn't bother to study it. She wasn't religious, but the cool air and dim light of the chapel brought a feeling of calm reverence. As she had grown older and closer to death, God was less the punishing tyrant she had been taught to fear and more a comforting presence she had learned to love. She whispered a prayer.

19

"No, for the last time, you cannot stay in my room," Kerry said. She and Toljy were in a cab headed to Rome. They had arrived at the Leonardo da Vinci International Airport that afternoon.

The evening before, Toljy had, to her surprise, kept his promise to behave. After the movie, they walked down Haymarket to get away from the crowds in Piccadilly Circus, talking about what had first drawn them to opera and their favorite singers. As they passed a club, he asked if she would like to go in for a drink.

"Just one," she said nervously.

They had a drink at the bar and continued their conversation. When, after half an hour, she said she wanted to leave, he didn't whine. He hailed a cab and gave her a friendly kiss on the cheek.

"Like a brother, no?" he said as he waved goodbye.

When she arrived at the hotel after the short cab ride, there was a message saying the next day's rehearsal had been canceled. It instructed her to meet three days hence in Spoleto. She immediately rebooked her flight to Rome.

At the airport the next morning, Toljy was waiting for the same flight. He was flying business class as befitted a brilliant young tenor with a recording contract.

"What's your seat? We are colleagues and should sit together," he pronounced.

She didn't respond, but her ticket protruded from the outside pocket of her purse, and he plucked it out.

"Economy? This is not acceptable."

"Give me that," she said, annoyed. He grinned and held the ticket high in the air. Jumping to grab it back would have been undignified.

"Give it back!"

"I will repair this," he said and strode to the ticket counter. "Please, miss," he said to the clerk, slapping Kerry's ticket down. "There has been terrible mistake. Please upgrade to business."

"No, Toljy," Kerry protested softly. "I can't afford it."

Rising tenors or coloratura sopranos had that kind of money, sure, especially if they had a touch of glamour and sex appeal and some marketing push behind them. Some of the baritone hunks, yes. But no basses, certainly not contraltos, and, with few exceptions, no mezzos.

"No problem, I do it for you."

"I can't let you do that. It's too much money."

"Not money, miles."

"What?"

"I have so many flyer miles. No money, no worry. Please let me. Why be lonely on the flight?"

"Okay, you win." After all, there was something to be said about maintaining good relations with your fellow cast members, especially Toljy, who was her partner in so much of the opera.

Once on the plane, Toljy ordered champagne and they drank to the success of the production. When he finished his drink, he wrapped himself in a blanket and fell asleep. She was reminded of Alice. When she was a baby, she would always fall asleep on a plane after drinking her bottle.

Once they were in the air, Kerry took out her score and tried to study, but she couldn't concentrate. She put it aside and looked out the window. Ahead already was the distant sprawl of Paris. The bright blue sky seemed to go on forever. The flight attendant came by and offered lunch. Kerry shook her head but accepted a second glass of champagne. As she drank, the silvery dot of Lake Geneva came and went and then they were passing Mont Blanc. Its deeply striated ice and snow reflected the sun as they skimmed over the pine forests and snow patches that were just visible between the hard, clean-looking peaks of the Alps.

When she was seventeen, she had come to Switzerland on a summer holiday with her parents. Fresh in the glow of her recent decision to become a singer, she wanted to go to one of Switzerland's many summer opera productions. She picked a performance of *Carmen*, the most hackneyed opera of all.

It was an inspired choice.

She would never forget the brilliant mezzo-soprano who sang the lead role. When she first came onstage, Kerry's heart sank. The singer was too large and too old for the role of the seductive gypsy girl, wore too much makeup, and had an ill-fitting wig. Then she began to sing. Kerry remembered almost every note of that glorious performance. She stood clapping and cheering with the rest of the audience for curtain call after curtain call until her father said it was time to leave. She walked out of the theater exhausted but exhilarated. There could be no higher calling than to be a singer who made people feel as she felt at that moment. In the years that passed, the realities of her chosen profession—the modest income, the constant travel, the lack of benefits or job security—had done nothing to dim her passion.

Her face was reflected back to her in the Plexiglas window. What would that idealistic girl think of the woman she had become? What would she think of the fact she constantly teetered on the brink of failure, of her decision to have a child, which set back her career by years, of her separation, and this foolish flirtation with a coworker? Would her teenage mouth curl down in disappointment and her unlined face frown with disapproval? Would she think her a failure?

Italy came into view and Kerry resolutely put that girl out of her mind.

Be grateful you're still singing and have a chance at success. Be happy you're not a checkout girl at Walmart, or a restless housewife with three kids and a philandering husband. Be glad you're not working all day at a keyboard in an ice-cold office, a permanent knot in your back, your slumping shoulders covered with a pastel cardigan and only a cat to come home to at night.

Every mile and every minute were bringing her closer to her complicated little family and a crossroads in her life. She had gambled her

marriage because she was desperate to succeed in her career. Could Spoleto really make a difference? She closed her eyes and thought of the next
few weeks, her chances of success or failure, of Michael and the work that
needed to be done if they were to repair their relationship, of Alice, and
of Jeanne and her troublesome heart.

The jet's engines changed pitch as they started their descent over the
roasted golden-brown Piedmontese plain and the peaceful blue waters of
the Ligurian Sea, then began the slow-falling parabola of the final fifty
miles into Fiumicino. The moment the plane bumped down on the run-
way, Toljy awoke, just as baby Alice used to at the end of a flight.

After retrieving their baggage, he seemed to realize for the first time
that he didn't have a hotel booking. He couldn't get through to his manager and tried calling some of the nicer hotels with no success.

"They could put a cot in your room," he pleaded with Kerry. "Just for
one night. Trust me. Like a brother. Please, be a good colleague." She
couldn't escape the feeling that his brotherly protestations were nothing
more than a lengthy lead-up to attempted seduction.

"I said no—now drop it. My husband and daughter are staying
there, too."

"Then it is easy. You stay with your husband. I have your room. Unless
this is problem?" he added craftily.

Kerry wasn't prepared to explain that one to him. "It's a huge city. I'm
sure you can find a room, even if it's not quite up to your usual standards."

They continued their fight in the taxi. Finally, Toljy folded his arms
over his chest, fixed his face in a dismal frown, and stared straight ahead.
She was torn between ignoring him and the desire not to make an enemy
of someone whom, to some extent, the most important role of her career
would depend upon. Finally, she relented.

"All right, you big baby. Come to my hotel. Maybe they can work
something out. But we're not sharing a room."

He smiled, leaned over in the taxi, and gave her a kiss on her cheek
while his hand somehow found its way to her knee.

20

Jeanne knew immediately that adding Toljy to their dinner party was a mistake and it was entirely her fault. She had insisted that Kerry bring him along.

"How often do we get to have dinner with a real opera star?" she had said. "Other than you, I mean."

Adding Kerry to their table for four was no problem. Adding Toljy, however, required that he squeeze in next to Kerry.

Of course, the success of any dinner attended by Michael, Kerry, and Alice in the current state of their relationship was a chancy proposition. Dealing in the wild card of Ernest could have gone either way. Throwing in Toljy, however—glamorously dressed, glitteringly handsome, glowing with arrogance—was an additional weight their little party could not bear. It didn't help that he flirted outrageously with their pretty, dark-haired waitress.

Alice relapsed into her monosyllabic ways. This could have been due to Kerry's unexpected presence or was perhaps a reaction to her parents' cold indifference to each other. More likely, watching her mother enjoy this egomaniacal foreigner's attentions triggered an unwonted surge of loyalty to her father. Her iPod and earbuds reappeared in public for the first time in two days.

Michael was unable to maintain any vestige of polite conversation in the face of the twin insults of Kerry's coolness to him and her warm rapport with Toljy. After a few abortive attempts at conversation, he lapsed into silence. Toljy only made matters worse. He sneered at the quality of the food and at Ernest's attempts at conversation. He kept joking with Kerry in a way that suggested great intimacy.

Kerry seemed eager to assure her family that Toljy was nothing more than a coworker—which should have been easy considering the fact it was the truth. There is no simple way, however, to communicate that you're not sleeping with the absurdly handsome man squeezed next to you, especially when the first thing you did upon arrival was try to get him a room in your hotel.

Under ordinary circumstances, Jeanne would have gently drawn out the other dinner guests. She was not herself, however, because she felt everyone at the table somehow knew she had slept with Ernest and was inwardly laughing at her. She imagined they saw all of his faults and none of his virtues. She was certain they were wondering why she was dallying with Ernest when she had traveled to Italy to meet John. Every time she thought of something to say, her cheeks grew warm and her heart palpitated and so she, too, remained quiet.

"Are those your opera glasses, Mom?" Kerry asked after a lengthy silence. Jeanne nodded and picked up the mother-of-pearl-covered opera glasses from the table. There was a jagged crack in one of the lenses.

"A friend gave them to me."

"They look old."

"They are."

"How'd they get that crack?"

"I dropped them, a long time ago," she replied, her finger tracing the crack.

It was left by default to Ernest to carry the conversational ball. The evening was especially warm and humid and his shirt was as wet as if he had just been dunked in the piazza's fountain—his complexion, not his most attractive feature in any case, had gone red and blotchy. He gamely gave it his best but seemed intent on living up to his Christian name by embarking on a series of solemn disquisitions on one arcane topic after another. He was, at the moment, deep into an arid discussion of a theoretical link between the eating habits of the ancient Romans and their political affiliations. Toljy rolled his eyes, which coaxed a stifled chuckle from Kerry.

Jeanne, seated next to Ernest, was at first grateful for his efforts, but, as he went on, her discomfiture grew. A dot of sauce appeared on his already soaked shirt and she fought an impulse to scrub it with a napkin and San Pellegrino. As the endless dinner wore on, she couldn't stand it any longer. She lowered her left wrist and surreptitiously checked the time. Ernest faltered in mid-oration. He forced out a few more words, and then clattered to a halt. An excruciating silence ensued. Jeanne wanted to help but couldn't think of anything to say. Ernest mopped his face with his handkerchief for so long it seemed as though he were trying to hide behind it. The only sounds were the scraping of forks on plates and conversation from diners at other tables.

"Did I tell you what we did today?" Jeanne finally said in a high, tight voice. She hadn't meant to tell anyone for fear they would misconstrue it, but, in her desperation, it popped out. She thought of changing the subject she had raised herself, but by now everyone was looking at her. Even Alice hit pause on her iPod.

"Tell us, Mom," Kerry said.

There were general murmurs of agreement. Anything but Ernest resuming his lecture.

"You know how I love the movie *Roman Holiday*, right?"

Michael and Kerry nodded.

"I had mentioned it to Sister Gertrude and she said there was a company that gave tours to the locations where the movie took place. Everybody rides on those Vespas, like in the movie."

"I can't believe you drove in this traffic on those little scooters," Kerry said, shaking her head.

"Well, young lady, we have photos to prove it," said Ernest.

"I can't wait to see them," Kerry said.

"I have one here," he said. He rooted around in the small backpack he carried.

Jeanne attempted to wave him off. "Oh, let's look at them later," she said.

Ernest paused uncertainly, finally catching her meaning, but Kerry took the folder from his hand. In it was a picture of Ernest and Jeanne standing next to their scooters, leaning in to give each other a kiss. The cardboard frame around the picture was in the shape of a heart and the caption underneath said, inevitably, "Roman Holiday." Kerry held it up and showed it to everyone.

"That's so sweet," said Alice, giving Michael a glance with raised eyebrows.

"Oh, yes, an adorable couple," Toljy said sarcastically.

"We're not a couple," Jeanne said, too quickly and sharply. "You know Italians," she added, trying for a light tone.

Ernest took a deep drink from his wineglass. No one else spoke.

"Well, they are Italian, so what can one expect?" he finally said. "They think everything is about love, *amore*. On the other hand, uh, although the word 'romantic' comes from the word 'Rome,' the Romans actually held such love in low esteem, they, well . . ." There was a thickening in his voice and it trailed off.

No one spoke. *"All silent and all damned,"* she thought. *If you remember your Wordsworth, Professor.*

Toljy finally spoke. "But the Italians are correct, I believe," he said, as though he had given the matter long thought. "What is more important than love? Not only between man and woman. Love of family, love of music, love of life." He put his hand on Kerry's and looked in her eyes. "When I hear you sing, I know you believe this too."

The pretty waitress was handing around dessert menus. Removing his hand from Kerry's, Toljy winked at the waitress and said, "No, I am wrong. Love of *i dolci*. This is the most important love of all." The waitress laughed, placed a hand on his shoulder, and poured him the last of the wine.

Jeanne touched her foot to Ernest's, but he moved away.

"I think I'm going to skip dessert," Alice said as she stood up. "I'm supposed to meet Justin and some of the other kids in a few minutes."

"Home by midnight, and text us where you are, okay?" Kerry said.

Alice didn't look at her. "I already told Dad I would." She gave him a kiss on the cheek and ran off.

"We better get going too," Jeanne mumbled to Ernest, placing a hand on his damp forearm.

"You know, Jeanne," he said, moving his arm away, "I suddenly find I am not quite the ticket."

"The tickets? Sorry?"

"Not feeling too well. Gippy tummy, I'm afraid. Must have been that squid. I seem to feel it wriggling round." He laughed harshly as he stood up, scraping his chair. "I'm afraid I'll have to beg off our opera tonight. So very sorry. Perhaps Kerry could go in my stead?"

"I should stay with you."

"No," he said quickly. "No need. I think just rest and a bicarb will see me right." He spoke hurriedly and began moving away. "This is probably goodbye, need to get an early start. Have to be in Perugia tomorrow. Probably should have been there a couple of days ago. Don't know what I was thinking, dawdling here in Rome."

He gave a wave and walked off.

"Oh, what a shame, I hope he feels better," Kerry said. They all looked at her. "His stomach, I mean."

"He forgot the photograph," said Michael absently.

"I'll take it," Jeanne said and slipped it in her purse.

"I'd be happy to go with you tonight," said Kerry.

"I would like that," Jeanne said.

The waitress reappeared. "*E per dolce?*"

"No dessert," Jeanne said. "*Il conto, per favore.*" The waitress sniffed and rolled her eyes in Toljy's direction, evidently contemptuous of the very idea of not having dessert and coffee. It was apparently an even worse offense than the fact that none of them smoked. She swayed off insolently. Toljy stood up, mumbled something about going to find the "tualete," and followed her into the restaurant. It was some time before she returned with their bill.

• • •

Hours later, Jeanne walked slowly through the Piazza Farnese. She and Kerry had returned to the hotel immediately after the opera. Jeanne, knowing she wouldn't be able to sleep, decided to take a walk around the piazza. Although the air was now cooler, every time she thought of Ernest, her face felt hot with embarrassment. She tried calling him, but it went straight to voicemail. She sent a text asking him to meet her in the piazza. "Please answer."

Almost immediately, her phone dinged with his response.

"Meet you there in five minutes."

She walked over to the sculpted fountain in the center of the square. The water from the fountain cascaded into granite stone basins that had once formed part of the Baths of Caracalla. A Renaissance palace loomed in the dark over the piazza.

Ernest appeared out of the darkness. He had changed his clothes and now wore khaki trousers and the loose-fitting dark cotton shirt Jeanne had bought him the day before in Trastevere. He squinted at the palace. "I hadn't noticed, the French embassy?"

"Mm-hmm. It's the Palazzo Farnese. If you remember your *Tosca*."

"Where she kills him."

"Right."

He looked as though he were trying to smile but had somehow lost the knack.

She caught his arm, drew him closer, and kissed him on the cheek. He smelled of soap and lotion and she guessed that he had showered and shaved. He gently disengaged and stepped back.

"I came because I acted like a lovelorn teenager," he began. "I wanted to apologize for dashing off like that, embarrassing you in front of your family."

"I embarrassed me in front of my family, not you. I'm so sorry."

"Thank you. And thank you for these last few days. I will remember them very fondly." He turned to leave.

"What—what are you doing?"

He turned to face her again. "Going back to my hotel. I really do have to leave early."

"But . . ."

"No, my dear. I did want to apologize and have a proper goodbye. But I don't think there's anything more to say."

"I thought that we could put this behind us and go on." There was a muted anger in her voice.

"Go where exactly?" he said equably.

"I don't know."

"Nor do I. After all, as you told Kerry, I'm just a man you met on a plane." He put out a hand and let water from the fountain run over it, then touched a few cool drops to his cheek.

"Surely whatever I did isn't completely unforgivable."

"No, Jeanne, not unforgivable, not at all. Just, I think, perhaps, I wasn't ready for an . . . involvement."

"Would you at least kiss me goodbye?"

"Jeanne—"

"Come on, Ernie." He winced at the diminutive. "A pity kiss, a wonderful American tradition."

He seemed to wrestle with his emotions but then turned and put his hands on her shoulders and kissed her lightly on the lips.

"Wow, that actually was a pity kiss."

He started to say something, but she interrupted. "Hey, I asked for it. At least you'll walk me home?"

"Of course."

They walked toward the Casa di Santa Brigida, a block away.

She tried again. "I'm new to this, too, you know. Maybe you'll give me another chance in a few days after you're settled in?"

"I think not, my dear. You have much to do, your son and granddaughter, Spoleto and the opera, not to mention your long-lost love."

"Don't call him that."

"Sorry. It's just, this way you can go to your meeting with him unencumbered as it were, as you should with someone who looms so large in your life."

"Ernest, you're making way too much of what I did," she said. "Surely you and your wife had problems during your marriage?"

"Of course. But as silly and as boring as I may seem to you, she adored me. I find I need that."

"I don't think you're *silly*."

He looked at her steadily.

"Well, no one is interesting all the time, Ernest, no matter how adorable."

"Fair enough." He laughed, wrinkling his forehead. "Good god, was I really lecturing your family on the eating habits of the ancient Romans?"

"I'm afraid so."

He shook his head. "That's damn dull, even for me. You know, it's an odd thing," he continued, "I expected by this age I'd be less nervy."

"That's not the way it works, my dear. You've lost the ability to protect yourself because it was unnecessary. It happened to me, too. And I've discovered—" She paused.

"Yes?"

"We're too old to ever get it back."

They were in front of the hotel.

"Now, Jeanne, I really do have to get on." He took her hand. At the touch, some of their passion from the night before stirred. They kissed again, arms around each other this time, and whatever she might have felt from him, it wasn't pity. They broke the kiss but continued to hold each other. He kissed her softly on both cheeks.

"Call me when you get to Perugia, just so I know you're okay?" Jeanne said.

"Mayhap I will," he said softly.

Ernest walked away. Just before he rounded the corner, he turned and boomed out a very loud and very English "cheerio." He waved to her and resumed walking down the street.

"Goodbye," she said softly to his retreating form.

21

Michael was in bed in his darkened hotel room but couldn't sleep. It was odd to be on the same floor of a hotel as his wife but in different rooms.

When Kerry told him she would be in Rome for a night, he thought of offering to share his room but was afraid she would say no. Better to wait and let her make the first move. He was hurt she hadn't. What if they had spent the night together? Would they have made love? Maybe she hadn't asked to share his room because of this Toljy. He squirmed under the cool linen sheets.

"Way too slick and pretty for me," she'd say if he asked her opinion of him. "Not my type," she would probably add.

Hard to believe, though. Wasn't he every woman's type—handsome, well-off, talented, a little dangerous?

Although Kerry and Toljy were playing lovers in the opera, Kerry had always assured him there was nothing sexual about onstage love scenes. A singer was only worried about singing. Kissing someone in stage makeup in front of a crowd of people was not erotic. Even so, it was very odd watching your wife seduce a man, kiss him, touch him, and make the sounds of ecstatic love. Although your mind insisted it was only make-believe, your heart didn't understand it was just an act.

She had never before given him cause to doubt her—until now. The guy was after her; it was so obvious. Working it so he sat next to her at dinner, their elbows touching, the way he fussed over her—pulling out her chair, pouring her wine, patting her hand, addressing all of his comments to her.

"When I hear you sing, I know you believe this."

This was the kind of cheesy comment that he and Kerry would have laughed at in better days. She hadn't laughed. She acted like she bought it.

He was angry at himself. He should have said something, set the guy straight, acted like her husband, for crissakes. But his courage leached out of him when he saw the way she enjoyed her costar's attention, smiled at him, laughed at his stupid jokes. Was that why she left him? So she could be with other men?

Cosi Fan Tutte.

"It means, 'women are all like that,'" Kerry had once explained.

"Like what?" he said.

"Oh, you know, vain, flighty, changeable, and unfaithful," she had laughed. "Mostly unfaithful."

It was four in the morning, but he didn't care—he slipped on his clothes, made his way down the dimly lit hall. There were voices. Were they coming from Kerry's room? He crept a few steps closer. The voices were definitely coming from her room. A woman's voice giggled and said something barely audible. A man's voice, louder, not caring who overheard, answered. Toljy! He couldn't mistake that silly accent. A shot of acid went through his stomach. He began panting as though he had just run a mile. Had they done it? Were they just about to? He couldn't hear their words, so what they were saying was left to his imagination. He froze, unable to go forward yet unable to retreat to safety, to oblivion.

Come on, Michael! Bang on the door right now! Barge in and yell, "What the hell is going on here?" But he was afraid that he wouldn't be able to speak—afraid most of all that she would tell him to go away.

He ran blindly down the stairs to the street and half walked, half ran to the corner and turned into the piazza. The restaurant where they had eaten dinner was still open, although all the outdoor tables and chairs were stacked in a corner. There were a few patrons sitting inside in dim light. He went in, walked straight to the bar, and asked for whiskey. When it came, he drank it down in a gulp and asked for another. The barman nodded and poured him a second.

His throat burned. "Soda, please," he said, "*por favor*."

The barman nodded. He grabbed a fresh glass and poured in the whiskey and a generous amount of San Pellegrino.

His pulse finally began to slow. He looked around the candlelit room. At a table in the center of the room, an old man with white hair sat alone, his face flushed and slightly sweaty. He was upright but swayed as though he were in a boat on a gentle sea. A nearly empty bottle of wine and a wineglass stood in front of him, along with a glass of water, a snifter of brandy, and a cup of coffee. He took small sips from each at intervals of metronomic regularity.

"Do I know you?" the old man said, his voice raspy and his eyes peering.

"Sorry, what?" he said.

"Something familiar about your face," the old man said.

"I don't think so," Michael said, though there was something familiar about him, too.

"Siddown," the man said, kicking a metal chair out from under his table. It screeched on the tile floor.

"No, that's okay." The old man was drunk. Michael hated drunks.

"Join me. Fellow American. Come on."

"No, really, I'm just having a quick drink, then on my way."

"Not having a 'quick drink' at four in the morning. Musta needed one pretty bad." He glanced at Michael's ring finger.

Michael wanted to be alone, but he needed to finish his drink. He remembered his father acting the same way when he was drunk, which was most of the time. The sooner he had given in to his father's pickled whim of the moment, the sooner he had been allowed to leave.

"Okay, just for a minute." He sat. Close up, he was sure there was something familiar about the old man's face. The old man waved at the barman and said a few words in rapid Italian. The barman brought him a large brandy and another whiskey and soda for Michael.

"I haven't finished this one."

"Gotta back 'em up. First rule of drinking."

"What's the second rule?"

The old man winked. "Get someone else to pay."

Michael laughed. Amazing. His wife was sleeping with another man and he could still laugh, still make conversation, still breathe. "You're drinking brandy with wine? Won't that make you sick?"

"Nah, they're both of viniferous extraction." The man stumbled over the words, then fumbled for a cigarette and, after several tries, lit it with a match. "Just took it up again. Want one?"

Michael shook his head and they drank.

"So, trouble at home?"

"Yeah." He finished his drink, pushed away the empty glass, and took a deep swallow of the one that the stranger had ordered. The alcohol simultaneously relaxed his body and increased his anxiety.

"Caught my wife with another guy in her room."

"Ouch! So what's next?"

"I don't know," Michael said.

"Tough one, buddy." The man took a long pull from his drink. "I live up north. North of here, I mean. Came down to Rome to buy a few things for this house I'm fixing up. Stay with the sisters, always do when I'm in town."

"Around the corner? That's where we're staying."

"They're the best, do anything for you. Last minute, I needed a bed for my assistant, Antonio—they fixed me right up with a different room." The stranger squinted at him again. "Sure we haven't met?"

He shook his head. "I don't think so."

"Look damn familiar, but I guess I'm pretty drunk."

At least he admitted it. Michael's father never did. The man stopped talking and lit another cigarette.

"You got it good, you just don't know it," the man said.

"How in the fuck do you figure I have it good?" He said it harshly. It made him feel better.

"But you do. Don't you understand?" the old man said. "You're young. And you still love her. That's everything. If you have love, you're still young enough to fix what you got with your wife. But if it can't be fixed, you're young enough to start again."

"Maybe."

"Not me," he said and started humming a song. "Know that one?" The man sang a line.

Michael shrugged. "Don't think so."

"'Your Cheatin' Heart.' Too young."

"Yeah, before my time."

"Not you," the old man said impatiently. "Hank Williams. He died too young." The man shook himself. "So you saw her with this guy? In the room, I mean?"

"I didn't actually see them, but I heard them talking."

"So maybe they didn't do it?"

"What are they doing at four o'clock in the morning in her room then? What the fuck are they talking about at four in the fucking morning?" With each repetition of the expletive, Michael felt—what was that word?—increasingly *testosteronic*.

"I'm not saying it looks good," the old man said.

The barman brought them their bill on a small silver tray, which also held two chocolate mints wrapped in foil. He said in English, "No more, gentlemen, no more." The old man grumbled and squinted at the handwritten check. "Uh, can I get your share, here? Twelve euro, I think." For one whiskey. Tourist prices.

Michael picked up the bill. Forty-seven euro. The old man had drunk an expensive bottle of wine. Well, it didn't much matter at this point. Either his mother was going to help him get back on his feet or it would all be over. "I got it," he said, reaching in his pocket and slapping his credit card on the plate.

"That so? Thanks." The old man smiled craftily. "See? Second rule of drinking."

Michael had to laugh. He glanced at his watch. It was nearly five. The dusty light of the Roman dawn crept through the streaked and yellowed windows of the restaurant. What was that song about the dawn?

"Hey, what's that song? Something about 'at dawn, I'll win,'" he asked the old man. "The big one Pavarotti's always singing at the soccer matches."

Opera. If they got divorced, he would never listen to another goddam opera.

The old man chuckled. "*Nessun Dorma*. 'No one shall sleep.'"

"I don't know the words," he said, crestfallen.

The old man recited, "*Fade stars, fade. At dawn, I will win.*"

"How's it go?"

The old man sang in a scratchy but accurate baritone, "*Tramontate, stelle. All'alba vincerò. Vincerò. Vincerò!*" hitting the high note on the penultimate syllable with a light but pleasing ring. He smiled and said, "By the way, name's Jack."

"Michael." They shook hands.

"Michael," Jack repeated, squinting at him and shaking his head. "*Andiamo, Michele.*"

They went outside and inhaled the cool morning air to clear their heads and lungs. They walked back to the hotel, sharing the kind of deep silence only too much drinking and too much talk can produce. Jack knocked and the night porter let them in. They walked through the lobby to the elevator past one of the sisters sleeping at the front desk.

"Sister Maria Teresa, gotta be over ninety. Sleeps there every night," Jack whispered. "What floor you on?"

"The third."

Jack hit the elevator call button with his closed fist, but Michael was too anxious to wait.

"I think I'll take the stairs."

He started toward the stairs but turned when Jack sang one last heroic "*Vincerò!*" Jack gave him a thumbs-up and said, "Good night and good luck."

"Same to you."

He ran up the stairs. The whiskey and their talk had heartened him. He was young. He was still in love. Why give up hope? Maybe the old man was right and nothing happened.

The old man was dead wrong.

Michael reached his floor and entered the corridor just in time to see Toljy leaving Kerry's room. He pulled the door closed with a careless thwack and a loud thud. He preened in a mirror hanging on the corridor wall. Smiling, he ran his fingers through his hair, shot his cuffs, and brushed a speck of dust off his jacket. Satisfied, he walked with a confident, wide-legged stride to the stairs on the other side of the corridor and vanished from view.

Michael's heart hammered and broke. So much for love. So much for hope.

PART IV

1947

22

Jeanne wished that their tour of the city could go on forever. They had strolled through Times Square, viewed the serrated skyline from the Empire State Building, walked through Radio City Music Hall, and seen a dozen other familiar sights. They were even better than the postcard pictures in her mind.

But as the bus rumbled north through Hell's Kitchen—whose blighted streets and demoralized tenements were satisfyingly depressing—she reread the observations she had written for John's article, then let her notebook flop to her lap. Her work seemed more like guidebook blather than incisive depiction. Writing something interesting was harder than it seemed.

"What's that?" Caroline said.

Jeanne covered the page with her hand. "Nothing, just some notes."

"Wouldn't it be easier to take pictures?" Caroline said.

"I'm doing that too," Jeanne said, opening her purse that contained her old Kodak Brownie.

Jeanne looked out the window. As they neared the shore, a huge cylindrical gas tower, several stories high, dominated their view. They turned onto West Fiftieth Street and headed toward the piers on the Hudson River.

"Look!" Caroline bounced up from her seat and pointed. "It's the *Queen Mary*!"

Jeanne felt a surge of excitement. The *Queen Mary* had been retro-fitted and returned to passenger service last July after dodging U-boats for seven years, filled with fifteen thousand soldiers a crossing, and was now the preferred transatlantic transportation for the country's elite. The huge ship was docked at the long, low terminal on Pier 90. Wisps of steam trailed from its three funnels. Cranes on the dock and deck of the ship were in operation, lifting supplies and luggage aboard. People walked along two gangplanks that stretched from the cruise terminal to the ship.

The bus stopped at a nearby pier, where students were to board the tour boat for a cruise around Bedloe's and Ellis Islands. Their guide climbed on the bus. He was a middle-aged man in a yachting cap and navy pea coat who introduced himself as John Cullerton. He was tall with graying hair and a dark slit of a mustache. "Wrap up, everyone, temperature is in the thirties and it'll be even colder on the water," he said.

He led them off the bus and waited while the students stood on the cracked asphalt adjusting their coats, hats, and scarves against the chill wind. Most of the boys wore suits and the girls all wore dresses and nylon stockings, the latter only recently available after wartime shortages.

Foam-hatted waves dotted the harbor. A flock of white-crested seagulls rested on the water and bobbed up and down like small, feath-ered buoys.

The tour boat was a sharp-prowed, surplus Coast Guard cutter that had been repainted blazing white with blue stripes. It had a single deck with a passenger cabin. In front of the cabin and several steps higher was an enclosed helm. On the forward deck, several dozen wooden folding chairs faced a podium at the bow.

Where is he? John had said he might make the tour. She bit her lip in frustration.

"He's not kidding—I'm freezing." Caroline had on her new coat and a tiny reversible hat, white on one side, leopard on the other. Jeanne wore a heavy coat and a black Navy surplus wool cap. Her silver-blond hair peeked out on either side of her face and hung free in the back.

"Come on, kids. Times a-wastin'," Cullerton yelled over the wind. The seventy-plus high school editors tromped up the wood and metal gangplank that bridged the gap between the dock and the open entry gate on the boat's rail. Jeanne trailed behind. In the distance, a tiny dot of a yellow cab appeared.

"Hurry," Cullerton said to Jeanne.

She took one last look at the approaching cab, then reluctantly walked up the gangplank. A sailor unhooked it as soon as she boarded.

"Eeeww, what's that smell?" said Caroline. She wrinkled her nose against the nauseating odor of diesel fumes and the sour cheese smell of the bilge.

Cullerton smiled. "It'll be better when we're underway."

The cab was closer now.

"Ready to cast off," Cullerton shouted to the boat's uniformed captain at the raised helm. The sailors released some of the tension from the dock lines and, with a practiced flick of their wrists, worked the spliced rope loops off the rusted iron-gray dock cleats. They hauled the dripping lines on board as the engine gave a low growl and the heavy boat began to inch away from the dock.

The cab's tires screeched in the parking lot. John leaped out. "Wait!" Jeanne called to Cullerton.

"Sorry, he's too late," he said.

John sprinted toward the boat, hat in hand. His coat was unbuttoned and trailed behind him like a cape. Cullerton divined his intent and yelled, "Don't try it, buddy."

John waved his hat and leaped over the widening gap between the dock and boat and landed with a tremendous crash. He somehow managed to stay upright as he slammed into the steel wall of the cabin.

Jeanne was sure he'd broken something. Cullerton ran to John, but when he saw he was unharmed, said in an aggrieved voice, "That was pretty stupid, mister."

John clapped his hat back on his head. "I know. Sorry." He smiled. "Heard this was a helluva tour. Didn't want to miss it."

"Great, a wise guy," Cullerton said and walked forward to the wide-open foredeck. He picked up a bullhorn and said dryly, "Well, kids, now that Captain Blood has joined us, let's begin." Jeanne smiled. He did look a little like Errol Flynn.

Cullerton stepped onto the podium and launched smoothly into his lecture, the boat rocking and pitching in the wind and waves. Some of the students looked sick and retreated to the cabin, but to Jeanne, the fresh air was delicious after the stuffy heat of the bus and the smell of the boat. They were sailing south on the river and Cullerton gave the history of Governors Island as they neared it.

"If you forgot your watch, no need to worry. You can always check the Colgate Clock. Fifty feet in diameter, it's the world's largest," Cullerton said, pointing toward Jersey City. It was three thirty.

Then, there it was—Bedloe's Island and the sight she had seen in her imagination since the day she was told she would be making this trip to New York—the Statue of Liberty.

She felt a rush of emotion. She opened her notebook and wrote, "America carried the lamp of hope for so many during the war. This statue is a reminder that it will always be a gateway to freedom for the people of the world and a refuge to the suffering."

Kind of corny, but it's a start.

A thin but melodic voice sounded beside her. "Tisn't something you'll soon forget, now is it?" It was Father Bernard.

She slapped her notebook shut. She could only guess what the sisters had said about her. She didn't trust herself to speak. It was one thing to be creative with the truth with cranky old nuns—it was quite another to lie to a priest.

"She is indeed 'the Mother of Exiles.'"

She nodded.

"Jeanne," he said sharply.

Her gaze snapped to him. "Yes, Father."

"The good sisters tell me you and I have something to discuss. Shall we say after supper this evening?"

She felt rather than saw him walk away. She wanted to drop through the deck and disappear into the ocean. Instead, she slunk inside the cabin where the evil odor was so thick it seemed like loathsome solid things were drifting in the overheated air.

Caroline stood by an untended table that held snacks and soft drinks, drinking a grape Nehi. A hand-lettered sign on the counter said, "Welcome Chicago Student Editors! Complimentary Refreshments!" Seasick students sat on metal chairs bolted to the deck, sipping tepid bottles of ginger ale. A rusted slop bucket had already been used at least once.

Jeanne walked to the counter and grabbed a bottle of Coca-Cola, popped off the top with a bottle opener attached to the counter by a slender silver chain, and took a gulp.

"He's in there," Caroline whispered, nodding toward a small companionway and anteroom just aft of the captain's station.

"Who is?"

"Mr. Wonderful." She snickered. "Really, just who does he think he is?"

Jeanne set the bottle down and walked to the companionway. She pulled off her wool hat, finger-fluffed her hair, then trotted up the metal stairs and stepped over the threshold of the watertight door to the anteroom where he stood. Just beyond him was the captain at the helm, facing forward. She and John looked at each other and began to laugh.

"I can't believe you jumped," she said.

"I guess I wanted to impress you."

"Why, Mr. McGrath, you'll turn my head."

"I have so much to tell you," he said and glanced around. The captain pushed the throttle lever forward and the engine responded with a deepened thrum. The stern of the boat settled and pushed faster through the water.

John turned back to Jeanne and, under cover of the increased engine noise, asked, "Did you see the *Queen Mary*?"

"Hard to miss her."

"She's leaving."

"When?"

He checked his watch. "Any minute. She was scheduled to go at three thirty. With over one hundred UN diplomats on board."

"What? Aren't they supposed to be here for the vote?"

"They put the vote off until Friday. But now even that isn't sure with all these guys leaving."

"What's going on?"

"I think they're scared."

"Scared?"

"They've been threatened."

"Really?"

"Yeah. A reporter for the *New York Times*, Tom Hamilton, tipped me off about this exodus. We interviewed some of them. Their story is they're going to a conference in London. None of 'em would admit it on the record, but three of the diplomats on board confirmed to me they'd had death threats."

He took his notebook out. "And just listen to who's on the ship. Vishinsky, the Russian ambassador, Bebler from Yugoslavia, Masaryk from Czechoslovakia—a dozen other ambassadors from the Soviet bloc countries, the Philippine and Greek ambassadors, the Turkish ambassador, another dozen from Latin America, Malik from Lebanon. There's something else. Thailand was a sure 'no' vote for the Arabs, but their ambassador, um, Svastivat—however you say it—never showed up for the session. Rumor is Thailand decided to change their vote from 'no' to 'yes.' One guess where Svastivat is right now."

"The *Queen Mary*?" she said.

"You got it. Oh, and get this, both of the chief British diplomats, McNeil and Shawcross, are on board. Why would they be leaving before the most important vote the UN's ever had? Britain can't wait to be rid of Palestine and this vote is their way out. One of them"—he checked his notebook—"McNeil didn't have a ticket until today. Came aboard at the last minute. It all adds up—they're getting out because they're frightened."

"Did you find out any more about the Syrians?"

"Not yet. I talked to that detective downtown, Michael Grogan. He said if I can bring him more proof, he'd start an investigation. I've got to keep working on this. Which reminds me, are you going to be able to write the article about your tour?"

"Sure, I've got notes of everything," she said, hoping he wouldn't ask to see them. "I even have pictures," she said, taking her Brownie out of her purse.

"You got snaps?" He laughed.

"You don't need to use them," she said defensively.

"No, that is perfect. Hershon will want to kiss me. Now there's a disgusting thought." They laughed. "I can use the AP wire photo service to send them if they come out. Their office is around the corner from the hotel."

"I'll write the story the minute we get back. I've already checked—the hotel has a typewriter I can use." She looked at him expectantly, hoping for a compliment.

"We better break this up."

"You're right. Father Bernard says I have to talk to him after supper. Can they really send me home?"

"I'm afraid so. We have to play it cool." Her eyes watered. "Look," he said, "it's only a few days, just till we get back to Chicago. Once the trip is over, we can have a real date. I'll pick you up at your house, bring flowers for your mother, shake hands with your dad, promise them I'll have you home by eleven—the whole nine yards."

"You mean it?"

"Cross my heart." He glanced at the captain and, when he turned back, she kissed him hard on the lips.

"Um, Jeanne. I think we need to discuss the meaning of the phrase 'play it cool.'"

She was shocked at herself but unrepentant. "Are we still meeting later?"

"You bet."

Cullerton was nearing the end of his well-practiced lecture about the Statue of Liberty. "We must be close to the dock at Bedloe's Island," John said. "You go first—I'll hang around here for a minute."

She walked down the stairs through the companionway to the cabin where Caroline was waiting. They went outside. Cullerton was just finishing his dutiful recitation of "The New Colossus."

At the moment he finished the sonnet, the boat bumped against the dock. It squealed along an array of old Jeep tires hung as fenders from the wood pilings. Sailors tossed the thick dock lines to waiting hands that secured them to foot-high cleats.

Cullerton ended his lecture with a short recitation of facts. "She's a tall girl, three hundred five feet if you include the pedestal. You'll have a chance to walk all the way to the top and look out the windows in the crown."

John stood near Cullerton. With a raised finger, he signaled Jeanne to wait. She and Caroline stayed behind while the deck cleared. Cullerton was joined by the captain and they stood at the bow. The captain was short, no more than five and a half feet tall. He wore rimless spectacles and was dressed in an old-fashioned naval uniform. They each lit a cigarette.

"You want to climb to the top?" Jeanne asked Caroline.

"Are you kidding? I just want to buy a postcard."

"You go ahead. I want to look at it from here for a few minutes."

"Yeah, sure," said Caroline, glancing at John, then following the others.

Jeanne went forward and climbed on the small podium and leaned back on its handrail to gaze at the statue, thrilled by its enormity. John squeezed next to her and leaned back against the rail, too.

"Thought we were supposed to play it cool," she whispered.

"The Catholic contingent got off the boat. Sister Mary looked pretty green if that makes you feel better," he said, gently elbowing her. "I remember seeing this when I shipped out in '44," he continued. "My sergeant said it'd help us remember what we were fighting for. It's funny," he said, his eyes distant. "Ike said almost the same thing to us at Buchenwald."

"You were at Buchenwald?" Like the rest of the world, she had been stunned by the revelations about the camps.

His face darkened. "Yeah."

She wanted to know what that was like, to climb inside his mind and see the things that he had seen. Everything seemed trivial compared to the horrors she had read about.

He went on without her prompting. "Patton got sick all over himself when he saw it. Ike was the real tough guy. He made himself go everywhere and see it all—the piles of bodies, mountains of gold fillings, the ovens, the mass graves, the dead kids. He ordered every unit within three hundred miles to go there. He said, 'We are told that the American soldier does not know what he was fighting for. Now, at least he will know what he is fighting against.'"

"I can't imagine." She put a hand on his arm.

"You could smell it for miles, the stink of the dead. Murrow came through and did his broadcast. When he said that tagline of his, 'good night, and good luck,' it sounded like a suicide note."

"This isn't just a story to you, is it?" she said quietly.

As though he hadn't heard her, he continued, "It reminds me of something Liliane said. They want to turn Palestine into a 'stinking pit of death.'"

"She sounds like she really cares."

Ignoring her comment, he answered her earlier question. "Damn right it means something to me." He turned to her. "I don't believe that crap they're probably teaching you about objective journalism. There aren't two sides to every story."

Three shattering horn blasts sounded. It was close to four o'clock and across the Hudson, the *Queen Mary* was being pushed and prodded into the river by tiny tugboats swarming like flies around a horse. She moved slowly through the upper bay heading toward the Atlantic, the water creaming white at her bow.

"And there they all go," he said. "Running away."

"If you can tell this story, you think it'll help?"

He turned to her. "Maybe. At least it'll show the world what these people are doing to rig the vote."

"Makes what we were talking about a little while ago, worrying about chaperones, seem pretty silly," she said.

Cullerton interrupted. "Hey, you two want me to take your picture?" They looked at each other, shy at being treated as though they were a couple. Jeanne handed Cullerton her Brownie.

"Sweetheart, point at something in the distance, like you just discovered America."

She pointed at the *Queen Mary*.

"Ready!" He snapped the picture, wound the film, and pointed the camera again. "One more for luck. Big smile." He snapped it again. "I think I got the statue right behind you. Even with all these clouds, should come out okay." He checked his watch. "Better get moving if you want to climb to the top."

"Ready?" John said to her.

"Yep, let's go."

• • •

Jeanne sat at the small writing desk near the window of her room at the Paramount Hotel. It was almost dinnertime. The bright marquees of the theaters on West Forty-Sixth Street and the constant sounds of traffic and car horns distracted her. She scratched her scalp with the eraser end of a pencil as she reread her article.

"Caroline," she called to her friend who was in the bathroom getting ready. "Did we go to Radio City before or after Central Park?"

"After," Caroline yelled through the closed door. "We went after."

"Thanks." She made a note with her pencil, erased it, blew away the eraser shreds. She read through the article again, moving her lips. It was typed on thick cream-colored hotel stationary using the classroom journalism style she had been taught—double-spaced text, multiple page numbers at the top and bottom. She had even typed "-30-" at the end.

"I have to get it to him in a few minutes." She lopped off some adjectives and exchanged some four-syllable words for simpler ones. When she was finished, she took an envelope from the desk drawer, folded the pages, and stuffed them inside. She called the front desk.

"Can someone deliver a letter to another room for me? Thanks."

She set the phone back in its cradle and it rang almost immediately. It was Sister Mary. Oh, god, her meeting with Father Bernard! She still had to get dressed.

"Father Bernard asked me to let you know something has come up and he will be unable to meet with you this evening. Please see him first thing in the morning before breakfast."

"Yes, Sister."

"You should have your room cleaned and your bags packed."

"Is that what Father Bernard said? Or just what you want?"

"No, he didn't say that, but I want you to know what to expect. That is all."

Jeanne slammed the phone back down. "Why that . . . that . . . *woman!*" she sputtered.

There was a knock on the door. She opened it and gave the messenger the envelope and a dime tip. "Right away, okay?"

John called her ten minutes later. "It's great. Hardly had to change anything. Just moved a couple of words around."

"Like what?"

"You'll barely notice when you read it in the paper tomorrow."

"What was wrong?"

"I'm telling you, it's fine. Maybe a little too literary is all. The *Sun* is a blue-collar paper. You're writing for *The New Yorker*."

"I love *The New Yorker*."

"Of course you do. I just . . . hang on a minute, somebody's at the door." When he came back, he said, "Delivery from the AP. It's your photos." There was the rustling of paper and then a low whistle. "Hey, these are pretty good."

"Surprised?"

"Yeah. It's not easy to take a good picture for a newspaper, especially using a Brownie instead of a Leica . . . Aww."

"What?"

"The picture of us on the boat. Oughta get that one framed. Man, you have a pretty smile. Thought so the first time I saw you."

You make me feel pretty, she thought, but "Thank you" was all she said. They were silent for a moment. She didn't want the call to end.

"Hey," he said abruptly. "I gotta get this to the AP and find Liliane. Bye."

"Be careful," she said, but he had already hung up.

It occurred to her that while thoughts of John now permeated her whole existence, his thoughts of her, though intermittently intense, were a part of his life he could easily put aside.

It was an uncomfortable thought.

23

After he called in the article Jeanne had written for Thursday's paper, John went to the Associated Press office in Rockefeller Center and dropped off the photos to be wired to the *Sun*. From there, he walked to the New York Times Building on West Forty-Third Street. It looked spectacularly out of place, a seventeenth-century French chateau crowbarred between city streets. Ungainly modernist extensions added to accommodate the newspaper's rapid growth hadn't improved its looks. He took the elevator to the eighth floor to see Tom Hamilton, the reporter he had met earlier. As he entered the newsroom, he was struck by the noise—typewriters snapping, the whoosh of pneumatic tubes carrying stories to compositors, yells and shouts from reporters and their editors, and, from somewhere deep down in the building, the rush and rumble of the massive presses.

He threaded his way through rows of wooden desks and tables occupied by dozens of reporters. The desks were littered with crumpled papers, telephones, typewriters, dirty cups and glasses, and overflowing ashtrays. Clouds of smoke drifted past small light globes hung on silver rods from the ceiling at geometric intervals. Hamilton was typing rapidly at a desk near one of the tall windows that faced the street. He was dressed in a gray vest and trousers, his maroon tie still neatly knotted. His suit jacket was on a coat rack.

"Almost finished?" John said.

Hamilton glanced up from his typewriter but didn't stop typing. A cigarette burned in a black enameled holder clutched between his teeth. He squinted against the smoke. "McGrath. What the hell you doing here?"

"You writing any of what I told you about the Mufti or those threats?"

Hamilton, still typing, shook his head. "If that's why you're here, you wasted a trip. Maybe if you had somebody on the record."

"That's what my editor says."

"He's right." He yanked the page out of the typewriter, made a couple of quick marks with a red pen, and placed the page on a short stack of paper, then yelled, "Copy!"

A copyboy not more than fourteen appeared, and Hamilton handed him the stack of papers. "Run it downstairs now." The boy studied the papers for a moment. "Come on, hurry. We can still make the city edition." The boy ran off. Hamilton took the holder from his mouth, tapped out the butt, and stubbed the cigarette in a glass ashtray. He fitted a new cigarette into the holder. "You're still here."

"Yeah, didn't want to interrupt the master at work."

"Cut the crap, McGrath—what do you want?"

"I need to know where the Syrian delegation is staying."

"Beats me."

"So where would I look for them?"

"What am I, traveler's aid?"

"Come on, Hamilton, help a guy out."

"Why should I?"

"I gave you my story today."

"What story? It's a few facts a good reporter might turn into a real story one day."

"When I do get it—and I'm going to get it—I'll share it with you."

"Lucky me," Hamilton said. He thought a moment. "You try the Waldorf?"

"The hotel?"

"No, the salad."

"You think they're staying there?"

Hamilton lit his cigarette. "Half the UN delegations live there, especially Middle East types. Hell, Dr. Weizmann himself has a suite at the top." Chaim Weizmann was one of the principal architects of the Zionist movement. "At each other's throats in Palestine but get along just fine in the Waldorf at a hundred bucks a night."

"Can I use the phone?"

"We don't have newsroom privileges for out-of-towners."

"Here's a nickel." He slapped one down on Hamilton's desk.

"Big spender. Go ahead." He scooped up John's nickel and put it in his vest pocket.

John sat on the edge of the nearby desk and picked up the phone. "Waldorf Astoria, how may I direct your call?" said a metallic female voice. He could hear dozens of other voices in the background repeating the same greeting in exactly the same tone.

"Can you tell me if a Houman al-Hafiz is a guest and what his room number is, please?"

"He is a guest, but I'm sorry, sir," the metallic voice said, "we're not allowed to give out room numbers. If you give me the message, I'm sure he'll call you back."

"No, thanks. How many rooms you have there, anyway?"

"Fourteen hundred."

Going door to door wasn't an option.

"Mind if I make one more?" he said to Hamilton's back.

"Oh, sure, why not?"

He called Grogan, the police detective he met that morning.

"Hey, it's me, John McGrath."

"Yeah?"

"I have a lead on where I can find"—he looked at Hamilton and lowered his voice—"the woman I mentioned. I'm pretty sure she's at the Waldorf, but I don't know which room."

"Why the hell should I help you?"

"Grogan, she could be in danger. I wouldn't bother you if it wasn't important. I know how busy you guys are. My dad was a cop."

He could hear someone yelling in the background.

"Okay," Grogan said quietly. "Give me your number. I'll call you in ten minutes."

"I'll walk you out," Hamilton said when he saw John's call was over. He got up and shrugged on his jacket.

"Um, I'm waiting for a call."

"Are you now?" Hamilton said. "That's nice. Anything else the *Times* can do for you? Coffee? A sandwich?"

The word "sandwich" reminded John he hadn't eaten since breakfast. He was ravenous. "You've got so much time to be a smart guy," he said, "why don't you figure out the real reason why a hundred UN diplomats hightailed it out of the city on the eve of the most important vote in its history."

"They have a conference in London like they told us. It's not a mystery," Hamilton said, sitting down again.

"Sure, and Teegan," John said, mentioning the name of a well-known heavyweight contender who'd been ducking the champ, "can't fight Louis at the Garden next month because he's got tickets to the ballet."

"You're giving me advice? How old are you, sixteen?"

John was saved from thinking up a clever retort by the telephone ringing. It was Grogan.

"Had me a word with the Waldorf house detective, ex-cop name of Sudowicz. That's Polish, by the way."

"I know, I'm from Chicago."

"Right. Anyway, told him why you're checking into this guy, al-Hafiz."

"You know Al's not his first name, right, Grogan?"

"Shut up and listen, smart aleck." Grogan sounded different. He seemed to be taking the whole thing seriously.

"Okay."

"Al-Hafiz and his people are in two of the Royal suites on the twenty-ninth floor, west tower. He's in the corner. The son and the security guy are directly opposite across the hall. Far as the house guy knows, the girl's with al-Hafiz, though no one's seen her since they checked in. Couldn't swear it was her, though, 'cuz she had one of them, whatchamacallits—"

"A niqab."

"Anyhow," Grogan went on, "Sudowicz says this al-Hafiz is nuts, walks around the hotel wearing an antique silver pistol and dresses up his guards like they're his favorite characters from *The Arabian Nights*—turbans, sashes, scimitars, the whole bit. Big shindigs at the Empire Room, keeps an open tab there. He's wearing out the local call girls and drinks himself under the table every night. If it's her, your Liliane's in the same suite."

"What's the setup?" he asked.

"The suites?"

"Yeah."

"I was in there once on a jewelry theft. Fancy as a Park Avenue apartment—sitting room, dining room for twelve, and a small kitchen."

"How do they get the stuff to the kitchen?"

"Service elevator off the main corridor in an enclosed elevator bay that opens to a side door for the kitchen. So the guests don't have to see all the dishes and carts going through the hall entry."

John was silent a moment.

"You might be able to swing it," Grogan said, "getting in and out that kitchen door without the guards seeing you."

"Read my mind."

"Sure, but that door'll be locked."

"Do you think the house guy—?"

"Could get you a key so you could do a B and E on one of the guests? Are all reporters as stupid as you?"

"Hey!"

"But there's a key guy."

"A what?"

"They got a guy, call him the 'key man.' In case a guest loses their key," Grogan chuckled. "He's a locksmith, like. Got a whole room in the basement of the Waldorf with the walls covered with hundreds of skeleton keys for all occasions. He's a guy known to do a favor from time to time."

"How much?"

"Double sawbuck."

"Jeez."

"Thought you were a big-deal reporter."

"Hey, this isn't just for a story, remember? It's to prevent a crime."

Hamilton stirred. Was he taking notes?

"You want his phone number or not?" Grogan said.

"Yeah." John jotted down the number. "We're still meeting at my hotel later tonight, right?"

"I got a thing. Won't be till maybe eleven, eleven thirty."

"See you then." They hung up. Eleven thirty would be cutting it close for his date with Jeanne, but it couldn't be helped.

He stood and turned to leave. "Thanks, Hamilton."

"Going to the Waldorf?" he asked, standing, too.

John smiled. "Why, want to tag along?"

Hamilton shook his head. "Nah. You'll let me know what you find out."

"Oh, sure."

"Hey, kid, you said you'd share."

"Did I? Thought you said it was a wild-goose chase."

• • •

Two hours later, John stood on the northwest corner of Park Avenue and Fiftieth Street, looking across the wide avenue at the broad-shouldered main building of the Waldorf Astoria Hotel. The gray brick and limestone structure squatted across the whole city block. The copper-capped Art Deco-style towers, triple the main building's height, hovered above and behind. Windows across its fourteen stories shone a bright patchwork of yellow in the evening darkness, overshadowing the dim glow of the mosaic dome and Byzantine arches of St. Bartholomew's to his left. The hotel's elegant doormen attended the continuous stream of taxicabs that flowed to and from the ornate main entrance. Their uniforms had a military air—shiny-brimmed captain's hats with the curlicued "WA" insignia, long wool coats with brass buttons, pants with a seam stripe—completed by white gloves and wing collars. They maneuvered a constant stream of women in bulky furs and men in long overcoats in and out of the taxis, ushering new arrivals through the endlessly revolving doors of nickel bronze.

The temperature had dropped below freezing and he stamped his heavy black wing tips to stay warm. He'd arranged to meet the key man at nine, but it was already ten after. To kill time, he sidled over to a news-stand on the corner.

"Got tomorrow's *Times*?" he asked.

"Yep, early city edition," the newsboy squeaked. He couldn't have been more than ten and wore a baseball cap and a thin wool sweater. His nose was running. What was he doing out this late and without a coat? John reached in his pocket, handed the kid a nickel, and picked up a copy of the paper. The boy offered him his two cents change.

"Keep it," he said.

"Two whole cents? Ya mean it? Oh, thanks so much, mister. Now my ma can get that operation she's been needin'."

Nothing on the front page. He opened the paper. Hamilton's article was on page 3.

SAILING DIPLOMATS CALL U.N. A VALVE
111 OFF ON QUEEN MARY—MOST HAIL
MEETING AS SAFETY VALVE—VISHINSKY
AGAIN DIGS AT US

There was a picture of the smiling Vishinsky and his daughter. She was holding a large bouquet of chrysanthemums. He scanned the article. It was filled with anodyne quotes affirming the value of the UN and a couple of nasty shots from the Russian at the US. When asked about the Palestine vote, several diplomats said they planned to listen to the General Assembly session on ship's radio. There was nothing about any threats. Hamilton hadn't dropped a hint of what John had told him. It was still his story. It wasn't solid enough for the *Times*.

There was a sidebar about the Thai representative. Thailand had been firmly in the Arab camp but was rumored to be on the brink of changing their vote to 'yes' due to a combination of Soviet and US pressure and promises. Its representative had disappeared from Wednesday's General Assembly session without explanation, only to appear later that day on the *Queen Mary*. He said he had been recalled by his government and did not plan to return to the UN this year.

John had just turned a page when someone tapped him from behind and said in a quiet voice, "McGrath?"

"Yeah?" He folded the paper and put it in his coat pocket.

"You got the twenty?" said a short man in a heavy overcoat. His hat was pushed low and a dark wool scarf just covered his chin. He carried a small paper bag.

John handed him the money and the man handed him the bag and started to walk away. John opened the bag. There was a silver key and a brass key inside.

"Wait," John called after him. "Which is which?"

"Silver one'll get you in the kitchen door for any of the suites. The brass one's for the entry door to the service elevator bays."

"Where's the service elevator bay?"

"Off the corridor just back of the restaurant on the promenade, the Peacock Alley. You can slip into the corridor through the swinging door. Watch you don't get on the elevator for the ballrooms." The man turned and vanished into the heavily bundled Thanksgiving Eve crowd.

Grogan had told him to call the house detective, Sudowicz, at ten o'clock to confirm that al-Hafiz, father and son, and Alfagari were making their nightly stand at the Empire Room, which would mean he'd have the chance to get in to see Liliane. He was a half hour early. He put the keys in his coat pocket, tossed the bag in the trash, and trotted across Park Avenue, dodging the evening traffic. He hurdled the low wrought iron fence and bushes at the center median and made his way to the side entrance on Fiftieth. Pulling open the heavy metal door to the tiny lobby, he noticed the private entrance for the Waldorf Towers to his left. Was that the door Liliane used?

Inside the lobby, there was a display case framed in the same nickel bronze as the entry doors with a poster advertising an "old-fashioned" Thanksgiving dinner in the hotel's Sert Room. His empty stomach drew his eyes to the dinner menu—three appetizers, including the famous Waldorf salad, Cape Cod oysters, giblet soup, four kinds of fish, and, of course, roast turkey with all the fixings, concluding with pumpkin, rhubarb, and blueberry pie.

Resolutely ignoring his hunger, he walked to Peacock Alley along the hotel hallways, their walls lined with mahogany and marble, the floors covered with Wilton carpets. In the north lobby, his feet tapped across the huge "Wheel of Life" mosaic floor that led to the broad promenade of the famous restaurant.

Peacock Alley was even more ostentatiously luxurious than the rest of the hotel and he felt shabby and out of place in his department store suit. The walls were polished walnut inlaid with ebony. Statues of Carrera marble adorned the numerous wall niches. A life-size portrait of some-one named "Oscar" hung on a wall.

The restaurant was jammed, the buzz of conversation extraordinarily loud. Clouds of tobacco smoke drifted toward the decorated ceilings twenty feet overhead and obscured the light from the recessed wall fix-tures and floor lamps. A pianist was playing something by Rodgers and Hart. The men were in evening clothes, the women in elaborate gowns. Some were seated on velvet-upholstered couches, others in cushioned chairs at tables covered in white damask.

To the right was a swinging door used by the wait staff. That had to be the door the key man told him about. There was a small round table against a wall with a "Reserved" placard. He slipped through the crowd, pocketed the card, and sat down. A red-jacketed waiter rushed over and asked for his drink order.

"Whiskey sour."

"May I recommend a New York Sour, sir?"

"A what?"

"We float a shot of red wine on top."

His stomach recoiled. "Um, no, just a regular one, thanks."

The waiter shrugged and walked off.

The next time the swinging door opened, he saw the corridor and the elevator. That had to be the one.

The maître d', dressed in an elaborate white-and-gold jacket, whis-pered to John's waiter, checked a list, and shook his head. The waiter brought John his drink. He jerked his head in the direction of the maître d' and said, "Boss says you got five minutes. Table's reserved."

"What do I owe?"

"Six bits."

"You're kidding." He'd never paid more than a quarter for a drink. "Here's a buck," he said finally. "Is there a house phone?"

"At the entrance to the alley." He gave a grimace meant to be a smile and hustled to another table. John waited a few minutes longer to see if anyone used the elevator, but no one did. The maître d' started toward him. No sense waiting any longer. He went to the restaurant entrance, picked up a house phone, and asked for the house detective.

"Sudowicz."

"This is John McGrath."

"The guests you're interested in have been in the Empire Room for the last hour. I'll tag along behind them when they leave, make sure they get to their room okay. No girls tonight, though. Don't know how long they'll stay. Usually, they have girls."

"I won't need long."

"You watch out. Those guards of his might look like they're dressed for Halloween, but the .45s they're carrying are real."

He hung up, walked back through the restaurant, and boldly stepped through the swinging door. The long corridor seemed to stretch forever in both directions. He crossed it and entered the elevator bay. The lighted floor display over the elevator only went to fourteen. This was the ballroom elevator.

He stepped back into the corridor and was nearly run over by a trio of waiters hurrying along with silver-covered trays held high. There was another elevator bay twenty-five feet farther along. He walked to it and saw it went all the way to the top of the towers. He blew out a breath and hit the call button.

The counterweighted elevator smoothly rocketed him to the twenty-ninth floor. With a silent prayer to whichever saint watched over reporters, he stepped out of the elevator. It was dark in the elevator bay, but a glimmer of light from the guest corridor came through the fire door's round window made of thick glass embedded with wire mesh. There was a kitchen door for each suite to his right and to his left.

He put his face to the round window cautiously.

Twenty-five feet away were the hall doors to each suite. Two guards stood on either side of Houman and Liliane's door to his right—large men, over six feet tall, broad and heavy. They were dressed, as Grogan had said, like extras from *The Road to Morocco*—turbans, white robes, turquoise sashes, gold scimitars on one hip, and, in a more modern touch, blue steel .45 caliber pistols in black leather holsters on the other.

He turned to the kitchen door for Liliane's suite and slipped in the key. With a twist and a turn of the knob, he was inside. It seemed pitch-black at first, but as his eyes adjusted, he saw a thin streak of light coming under the door from the next room. He opened it and found himself in a dining room with a rectangular polished wood table. He walked through the dining room and pushed open the door to the sitting room.

A lone table lamp illuminated the room, which was furnished like an eighteenth-century London town house complete with overstuffed sofas, rounded polished mahogany chests of drawers, and inlaid gilded chairs. Satin drapes covered the arched windows and oil paintings hung on the creamy yellow walls. Fresh flowers overflowed ceramic vases placed throughout the room. There was a working fireplace. Despite the crowded warmth of the materials, the room had a chilly feel, like a stage set. At its center, Liliane was perched on a small sofa.

She wasn't dressed in a robe and niqab like the first time they met or in a nightgown like the evening before. Instead, she wore an expensive black cocktail dress, like one he'd seen in a shop window in the Waldorf lobby. The bodice had a low scalloped neckline. It was drawn in at the waist and secured at the midline by a row of tiny buttons that looked like black pearls. The skirt was crepe silk covered by a matching over-skirt with glittering stones sewn in, spaced at irregular intervals. Not diamonds, surely? He walked into the room. She looked startled; then her face relaxed into a smile.

"I knew you would come. They're all in the nightclub," she said. "Alfagari too."

The nearby lamp created a soft sheen of light across her face. "Liliane, we don't have a lot of time. Did you find out anything else that can help me?" Her face hardened in disappointment. "Yes, John. I listened to Alfagari on the telephone today. He was in our suite. Houman and I were in our room for a time." She looked down. "When Houman was sleeping, Alfagari used the telephone. I listened on the extension."

"That was dangerous."

"No more than this. I don't know who he was talking to, but Alfagari said he couldn't find a man he was supposed to kill today."

A surge of excitement went through him. "He say a name?"

"A Britisher, McNeil. He talked about another too. 'He went over to the Zionists,' he said."

This was it, the confirmation he needed. They had meant to kill McNeil today. Somehow, McNeil had found out about the threat and decided to leave town with the other diplomats. The other man might be the Thai diplomat who took refuge on the *Queen Mary*.

"What else did they say?"

"The man he spoke to said someone else will finish this task."

"How? McNeil's on the *Queen Mary* in the middle of the Atlantic."

"That won't stop them."

"Thank you, Liliane. That's a big help."

"There is more. Alfagari received a telegram from the Mufti today. I didn't see it, but"—she shrugged—"he keeps his papers in a silver dispatch case."

"It's worth a try." He held up the passkey. "I can get into his room through the kitchen. The guards won't see me."

She stood. "I will go with you."

"What? No."

"And how will you read his documents?"

She was right. "Okay, let's go."

She walked toward him. The skirt of her dress flared from her body and swayed with her movement. As she neared, he could just see the swell of her breasts above the neckline of her dress. He had an urge to touch her, to take her hand, to kiss her.

They walked in careful silence back into the elevator bay. He used his key on the other suite's kitchen door and walked in, rigid with tension, every hair on his skin alive. It was the exact reciprocal of Liliane's suite and they quickly found Alfagari's bedroom. Its door was open. There was no sign of the dispatch box.

"The closet?" he whispered. She raised her eyebrows in question. He opened the door of the walk-in closet. It had the military neatness one would expect of a soldier. Suits and shirts were hung in an orderly row, several pairs of shoes neatly arrayed below them. Two large suitcases occupied one corner of the closet. A cylindrical leather case, four feet long, occupied another.

Alfagari will be babysitting al-Hafiz for hours, he told himself. *There's all the time in the world. Keep moving.* He searched the closet and a chest of drawers. Nothing.

A shelf ran around the circumference of the closet just above eye level. He felt along it until his hand hit something hard. He reached up both hands and carefully lowered the box from the shelf.

"Liliane," he whispered, walking back into the bedroom. He set the silver box on the bed and tried the catch.

"Locked," he whispered.

"Can you open it?"

He studied the lock. "I can probably break it."

"Then he'll know." Her face was still.

"He'll know anyway if I take something."

She looked at the box as though weighing the consequences. "Break it, John."

He opened the screwdriver blade of his pocketknife and slipped it in the lock. He turned it gently, steadily applying more force, but the knife slipped and scratched the lock. He stopped to adjust his grip on the knife, then turned it sharply. There was a loud crack as the lock broke and he opened the box. There were papers and envelopes of various sizes. Liliane took the box from him, sat on the bed, and quickly rifled through them in the dim light.

"This is from Jerusalem. It came today," she said, holding a thin brown envelope.

He sat next to her on the bed. She opened the envelope and pulled out a postal telegram. At the top, there was preprinted text in French and Arabic. The body of the telegram was in Arabic, except for one word.

"It is the Mufti. There is his name, Hajj Amin al-Husayni."

"What does it say?"

Her hand tremored. "It says, 'Mohammed: You are sworn to resist the creation of a Jewish state. Eliminate *la cérat*.'. . . uh . . . 'the salve . . . as planned. May Allah grant you success.' I don't know why the word 'salve' is in French."

He took out his pad and wrote down the words. "What does that mean, 'eliminate the salve'? You sure you're translating it right?"

She nodded.

"And 'success'? Success in what?"

She looked in his eyes. "In killing. What else?"

"Could it mean Lake Success?"

She shook her head, looking at the telegram. "It is the same word, but I don't think so." She shrugged. "They are worried their threats are not enough. Now they must kill to disrupt the vote."

"I think you're right." He took the telegram from her and put it in his inside pocket, then took her hand. "You know I can't sit on this. I have to report it."

"I know. But Alfagari is already suspicious. I can tell how he looks at me. Have you been indiscreet, John?"

"No, no," he said passionately, wanting to put his arms around her. "I haven't even told my editor. You're an unnamed source." He waited tensely for her approval and added, "But I might have to tell the police."

She shook her head, but said, "Very well. I trust you."

He had his proof—the rifle, the telegram calling for action of some kind, the telephone conversation about McNeil—and a witness. That should be enough for Hershon and for Grogan. He had to get back to the hotel, call in the story, and get it published. This could make his career. But how much should he tell Grogan? He might give the information to another reporter.

"We better get going," he said. They stood up. "You can't stay with him."

She stepped toward him. "I know. I am going to leave him. I will stay in New York."

"Will he let you go?"

"Never. It will be an insult. He will kill me."

She moved closer to him. Now they were only inches apart. Despite the armed guards twenty feet away and against all reason, he took her hand. When she didn't resist, he pulled her gently to him and kissed her. Her lips tasted sweet. He pulled back for a moment to look in her eyes, then kissed her again. "Come with me now," he said softly. "I can get you away."

She shook her head slowly. "No. I have a friend from Syria in this city. I have already made my plans."

"I'm afraid for you."

"I am afraid too. But I know how to be secret. Remember, I was a courier for the British during the war."

"Yeah, until you were caught."

"I was careless then. I won't be now."

"Call me the second you get away." He wrote down the number of his hotel on his pad, ripped out the page, and gave it to her. "I'll be at the hotel until Sunday. If something goes wrong, call the police." He took the page back, wrote Grogan's number, and handed it to her. "Grogan knows about this. He'll help you."

A key slid into the lock of the suite's hall door and they froze.

Alfagari had returned. The door closed. Heavy steps crossed the sitting room. There was nowhere to run. He stepped in front of Liliane. Sweat broke out all over his body.

"Hall porter," a man's voice called. "Evening service. Anyone in?"

They looked at each other in relief. "Stay here," John whispered.

He snatched all of the papers from the dispatch box and threw them in a small wastebasket. Gambling that the porter wouldn't know the room's occupants, he stepped out of the bedroom carrying the wastebasket.

The porter was a stocky man dressed in a bright red jacket, white shirt, and black pants. He was refilling the liquor cabinet with bottles from a small cart. He turned at the sound of John's footsteps.

John gave him a friendly smile. "Hey, would you mind emptying this wastebasket?"

The porter eyed him carefully and he was afraid for a moment that the porter knew it wasn't his room. "Sure, sir. There's a trash chute in the kitchen. Let me take it for you. I'll just be another minute."

"Oh, right, jeez, I forgot. I'll take care of it."

He walked into the kitchen, calling over his shoulder, "Thanks." He quickly found the trash chute and threw the papers down it. He returned to the bedroom, grabbed the dispatch box, and threw it down the chute as well. There wasn't much chance Alfagari would connect Liliane with its disappearance. John returned to the bedroom and they waited.

"Night, sir," the porter finally called as he left and relocked the hall door.

Outside the suite, the porter said something and one of the guards replied. The door to Liliane's suite across the hall opened and closed.

"We should go," John said. "We can wait in the elevator bay until the porter is finished in your room."

She nodded and followed him to the kitchen. He pointed to the trash chute. "I threw the box and all the other papers down the chute. Better he thinks someone stole the whole box rather than know which paper was taken."

They were walking out the kitchen door into the elevator bay when a gunshot exploded in the corridor. He shoved Liliane to the floor and covered her with his body. She turned her head and opened her mouth to speak. He shook his head, placing a finger to her lips. There were shouts in a foreign language from the corridor and a squeal of terror.

"Houman," she mouthed.

"No, sir, stop, please, I didn't do anything!"

It was the hall porter's voice. John crept to the corridor door and pressed his face against the little round window so he could see through the wire mesh embedded in the glass.

Houman al-Hafiz was at the door to his suite. The muzzle of his antique silver revolver was jammed against the head of the terrified porter who was in the vise grip of one of the turbaned guards. The other guard stood to his side. Alfagari was several feet away, back to a wall, in profile to John, hands at his sides. Seeing him, John felt a surge of anger.

Al-Hafiz wore a long robe of patterned gray silk, and a wide black sash draped over one shoulder and looped around the hips. His white headdress reached nearly to his waist and was held in place by a braided and jeweled headband.

Feet pounded around the corner and two men in suits ran into the hall and stopped short. "Sir, put down your weapon," the first man ordered. His jacket was unbuttoned and his hands were at his side.

Al-Hafiz responded with what sounded like a string of curses.

"Sir, if we could just speak English," said the man, "I'm sure we can work this out. Please put that gun down now."

"This servant," al-Hafiz hissed, switching to heavily accented English, "has dishonored my woman. He must die." He was slurring his words and his eyes were red and glassy. His finger twitched within the pistol's trigger guard and the muzzle danced against the porter's temple. Liliane came to stand by John.

The porter was bent backward by the guard's tight grip and held his hands stiff and high over his head in a way that made his red waiter's jacket and white shirt ride up over his substantial midsection, exposing an unusually hairy stomach. It would have been comical if the situation weren't so serious.

The man who had spoken had a name tag just below his pocket handkerchief that said, "Sudowicz," in large gold letters. His partner stood a few steps behind him.

"Sir, I'm sure that's not the case," Sudowicz said, his voice calm. "He was simply doing his job, cleaning the room for the evening and restocking the bar. He does that for all the rooms on this floor and our staff know they're not to be in any room with your, uh, guest. Your guards must have told him that the sitting room was empty and he could do his work."

The guard holding the porter nodded imperceptibly to the detective who caught the gesture.

Al-Hafiz shook his head. "That's a lie," he said venomously, trying to focus on Sudowicz.

"That's for Chief Jennings to decide, sir. You're going to have to come downstairs with me to sort this out."

"I have diplomatic immunity," al-Hafiz said.

"Sure you do. We're not police, just hotel security. I'm not arresting you," Sudowicz said. "But you pointed a gun at one of our employees. There was a shot fired. Until we get this cleared up, I need to take that gun and you have to come with me."

John admired his calm authority. Neither Sudowicz nor his assistant had drawn their weapons, which would have made matters worse, possibly fatal. John's forehead hurt because it was pressed so hard against the small window. He stepped aside and Liliane took his place, looked through the window for a moment, and then pulled back, shaking her head in disgust. John returned to the window.

"I refuse. They," al-Hafiz said, indicating the guards, "will not permit such an outrage."

"Then I'm calling the police, sir. They won't care about any immunity. If you don't put your gun down, they'll shoot you dead. Your men too."

The guards shifted uncomfortably.

"If they don't shoot you, they'll take you down to the station until your ambassador can vouch for you. The press will get involved and it'll be in all the papers." Sudowicz's voice got hard. "Someone might even tell your ambassador about all the booze and women you've been enjoying. That'll be in the papers too. You don't want that, now do you? Give me the gun, come downstairs, I'll make a report, and you'll be back in your room in no time."

Al-Hafiz weaved a little and his finger moved on the trigger. John held his breath.

"If I come with you, no word to my ambassador about . . . all that?"

"Not from me, no sir,"

"No police or newspapers?"

"No, sir. Now give me the gun." Sudowicz put his hand out slowly, palm up. Al-Hafiz lowered the gun. His finger was still near the trigger. John was afraid he'd shoot somebody by accident. The guard not holding the porter must have had the same thought. He took the gun from al-Hafiz's hand in the careful way you take a sharp object from a small child. Once he had it, he expertly popped out the cylinder and emptied it of shells. He poured them into Sudowicz's outstretched hand, then gave him the pistol, butt first. The detective sniffed the barrel and nodded. He dropped the pistol in one of his jacket pockets and the shells in another.

The other guard released the terrified porter. Sudowicz whispered something to him. The porter pulled his jacket into place with trembling hands and walked around the corner.

"You two," Sudowicz snapped at the guards. "That suite's a crime scene until it's been cleared by me. I need to take some pictures and dig the slug out of the wall. Neither one of you goes in there without my say-so, got it?"

They both nodded.

"Anybody else tries to go in, you call me. You don't and I'll have both your asses thrown in jail as accessories to attempted murder. You don't have any immunity. I'll see that you both spend a couple years in prison. Understood?"

They both nodded. "We don't want any trouble," one said.

"Now, sir," Sudowicz said to al-Hafiz, "you and your friend"—he nodded to Alfagari—"should go to the elevator with my associate." Alfagari took al-Hafiz by the elbow and steered him down the corridor and around the corner to the public elevator.

"You have to come with me," John whispered to Liliane. "The guy's crazy!"

She put a hand on his cheek but shook her head. "Soon. I will call you tomorrow."

"Then let's get you back to your room." He opened the kitchen door to her suite and led her to the sitting room.

There was the muffled sound of a man's voice in the hall and a knock on the door. One of the guards said something in Arabic. Liliane replied in the same language, then whispered to John, "Go the way you came. I told them to wait."

"Miss, uh, Hafiz? Are you—?" It was Sudowicz. "Would it be okay, I mean, could you let us in please? I just need to look around a little."

She didn't reply.

"Miss Hafiz," Sudowicz tried again after a moment. "I don't want to force things, but we have to get in there. We want to make sure not to offend you. Do you understand?"

John put a hand on her shoulder and whispered, "Tell him to give you a few minutes. You'll open the door, but he has to give you time to get back to your room."

She nodded and, despite her tension, smiled.

"Make sure you call me," he said, still whispering. "I have to know you're okay."

"I will. Don't worry." They touched hands and he turned and went to the dining room and out the kitchen door. She called to Sudowicz. "I will unlock the door, but you must give me time to return to my room. Do you agree?"

"Yes, ma'am, that's fine," Sudowicz said, sounding relieved.

When John was out of the suite, he locked the kitchen door and touched the button for the elevator. While he waited, he stole a look through the fire door window. Sudowicz was standing in front of the suite. As the elevator doors rumbled open, one of the guards looked in John's direction, peered carefully, then started walking toward him, his hand moving toward his gun.

All the tension he had been suppressing since entering Liliane's suite seemed to explode. John backed away from the window, jumped in the elevator, and pushed the button for the first floor. It took forever for the door to close. He stabbed the button for the first floor repeatedly. It finally closed just as the hall door was thrown open.

He reached the first floor and burst out of the service corridor, trotted along Peacock Alley into the main lobby, and across the mosaic floor. He whirled through the revolving door of the Waldorf's Park Avenue exit and yelled to the doorman for a cab. The doorman blew his whistle and a Zenith yellow cab careened to the curb. The doorman opened the passenger door. John jumped in and slammed the door shut.

"Drive, buddy!" He looked back. No one was following him. He told the driver to turn left on West Fifty-First Street and began to breathe easier.

He checked his watch as his pulse slowed. It was only eleven. The entire episode in the Waldorf had lasted barely an hour. There was plenty of time to phone in his story to the *Sun*, make his meeting with Grogan and his date with Jeanne. He took out his pad and made notes of everything Liliane had told him, then put the rest of his notes from the day in order. When he arrived at the Paramount, he went straight to a telephone booth in the lobby, called the *Sun*, reversing the charges, and dictated his story to the stenographer on duty. "Have the night editor call me the second he reads it." He gave her his room number.

He grabbed a red apple from a bowl on the reception counter and devoured it as he rode the elevator to his room. He was sweaty and disheveled after the long day that had started on the train before dawn. In his room, he undressed and stood under a hot shower for several minutes. When he got out, he wiped the steam off the mirror and shaved. Just as he finished, the telephone rang. He walked to the nightstand, a towel around his waist, and answered it.

A man's voice said, "McGrath, this is Janus Pilch. Editor on duty tonight."

Night desk or "bullpen" editors worked the night shift at the *Sun*, taking turns handling late stories. They were usually burnouts who could no longer handle the pace of the day. They often drank.

Pilch was probably working from the glassed-in office John had used for his meeting with Mahmoud Haleem. Would Haleem ever know what he had set in motion?

"Just finished your story," Pilch continued. "Like you told the girl, this is hot all right. I'm gonna put it on the front page. Lemme read it back to you. I have to lock it now. The print run is taking longer on account of the strike. How's this for a headline, 'Assassins in Lake Success? Link to Palestine Vote Suspected.'"

"Couldn't be better, but don't you have to get Hershon's okay?"

"Nope, it's my decision." He sounded insulted. "I've got full authority on nights. This is solid, right? You have an inside man who confirms it?"

Or woman. "Absolutely."

"So we go with it," Pilch went on, "unless you're telling me you're not sure."

"No, sir, I'm a hundred percent sure."

"Okay, listen up.

"With the many acts of terror that have occurred during the last year in Palestine, the Halloween bombing of the British embassy in Rome, and numerous published accounts of Jewish and Arab killers walking the streets of London, it should come as no surprise that assassins have come to United Nations headquarters on the shores of Lake Success, New York, to carry on their deadly work.

"The Sun *has confirmed that death threats have been made against UN diplomats who favor partition by a Palestinian known as the Mufti of Jerusalem, a virulent anti-Zionist who worked with the Nazis during the war. Links to other acts of violence have been discovered between the Mufti and a member of the Syrian delegation, Mohammed Alfagari. There is evidence that attempts on the lives of other diplomats have been or soon will be made."*

The article went on to describe the purchase of the rifle in Chicago. It concluded with quotes of the Mufti's threats against any supporter of the partition vote and his implacable hatred of Jews.

John approved Pilch's edits and dictated a few of his own. "It's good to go," he said.

"Great. Hey, this means you'll have two stories in tomorrow morning's paper. We have that one on the kids you sent in earlier. Put it in the women's section, but it'll still get good play. Great photos, by the way, especially the one of you and the young lady. You're some hotshot, you know that? Babysitting those students the same time you're chasing down an international assassination plot."

He wished he could confess that Jeanne had written the article about the school trip but was more than a little surprised that Pilch hadn't noticed a difference in quality between the two articles. Something Pilch said stuck in his mind.

"Wait a minute. What young lady?"

"The one in the photo with Lady Liberty behind you. Great shot!"

He hadn't meant to send the photo Cullerton had taken of him and Jeanne, just the one with the students in Times Square. The AP must have screwed up.

"Something wrong?" Pilch asked. "We gotta hurry here."

John thought for a minute. "Nope, nothing at all, Mr. Pilch. Run 'em both."

Why shouldn't her picture be in the paper? No one at the *Sun* knew of their friendship. It was a way to pay her back for writing the article.

At the thought of Jeanne, he had a sudden pang of guilt. He'd never kissed two women in the same month, much less on the same day. And he was supposed to see Jeanne again in less than an hour. He tried to reassure himself that there was no reason for either of them to be upset but was dimly aware that reason might not have anything to do with it.

To distract himself from his uncomfortable train of thought, he asked Pilch, "So, the printer's strike is still on?"

"Yeah," the editor answered, "but there's a way they can engrave the newspaper instead of using the linotype. Management's fed up, talking about just firing all the printers."

"It'll never work," he said. "The A.F. of L. will get all the other unions involved. We wouldn't be able to put out a flyer."

"Well, tomorrow's paper will get out, don't you worry about that. I'm going to get the AP to pick up this assassination story under your byline. Might see it in some of the New York papers tomorrow afternoon."

"Gee, thanks, Mr. Pilch."

"No thanks necessary. This is an important story. Everyone's going to want it. Even the *Trib* will have to report it. You'll be famous."

• • •

Pilch's words kept going through his mind as he dressed in the same tired suit, but with a clean shirt and a fresh tie. It was nearly eleven thirty. He went to the lobby and down a short flight of stairs to the basement bar outside the subterranean Diamond Horseshoe nightclub.

He took a corner table and a waiter came over.

"Large beer and"—he remembered the menu he'd seen at the Waldorf—"roast turkey?"

"Thanksgiving's not till tomorrow, pal. Turkey sandwich?"

"Fine, turkey and Swiss on rye, extra mustard."

"Anything else?"

"Waldorf salad?"

"Cole slaw or potato salad, buddy."

"Both. Double portion."

"Coming up." The waiter jammed his pad in his apron and yelled to the bartender. "Large beer."

His food and beer came almost instantly. While he ate and drank with one hand, he added to his notes from his talk with Liliane with the other. He was just finishing when a man walked into the bar in full police uniform.

"Hey, hotshot," Grogan said, tossing his hat on the table next to John's glass and empty plate. "Busy night?"

"You call Sudowicz?" John said.

"Of course."

"Then why ask?"

Grogan was thick and tall with gray hair buzzed close. He reminded John of his father. He had the same no-nonsense confidence and authority. His face was parchment white, shot through with red veins, his eyes a vivid black, shrewd and humorous. He had the air of someone who knew who he was and had decided he could live with it. The uniform surprised John. Grogan had been in plain clothes when they met earlier in the day.

"You been on parade?"

"Nah, we had a retirement racket for one of the guys. Chief of Ds wanted us in uniform."

"Get you a beer?"

"You have to ask?"

The waiter reappeared and John ordered a beer for Grogan and another for himself. Grogan raised his eyebrows expectantly and John couldn't hold back.

"I got it."

"You got what?"

"Proof." He told him what he had learned from Liliane as he slipped the telegram out of his pocket and laid it on the table. "So investigate."

Grogan pulled out a pair of reading glasses, looked at the telegram, and took them off again. "What the hell's it say?" The waiter returned and set down two draft beers and took away John's empty glass.

John pointed. "That's the name of the man who sent it, this Mufti guy, a well-known anti-Zionist Palestinian." He read the words Liliane had translated for him.

Grogan looked at him and nodded. "What else do you have?"

He told him about the conversation Liliane had overheard and the diplomats leaving on the *Queen Mary.*

"What else?"

"The rifle."

"You already told me about that. I need to know who told you all this."

John understood. A large part of the value of any information was its source. There wasn't any choice. "It's the guy's girlfriend, Liliane al-Haffar. She overheard this Alfagari talking on the telephone extension. They're going after two of the guys on the *Queen Mary.* And you should know, Grogan, you don't have a lot of time before this is public. I've already filed my story. It'll be in the morning *Sun*. Probably in the New York papers in the afternoon."

"Will she give us a statement?"

John shook his head slowly. "I don't know. Al-Hafiz and his guards keep her close and they're crazy protective of their women. If you tried to see her, there'd be an international incident. She said she's going to get away from them, wants to stay in New York."

"We could help her if she helps us."

"I offered, but she said no."

"Due respect, kid, we might just be able to help more than you."

"I hope you can. I hated leaving her with that madman, but she wouldn't go," John said. "But what about Alfagari? Can't you pick him up? We got him buying the rifle."

"Nothing illegal about that and anyway, he's part of the delegation and he's got immunity. But even if he didn't, I don't think I could hold him. I'll open the investigation, but I don't know what we got. Not as sure as you are what that telegram means. Is it political palaver or a plot? Why's the one word in French? Doesn't make any sense. We could watch this Alfagari, but the two guys you say he's going after are in the middle of the ocean. Can't put a guard on every diplomat here. By the way, did you see the rifle when you searched his place?"

"I didn't look."

"Are you kidding me? Jesus, kid."

"Shit, I shoulda thought."

"You're not a cop, calm down. I'm going to pay a call on the Syrians first thing tomorrow, even if it is Thanksgiving. My wife'll be glad to have me out of the house while she's cooking. I'll get my pal at the FBI to come with us and I'll bring a policewoman. We'll try to get a statement from the girl and if she wants to leave, I'll bring her out."

John felt enormously relieved. Tough, competent Detective Grogan would make sure Liliane was safe.

Grogan looked thoughtful. "But like I said, they have immunity."

"Doesn't mean you let them commit murder," John said.

"I don't need a punk reporter from Chicago telling me my job."

John looked down, abashed.

"No, it doesn't mean that," Grogan said, having made his point. "But they can't be arrested. They don't have to cooperate. But if we can get her on record, I can talk to the State Department. We'll confine Alfagari to the hotel, keep a watch on all of 'em, maybe boot their asses out of the country. By the way, I got hold of the UN security guys today. They weren't too impressed. They've been getting threats every day for a year over this Palestine thing. They were gonna add security for the vote, anyway."

"I guess that'll have to do," John said.

"By the way, do you think this al-Hafiz knows what Alfagari is up to?"

"Liliane doesn't seem to think so."

"Right. Anyway, you and the kids going out to Lake Success in the morning?"

"Yeah, that's the plan," John said. "We're watching the parade, then heading out there for a tour."

"The Macy's parade? You're gonna freeze your ass off. Doesn't matter what you do. I tried everything when I was on patrol. Long johns, hats, gloves, earmuffs, two pairs of socks, newspaper in the shoes, flask of brandy, you name it. Still froze."

"I can handle cold. I'm from Chicago."

"Whyn't you watch it on television, for Pete's sake? Local NBC station has it on."

"Wouldn't make much of a holiday picture for the *Sun*, the kids gathered around a fuzzy television receiver," John said glumly. "Nah, they want the whole *Miracle on 34th Street* angle."

"Loved that movie. Love anything with Maureen O'Hara." Grogan drained his beer and got up to leave. "You got this?"

"Yeah, god forbid a New York City cop should pay for a drink."

Grogan laughed.

"Just kidding, I'm on expenses."

"Hey, McGrath," Grogan said seriously.

"Yeah?"

"I'm not running with this to another reporter in case you're worried. And I'll give you first crack at anything I find."

It was a valuable concession. "Thanks, Detective."

"Only fair. You didn't have to bring this to us."

"Maybe because my dad was a cop."

Grogan looked at him kindly. "Yeah, you said."

"It's not just that, though." He shook his head. "Since the war, I just can't stand on the sidelines."

"Your pop would be proud. You're a credit to the Irish, boyo," Grogan said with a faint brogue.

"Oh, faith and begorra, I suppose that's all that counts," he said, irritated.

"Don't be such a smart aleck," Grogan snapped. "Not so long ago you wouldn't have been able to get a job in this city 'cause you're Irish."

"I know."

Grogan was like his father, like all of his relatives in Chicago. They were tribal and the tribe came first. It didn't matter how many generations back your people had come to America; you were still the Irish kid or the Polish boy, the Jewish guy or the Italian man, the Greek or the Swede, the German or the Finn, and so on. Whatever else you became, you were a member of your tribe first.

"Call me late morning, I'll fill you in," Grogan said. "Enjoy the frostbite." Grogan put his policeman's hat square on his head and the big Irishman walked out of the bar.

24

Jeanne waited nervously on the sidewalk at the entrance of The 3 Deuces on West Fifty-Second Street, standing near a sandwich board that read, "Charlie Parker Quintet Tonight." It was nearly one in the morning on Thanksgiving Day. Despite the hour, people were going in and out of the club. She had just decided John must be waiting for her inside when he rushed up.

"Sorry, sorry. I got held up."

"It's okay," she said, relieved to see him.

"I hope you weren't waiting long." He smelled of Barbasol and soap and she was pleased to think he'd showered and shaved for her.

"Just a few minutes," she fibbed. "Carolyn and Tony were headed uptown, so they walked me over here. If they do a bed check in our room, we're both getting sent to reform school."

He laughed and said, "You ready?"

She nodded with a confidence she didn't feel as they went in. This was her first time in a real nightclub. As her eyes adjusted to the dim lights, everything about the low-ceilinged room—its moist heat, the smell of smoke and bodies, people talking loudly—was intensely exotic. The men wore suits in a wide range of styles and their shirts and ties were bright bursts of color. The women displayed a variety of fashions designed to be as revealing as possible. Everybody seemed to be smoking.

"Hey, how about a Brandy Alexander?" John smiled after they found a seat at a tiny cocktail table near a wall.

Her stomach flipped at the thought. "Uh, maybe just a pop?"

"Sure, I was kidding," he said, speaking loudly so as to be heard over the crowd. He signaled to a waiter and ordered two Cokes.

She leaned closer so as to be heard. "I'm dying to hear what happened tonight. Did you find Liliane?"

He stiffened. "I did."

"And? Was she able to tell you anything? Are you going to write a story about it?"

"You know, it's too noisy in here to really talk and they'll be starting to play in a minute. I'll tell you all about it later."

"Okay."

They were silent for a moment; then Jeanne said, "What's she like? I've never met someone from that part of the world."

"She's nice, just like anybody. Very brave."

"Did she wear a veil, like in the movies?"

"Uh, no, just a regular dress." He craned his head around. "I'm not sure where that waiter went. I'll get some Cokes from the bar. You okay for a minute?"

She nodded, disappointed at his reticence. He got up and walked to the bar, which was at the opposite end of the room. She could see him making his way through a group of men who all seemed to know each other. They were drinking, laughing loudly, and slapping each other on the back. He returned and set their drinks on the table next to a candle that provided almost no light.

"I can barely see you," she said, waving her hands as though they could dispel the smoke and darkness.

John scooted his chair closer until they were almost touching. "This better?"

She put a hand on his and nodded.

"Any trouble giving the sisters the slip?" he said, removing his hand to pick up his drink.

"Not at all. Oh, look, somebody's on the stage."

A clean-cut young man dressed in a conservative suit and striped tie had stepped onto the stage at the front of the room and adjusted a sleek silver microphone on a thin stand. The stage was only a foot higher than the floor. Portable sound partitions made of stuffed vinyl and irregularly placed brass studs were grouped around the bandstand, leaving just enough room for a drum kit, an upright piano, and the band members.

The man raised the microphone until it was even with his chin and said, "Uh, ladies and gentlemen. If I could just have your attention for a few minutes." The room quieted for a moment and a few people looked up but then resumed their conversations. Although the man was only of middle height, his head nearly touched the exposed steel beams on the unfinished ceiling. He peered at the crowd through rimless glasses as though trying to size them up. He tapped on the microphone and coughed and a spotlight snapped on. He blinked. "Uh, believe me, I know who you're here to see and it's not some comedian, but I promise I'll get Bird up here before you know it."

The crowd slowly quieted.

"How's everybody doing tonight? I'm Sam Levenson. I know, what's a guy named Levenson doing in a place like this? I'm not sure, to tell you the truth." There were a few chuckles and, thus encouraged, Levenson launched into a series of funny stories about his life growing up in Brooklyn. He was frequently drowned out by bursts of conversation and laughter not related to his act, but he soldiered on. After less than ten minutes, he checked his watch. "I'm sorry, folks, but I see my time is up."

There was a loose round of applause.

"Boy, tough crowd. I think on that note I'll say good night. Now, help me give a warm 3 Deuces welcome to Duke Jordan on piano." There was some clapping as Jordan and two others made their way to the bandstand. "Tommy Potter on bass."

The applause grew.

"Max Roach on drums." Roach gave a hard rat-a-tat ruffle on his snare drum. There was more applause and now some shouting.

"Miles Davis on trumpet."

More clapping and shouts as a thick young man with a broad smiling face strode to the bandstand like a boxer rushing toward the ring. The crowd was now shouting, clapping, and stamping their feet.

"Ladies and gentlemen, the Yardbird himself, Chaaaarrr-lleee Paarr-kerr!"

Parker stepped up on the small stage, holding his alto saxophone. In his huge hands, it looked like a child's toy. He was wearing a striped suit with wide lapels and a flowered tie. Without announcing the title of the song or giving a glance at the audience or each other, the band launched into a hard, fast, swinging torrent of sound. When the first song was done, without saying a word or waiting for applause to end, they burst into the next one.

Jeanne was bewildered. She shouted in John's ear. "I don't know how they can play that fast. I can't even think that fast."

Although she had read about bebop, she had never heard it. It was nothing like the gentle swing of her favorite big bands, or the smooth singing of Frank Sinatra. Song after song, the sound swept over her like an assault. She was ready to write it off completely when the band changed pace. Roach switched from sticks to brushes and they played a slow, sensuous version of "Embraceable You." Parker, his eyes closed, played the melody straight through, then played it again, adding a dizzying array of notes. He soloed through a few choruses, then repeated the melody with a warm breathy tone. The rest of the band played barely above a whisper. When he finished, there was a moment of quiet followed by a roar of applause. With brief nods, the band left the stage. All of them, except Parker, headed for the bar.

"So, what do you think? You wish we went to see Sinatra, right?" John said. Before she could answer, a waiter came by.

"Two Cokes, please," she said quickly.

"So?" John said again.

"I liked that last one, 'Embraceable You.'"

"You hated the rest?"

"No, I mean, it was . . . interesting."

"Well, it's not for everyone."

Their Cokes came and before he could pay, Jeanne handed the waiter a quarter and signaled for him to keep the change. "Hey," John protested.

"What, I can't have you paying for everything. What would people think of me?" she said.

He laughed. "You're so Chicago."

"What's that supposed to mean?"

"Just that you know how to act. You know who you are." He checked his watch. "Oh, jeez, it's late. We gotta get going. We have to be up at the crack of dawn to watch that ever-lovin' parade. Wish there was a way out of it."

"Don't say that, I'm looking forward to it."

They finished their Cokes and walked out onto West Fifty-Second Street. The clean cold air felt glorious after the hot, smoke-filled club. A string of neon signs for other jazz clubs stretched from Broadway to Tenth Avenue. There was a noisy crowd on the street despite the cold and the late hour.

John put his face close to hers. "Let's go home."

That phrase unleashed a flush of warmth in her.

"Sure," she said. She put her arms around him and he put his hands on her shoulders. She stood on her toes and kissed him quickly. "You better take me around back at the stairs." They walked down Eighth Avenue.

"There's the alley," he said. "I'll wait till you're inside." She went down the alley, grabbed the handle of the metal door, and pulled. It didn't open. Puzzled, she tried again, but it didn't budge. She trotted back to John.

"It's locked."

He went to the door but couldn't open it, either. "Guess you'll have to go through the front."

She gave him a worried look.

"They have to be asleep," he said.

"You're right." They walked around to the Paramount Hotel's front entrance. The theaters on the street were dark now. The windowless brick façade of the warehouse across the street loomed gloomy and ominous.

"See you at the parade," she whispered but stood rooted to the sidewalk, gathering her courage.

"Go on—it'll be okay. I'll wait a few minutes."

She walked through the revolving door, half expecting the chaperones to be there, holding pitchforks, tar, and feathers. The lobby was empty. Her shoulders relaxed as she walked to the elevator and pressed the call button. She gave a huge yawn and covered her mouth with her hand. While she waited, Father Bernard walked up and stood beside her.

"Well, if it isn't Jeanne. A very good morning to you," he said. "An early riser?" He allowed his eyes to travel up and down her outfit. "Or perhaps you've not been to sleep?"

"I know we're supposed to have a talk," she said, stifling another yawn, "but can we do it tomorrow, please?"

"It is tomorrow, Jeanne. It's time we talked or the sisters will be having my head." He pointed across the lobby. "Let's go to the coffee shop. I could use a cup and you look like you could too." He set off without looking to see if she followed.

She trudged after him, forcing her tired mind to devise her defense.

They took a booth in the dimly lit restaurant and Father Bernard ordered coffee. He was wearing the same heavy overcoat as when he was introduced at the train station in Chicago. His brown eyes were watery behind steel-rimmed glasses and his stiff gray hair stood like a bristly hedgerow along the strong ridges of his forehead. She was surprised to see that his dour mouth seemed to be flirting with a smile.

He looked out the window at the street toward the windowless warehouse. "Well, my dear, what do you have to say for yourself? Perhaps starting with what you were doing out until all hours tonight and working backward."

She took a breath and said, "Father, I've done nothing wrong. Yes, I know we're not supposed to go out on our own, but all I did was listen to music with a friend a few blocks away."

Father Bernard turned from the window and leaned against his chair. He ran his hand back and forth over his short hair like he was polishing his palm.

"Music, eh? Who did you see?"

"Um, Charlie Parker."

"All that jazz is over my poor head." He lowered his voice. "I must confess, I was just getting in myself. An old friend of mine had a table at the Roosevelt Grill and we had a very nice time listening to Guy Lombardo. But we're not here to talk about music, are we?" He shook himself. "Yes, well, to business. Sister Rose thinks the worst, of course, and Sister Mary was so uncharitable as to call you a pretty little liar."

"She didn't! Who does she think—"

"Hold on, hold on." He paused while the waitress delivered his coffee, then cleared his throat and said, "Do you promise me you were doing nothing you'd be ashamed to tell your parents or your priest?"

"Can I ask you a question first?"

"Ah, a question in answer to a question. You sound like a Jesuit."

Jeanne looked down.

"Ask your question."

"Is kissing someone wrong, Father?"

"Well, as we say where I come from, 'It's not the kissing—it's what comes after.'"

Jeanne felt herself blush.

"Is he someone you care for and who cares for you?" She nodded. He looked out the window again and said, "All right, then. I'm probably abetting your malfeasance, but I'll tell the sisters that whatever they think they saw on the train, we'll let it go just this once." He frowned. "And I'll leave out the exact circumstances of our meeting this morning, if you promise you'll go to confession the moment you get home. Agreed?"

"Oh, thank you."

"This is a rare opportunity, Jeanne. I hope you're taking full advantage."

"I am."

"Our trip to the United Nations is what I was referring to."

She looked at him guilelessly. "Of course. That's what I meant too."

His eyes narrowed, but there was a veiled gleam.

"May I go now?"

"Yes." He traced a lazy cross in the air. "And, Jeanne."

"Yes, Father?"

"For Heaven's sake, get some sleep. You've great dark circles under your eyes."

Her hand went involuntarily to her face and she frowned. "I'll try."

• • •

The student group watched the parade from Columbus Circle. The assembled crowd was enormous. Jeanne found a discarded wooden box to stand on and placed it next to a traffic light. She was so excited she barely noticed the biting cold. A small girl dressed in a plaid coat tugged at her skirt.

"Please, miss, can I stand on your box, too? I won't take hardly any room."

"Sure, climb up."

The little girl scrambled up and looped her arm around the traffic light pole.

"What's your name?"

"Gabrielle Benda."

"How old are you?"

"Seven."

"Where are your parents?"

"At home. We live just around the block. My dad didn't want to come. He says he tries to avoid two million people whenever he can."

Two million people—more than the population of many states and most cities, gathered in one place just to watch the parade.

Jeanne loved it all—the American Legion marching band, the uniformed New York policemen good-naturedly holding back the huge crowd, and, best of all, the helium-filled floating figures kept tethered to the earth by ropes held by walking groups of handlers. There was the huge Comical Cop, the Three Little Pigs, Peter Rabbit, a forty-six-foot candy cane, a flag float with flags of all forty-eight states, and a cone-shaped gnome. There was an enormous pirate whose handlers were all dressed in pirate garb, an even larger panda bear, and, of course, a human Santa Claus. Gabrielle began to jump up and down when he appeared, nearly knocking Jeanne off the wooden box. His shouts of "Happy Thanksgiving" and "Merry Christmas" were amplified through a microphone under his beard and echoed against the tall apartment buildings on Central Park West.

"He really is Santa," Gabrielle said. "Just like in the movie."

Just before noon, the last float and the final marching band of the 1947 Macy's Thanksgiving Day Parade passed by Jeanne and her companions. They made their way as quickly as their frozen bodies were able to their waiting bus. The chaperones passed around waxed paper cups filled with hot tea, coffee, or chocolate poured from thermoses. The drinks, together with the warm air pouring from the bus's heater, worked to ease their shivers and quiet their chattering teeth.

Caroline and Tony sat together and John sat in the row behind them. Jeanne decided to join him, despite the stares from the two sisters who were seated at the rear of the bus, the better to espy any shenanigans among their young charges.

Jeanne said to Caroline, "I can't believe they can make those balloons so big."

"You know who invented animal balloons?" said Tony.

Jeanne shook her head.

"Leonardo da Vinci."

"You're kidding," Jeanne said.

"Nope, you could look it up. He sculpted hollow figures in wax, filled them with air, and they floated."

"You'll have to excuse Tony," Caroline said. "He knows more useless information than anyone I've ever met." She scrunched her face and looked at Jeanne. "Except maybe you. But he's just so darn cute I don't mind at all."

John took the opportunity to give Jeanne a heavily abridged outline of his adventures at the Waldorf and his meeting with Grogan. She was touched that he had done so much—even been in danger—but had kept his promise to meet her at The 3 Deuces, showered and clean-shaven.

"Seen today's *Sun*?" he said.

"How could I?"

"Oh, right. Here, take a look." He handed her a tear sheet of the article she had written. It was illustrated with the photograph of the two of them, as well as the one she took of the students in Times Square.

"Oh my gosh," she said. "Everyone I know will see this. Is it really going to be in the paper?"

"Already is. A couple of hundred thousand people are reading it right now with their morning coffee."

"Can I tell my parents I helped you on the article?"

"Hell no." He paused, smiling. "Tell 'em the truth—tell them you wrote it."

She kept looking at her article, then at the photograph, then back at the article. She shook her head. "I can't believe that picture—it's perfect." She was already envisioning it pasted in the scrapbook she had decided to create, memorializing this trip.

"Do you have your story, too?" she asked.

"Yep." He handed her several more sheets of thin curling paper from his overcoat pocket. There was a telephone message from Janus Pilch clipped at the top. "AP picked it up. You'll be in the New York afternoon dailies. Congrats."

She read his story and was filled with admiration. "It's so good. And, that quote is chilling." She found the place in the article and read the statement of Jamal al-Husseini, the chairman of the delegation of the Arab Higher Committee. "'The Arabs of Palestine will die to the last man to resist the creation of a Jewish state. By imposing partition on Palestine, you will precipitate the country into a virtual bloodbath. We have nothing more to lose but our lives.'"

"I think they mean it," John said. "I'm really worried they're going to do something at the session tomorrow."

"Did you hear from Grogan this morning?"

He shook his head. "I tried calling him while we were at the parade. I'm worried about Liliane at the mercy of that crazy guy."

"She must be terrified."

"Maybe. She's pretty gutsy."

Jeanne was torn between concern for Liliane and a painful sliver of jealousy. She suspected he found Liliane to be attractive because he studiously avoided commenting on her appearance. She must seem commonplace in comparison. "So Chicago," he had said last night, which was probably code for "extremely dull." In her lively imagination, Liliane had morphed into a shapely Technicolor beauty, an exotic Arabian princess. She hoped he wouldn't have to see her again. Perhaps Liliane would just gracefully step aside and vanish from their lives.

•••

It was early afternoon when their bus reached Lake Success and turned off the highway onto Lakeville Road. It slowly made its way toward the object of their journey—the United Nations headquarters.

Lakeville Road took them past the small glacier-made lake that had given the village its name. It was surrounded by trees and bushes that were now brown and leafless. The first flakes from the first snow of the season dusted the shore. A glistening sheen of ice extended a dozen feet out over water that was otherwise dark with sediment. The weak autumn sun was reflected by tiny rippling waves. The lake's shore was dotted with elaborate summer cottages, shuttered now and half-hidden by trees.

The bus lurched left and then, they had arrived. A line of large flags planted on long poles snapped in the breeze just over a stand of bare trees. The flags were the only sign that the undistinguished, three-story, glass-fronted building was not what it had in fact been before—the site of a military industrial operation known as the Sperry Gyroscope Plant.

The plant was built to manufacture gyroscopes, bombsights, and radar equipment. The darkened windows lining the three floors had previously concealed wartime engineers designing increasingly more efficient methods of killing people. They now hid the architects of world peace as they struggled to make those modern mechanisms of murder obsolete.

A multihued group of people emerged from the main entrance of the building and walked in a tight knot toward the bus, like a welcoming committee. There was a woman in a light-colored sari; a man in a white tunic, dark billowing pants, a wide black belt, soft leather boots laced up nearly to his knees; and another man wearing a multicolored African caftan and sandals despite the cold. As the group approached, it slowed and some of its members looked in the students' direction. They then turned onto another walkway. As they moved away, a slender young man detached himself from the group and hopped onto the bus. He had blond hair and wore a navy blue blazer, a black-and-white silk tie, and charcoal slacks.

"Hello and welcome to the United Nations. I'm Benjamin Cohen, an assistant in the UN Department of Information. It's my honor to be your tour guide here at our UN headquarters. Tomorrow, we'll go to the General Assembly Hall in Queens, about ten miles west of here. Today, we'll have lunch in the same cafeteria where many of the delegates and their staff take their meals, but first, a little business." He held up a brown cardboard box. "Identity bands and tickets. If you would, please take one of each and then follow me."

He got off the bus and stood waiting on the sidewalk nearby. Each of the students took a blue paper wristband that read, "United Nations—Nations Unies," and a ticket that had the date and the words "UNITED NATIONS—Admit One to Lake Success New York." More items for the scrapbook.

John and Jeanne got off the bus.

"You're Mr. McGrath?" Benjamin Cohen asked John.

"Yes."

"There's a message for you to call Detective Michael Grogan."

"Is there a telephone booth?"

"Right inside the entry doors."

"Jeanne, can you . . . ?" John waved his hand at Cohen and the group as he dashed off. She understood he meant she should take notes of anything he might want to include in his article about the day's activities. She fought the urge to follow him. She nodded brightly at his back as he vanished into the building.

25

"The girl's disappeared," Grogan said.

"No!"

"We went to the hotel this morning and searched both suites. Talked to the son, Adnan. He said his father was at Lake Success but Liliane was gone, he didn't know where."

John blew out a breath, which misted the glass of the phone booth he stood in. Had she tried to call him? "She said she was going to leave, but I'm worried about her. Can the FBI man help?"

"Useless bugger, didn't even show up today. Said Truman gave them the day off," Grogan said harshly. "I put out her description. We'll keep looking. There's something else you should know."

"Yeah?"

"A bomb went off at the British consulate here this morning."

"What?"

"Nobody was hurt. There was a warning call yesterday and the building was mostly empty anyway because of the holiday. Bomb exploded inside an empty office of a fellow, name of"—there was a rattle of paper—"McNeil."

Hector McNeil. John's relief that McNeil hadn't been killed out-gunned his gratitude that his reporting had been proven accurate. "Grogan, he's on the *Queen Mary*. He's one of the guys Liliane told me they're after. This confirms it."

"Maybe."

"What do you mean, 'maybe'?"

"Not so fast, my boy. I talked to the British security man. He thinks it was Zionists."

"What?"

"You really don't know so much about Middle East politics, do you? Arabs and Jews may hate each other something fierce, but they hate the British too. Some of them even tried to fight on Hitler's side during the war."

He remembered Liliane saying to him on the train, "You are surprised? The Arabs have death lists; the Jews have death lists."

"You think it's them?"

"You heard about the bomb at the King David Hotel last year? Nearly a hundred dead, most of them British. That was them. Same pattern here—warnings the day before, then, boom."

John remembered the picture of the collapsed wing of the hotel. A Jewish underground group known as the Irgun had taken credit for the killings. He hadn't paid much attention at the time. Just more noise in the constant din of violence in the region.

John wasn't the first person to be flummoxed by the complexities of Middle East politics. Had McNeil fled because of the Arab threats? Zionist ones? Or both?

Grogan continued. "The Irgun are dangerous. Murdered two British policemen just this summer. I'd say this bomb was the Jews."

"There's no way they'd do something like that in this country and risk turning us against them."

"Maybe. So where does that put us?" Grogan said.

"No clue."

"That makes two of us, boyo. Listen, I'm coordinating with the local precinct and the FBI. Call me at home later, where I hope to be eating my Thanksgiving dinner. I might have some news." Grogan gave him his home number.

Jeanne knocked on the glass door of the booth. He waved at her to wait. "Hey, Grogan."

"Yeah?"

"Which horse you backing in this Palestine thing?"

"Why?"

"Just curious."

"Off the record, Johnny?"

"Off the record, Detective."

"Easy, then. The Jews."

"Yeah, why?"

"The Irish and the Jews have a lot in common."

"Like what?"

"Suffering, my boy. We both know suffering. And neither of us have any use for the English." He paused a moment. "Doesn't make a blind bit of difference, you know. Fish or flesh, I'll catch whoever did this and put them away for a good long time."

"Listen, I've got to write this up for the paper. Can I quote you on the bombing?"

"Nah, I can't be your source. There's a lot of politics in the department about the whole Palestine thing."

"How about if I don't name you?"

"Anonymous NYPD source?" Grogan chuckled. "Yeah, that's fine. As far as we're concerned, that's just another way of a reporter saying he made it up."

John laughed. "Thanks. I'll call you later."

He hung up and stepped out of the phone booth. Jeanne was waiting, an anxious look on her face. He started to relay what Grogan had said, but she interrupted.

"You have to come quick," she said.

"What is it?"

She was already running down the hallway. "Hurry."

He followed her to a large conference room. There was a table at the front and Houman al-Hafiz was seated behind it, dressed in a business suit. He was flanked by the Syrian delegation's spokesman on one side and by the widely respected Syrian ambassador to the UN, Faris al-Khoury, on the other. A group of reporters was there. Flashes went off as photographers, including the one from the *Sun*, took pictures. Al-Hafiz spoke.

"We have called this news conference to address false and malicious reports of a supposed assassination plot, which have appeared in a Chicago newspaper and which will appear in some New York papers this afternoon. Those reports accuse the Mufti of Jerusalem, as well as a member of our delegation, Mohammed Alfagari, of planning to commit the murder of United Nations diplomats."

Al-Hafiz spoke deliberately in a low and reasonable tone. He was cold sober.

"My ambassador has asked me to express our shock and indignation over this report. Let me be entirely clear, neither Mr. Alfagari nor any other member of our delegation is part of any 'assassination plot.' The Mufti is a highly respected religious leader of impeccable reputation, not a murderer. This story has been completely fabricated by the reporter." Here, al-Hafiz by tone and raised eyebrows conveyed his contempt. "It is, gentlemen, completely ludicrous."

Al-Hafiz gave every indication he was telling the truth. He probably believed he was. John remembered Liliane telling him that Alfagari and the Mufti wouldn't trust al-Hafiz with something like this.

"Nevertheless," he continued in a loud voice, "Mr. Alfagari has informed me that he wishes to avoid giving credence to these rumors. Although it will compromise his ability to perform his duties, he will remain in his hotel until this session of the General Assembly adjourns in the next few days. He will be dining on the excellent room service at the Waldorf, not"—he allowed himself a mild chuckle—"roaming the city with a souvenir rifle."

His face resumed a serious expression. "I am told that the reporter is a young man steeped in the violence of the Chicago criminal classes," al-Hafiz continued, "and is entirely ignorant of this organization and its issues. He could easily be duped by Zionist lies."

John was fuming.

Al-Hafiz checked his notes. "His story claims it is based on the word of an 'unnamed source.' Who is this mystery man? Surely such a monstrous accusation should come from someone prepared to stand up and, as your Mr. Truman would say, take the heat. I challenge the *Chicago Sun* to produce this person and proof of their allegation. When—and I say *when*, not *if*—they cannot"—here his voice rose in outraged rectitude—"I hope they will have the decency to report that failure with the same large headlines they have used to slander us. Thank you, gentlemen. I will take your questions."

Several reporters spoke at once. One, louder than the others, asked, "Have you heard about the bomb at the British consulate today?"

Al-Hafiz looked grim. "I am sickened by it. On behalf of my government, we deplore this act of violence."

"Who do you think did it?" several reporters shouted.

Al-Hafiz shrugged. "Ask the Zionists. They and their American agents are actively buying votes with tens of millions of dollars. And where their bribes do not work, they have proven themselves willing to shed blood."

His voice rose again. "Ask the members of the United Nations committee on partition who visited Palestine this year and were shocked at the obscene level of Zionist violence. Ask the families of the British policemen who were killed by them this summer. Ask the dead and maimed at the King David Hotel." Al-Hafiz checked his notes again and it struck John that this peroration wasn't spontaneous. "If they could speak, the blood of those victims would cry out." His voice shook with emotion. "Go ask the Zionists about this violence."

John couldn't stay quiet any longer. "Mr. al-Hafiz, you're kind of a violent fellow yourself, aren't you?"

Al-Hafiz stared but didn't respond.

"Isn't it true you took a drunken shot at a hotel porter at the Waldorf last night?"

There were gasps from some of the reporters.

"And that the only reason you're not in a New York City jail this minute is because you claimed diplomatic immunity?"

Al-Hafiz froze. Faris al-Khoury stared at him. Al-Hafiz looked ill but recovered enough to say, "Your name, sir?"

"John McGrath, *Chicago Sun*."

Al-Hafiz gave a condescending smile. "Ah, you are the man who invented this story."

"Well, as we say in Chicago, sez you. But now that we've been introduced, can you answer my question, sir?"

"Mr. McGrath, that insinuation is as false as your story. I suppose we are dealing here with another of your shy and retiring unnamed sources?"

There was a ripple of laughter.

"No, sir. I'm the source."

The laughter stopped. The room was silent, expectant.

"I saw it all. And let me remind you in case you were too drunk to remember, you were pointing your antique silver pistol at the porter's head. That's what we young crime reporters call assault with a deadly weapon."

The Syrian's face was filled with fury. "Where I come from, you would be whipped for telling such lies."

"Where I come from, pointing a gun at a guy's head gets you three to five in Joliet. Sir."

As al-Hafiz leaped to his feet, he knocked over a water pitcher. Al-Khoury tried to restrain him with a hand on his arm, but al-Hafiz was too furious. Several reporters shouted at once. "Is it true? Can we see the gun?"

Faris al-Khoury, shaking his head in disgust, walked out of the room. There were more questions, but the Syrian spokesman shouted, "This conference is over, gentlemen." He half pushed, half dragged al-Hafiz out of the room, several reporters in pursuit. The rest gathered around John, peppering him with questions.

"Sorry, guys. You can read all about it in tomorrow's *Sun*."

"Where you off to, McGrath?" a man asked after the others had left. It was Hamilton, the reporter from the *New York Times*.

"Hi, Hamilton. I'm told I need to bone up on the UN. This seems like a good place to start."

26

At five o'clock Friday morning, Mohammed Alfagari was alone in the sitting room of the two-bedroom suite he occupied with Adnan al-Hafiz, Houman's son. Despite the early hour, he was dressed in a plain dark wool suit, white shirt, and quiet tie. Adnan was asleep in the larger of the two bedrooms, having stumbled in only an hour ago. Adnan had few official duties and had spent most of his time in New York indulging his weakness for women and alcohol. His thick snores echoed through the room.

Just like his father. After today, the father at least will no longer be an embarrassment to us. He was seated at a dining table and there was a disassembled rifle of Japanese manufacture on it, along with a rag and bottles of machine oil and cleaning fluid. He had protected the table with a canvas drop cloth. Alfagari had wanted to use his own rifle, a German-made Mauser, but had been overruled.

"To carry a rifle out of the hall after shooting would be impossible," the Mufti had told him three months ago in Damascus. "And if you leave it, it will be linked to you. You would be arrested. We want no connection between you and this act until you have left the country. Guns are plentiful in America. It will be easy for you to obtain an adequate one. Leave it after you have used it. When you return home, I will announce your deed to the world and you will be a hero."

During the Syrian delegation's cultural trip to Chicago, he had found the perfect weapon in the store next to the Palestinian restaurant. It

was unlikely it could be traced, but Alfagari had nonetheless filed the
serial numbers off the rifle and scope. He left the engraved sixteen-petal
chrysanthemum flower seal on the rifle's steel barrel because he found it
beautiful.

The rifle was a 1939 Kokura Type 97 sniper rifle with a factory-
installed 2.5 power matching telescopic sight. It had a range of eight
hundred meters—far more than he would need. It was in perfect condition. Its four-foot length fit easily in the cylindrical camera tripod case
in which he would carry it. The rifle took a 6.5mm cartridge, slightly
larger than a .22, and held five of them in its magazine. Although it had
come with a five-shot stripper clip, he would load the magazine manually
to reduce the possibility of jamming. He also removed the one-legged
sniper stand because it was unsteady. He had found a far more satisfactory two-legged stand in a New York gun store. He test-fired the rifle
and sighted in the scope in an abandoned warehouse near the East River.

He was dismayed but not deterred by the newspaper article in the
Sun and the missing dispatch box. No one but the Mufti knew their plan
and there was nothing in the box that could reveal it unless someone
knew their code. As they agreed, he would station himself in one of the
small booths in the side balcony near the rear of the General Assembly auditorium. They were meant for cameramen and were enclosed at
their rear by a heavy curtain, which would ensure privacy. At the Mufti's
request, the Syrian delegation had reserved one for use by its official
photographer. Alfagari had obtained an identification card in another
name identifying him as such. From the booth, he would have a clear
shot at his targets on the auditorium floor. Entering and hiding himself
at the United Nations would not be a problem. Security at the Assembly Hall was lax. Doors were unlocked at six in the morning. They were
unattended until one hour before the meeting of the General Assembly
commenced. The attendants who manned the doors were unarmed. They
were there to control access to the auditorium. There would be no difficulty entering early in the day with his camera tripod case and concealing
himself in the booth.

He cleaned and oiled the bolt, the bore, and the receiver of the rifle,
although he had only fired one shot since its last cleaning. One shot was

all he had needed. When he was finished, he reassembled the rifle and tested the bolt action. It slipped in and out easily with a satisfying click. He slipped the rifle into a long cloth bag and buttoned it, then put the cloth case and the box of ammunition in the tripod case. He checked his watch. It was five thirty and a flitter of light streamed through gaps in the heavy curtains. A car would be waiting for him at Fiftieth and Lexington. He would be in Flushing Meadows in less than an hour.

He put on his overcoat, a thin pair of gloves, and pulled a hat low on his head. He opened the suite door and looked both ways. No one was in the corridor. The fire escape stairs would allow him to avoid the lobby. Adnan's snores rattled through the suite. It would be so easy to put a bullet in his head. He fingered the butt of the revolver in its holster under his jacket. A pillow over Adnan's face would muffle the shot. He was a loose end. Even someone as foolish as Adnan would know his father had been targeted for death and would seek revenge. It would be better to finish him now, but that was not his decision.

With a last look around the room, he picked up the tripod case by its handle. It was time to go. He closed and locked the door of the suite and made the long walk down twenty-nine flights of stairs.

27

At nine o'clock Friday morning, Jeanne and the other student editors were seated on the main floor of the General Assembly Hall of the United Nations. The General Assembly Hall was in Corona Park, Queens, about ten miles from the UN Headquarters in Lake Success they had toured yesterday. The building had originally been constructed for the 1939 World's Fair.

The approach to the General Assembly Hall was dominated by a large circular drive and the building itself was fronted by a colonnade, punctuated by white limestone pilasters and dark polished granite. The lawn inside the circle was now a seedy autumn brown. The flags of the fifty-seven member nations hung on fifty-foot flagpoles that ringed the drive.

The students entered the hall through the high-ceilinged lobby. Various wings and additions had been built to house a pressroom, a bar and restaurant, and offices for UN officials. In an effort to instill some grandeur, there was a paneled wooden dais eight feet tall and twenty feet wide on the front stage. Behind the dais hung an enormous replica of the United Nations emblem, a polar view of the world that rose fifty feet. Dark curtains on either side of the emblem ran from the stage floor to the ceiling.

There were four hundred padded seats, divided into three sections. The front of the hall, where the students now sat, was reserved for delegates. Each seat had a wooden desk in front of it. Near the rear of the hall, a large balcony extended out with seats for another two hundred. There was a large clock embedded in the front of the balcony facing the stage.

There were two tiers of covered balconies on each side, divided into booths, like boxes in a theater. The larger booths provided seating for important visitors. The smaller side booths near the rear of the hall were no more than four feet wide. They were assigned to photographers from the delegations and from the press.

Jeanne hadn't seen John since they had returned to the hotel yesterday. He immediately went to his room to write his article and hadn't reappeared. She had tried calling him after dinner. He hadn't answered nor was he on the bus this morning. Jeanne and the rest of the students had spent the rest of Thursday ice-skating at Rockefeller Center, then eaten an elaborate Thanksgiving feast at the Tavern on the Green in Central Park. She was exploding with questions. Was he following a new lead? Meeting with Detective Grogan? Or that Liliane?

Jeanne picked up the headphones for simultaneous translation plugged into the armrest of the chair where she sat in the front row. There was a dial with five numbers directly beside the headphone jack, one for each of the five official languages of the United Nations— French, English, Russian, Spanish, and Chinese. According to the itinerary of the day's events they'd been given that morning, the debate on the Palestinian question was scheduled to begin at eleven, and the vote would occur at three. None of the UN delegates were in the Assembly Hall yet, but numerous staff members filtered in and out preparing for the day's session.

Benjamin Cohen, the UN information officer, stood facing them.

"I hope you all had a nice Thanksgiving. Now, back to work. I want to explain the mechanics of the vote. You may have heard that it will create the Jewish state of Israel. Well, not exactly. Technically, the Assembly is voting on Resolution 181, which provides an outline for the future governance of Palestine. The vote's main purpose is to relieve the British from the responsibility of governing the region and to begin the process of separating the Arab and Jewish populations, so that they may create their own states while, at the same time, preserving the peace and the world's access to the many holy places of the region."

Caroline called out, "Do they know who's going to win?"

Cohen shook his head. "Nope. We just know it's going to be close. This is how it works."

Jeanne leaned over her notebook on the wood desk, taking notes in case John needed her to write his article for the day. He should have at least sent her a message.

"The resolution requires a two-thirds majority to pass. That means two-thirds of those present and voting. This is important because that means that members who are not here—"

Like the representative from Thailand who sailed away two days ago.

"—or who abstain are not counted in determining the outcome. So let me ask you, if all fifty-seven members were here and voted, how many votes would the resolution need to pass? Any math majors?"

Several hands were raised. Cohen pointed to Tony, Caroline's new friend. "Thirty-eight."

"Exactly right. But now it gets complicated. There are sure to be some abstentions. Mathematically, for every three abstentions, the number of votes needed for the two-thirds majority is reduced by two. Everyone with me?"

Some heads nodded.

"The no votes are, by and large, the Arab and Muslim nations, of which there are ten. The yes votes consist mostly of the United States and the Soviet Union and their allies, call it twenty votes. That leaves a lot of votes up for grabs. Those countries have been the subject of vigorous efforts to persuade."

Jeanne asked, "Are any countries especially important? I mean, are some more influential than others?"

"Yes, Britain and France."

"But why?" Caroline said.

"The old colonial powers," said Tony.

"Exactly," said Cohen. "Britain wants the partition and has the Commonwealth countries who will follow her lead. France has a number of close allies who will follow hers. France has been vocal in its opposition to the resolution, but many now believe they are bending to US pressure to change their vote to 'yes.' If they do so, France may carry several of those allies with her, which will put the yesses very close to the required majority."

"So France's vote is crucial?" Jeanne asked.

Cohen nodded. "Absolutely." He looked at the clock embedded in the mezzanine.

Jeanne craned her head around, looking for John. The clock at the back of the hall read ten thirty.

"Now, we have a special guest," Cohen said, as he walked to the wood barrier that separated the audience from the rostrum. He whispered to a woman at one of the desks. She nodded, picked up a telephone, and spoke into it quietly. Cohen returned to his position in front of the group. Jeanne wondered who they were waiting for.

A few moments later, a tall, dignified woman walked through the curtains on the left of the stage and onto the speaker's rostrum. She stood there a moment, seeming to survey the entire auditorium before focusing on the student group. Her short, wispy, brown hair seemed to have been lacquered into place. She wore a light-colored wool suit. There was a fur boa around her shoulders and three strands of pearls at her neck.

"They said I should speak to you from up here," she said in round tones and a patrician accent. "I can't think why." She walked gracefully to the left side of the stage and down a short flight of stairs.

Jeanne recognized her immediately. Eleanor Roosevelt was one of her heroines. She stood and clapped. No one joined her. Her face grew hot and she sank into her seat. Mrs. Roosevelt walked to her. She was a tall woman, but to Jeanne, slumped down in her seat in embarrassment, she seemed even taller.

Mrs. Roosevelt looked down and said gently, "What is your name, young lady?"

Jeanne mumbled her name.

"Well, Miss Cooper, I must thank you for your warm welcome. I hope when I'm finished speaking, you will still feel like applauding."

"I . . . I'm sure I will," Jeanne managed to say.

Caroline elbowed her and whispered, "Way to go, silly!"

"Thank you all for coming today and my thanks to the *Chicago Sun* for providing you this opportunity." She gave a practiced smile, then continued in her slow, high-pitched voice. "I have devoted much of my time in the last several years to this organization and I can tell you that the best way to make the UN fail is to spread the idea—the false idea—that it *is* failing. You, the future members of the press, must spread the truth. The United Nations is not failing; it is flourishing. You are here today for the most important vote of this organization's young history. And thanks to the UN, the people of the region most involved are talking here in New York, and not shooting at each other in Jerusalem or Aleppo or Beirut or Cairo. That, in and of itself, is a miracle. This is an oasis of peace. In some parts of the world, we would need armed guards. But here we need none of that."

Won't we?

"Our members are dedicated to peace. They may disagree but with words, not bullets. Let me conclude by saying that the fundamental change which must come about is not a change in the law but a change in the hearts of everyone everywhere. I hope you will resolve, here and today, to be a part of that change for the good. Thank you for being here to support us. God bless you all."

Jeanne stood again and clapped. This time she was not alone. Mrs. Roosevelt, to Jeanne's everlasting gratitude, walked over and shook her hand.

"Thank you, my dear."

As Mrs. Roosevelt walked off, Caroline elbowed her again. "She likes you!"

28

John reread his article detailing the Thanksgiving Day news conference given by al-Hafiz and the bombing of the British consulate as he traveled by cab to the UN General Assembly Hall in Queens. He had stayed at the hotel as late as possible, hoping for news of Liliane. He was glad to be alone with his worries rather than on the bus with Jeanne.

He shook his head as he went through the story. As his editor Henry Hershon pointed out, it was not quite the bombshell his article the day before had been. While it was amusing, it was short on any new facts on the assassination plot. "And you left out the one thing that would have been interesting—the fact the broad is gone. You ain't gone soft on her, have you?"

"No," John replied, "it's just it's not the right time. Wait till we find out what happened to her. She might be on a visit or something; then we'd look flaky."

"Too late for that," Hershon muttered. "The only good thing about the article is the photo you sent." Hershon had tried to obscure the weakness of the article by putting the absolutely smashing photograph that accompanied it on the front page.

The *Sun* photographer had snapped Houman al-Hafiz at the news conference as he leaped up. It showed him half out of his chair. Embarrassment was written on his face. His glasses were falling off. He had knocked over a carafe of water and a flood of liquid in mid-flight seemed to be erupting from the table. The expression on the face of Faris al-Khoury, seated next to al-Hafiz, was a priceless mixture of shock, chagrin, contempt, and disbelief.

The photo had almost not made it to the *Sun* by deadline. The AP wire was down. Only a last-minute taxi run by John from Lake Success to LaGuardia Airport saved the day. He managed to get the film aboard the TWA Constellation service to Chicago. The Constellation was the TWA's newest, fastest, and swankiest passenger plane.

"Pilch never should have let you print the last article," Hershon said. "But now it's out, we gotta back it up. And the only way to do it is get your source on record."

"No."

"I'm getting a lot of pressure."

"Pressure? From the Arabs?"

"No, it's the Jewish groups."

"Why?"

"Jeez, you're stupid. Because the worse the Arabs look, the better the Jews look. They think it'll help the vote. And your story makes the Arabs look real bad."

"I get it, Henry. But I can't do it. If I publish the name of the source, the source is dead."

Hershon chewed on that one for a while, then said softly, "Maybe she already is."

Was Hershon right? If she was alive, why hadn't she called?

"I'm right, aren't I?" Hershon went on. "It's the broad?"

John was nearly overcome by fear.

"Listen, you're young—new to this type of thing. If you want to finish the job you've started and get back to working the crime beat here, you do what I tell you. Write tomorrow's article and name her."

"I gave her my word, Henry."

"Fuck your word. Think about your career."

John said, "Fuck my career."

"You don't mean that, kid. Christ, you're twenty-one—you got a future. Don't be a jerk. You give me an article with her name in it for tomorrow or all you'll ever cover here is Miss Photo Flash."

"I'd rather quit."

"Be my guest."

John cursed, Hershon swore, and they both hung up.

John had arrived at the United Nations General Assembly Hall where the future of generations of Arabs and Jews would soon be decided. He got out of the cab quickly. Maybe Grogan would have news.

29

ater that same afternoon, Grogan and John McGrath circled the perimeter of the General Assembly Hall for what seemed to be the hundredth time. Grogan had recruited twenty police officers from local departments, including the entire three-man Lake Success outpost. They were stationed at various locations inside the building. Nothing out of the ordinary had been seen or heard. John spent most of his time keeping a watch on the Syrian delegation. Al-Hafiz was there on the main floor, sitting upright in a chair and looking like a scolded schoolboy afraid to move. He hadn't spoken a word, although several reporters had shouted questions at him in violation of UN rules.

"Still no Alfagari?" he asked Grogan.

"No, I told you, he's not here. We would've seen him. He hasn't left the hotel, according to Sudowicz."

"You sure?"

"Sudowicz says he's still in his suite."

"I still think you should have frisked the Syrians," he groused.

"Yeah, well, me too, but it's not allowed. I asked the UN security guys if they would help. Know what they said? 'Don't worry, no one would ever do something like that here.' That's their security plan."

"At least they have a plan. Do you?"

"Right now, I'm gonna call the station and see if they've found your Liliane."

John's stomach clenched. Had she gotten away?

They walked into the lobby. Grogan moved to the bank of telephone booths.

"I'm going to grab a sandwich," John said. "Want one?"

Grogan, already speaking into the telephone, shook his head.

The Cuban delegate's voice droned on over the loudspeaker as John headed for the press bar, just off the lobby.

"John?"

It was Jeanne. She looked fresh, pretty, and happy to see him. His heart lifted. Her blond hair hung free around her face and she was wearing a black jumper over a long-sleeved white sweater of lambs' wool. Her cheeks had a healthy blush as though she'd just come in from the cold.

"I saw you with Detective Grogan," she said. "Is there news?"

He shook his head. "Nothing."

Her words poured out in a rush. "What about Liliane? Did you see her yesterday? I missed you at dinner."

"Nothing new. He's checking again. I was just heading to the press bar to get something to eat. Want to come? You can still hear the speeches."

"Four years of Spanish, but I can't understand a word he's saying," she said.

"They have the translation headphones in there. Hell, a guy told me that half of the reporters covering the UN have never even been on the floor. They do all their reporting from the bar with a drink in one hand, a pencil in the other, and the headphones over one ear."

He opened a tall, heavy door at one end of the lobby and they walked into the high-ceilinged room. It was crowded. There was a murmur of voices accompanied by the rattle of plates and silverware. Two loudspeakers in either corner of the long, curved bar broadcast the audio feed from the assembly floor. Waiters in white shirts, black bow ties, and long white aprons, tied with double-wrapped cloth strings, hustled in and out of the kitchen doors. Stools lined the front of the bar and there were a dozen tables scattered around the room. Most of them were occupied. Some of the reporters were pecking away at typewriters. John spotted an open table and nudged Jeanne in its direction.

He handed her a headset. "We can listen and talk at the same time." They put them on and turned the dial to English. The Cuban representative had finished and Prince Saif al Islam Abdullah of Yemen was delivering a stern warning against passage of the resolution. John turned down the volume so it was barely audible.

A tall man with salt-and-pepper hair and a well-trimmed mustache approached them. He looked familiar. "Excuse me," the man said, "are you the young gentleman who wrote the articles for the *Chicago Sun* about the Mufti?" His voice sounded hoarse from too much talking. He had a slight Russian accent. He was looking directly at John, but he seemed at the same time to be aware of everything taking place in the room, as though he were a sentry standing post in a war zone.

"That's me. What can I do for you?"

The man smiled, which made his mustache stretch. "I just want to thank you. I am very sorry to have missed that news conference yesterday." He held out his hand. "My name is Shertok, Moshe Shertok." John stood up and they shook.

"Oh, good lord. I'm so sorry I didn't recognize you, sir. I mean, you look—"

"Older than my pictures?" Shertok chuckled.

"Let's say more distinguished. It's truly an honor to meet you."

Shertok gave a polite declination of his head as if agreeing that, yes, indeed, it was John's privilege.

"And who is this pretty young lady?"

"May I present Miss Jeanne Cooper of Chicago."

"A pleasure."

"Jeanne, Mr. Shertok is—"

"Is one of the leaders of the Zionist movement and the mastermind behind the partition vote," she said, standing. "Of course, I know."

"Mastermind?" Shertok shrugged and smiled.

"I read an interview you gave to Dorothy Thompson last month for the *Herald Tribune*," she said. "It was the best case for the partition I've read."

"Why thank you. She is an excellent reporter."

"I think she's the best."

He squinted at her kindly. "My daughter Yael is about your age."

"Is she here?"

"Here in New York with us at the Berkshire Hotel, but not here at the Assembly."

"Would you care to join us?" John said.

"Considering this is the only open table, sure, why not?" He seemed to realize his comment might be impolite. "I would be delighted, of course." They all sat and Shertok picked up a set of headphones and put them on.

"I apologize, but I must hear all of it."

A waiter came up. "What can I get you?"

"Young lady?" Shertok said politely.

"Oh, um, a glass of milk, I guess."

"Coffee for me," said John. "And can you bring some sandwiches? Whatever you have."

"Tea, please, and biscuits," said Shertok.

The waiter scribbled on his pad and hurried off. They listened to the translation of the speaker for a while. Shertok took a watch from a small pocket in his trousers. He absently wound it for a while, then set it on the table where he could see its face.

"I have to ask, sir, off the record, of course; will the vote go your way?" John said.

Shertok gave a rueful laugh. "On the record is fine because all I can say is, you tell me." He shrugged. "I think so. I have been counting votes, cracking heads, and kissing feet for three months and I still don't know for sure. Aranha"—referring to the president of the General Assembly, Oswaldo Aranha—"said at breakfast this morning he thought we would lose. Then, at lunch, he said he thought we would win. Maybe he knows more than I do. I didn't think we had it two days ago. That's the reason we put off the vote Wednesday. Maybe now we do. We'll see this afternoon." He shook his head and stared into the middle distance.

The waiter returned with their orders, including a stack of sandwiches cut into quarters with toothpicks stuck through the quarter sections. Each of them had a tiny flag of one of the UN member countries.

"Trygve Lie's proudest accomplishment," Shertok murmured.

"What's that?" Jeanne asked.

"The little flags on the toothpicks. Our esteemed secretary-general's best idea. Maybe his only one."

"He hasn't been much help?" John said.

Shertok shook his head. "None at all. He wants to 'preserve his credibility with all sides.' Which means he does nothing for anyone."

"Yeah, but he got you the flags on your toothpicks," John said.

"Yes," Shertok said, "he did do that."

"Will they have the vote today?" Jeanne said.

"Yes, as soon as they're done speaking. We don't know if we'll win." He seemed to be doing the sums in his head as he ticked off the countries one by one, touching his right forefinger to the fingers of his other hand.

"Paraguay still has no instructions from its government. Liberia, as of"—he looked down at his watch—"ten a.m. was still unsure. Greece was a yes but told me this morning they are now a no. Belgium, the Netherlands, and New Zealand, who planned to abstain, may have been convinced to vote yes. But—"

"But changing three abstentions to three yesses is a net gain of only one vote," Jeanne finished for him. "We did the math this morning."

"You're right. In any case, Thailand was yes but now is gone. Haiti, was a yes, then argued for no on Wednesday, now may vote yes. Chile was a very strong yes but now will abstain, and the Philippines is probably a no. That is why General Romulo, my old friend, left us. He was embarrassed. As for the others who left Wednesday, who knows?" he said and looked at John. "It seems they were frightened off. Maybe others will leave. But in the end, it will come down to France and France is still full of powerful people who hate Jews. Other countries will follow France's lead. And so, France will decide this vote. I tell you, if it doesn't go our way, every man, woman, and child of the six hundred thousand Jews already in Palestine will rise in revolt," he finished, sounding not unlike his Arab opponents. He blinked several times and took a big swallow of his tea. "I'm sorry. This is all I think about."

Tom Hamilton, the *New York Times* reporter, rushed up to John.

"McGrath, did you hear?"

"Hear what?"

"Just came over the wire. Hector McNeil, the British representative, fell overboard from the *Queen Mary*; he's lost at sea," Hamilton said.

"Fell?" John said. "No way he fell. He left here because he'd been threatened. My source said they'd still go after him. You should've put it in your article, Tom."

"I'm going to write this up right now," Hamilton said. "I'll beat you to it."

"Not in Chicago, you won't," John said as Hamilton walked off.

John turned to Shertok. "Do you believe what I wrote?"

Shertok nodded. "Of course I do. Even before what we just heard."

"So why don't you people do something about it?"

"Like what? Run and hide? Call off the vote?"

"No. I mean really do something about it, sir," he said, sounding like the soldier he'd once been.

"Ah, I see." Shertok slowly nodded. "You mean eliminate this Alfagari? Why not assassinate al-Khoury, while we're at it? Or Trygve Lie?" He shook his head sadly. "We could. We have resources."

John felt Jeanne stiffen and he glanced at her. She must be frightened, hearing them quietly discuss having men killed.

"Here in New York?" John asked.

"Here, there, everywhere. But where does it end, Mr. McGrath?" Shertok spoke in a quiet voice that slowly grew in intensity but not in volume. "They kill us . . . we kill them . . . we both kill the British. Where does it end? No!" He pointed his finger at John. "There must be no question about this decision. It is the most important moment for our people in two thousand years. It must be done in open session, for all the world to see. It cannot be the product of violence. That's what so many—even my own people—don't understand. We are so close. But we must have the world's blessing if we are to have any chance to survive." He smacked his hand on the table. "There can be no violence."

He forced a smile and apologized to Jeanne for his vehemence. "I have to go." He picked up his watch, put it in his pocket, and stood. "Somewhere, there must be a few more votes." Shertok bent his head to John and said softly, "These Arabs are proud people, Mr. McGrath. You have humiliated them. I hope you will be careful."

"Careful what I write?"

"No, Mr. McGrath, careful of your life."

30

Mohammed Alfagari was perched patiently in the small photographers' booth on the second level of the auditorium's side balconies. His chair was at the heavy curtain at the back of the booth so he was in the shadows, invisible. No one had questioned him or asked to see his identification card. Uniformed police officers drifted in and out of the auditorium continuously, but none had even looked in his direction. He remained alert, although the drone of the seventh speaker of the afternoon, the representative from Paraguay, had put President Aranha to sleep. Aranha was seated in the center of the three chairs atop the dais. Trygve Lie, seated to his right, was also dozing. The assistant secretary-general Andrew Cordier, an American seated to Aranha's left, seemed to be listening.

Alfagari was not in a hurry. He would not act until after they had commenced the final vote. He checked his watch. The vote had been scheduled for three, but it was now after five. It would be soon. He stood and inched forward, and imagined holding the rifle and setting the bipod stand on the wood rail that topped the four-foot wall at the front of the booth. He pictured sighting through the scope and pulling the trigger and chaos erupting.

He moved back into the shadows and sat down again. He decided he could risk a cigarette. He lit it with a match, shielding its flare with his hand. He inhaled with relief. He had not left the booth since early that morning. After the newspaper revelations, he could not risk being seen in the building. He had had nothing to eat or drink since he left the hotel. It did not matter. He had gone much longer without food or water when on an assignment. There was the time he sat in an apartment near the Street of the Prophets in Jerusalem for a day and a night, waiting to ambush three members of the murderous Lehi. There had been no food or water then, no chair to sit on. Yet, when his quarry appeared, he had acted instantly and effectively. All three men had died. So it would be today.

When the vote proceeded, the French ambassador to the United Nations, Alexandre Parodi—whose code name in the French Resistance was *cérat*, French for "salve"—would die before he could vote, as the Mufti's telegram had instructed. The fool, Houman al-Hafiz, would die a second later.

His task was made easier by the fact that the French and Syrian delegations sat side by side, a fact that was providential but curious. France's cruel twenty-five-year occupation of Syria had just ended and there was great enmity between their people, yet here the two sat as neighbors. It was as if Allah had decided to help him. Two shots, closely grouped, and it would be done. Two dead and history would be forever altered. The resolution would go down to defeat and the Jews would be forced to look elsewhere for their homeland. He had a rare humorous thought. The United States strongly supported the Zionists' right to a homeland, did they not? Fine. Perhaps they would give them New Jersey.

He stretched his back. Another delegate had finished his speech and returned to his seat in the auditorium. President Aranha, Trygve Lie, and Andrew Cordier were conferring on the dais, their hands held over their microphones.

Alfagari verified that the heavy curtain behind him was still securely in place, then opened the tripod case, unbuttoned the gun cover, and removed the rifle. He slipped the bipod stand onto the barrel six inches from the muzzle. He moved his chair to the rail. No one would be looking in his direction now. He sat down, calculating where to rest the stand on the rail. Satisfied, he put the rifle on his lap, out of view, and looked down on the auditorium floor. Al-Hafiz was sitting in the same position he had occupied all day, behind and to the right of Faris al-Khoury. The French delegate, Parodi, was next to them. The Syrian ambassador, al-Khoury, was not in the line of fire. In a moment, he would place the rifle in position.

As a soldier of the jihad, his well-being was unimportant. However, the Mufti had said that his safe return would be a great propaganda coup. There was a good chance he would be able to escape down the emergency stairway directly behind his post. He would leave the rifle in the booth, walk down the stairs and out of the auditorium. He would be swept along in the crowd of people rushing out in the ensuing panic. He would be out of the country tonight.

It would be so easy.

31

ohn saw Grogan enter the press bar, his face grim. He waved John over.

"It's not good, kid," Grogan said. "Liliane was found in an alley a block from Washington Square about twelve hours ago. They just ID'd her. She's been shot in the head."

"Dead?" John shouted.

Grogan grabbed his forearm and gripped it hard. "Quiet down. She's not dead."

"But you said—ow, hey." Grogan's pressure on his arm increased. He tried to jerk away, but Grogan kept his iron grip.

"Come sit down."

John allowed himself to be led to the table where Jeanne sat. Grogan asked, "Can you listen now?"

John nodded. He was shaking.

"Cabbie found her and took her to Bellevue. She's alive, but just barely. A couple of detectives are guarding her. The doctor said—" He looked at Jeanne. "Sure you want to hear this?"

"Very sure, Detective."

"The bullet was small, like a .22. It went through the left side of her brain. It came out clean, no debris, they think. There was a lot of swelling, but they were able to operate to relieve the pressure. They took out a little bit of the skull—"

John felt sick and put his handkerchief to his mouth, but nothing came out.

"It's tough to hear, kid, I know."

John's insides were burning. He fought to keep from crying, but a single tear escaped and ran down his cheek. He brushed it away. It was his fault. He should have forced her to leave Wednesday night. But he was in such a hurry to phone in his article he let himself believe that she could get away. Oh, he'd thought he was so clever, quoting his confidential source, reassuring himself they'd never know. That little trick hadn't fooled them for a minute. Because he'd been so full of himself, so thrilled to play the dashing romantic international reporter, that brave, beautiful woman was lying in a hospital with a bullet through her brain.

Jeanne put a comforting hand over his. John jerked his hand away. He didn't deserve her sympathy.

Grogan went on in a quiet voice. "If the swelling goes down in the next few days, doc thinks she'll live, but she'll need a lot of care. She'll have some pretty serious problems, you know, walking, talking, that could last for weeks or months."

"It's a miracle she's even alive," Jeanne said.

Before John could respond, President Aranha's voice boomed through the loudspeakers in the bar. He spoke in heavily accented English. "Thank you to the distinguished representative from Paraguay for his most interesting remarks. We have no further speakers and we have reached the time for the vote." Aranha's words momentarily snapped John out of his despair.

"This is it," Jeanne said excitedly.

"We have to get to the floor," John said as he rose. His legs were trembling. He and Jeanne headed into the auditorium along with the rest of those in the press bar. Every seat was filled, so John and Jeanne stood against the back wall. Moshe Shertok was a few yards in front of them, seated in the last row on the aisle.

Jeanne's hand sought John's and gripped it fiercely. He returned her pressure, suddenly grateful for her unquestioning affection. They stood together, wordless, at this crossroads in the life of the world.

32

Alfagari moved his chair again to the front of his booth and checked on his targets. To his surprise, the headdress of al-Khoury and the bald pate of Alexandre Parodi were nearly touching. That wouldn't be a problem, even if al-Khoury didn't move. His shot at the woman yesterday proved he could still hit a target at two hundred yards and this was less than half that distance. The two men were deep in conversation. After another minute, Parodi rose to speak.

President Aranha said, "We recognize the distinguished representative from France, Monsieur Parodi."

Alfagari inched forward in his seat, ready to be a hero. He allowed himself a slight smile.

• • •

"What's Parodi doing?" John said, still gripping Jeanne's hand. "There aren't supposed to be any more speakers."

"Mr. President," Parodi began, speaking English with a Parisian accent. His voice echoed throughout the auditorium. "I have just been informed that representatives of the countries opposing this resolution have proposed a compromise. They would like the opportunity to present this compromise to this distinguished assembly as a substitute for partition. May I suggest that the decision before us is too grave to overlook even a faint chance of an agreement acceptable to both the

Zionists and the Arabs. I therefore move for a twenty-four-hour delay on the vote."

There was a loud buzz in the auditorium. Voices shouted yes and no in a dozen languages. President Aranha had to speak up to be heard. "Very well, I call for a vote."

• • •

Alfagari's smile vanished. He lifted the rifle and balanced the stand on the balcony. He locked the stock to his right shoulder. Al-Khoury had moved away from Parodi and was still standing. Good! That would make this easier. His finger closed around the trigger.

"Not," Aranha shouted, "a vote on partition. Only on the French motion for a delay."

Alfagari took his finger off the trigger but stayed in position, hopeful the French motion would fail. There were further delays as delegates sought instructions from their ambassadors. After a half hour, Aranha called again for a vote and the motion for delay passed, 25 to 14. The Assembly would reconvene the next morning, Saturday. Alfagari exhaled and slowly put the rifle back into its cover and the cover into the tripod case. He moved the chair back into the shadows. He couldn't leave until just before the doors closed at 10 p.m. He would sneak back to his hotel and return early tomorrow.

• • •

Moshe Shertok popped out of his seat. He looked furious. He passed Jeanne and John as he stalked out of the auditorium.

"What the hell happened?" John asked.

"We had it. They knew we had it," Shertok snapped. "God only knows where we'll be tomorrow. It's going to be a long night trying to hold this together!"

PART V

2003

33

"Still on for lunch?"

It was a text from John. It was Wednesday, June 25, the day they had agreed to meet, so the answer was yes, of course, but Jeanne didn't reply. She had waited thirty years. He could wait thirty minutes.

Jeanne, Michael, and Alice were on the train from Rome to Umbria. Outside the window, the clutter of Rome slowly gave way to green hills and brown fields baking in the morning sun. Michael faced her across a narrow table. Alice sat by the window. They would be at Terni by nine thirty and would change trains there for the short ride to Todi. Kerry was not with them—she had driven to Spoleto with Toljy earlier that morning in a rented Ferrari.

How could their meeting be so casually arranged? She wanted poetry, not the breezy exchange of electronic prose that had sifted between them for the last two months. Maybe they should have talked on the phone.

What did he sound like now? She had loved his voice when they were younger—resonant, energetic, and confident. Had it dried into a low, rattling, old-man voice, parched and querulous?

She teasingly told herself she could back out. She would still have sightseeing in Rome, hearing Kerry sing in Spoleto, precious time with Alice, even the memory of a summertime fling. Sure, there would be questions asked, jokes at her expense, self-deprecation at her indecision. John would be disappointed, but she was certain he would understand.

Kerry had said there was nothing to be afraid of, that at worst she would have an awkward lunch, but that wasn't what she feared. Her greatest fear was that she would feel nothing for him, nothing more than the momentary glow she might feel walking by the house she lived in when she was a child.

She had decided to ask him what she wanted to know immediately. Once they had navigated that landmine, then what? Kids, work, and—inevitably, at their age—their health.

She wasn't worried about her appearance. After all, she had been able to attract a charming, intelligent man nearly ten years her junior without half trying. She had a sharp tug of regret at the thought of Ernest.

Kerry and Alice were inordinately interested in what she would wear. "I refuse to obsess about my appearance," was all that she would say, but she had planned her outfit exactly. She bought a simple sleeveless V-neck linen dress at a shop in Trastevere when she was there with Ernest. It was light blue, loosely gathered at the waist, and came just below the knee. She would pull her hair behind her ears and wear her usual light makeup and clear nail polish. She had a simple, comfortable pair of slingbacks with one-inch heels she had brought from home. She would have to wear sunglasses, of course, and her wide-brimmed straw hat as protection from Italy's summer sun. She frowned. She didn't look good in hats.

The train bumped and jerked through a turn as it headed through the hills north of Rome and her knee cracked painfully against the metal leg of the table. She rubbed it, drew back, and settled deeper into her seat.

Her memory of their time together was a volatile mix of excitement, doubt, and pain. He had hurt her deeply both times they had parted and what hurt most was her conviction that he had never told her the real reason.

At the end of their trip to the United Nations in 1947, John had accepted a newspaper job in New York. It was an astonishing opportunity for him and they planned that Jeanne would join him that summer. On a cold afternoon the Sunday after Thanksgiving, they had a romantic goodbye on a train platform at Penn Station.

"I'll be back in Chicago at Christmas," he'd said. "It's only three weeks away."

Three weeks sounded like three years.

"I'll write every day," she said and they had kissed goodbye.

John made it home for Christmas as promised, although his train got stuck in Indiana for a day due to a heavy snowstorm. As disappointed as she was at the delay, it was almost worth it to have the usually grimy Chicago streets transformed into a postcard paradise of glittering fresh snow. Cars and trolleys couldn't move, but John scrounged an Army Jeep with canvas sides and top and they roamed the city at will. What the Jeep lacked in modern conveniences—such as heat—it made up for by its ability to go everywhere.

It was an epic week. They went shopping on Michigan Avenue, sledding near Soldier Field, and ice-skating along the frozen lakeshore. The second night, true to his promise, he took her on a real date. He picked her up at home, brought her mother flowers, and promised her father he would have her back by midnight.

They went to The Cape Cod Room in the Drake Hotel, where he was staying. It was the best seafood restaurant in the city. Seated in a corner near a window, they talked nonstop. They were completely, sweetly full of themselves and each other.

"You won't believe how different it is working at the *Herald*. I'm kind of in the salt mines now, rewriting wire copy for the international desk, but my boss promised me a promotion soon, maybe even a post in Europe as a foreign correspondent."

Her heart sank at the thought of him going abroad.

"I applied to Hunter College in Manhattan," she said. "They don't have dormitories, so I'll need to find a room. Where do you think I should live?"

"Near school, I guess." *Why not near him?*

"Is Liliane getting better?"

He paused a moment, then said, "It was touch and go for a while, but the new doctor helped a lot. She's walking and talking some, which is a really good sign. I got her into a military rehab hospital on Long Island. They're used to helping people recover from that kind of injury. She's looking more like herself."

"That's good." She couldn't help adding, "You said she was beautiful." He hadn't ever said that, but he didn't correct her. "I guess you see her a lot?"

"I've kind of taken responsibility for her. I got that guy we met at the UN, Benjamin Cohen, to help her apply for asylum, but our government is dragging its feet and the Syrian embassy won't lift a finger."

"She's not, you know," she said quietly, looking down at the checked tablecloth. "Your responsibility."

He shook his head slowly. "I have to help her."

No, you don't!

"It wasn't your fault, John," she managed to say calmly.

"Even if that were true, you know I'm doing the right thing."

She gave a rueful laugh. "I know. That's one of the reasons I—like you so much."

Although they were in the fresh flush of first love, they hadn't said the words. She had decided he should be the one to say it first. She was sure it would happen any day now, maybe even tonight. She checked her watch.

"Is it late?" he said.

"Not even ten."

"I could get you home early, make your folks happy."

She shook her head again, blushing with anticipation.

"A walk then? Some of the stores are open late."

"It's too cold."

He frowned for a moment, then said, "Would you like to see my room?"

A fire started in her center and spread its heat through her body. "Yes."

At the door to his room, she put her arm around his waist and leaned her head against his shoulder as he opened the door. Inside the room, the door swung shut and they dropped their coats on the floor and fell into each other's arms. After a while, she pulled back, holding his hands, and whispered, "Just a minute."

She went into the bathroom and shut the door. She took off all her clothes except a cream-colored slip with thin straps and lace at the bodice. She looked in the mirror and fluffed her hair. *Don't stop to think.* She turned off the bathroom light and opened the door. A dim light came from streetlamps through the curtains. He had turned down the covers on the bed and sat on its edge, feet on the floor, wearing only his T-shirt and boxer shorts.

"Are you sure, Jeanne?" he asked.

"Yes," she said in a whisper.

He took her hand and pulled her onto his lap. She put her arms around his neck and they kissed. She put her weight against him and he slowly lay back. They swung their legs onto the bed and Jeanne lay on top, still kissing him. He ran his hands down her back and pressed her against him. Her breathing came faster as she turned and shifted underneath him. She was overwhelmed by her feeling of warmth for him and the thrill of being the object of such intense attention.

• • •

Afterward, as their heat faded, her emotion seemed to grow. They lay on their sides under the covers, facing each other, she with her knees drawn up, he propped on an elbow. His free hand grasped one of hers and he brought it to his lips.

"You okay?"

She nodded and smiled. "More than okay."

"You're very precious to me, you know." He brushed back a lock of hair from her eyes.

"You are too."

This is it. This is when we say, "I love you."

"I'm glad of that," he said.

She tried to think of a way to make him say the words, but then she remembered a phrase she had once read. "Don't be importunate. Where love is concerned, never be importunate." She would wait.

He kissed her gently and they pressed their bodies together.

"We should probably get dressed if I'm going to get you home by midnight."

"It's still early," she whispered as their heat returned and they made love again. When they were finished, she went to the bathroom and washed and dressed. She noticed her reflection in the mirror. How could it be that there was no sign of this cataclysmic event? But if there was no new-born look of maturity or wisdom, neither did she feel any damage, taint, or shame.

They rode down the elevator alone, holding hands.

John smiled and said, "Uh, Jeanne, I'm thinking that when your parents ask about our date—"

"We should probably leave this part out."

They laughed and walked out of the elevator and into the night. The temperature had dropped into the low teens, so they left the Jeep at the hotel and took a cab. In the back seat, they held each other the whole way. They walked through her door on Diversey exactly at midnight.

The next day was Christmas Eve. They spent it visiting her relatives. He came over again Christmas morning and they exchanged gifts. John gave her a glossy copy of the picture of the two of them with the Statue of Liberty in a heart-shaped frame. She gave him a navy blue cashmere scarf. There was a plain cardboard package that had been mailed from New York, addressed to her. It said in large letters, "Do Not Open Until Christmas." The return address was the UN Headquarters at Lake Success. There was no name. Jeanne opened it eagerly and pulled out a heavy object wrapped in old newspaper. She stripped off the paper and laughed. It was a pair of well-worn opera glasses with a crack in one of the lenses and a deep scratch on the mother-of-pearl case.

"What are those?" John asked.

She laughed again. "These are Mr. Shertok's opera glasses. Remember, he lent them to me the day of the vote?" She shook her head. "I don't remember giving them back."

"There was a lot going on that day."

"I'll say."

"Look, there's a note," John said. He unfolded the heavy paper and read—

Dear Ms. Cooper,

I hope this finds you well after your eventful trip to New York. Please accept these old glasses of mine as a souvenir of the moment my dream of a country became a reality. May they always remind you of that happy day and the part you and your friend played.

Sincerely,
Moshe Shertok

"How thoughtful," she exclaimed.

Jeanne's mother cooked a huge Christmas dinner for a couple of dozen aunts, uncles, cousins, and neighbors spread throughout the house. After dinner, John and Jeanne put away the card tables and folding chairs and slipped out for a walk under the cold, clear evening sky.

"I wish we could go back to your hotel," Jeanne said, slipping her arm through his.

"Me too," he said.

"I can't believe I'm not going to see you until summer."

"Maybe you can visit around Easter?"

She shook her head. "My parents wouldn't let me travel by myself. Could you come here?"

"Probably not. I just started. I'm not due for vacation for at least a year. And the *Herald* might even send me overseas."

"But you'll come back by June if you do?"

He smiled. "I'll make sure of it."

• • •

Jeanne's parents drove John to the train station the next day.

"Thank you so much," he said as he and Jeanne got his bags out of the trunk. "I haven't had a family Christmas in a long time." He hugged her mother and shook hands with her father.

"I'm just going to walk him inside," Jeanne told them. "I'll be right back."

They walked hand in hand into the station. Once inside, she flung her arms around him and they kissed.

"Write every day," she said.

He laughed. "You know I have a job, right?"

"Well, then as much as you can. I will. I won't mean to, but it'll happen because I won't be able to stop thinking about you. I'll use the typewriter my parents got me for Christmas. You won't mind, will you, that they're not handwritten?"

He picked up his bags and kissed her quickly. "Nope. Gotta go. See you soon."

Not exactly "Parting is such sweet sorrow."

"Not for six months. I may die."

He laughed uncertainly. "Maybe we can figure something out around Easter. But you'll be so busy with school and the paper it'll go by like nothing. This is your last year of high school. Make the most of it."

She tried to be brave. "I will. I have so much to do to get ready to move this summer. Maybe you're right."

They kissed one last time and he walked away.

In the months following Christmas, Jeanne made ready to move to New York. She was accepted at Hunter College. When she discovered that it had been used by the United Nations for its first Security Council meeting in 1946, she took it as another favorable sign. She wrote several letters a week to John. He responded occasionally, usually in the form of newspaper clippings of his articles with short notes to her scribbled in the margins in blue ink. It didn't worry her. He was busy.

She loved packing because it made her feel close to him. Her summer clothes went in suitcases; winter clothes and personal items she'd ship in boxes. Through Hunter, she found lodging near campus. She was entirely packed a month before graduation when she received a telegram from John.

1948 MAY 28
JEANNE COOPER
6656 WEST DIVERSEY AVE CHICAGO ILLINOIS

DEAR JEANNE HERALD POSTING ME ABROAD FOR 2 YEARS MAYBE LONGER STOP MUST LEAVE IMMEDIATELY STOP SO SORRY I HAVE TO GO STOP LETTER FOLLOWS

JOHN

Jeanne's head began to throb. She reread the telegram again and again as though it were a cipher that, when decoded, would reveal a different meaning. Her insides twisted in tight, painful cramps. She dialed his number, but there was no answer at his apartment. She called the paper, but he was already gone.

She told no one about the telegram and spent three days awash in illness, awaiting his letter. When it came, it was merciless. He explained he was being sent to Paris and then Brussels to cover the formation of a mutual defense organization among the Western powers. The posting would last at least two years and would probably be extended. He would be constantly traveling. After much painful reflection, he had decided that maintaining their relationship wouldn't be fair to her. "This is something I have to do." He wished her every success and happiness. "I know this will hurt you, but whatever life might bring, I will never know anyone finer than you."

She locked herself in her room to avoid her mother's looks, her father's words of comfort, and Caroline's hollow assurances that she would find someone better. With manic calm, she carefully unpacked her clothes and unboxed her things. She typed out a polite letter to Hunter College thanking them for their acceptance and explained that, unfortunately, she would not be able to attend due to a change in circumstances.

She told her mother she would not attend her graduation, but on the day of the ceremony, Caroline came over and made her get ready.

"You have to go. You'll always be sorry if you don't. Don't let the bastard ruin your life. Please, Jeanne."

Jeanne stood listlessly, her eyes dry. She had run out of tears. "Okay."

In the months that followed, she slowly returned to something resembling life. She went on a few dates and occasional outings with friends. She enrolled in Roosevelt University, a new college named for the late president. She completed a two-year course of business classes. After graduation, she got a job as a secretary at a small local paper, the *Montclare Herald*. During the next several years, she was promoted to copywriter, then reporter, and, finally, editor.

In 1962, she met Michael Hanson, a hard-drinking reporter at the paper who had dreams of becoming a screenwriter. They were married six months later, mainly because she was pregnant. They moved to Los Angeles and arrived New Year's Day 1963. After Michael was born, she went to work at a local community college as an English teacher. As the years went by, the sharp pain John had caused her faded to a recurrent ache. In 1971, she and her husband separated.

In early 1973, there was a banner headline in the local afternoon paper, the *Los Angeles Herald Examiner*, trumpeting the signing of the Paris Peace Accords, ending the Vietnam War. A wave of relief swept through her. Some of her former students were serving over there. The article had a clean, slyly skeptical style and was blessedly free of clichés. She glanced at the byline and froze.

"By Jack McGrath." That was what he was called now.

At the end of the article, there was a brief note in italics saying that, after twenty-five years as a foreign correspondent, the *Herald* was pleased to announce that Mr. McGrath had accepted a position as assistant editor and would be relocating to their office in Los Angeles.

The ache returned.

Don't be ridiculous! It's been twenty-five years. He forgot you ten minutes after he wrote that letter. He's probably married or has a girlfriend—or both.

She kept thinking about him, though. She was lonely. She hadn't gone on a date since she had separated from Michael's father. The following Friday afternoon, she screwed up her courage and called the *Herald*.

"John, uh, Jack McGrath, please."

"I'll connect you."

"McGrath," said a low, easy voice.

"Uh, John?"

"Yes, who's this?"

"John, it's Jeanne, Jeanne Cooper? Well, Hanson, now." Her voice was high and tight. "Do you remember me?"

He coughed to clear his throat. "God, yes, I . . . of course I do. How could I forget?"

"Well, it has been twenty-five years. I live in LA and I saw your name in the paper. I wasn't sure you'd remember me." She had hoped to be less nervous.

"Has it? I think of you so often it just doesn't seem like it."

She laughed, disbelieving. "You think of me?"

"Are you kidding, Jeanne?"

It was a relief to hear him say that and say her name in a way that was familiar and intimate.

"Of course I do. I always thought that week in New York would make a great thriller, you know, like the *Day of the Jackal*," he continued, mentioning a recent bestseller about a political assassination. "My god, it was epic. I've always been so sorry that I, you know, how we ended."

"Forget it," she said as though she really had.

"Yeah?"

"You're forgiven." She laughed as though he really were.

"That's good to hear," he said as if he believed her.

"It was a long time ago," she said. "We were young and foolish. You did what you needed to do." For some reason she was making his excuses for him.

"Thanks, I guess."

They were silent for an uncomfortable moment; then John said, "This may sound crazy, but is there any chance I could see you? Let me buy you dinner."

"Won't make up for dumping me."

"Yes, well, no. I mean"—he laughed nervously—"it would be a down payment. Wait a minute, though. Hanson, you said. You're married?"

"We're separated, getting divorced. California passed no-fault, finally, so it's not as messy as it used to be. How about you?"

"I'm separated, too."

"Really?" She was relieved. "It must be going around. What happened?"

"It's a long story."

"Mine too. I guess they're all sort of the same story, though." He didn't answer.

"Where are you living?" she asked.

"A hotel for now, that tall, round one by the 405 and Sunset."

"Is it nice?"

"Not bad. I'm supposed to find an apartment, but the hotel is so reasonable I might just stay on. How about you?"

"We have an apartment in Santa Monica. Me and Michael, my ten-year-old. I teach nearby."

"You have a son? That's wonderful."

"You have kids?"

"Um, well, yeah, a son, my wife's son, actually. I'm basically his dad. He's grown, though, twenty-four."

"Twenty-four. She married young."

"She did."

"What does he do?"

"He's working in Paris. One of those international organizations."

"How exciting."

"So, what about dinner? I'll be done in an hour. Are you free tonight?"

She panicked. Did she really want to see him again? What was she doing? What would she wear? What does he look like? What would he think of her? Forty-three was a long way from seventeen.

"Tonight, wow, I don't know, I mean—"

"Sure, I understand. Hell, you're probably still mad at me."

"John, come on, it's been twenty-five years. Who could stay mad that long?"

Me. That's who.

"Yeah? That's good to hear. If tonight's no good, maybe another time?" She didn't want to wait. She didn't care if it was a bad idea.

"Not so fast. I just had to think about logistics. Look, I can get Michael to his sleepover and be back by six. Can you come out my way? I'll make a reservation somewhere nearby, nothing fancy."

"Great. Pick you up around seven?"

"Perfect," she chirped. She gave him her address and got moving.

• • •

John rang the bell of her second-floor apartment at seven exactly. She put her eye to the peephole. He was older, sure, but still tall, still handsome. He wore a wrinkled, wide-lapelled tan suit, a blue-and-white-striped shirt, no tie. His unfashionably short hair was beginning to go gray.

"Do I pass inspection?" he called out.

Embarrassed, she opened the door. "Wow, look at you," he said, which was exactly the right thing to say.

She wore a long, sheer dress, cut on the bias, with a pastel floral pattern and high strappy heels. She had a slip underneath but no bra. Her hair was done in a fluffy pixie cut. She wore almost no makeup. Her only jewelry was a pair of small diamond studs in her pierced ears.

He held out his hand and she took it. She had wondered if he'd try to kiss her and if she would let him.

"It's good to see you," she said.

"You too. Hey, you cut your hair."

"Yeah, like ten years ago."

"It's nice."

"Thanks. You look good, too."

"Bullshit. I'm wrinkled and rumpled. But, hey, I'm on time."

"You're twenty-five years late." She laughed to show she meant it as a joke. "This is crazy, John. Surreal."

"It really is."

She stepped out of the apartment and closed the door behind her. It was a mess inside.

They walked down the stairs. There was a loud argument going on between a man and a woman in the apartment below. "They do that all the time," she said.

"Must drive you crazy."

"It does, kind of, but mostly I hate Michael hearing it. He heard enough of that from his father and me."

"That's rough. Thought about moving?"

"Sure. I'm looking for a house."

"Ambitious."

"A girl's got to dream, right? There are some places in Santa Monica Canyon that aren't too pricey. Lots of artists and writer types live there."

He directed her to a tan Oldsmobile Cutlass parked on the street. "Company car," he said. "Could it be any more bourgeois?"

He held open her door, then got in the driver's side. The car was clean but smelled of cigarette smoke. An open carton of Gitanes sat in the bench seat.

"French cigarettes, very sophisticated," she said.

"Yeah, smoke like a chimney. I'm gonna quit soon, though. Hard to over there—everybody smokes." He tapped a cigarette from a pack. "Do you mind?"

"No. I always loved the smell; it reminds me of my dad."

He lit the cigarette from the dash and rolled down the window a couple of inches to let out the smoke. "Where to?"

"There's a little seafood restaurant a mile south of the pier." She gave him directions, but otherwise they didn't talk as he drove. When they arrived, he parked on a side street near Pacific Coast Highway and they walked a block to the restaurant. The dining room was small, a dozen wooden tables covered with checkered tablecloths. There were only a few other diners. A waiter seated them in a booth by a large window facing the wide beach and the dark ocean beyond.

"Cocktails to start?" the waiter asked.

"Can you make a Brandy Alexander?" She smiled and looked expectantly at John. His face was impassive.

"Of course. You, sir?" the waiter replied.

"Whiskey sour."

After their drinks came, John raised his glass. "Guess we should drink to Los Angeles," he said.

"Not 'love and joy'?" she teased.

They clinked glasses and sipped their drinks.

"Thought you would have had enough of those to last a lifetime," he said.

She laughed and almost spit out her mouthful. "I thought you forgot."

"The first night on the train. You drank a pitcher full of the stuff and threw up half the night. Hard to forget."

"I did not throw up."

"Well, that's how I remember it."

"Then you have a pretty bad memory. God, I felt sick, though."

"But very funny and totally adorable."

"I remember you taking care of me. You were pretty dashing, kind of Errol Flynn with a maternal instinct."

She had worried their conversation would be stilted, but it was nothing of the sort. Having a past in common, even one that ended badly, enabled them to relax in a way they never could have with a stranger. They talked about their lives, their work, their children, and moved on to the war and Watergate.

They lingered over coffee and after-dinner drinks. Neither of them wanted dessert. She took a sip of her drink and said, "Well, think we've talked about every subject but two."

"Which are?"

"Well, first, what do you think of our weather out here?"

He nodded soberly. "It's great. And second?"

She rested her chin on her hands. "Tell me about your marriage."

"Really great weather," he said, looking out the window.

"Come on," she said softly. She put her left hand over his right where it lay on the table and squeezed. He took a long drag from the cigarette in his other hand.

"Okay," he said finally. "We were married a long time ago. We haven't lived together for five years. She's in New York. Our son lived with us until he went to university."

"Your stepson?"

He paused, then said, "Right."

"Why didn't you divorce?"

"I can't."

"But why?"

"I promised her I wouldn't."

"That's not a reason. Everyone promises that, 'til death do us part."

"I know," he said, stubbing out his cigarette and returning her gaze. "But I meant it."

She looked down, deflated. There were things he wasn't saying, but there was no way to know if they were important things.

"Can we change the subject?" he said.

"Sure. Hey, I thought of a third topic."

"Thank God. What is it?"

"Loneliness."

"Yeah?"

She looked at him appraisingly. "I think you must get lonely."

"Sometimes." He shrugged. "But what are you gonna do?"

"I was thinking more like, what are we going to do?" She arched her back. "I hear there's a great view from that hotel of yours."

"Not from my room. All I see is the freeway." He called for the check. "You're pretty direct."

"I'm not seventeen anymore," she said.

Outside, they walked down the street, occasionally bumping shoulders, enjoying the smell and feel of the chill sea air. When they got to the car, he opened her door. She rested her hands on the crooks of his arms and kissed him. They drove to his hotel. When they arrived, they went straight to his room and, with very little preamble, made love. It was both very familiar and completely new.

After that night, they saw each other regularly. Willfully, with her eyes wide open, she let herself fall in love with him all over again. For nearly a year, it worked. They learned each other's needs and rhythms, and gingerly made plans for a future, living together, even buying a home.

It all fell apart one night at his hotel. They had come back late from a party and been up most of the night making love and talking and arguing about his refusal to divorce his wife. It was early morning.

"We're buying a house, Jeanne," he said, trying to put an end to their discussion. "Which means we'll always be together." She was sitting up in bed in her nightgown. Something about the way he said it caused all of the things she had been trying to forget to rise to the surface.

"If you mean that, then why won't you get the divorce?" she cried out angrily. "You haven't lived together for six years. You say you never talk."

He flared to anger. "We don't. But I can't get divorced. I told you that from the beginning and a million times since. She's three thousand miles away. You never have to think about her—it'll never affect our lives in any way. You have me. I'm with you."

"But she exists. If we have any chance of working, I can't share you."

"You won't have to, I promise."

"If you could just explain it to me," she said, fighting not to cry. Her feet were on the floor now.

He shook his head. "There's no more to say."

She stood up, jamming her clothes on over her nightgown. "I'm going. I can't do this anymore."

"What about the house?"

"Don't worry about my house."

"Okay, fine, if that's what you want."

It wasn't what she wanted, but it was what she had to do. She walked out and slammed the door.

Don't worry about my house. Easy to say, but it wasn't easy to do. She spent hours reapplying for mortgages in her name only and trying to cobble together enough money for the down payment. A day before she was required to have all of the money in escrow, the mortgage came through, but she was still short of the down payment. She drove to the house and parked in front of it. And began to cry. After a while, the owner of the house came out. They talked and he agreed to take back a second mortgage for the down payment. Two weeks later, she moved in and started her new life with Michael.

• • •

The train screeched around a corner and Jeanne snapped back to the present, where Michael was a difficult adult, not a pliable child. She tried to catch his eye across the table, but he was reading *The Da Vinci Code*. The heavy book jiggled with the motion of the train. Something must have happened between Michael and Kerry. Was it Toljy? What was the story there?

John had offered to pick them up at the station, but she'd said no. Twenty minutes had passed since his text. She could answer him now.

"Sure. What time?"

"12:30?" His text zoomed back in seconds. He clearly wasn't afraid of seeming eager. Texting was still a laborious procedure for her, tapping the tiny raised letters of her keyboard. What type of phone did John have? Did he use his thumbs to type? What did his hands look like now? She remembered them—rough and strong but surprisingly tender.

Minutes passed. She should reply. She didn't want him to think she was playing games.

"Perfect," she typed, but then deleted it. Too chirpy. Alice would have just sent the letter "K."

"Okay," she typed.

"Perfect," he replied immediately. "See you soon."

He didn't seem to mind being chirpy. In fact, he was maddeningly offhand, as though they saw each other every day rather than every quarter century or so.

Michael and Alice were thrilled by the hotel and no wonder. It was a beautifully restored twelfth-century monastery that combined the Italian architecture and furnishings of the period with every up-to-date modern convenience. Michael expressed no interest in seeing the town. "Enjoy your lunch," he said with an edge of hostility and locked himself in his room.

Jeanne and Alice went outside. The valley floor and green hills stretched for miles in the misty air. Alice pointed and exclaimed, "Look at the pool. It's so beautiful!" Its sapphire water was surrounded by stone tiles. One side of the pool was shaped like the outline of the dome of the nearby church. Despite the early hour, there were a few people scattered at tables and lounge chairs.

"I'll be right back." Alice hustled to her room and returned wearing a V-neck white mesh tunic over her bathing suit.

"You should go in," Alice said. "Plenty of time before the big date."

I am so tired of those jokes. Jeanne managed to say politely, "No, honey, you go ahead."

"'Kay, bye." Alice surveyed the area like a general choosing a battleground and selected a chaise longue with a table and umbrella that had a view of the pool and the surrounding hills.

Jeanne went to her room and unpacked, hanging her things in an ancient armoire and spreading her toiletries on the bathroom's marble countertop. When she was finished, she walked onto her terrace, which overlooked the pool.

A stream of young men dressed in white polo shirts and khaki shorts danced attendance on Alice, bringing her towels and serving her cold drinks and snacks. One squatted next to her and gave her sunglasses a good, long cleaning, all the while looking into her eyes and keeping up a steady stream of chatter. As a bonus, a lithe, dark-haired young man with an impossibly chiseled torso greeted her as he swam up to the edge of the pool, leaned on the coping, and idly kicked his feet in the water. He said something. Alice laughed and shook her head. He gestured at the hot sun and flicked a few drops of water on her. Alice retaliated by tossing flecks of ice from her drink at him.

Their interest in Alice was not a mystery. Since the last time Jeanne had seen her in a bathing suit, she had grown into a young woman, a fact she hid beneath shapeless school uniform sweaters, bulky coats, large men's shirts, and baggy pants. Her daring bikini showed her curved figure to maximum advantage. Her untamable hair miraculously seemed to benefit from Todi's heat and humidity and had settled into soft springing curls that bounced when she moved.

Jeanne went inside, grateful for the air-conditioning that switched on when she closed the sliding door. It was already eighty-five degrees, although it was only eleven. She decided to get dressed and walk to the town square. She shook out her linen dress and slipped it on, then leaned against the chair by the writing desk to put on her shoes. They had fit perfectly when she bought them two months ago at a spring sale, but her feet were swollen. She sat down on the chair, bent over, and loosened the straps a notch. She used her finger to pry them on, then sat up, dizzy and breathing heavily from the minor exertion. She struggled not to cry.

She didn't think she could walk all the way into town. There was a brochure on the table about the nearby sixteenth-century church called Tempio di Santa Maria della Consolazione. It had supposedly been designed by Leonardo. She could sit inside in the cool darkness. She hoped they wouldn't have to walk to lunch. She tried on her hat in front of a mirror, setting it at various angles, none of which looked right. She would wear it on her walk but not for lunch. She started to leave, but at the last minute, remembering European religiosity, went to the armoire and put on a teal-colored shawl that covered her bare arms.

• • •

Jeanne went out of the hotel through the ornate lobby and walked up the slight incline of the narrow road. The white church stood alone at the top of a small rise, surrounded by green grass. There was a view of the Tiber

Valley to her right. By the time she was halfway there, though, she was
puffing hard, her stomach had cramped, and her heart was pounding. A
trickle of sweat ran down her back.

Damn it.

She pretended to admire the view while she paused to catch her
breath. A drift of wind ruffled her dress and cooled her. Her heart's
pounding slowed. She took a deep breath and walked the rest of the way
to the church.

It was larger than it looked from a distance. Its dome rose two hundred feet into the air and was topped by a massive cross. The church
was polygonal and made entirely of white stone with decorative cornices
around the roofline. There was a wooden door just off the road. It was
open and she went in.

She had expected shade and shadows and was surprised by the
abundant natural light that streamed through the oculus in the dome
and rows of rectangular windows. She picked up a small guidebook
from a table at the entrance and dropped a few coins in an old Lavazza
coffee can. No one was inside. A handful of short wooden pews faced
an elaborate altar. She sat near the front and began reading the history
of the church. As she read, her pulse dropped as close to normal as it
got these days.

A priest and a small group of people, well dressed in dark suits and
formal dresses, entered from a side door. The priest went to the altar
and the group gathered in a semicircle facing him.

The priest nodded and a white-haired man in the group smiled.
He went to the door from where the group had entered and escorted
a woman in a simple off-white dress to the altar. It was a wedding. The
bride was in her early forties. Her bridegroom was older. He took her
hand and together they faced the priest.

It was obviously meant to be a private ceremony. Jeanne tried to
slip out quietly, but when she stood, the wooden pew scraped the floor
and made a hideous sound. The priest frowned and the group turned
to stare.

"Sorry," she said in a loud whisper, stumbling and knocking against
the pew again. Her face grew hot and she began to sweat. "Uh, *dispiace*."

The bridegroom smiled and said, "*Signora, per favore, Lei stia qui fino al matrimonio.*"

"Sorry?" she said.

A voice behind her growled in a resonant whiskey-rough baritone, "He asked would you please stay here until the wedding is over, Jeanne."

Her heart knocked and clattered as though she had run up a flight of stairs. Her pills didn't help. She turned. He was as tall and straight as she remembered. His clean-shaven face was burned brown from the sun and there were deep grooves at the corners of his eyes. The dimples she had loved were reduced to slashes, as though they were no longer needed. He was wearing the same white shirt he had on in the photograph he had sent her. She could tell now it was loosely woven linen. The sleeves were rolled halfway up his muscled forearms. He wore faded jeans and black leather sandals without socks.

She slipped her hat off and smoothed her hair while she blinked back tears. A smile played on his lips. He twice cocked his head to the side as though he wanted to say something. She couldn't stop looking into his eyes.

The priest grunted and spoke sharply.

John cleared his throat and said hoarsely, "He wants to know, are we coming or going?"

She gave a bewildered laugh. "I wish I knew."

"Let's stay."

She nodded. It would give her time to adjust to the reality of him. He said something to the priest, who looked annoyed, then turned back to his little flock.

"We better sit before he has us burned at the stake. Mind scooting over?"

They sat in the hard wooden pew, side by side. With the weight off her legs, she realized they had been shaking.

The ceremony was simple and lovely. John occasionally leaned close and whispered a translation, but it was mostly unnecessary for some-one raised a Catholic. The fresh scent of soap mixed with lemon and cedar drifted to her—and something else. Cigarette smoke? *Are you kidding me?*

Weddings usually made her weepy and, with John sitting next to her, it took a determined effort not to cry. But, as she leaned toward him while he whispered to her, a furtive tear slipped down her cheek and dropped onto the dry brown wood of the pew between them. John's right hand slid tentatively toward her. Almost of its own volition, her left hand moved and when they were close, their hands snapped together. They still fit as if they remembered each other's every line and whorl. His hand was spotted and weathered now but was still firm and steady. Her heart grew quiet. The priest gave his final blessing and the ceremony was over. They followed the wedding party outside and stood blinking in the hot sun as the bridal couple stuffed themselves into a shiny top-down Fiat and roared away. The rest of the group crowded into an ancient white Volkswagen van and followed them.

Jeanne moved along the grass to the shade of the church to escape the sun and John followed. He seemed nervous. She was surprised to find she wasn't. It was easier standing side by side looking out over the valley than it would have been staring at each other in a restaurant—less confrontational. She had thought so much about what she would say that she was afraid it would all come out in a rushed jumble. She told herself there was no need to hurry.

"Nice place for a wedding," he offered.

She nodded. "Very nice."

"Great view, huh? My house is over there," he added, pointing. "Can't see it from here, of course." He checked his watch. "Um, lunch isn't for a while."

"Okay."

"You're probably wondering what I was doing here at the Santa Maria."

"Not really."

"Just killing time, to tell the truth."

There was a stone bench against the outer wall of the church. Jeanne sat. John hesitated, then followed suit. She could feel his tension. "You're still mad," he said.

"Yes."

"But you came anyway."

"I came anyway."

"Can I ask why?"

She took a deep breath. "Because you ruined me, John." She had rehearsed that phrase many times, but she hadn't meant to say it right out of the box.

He looked stricken. "What?"

"You heard me."

"I ruined you? Because . . . because you were, it was your first time, you mean?"

"Not because of that. That was wonderful. It was all wonderful. Our week in New York, falling in love in late autumn in the greatest city in the world, witnessing world-shaking events, it was the best. And then our time together in Chicago, the city covered with snow, Christmas everywhere, making love every day."

"How did that—?"

"Ruin me? Because no one could ever compete with that. And they would never have had to if we'd stayed together. We were supposed to be together forever, John. But you ruined it."

"Oh."

"Yeah, 'oh.'"

"Was it as wonderful as all that?"

She looked at him.

"I know," he said hastily. "It was for me, too. It was perfect, maybe too perfect."

"Really?"

"Are you kidding? Everything you said, plus we were present at one of the seminal moments in history, met important statesmen, worked with a big-city detective. It had everything. I don't think even you and I could compete with those two months. If we'd stayed together, the rest of our life would have been a letdown."

"We should have had the chance to find out."

"You're right."

"Everything after was second best."

"Even us," he said.

"You mean in LA? That's probably true. The man you had become was definitely competing with the man I remembered."

He shook his head. "Who won?"

"Not me, that's for sure."

"You sound so sad."

"I'm not. Not really, John. I've been very lucky in a lot of ways. I was married to a wonderful man for seventeen years. I have a good son, a darling granddaughter; I'm comfortable financially. So I've had some heartbreak. Big deal. Show me somebody who hasn't."

He put a finger on her chin and gently turned her face toward him. "I'm sorry for hurting you. I needed to say that to you face-to-face. One reason why I wanted to see you."

"You lied to me." She turned away.

"Jeanne—"

"What I need—what I'd like—is the truth. Why you broke up with me the first time, why you wouldn't divorce your wife the second time around. It's no use going any further with this if you won't tell me."

He looked at his hands and sighed. "Right now, you mean?"

"I'm not getting any younger. Neither are you, jack."

He tried to laugh, but it was more of a swallowed chuckle. "Okay. Can we at least have lunch?"

"John—"

"Please? I promise I'll tell you everything."

"Okay."

"I could really use a drink."

"And a cigarette?" she needled.

He looked embarrassed.

"You're busted, McGrath."

"I hardly ever smoke anymore."

"You were just nervous, I suppose."

"You weren't?"

"Oh, yeah," she admitted, exhaling.

"I'll get my car. It's on the other side of the church."

"It's not a convertible, is it?"

"I should be so lucky," he said, standing.

Good, at least she wouldn't have a sweaty walk to town or a hot ride in an open car. She wouldn't have to wear the unbecoming hat.

He moved across the bright green lawn. Except for his white hair, he looked the same from behind as he always had—the same erect posture and broad shoulders, the same long stride. Would it still feel as wonderful to touch and kiss and hold each other? She was surprised to find she was enjoying herself.

"How about a hint?" she called gaily just before he went out of sight.

He stopped and turned, his face sad and serious.

"Do you remember the woman named Liliane they found facedown in an alley, shot through the head?"

She froze.

"It all had to do with her," he said as he vanished around the corner.

34

John's cell phone buzzed as they drove through the Umbrian hills in his ancient Alfa Romeo sedan but stopped almost immediately as though the signal had been lost. The phone, an old gray Nokia, was in a cradle mounted on the dash with rusted silver screws that split the faded wood. A thin black cord hanging from the phone was plugged into the cigarette lighter.

Neither of them had said a word since getting in the car. Jeanne had experienced a spasm of jealousy when he said Liliane's name like the fevered heat of an old illness shotgunning through her body. She was sweating through her dress, especially where her back and thighs pressed against the cracked black leather seats. It didn't help that the car's air-conditioning was broken. The narrow road was full of curves and seemed extremely perilous. Cars coming the opposite way could barely squeeze by. She rolled down the window and leaned forward to let the warm air flow around her.

Fields of yellow sunflowers riffling in the breeze were interspersed with vineyards and patches of brown dirt. There were trees everywhere— olive, cypress, birch, and maple. Spoleto, where Kerry was in final rehearsals, was hidden in the hills to the east. Beyond those hills, outlined through the smoke of distant clouds, stretched the Sibillini Mountains.

The cell phone buzzed again. John downshifted and as his hand came off the gearshift, he pressed the speaker button.

"Signor Jack?" a voice crackled.

"Antonio?"

"Yes, *padrone.*"

"*Tutti pronti?*"

"C'mon, English, Signor Jack, so I learn. *Per gli ospiti*, you know, for the guests."

"Okay, English. We'll be there in twenty minutes. Is everything ready?"

"Sure, all ready. But they don't finish the upstairs bedrooms. Ricci tell them no more work."

"Why?"

"Money, he say."

"But I paid them. He still there?"

"No, gone a lunch, *ritorna* two *ore*, maybe three."

"Fine, just make sure everything's ready."

"Okay, ciao," Antonio said.

"Ciao."

She couldn't help smiling. "Ciao," she said, drawing out the word.

John glanced at her and appeared to shake off his frustration. "My god, do you remember that woman?"

She pulled back her shoulders and shimmied them back and forth. Her voice went breathy. "*Ciao, bambini. Grazie a tutti.*"

John glanced at her. "I remember you doing that voice. It killed me. That's why you said 'ciao' in your email, right?"

"I wondered if you'd remember."

"Took me a while, but, yeah, I finally figured it out." He glanced at her again. "I figured it was your way of saying you really did want to see me, that you weren't just being polite."

"You're pretty smart."

"Some days."

"I remember her like it was yesterday," she said.

"Me too. It's yesterday I forget sometimes."

"I kept thinking her boobs were going to pop out of that dress. They were spectacular."

"Were they?"

"Sweet of you to pretend," she said.

"Nothing could make up for having to listen to her. Why did we?"

"She was your editor's new girlfriend."

"Shit, that's right. So my fault."

"The least of your sins."

"Je-eanne," he said, drawing it out. "You keep taking shots."

"Jo-ohn," she replied. "It was just a joke."

"Freud said there are no jokes."

"Nobody quotes Freud anymore."

"I still can't believe you're here. I'm so glad to see you."

"I know." She paused.

He gave her another glance.

"Okay, I'm glad to see you, too. Who's Antonio?" she said, gesturing at his phone.

"He works for me at the house."

"We're going to your house for lunch? Not a restaurant?"

"Yes—hope that's okay?"

She frowned. "Well—"

"I mean, technically, it is a restaurant. We're going to be serving food to our guests."

"How far is it?"

"In miles? Nine or ten. But I count it in curves."

"What?"

"I've driven between the house and Todi a million times. There are a hundred and ninety-seven curves between them."

"Good thing I don't get carsick."

"I wanted you to see it. I'm pretty proud of the work we've done." They were quiet for a while as the car spun through curve after curve.

"I don't have to call you Jack, do I?" she said suddenly.

"Good god, no."

"What did Liliane call you?"

He didn't answer, keeping his eyes on the road through several hairpin turns.

"Why did you change it?"

"It wasn't my idea. When I started working in Paris, after—"

"You dumped me."

"Um—"

"There I go again."

"It's okay. Anyway, an Irish guy in the office, my boss, started calling me Jack and it kinda stuck and they changed my byline."

John spun the wheel, downshifted, and rounded another hill.

"We're here. Casale Leonardo," he said, switching off the engine. They were on a small rise on a packed dirt road. The road led down a gentle slope to a stone drive lined with cypress trees. She opened her door and stepped into the baking heat.

The white stone walls and rust-red tiles of the two-story house glowed in the afternoon sun. The combined fragrances of roses and lilac, lavender and lemon, rosemary and cypress, and blackberry and wisteria blended into a single heady scent.

"It seems to have been here forever," she said softly.

"It's over five hundred years old."

Despite her resentment at being manipulated into this visit, she couldn't deny him the praise he was due. "Those pictures you sent didn't do it justice."

"Can I show you around?"

"Sure."

"The pool's around back. Let's start there."

He held out his arm and, after a brief hesitation, she slipped her arm comfortably through his. As they neared the house, a curved stone path lined with brick split off from the drive. They followed it to the turquoise water and rounded stone coping of the pool, stopping at a low stone fence that separated the grounds from an olive grove. The silver-green olive leaves shimmered.

"Every fall, they harvest the olives and send them to a local olive mill. They get maybe a couple hundred gallons of oil. I'm told we can double that. We'll use it here, in the kitchen."

She gently disengaged her arm and ran her hands along the rough stones on the wall.

He touched her shoulder lightly to direct her attention to a small plot of dirt lined with terra cotta flowerpots. "Over here, we're growing vegetables. And in that corner, we'll have an herb garden."

"The last thing I ever thought you'd become is a farmer."

They walked the other way around, past the oak trees, along another stone wall, this one lined with wisteria.

"This way, under the arch," he said.

A stone arch extended from one of the two-story walls like a flying buttress, though it had no discernable function. There was a sharp incline. She panted as they climbed but refused to stop before reaching the top.

"Are you okay?" he said.

"I'm fine," she said sharply. She tried to take a deep breath, but her stomach knotted. She winced, more in fear than in pain. "Little out of shape. And I'm seventy-three."

He looked concerned. "Something's wrong."

"Nothing's wrong." He had his secrets—she could have hers.

"Okay."

He led her through the double doors into the *soggiorno*. Despite the heat and the ample sunlight shining through the arched windows, this main room of the house was cool.

She suddenly felt better. "It's so comfortable in here."

"The walls are three feet thick. It was built to stay cool in the summer, warm in the winter, and, no kidding, to repel invaders."

"I love this floor tile. Is it original?"

"No, but they're handmade. I put 'em in. One of those beams"—he pointed to the ceiling—"fell while we were working and broke some of the tiles. Almost killed me, but we were able to repair it."

"It's marvelous."

Her approval seemed to relax him. He gestured to a door on the opposite end of the room. "Let me show you the kitchen."

The kitchen was one of the largest she'd ever seen in a private home. There was a six-burner gas range with cast-iron grates in one corner, copper pots hanging from hooks on the walls, cabinets filled with food, glassware, crockery, and spices, and a huge refrigerator with a wooden door that took up an entire corner of the room. There was a large brick oven and, next to it, an open-hearth fireplace with a roasting spit.

"The oven and fireplace have been here over four hundred years. They burn wood, but we added gas."

A farmhouse table with eight chairs dominated the center of the kitchen. She could imagine cooking breakfast on a cold morning in the early light and the smell of oranges and coffee and fresh-baked bread.

He let her enjoy the room for a while and then said, "Let's go upstairs," in the voice a man might use to invite a woman to his bedroom.

Stop it. He's not in love with you—he's in love with his house.

They walked up the stairway. At the top of the stairs, a long hallway stretched the length of the house. "My bedroom plus five for guests."

He stopped at a floor-to-ceiling door of solid oak, stained dark, with heavy iron hinges and handles. He pushed it open and, with a slow sweep of his arm, invited her to enter. It was the master bedroom. The room glowed with sunlight. An en suite bathroom was visible through a partially open door. A pair of bookshelves stood along the plaster walls on either side of a stone fireplace. French doors led to a stone tile terrace and there was a huge wood-frame bed with a carved headboard.

It was exciting to be standing alone with him in his bedroom. She almost expected him to fold her into his arms, kiss her, and lay her gently on his bed. The moment passed but left her confused.

Carefully controlling her voice, she said, "It smells so good. Cedar?"

"Italian cypress. Ricci's idea."

"Who is this Ricci?"

"My construction guy. He says he always makes his clients rich. A pun on his name," he explained. "'Ricco' in Italian means 'rich.'"

She raised a brow.

"He's drunk half the time, but he's really good." He opened the French doors and they stepped onto the terrace. There was a broad view of the neighboring fields and hills. They were dotted with sheep. They stood at the railing. She was sure he wanted to take her hand.

"It really is lovely, John," she finally said. "You've done a good thing here."

"I'm so glad to hear you say that."

It was obvious he wanted to say more.

I love this house. Could I be happy here?

"Let's go outside," he said. "I think lunch is ready."

As they walked down the long hall, she noticed the doors of the guest rooms were closed.

"Can we see them?" she asked.

"Ah, they're not quite finished."

She remembered his call with Antonio about the workers. What was the story there? Was he having financial trouble? It made her think of Michael and his real estate problems.

At the end of the hall, they went through a door that led to the exterior stairway on the side of the house. At the bottom of the stairway near the kitchen door, there was a wooden pergola laced with climbing vines. Underneath, there was a long trestle table lined on either side with a dozen padded, canvas-backed chairs. At the end nearest the kitchen, it was set for two with white tablecloth, silver, crystal, and white china. A bottle of wine with its cork out perspired in the heat.

"Hungry?"

"I am." She hadn't eaten breakfast before leaving Rome and had been too nervous to eat since. "Thirsty, too."

A dark-haired young man dressed in a short-sleeve white shirt and black pants and shoes emerged from the kitchen door.

"*Signori*, lunch is ready."

"Thanks, Antonio," John said. The young man gave a slight bow and vanished back into the house.

John pulled out her chair and she sat. He walked to the other side of the table and sat too. She drank from her water glass. As she set the glass down, she squinted at a bug floating on an ice cube like a tiny castaway on a raft.

Nothing's perfect. She dipped a finger in the glass and removed it.

"Antonio cooks real Umbrian style, learned it from his grandmother. Try the wine?" John asked, holding the unlabeled bottle. "It's from a winery around the corner."

"Just a little," she said. After he poured, she raised her glass. "To Casale Leonardo."

They touched glasses and drank.

Their meal started with plates of *salumi*—small bites of cured meats such as prosciutto, salami, and mortadella—served with fresh bread and olive oil. The prosciutto was pink, tender, and tasty, nothing like what she had eaten in the States.

"That's because it's real prosciutto from a butcher shop nearby. Takes 'em three years," John said like a proud father describing the latest accomplishment of his prodigy. "The stuff you get in the States, it's all made by machine in just a few months."

Bruschetta followed, some topped with tomatoes and basil, others coated with a mixture of wild mushrooms and calf's liver.

Their eyes met and she smiled at memories of other meals together. Was he thinking of those times too? He poured her more of the cool red wine. It was dark, almost black, and its fruity smell was overpowering.

The pasta course followed, thick handmade spaghetti with wild boar sauce that had been cooked for hours with local vegetables to form a creamy liquid. They ate in silence until she finally pushed her plate away.

"I can't eat another bite."

Dessert was blessedly simple, tiny bites of plain cake, served with fresh strawberries and cream. On a separate plate were small pieces of pecorino cheese made from sheep's milk, served as a digestive.

"It was wonderful," she said. "You are going to have some very happy guests."

"I hope so. We need it. We're supposed to open in two weeks. We should have opened last month, but, like everything in Italy, there were delays. I need the place to start paying for itself."

"Is it expensive?"

"Much more than I thought, and I still need to staff up. I was in Rome a few days ago and spent a fortune on things for the house."

"We were there too."

"I know, you mentioned," he said.

Antonio had cleared the dishes. The afternoon was warm, but she was comfortable in the shade of the pergola. The food and wine had relaxed her. She was ready to hear what he had to say.

"Tell me about Liliane."

He turned away and stared at the afternoon sky. The wind had picked up. Clouds had appeared and blocked the sun. "She's gone, you know."

"How could I know?"

"Passed away two years ago."

"I'm sorry," she said with a sudden foreknowledge of what he was going to say.

"Liliane was my wife."

It seemed to her she had always known. Her shoulders tensed, but she tried to remain impassive. He looked at her to gauge her reaction.

"We were married on November 25, 1948, so for"—he cocked his head as if to calculate—"more than fifty-two years."

"November 25?"

He nodded. "Exactly a year from the day you and I took that train to New York. Some of this could be hard to hear."

"It's okay." This was why she had come.

"Mind if I smoke?"

"Your funeral."

"You know, a man once told me, 'Jack, there is no pleasure on earth worth denying yourself for a couple of extra years in an old age home.' Hey, Antonio?" he called loudly.

The young man appeared immediately.

"Coffee, please, and do we still have that bottle of Strega?"

"*Sì*, boss."

"Bring the bottle and the good glasses. Oh," he added as if it were an afterthought, "and my cigarettes."

"*Certamente.*" He disappeared and returned a few moments later. He had a small bottle, two glasses, and a pack of Marlboro Reds on a polished wood tray. He set the tray in front of John and left only to return moments later with a silver coffee service.

John poured them both coffee and a small glass of Strega. He refreshed their water glasses from a nearby pitcher. He lit a cigarette and blew out a plume of smoke that was whipped away by the wind.

"There was something between us from the moment we met. Not, like what you and I had, but it was there."

He drew on his cigarette. His eyes narrowed against the smoke as he exhaled, watching her.

She bit her lip.

"The night I saw her at the hotel, she told me the details of their plans. Lots of those details ended up in my articles. And . . . we kissed."

"I knew something happened between you."

"There was more to it than that. She so badly wanted to end the violence in the Middle East, but she was trapped, practically a prisoner. So when I dropped from the sky, she helped me. I offered to get her away from them, but she refused my help, said she had her own escape plans. I should have insisted."

"She made her own choices."

"I've told myself that a million times."

The smell of his cigarette reminded her of her father sitting in his leather wingback chair in the small parlor of their home on Diversey Avenue in Chicago, smoking while he read the newspaper in the morning or listened to the radio after dinner. She loved the smell of the phosphorus match and the burning paper and tobacco.

"What happened to her was my fault."

She remembered his reaction when they heard the news. "You didn't shoot her."

"I might as well have. She was the source for my articles. I should have realized they would know it was her. But I . . . I wanted that story."

She was silent. If he wanted absolution, he wasn't going to get it from her.

"Anyway, she was in bad shape. I stayed with her in the hospital as much as I could. She didn't have anybody else. I found her a better doctor and I got her into a rehab place and some help with the expense. From Mr. Shertok, remember him?"

"Of course. He changed his name to Sharett, you know," Jeanne said.

"Sure, long time ago, before he became prime minister in the fifties, but I always think of him as Shertok. Do you still have his opera glasses?"

Jeanne smiled and nodded.

"Anyway," John continued, "two or three times a week, I'd take the train out to the rehab center in Long Island and sit, maybe read the paper to her, just so she wouldn't be alone. After a few weeks, she began to respond."

"So, when you came home that Christmas, you had been seeing her every day?"

"Not every day," he said quietly, as if it made a difference.

"You were falling for her."

"Absolutely not. I admired her, sure, and I felt sorry for her."

"John—"

"I had to take care of her," he said loudly, chopping the air with one hand. "I knew that at least, so that's what I did." He paused, then continued. "Later, after Christmas, she got better faster than the doctors thought she would."

"You started dating?"

"No. She still couldn't walk very well, and she couldn't get words out when she wanted. And sometimes her mind wandered. She would just go blank for a while."

"So, just friends, huh?"

"Yes. But by March she had recovered. They released her from the rehab place. She had no money, nowhere to go. I told her she could stay with me."

He looked at her, then away. "That's when we started. She said she loved me and maybe she did. I know she needed me. I should have stopped it, but I didn't."

"Why didn't you tell me?"

"I didn't know how."

"Did you love her?"

He shook his head slowly. "No. Not then. As the years went on, of course. She was a very special person." He shook his head again. "But not then. I was in love with you."

"But you sent me that horrible telegram. Did the paper really give you the new job or did you ask to be transferred to get away from me?"

"What? No, it killed me to send that telegram. Absolutely they gave me the new job."

"So what was it? Why did you choose her instead of me? If it wasn't love, what was it?" Her voice broke, but she forced out the question she had come six thousand miles and waited fifty years to ask. "Why did you break my heart?"

"We found out she was going to have a baby."

She was suddenly nauseated. A gust of wind blew her hair across her face. She held it back with one hand and put her napkin to her mouth with the other, expecting to vomit. She was disappointed when she didn't because doing so might have emptied her of her anger over this miscarriage of justice—another woman having his baby, the baby who should have been hers. He moved to comfort her, but she brushed him aside and walked unseeing on a path along the stone boundary wall, her hand tracing its rough stones. Her finger caught on a jagged rock and began to bleed, but she ignored it. Yellow roses and red ones grew near the wall in soft, dark dirt. They were like those in her own garden in Santa Monica. Why hadn't she stayed home?

She followed the path toward the rear of the house until she came to a large, spreading oak. There was a pair of wooden slat chairs, painted green, beneath it. She sat in the shade and waited for her heart to slow, her stomach to unclench, and her tears to dry.

She had wanted answers; now she had them. It was worse than she'd feared but better too. He was the good man she had fallen in love with, not the feckless one he had appeared to be. Out of a stew of guilt, responsibility, generosity, and, yes, desire and love, he had devoted a large part of his life to another woman because he had injured her, because they had a child together, and because she needed him. That Thanksgiving weekend so long ago, Jeanne had fervently wished that Liliane would have the good grace to step aside. Well, now she was gone and what did it matter?

Her finger had stopped bleeding. She dabbed at it with the napkin that was somehow still in her hand. She rose wearily and returned along the same path. John was leaning forward, his elbows on the table, his head in his hands. A surge of affection filled her and battled with the fresh anger she felt. Yes, he'd broken her heart, but it was because he had tried to help someone who had suffered grievous harm, because he had made mistakes and tried to rectify them.

She came up behind him and placed a hand on his arm. She was surprised to feel how firm his muscles were through the smooth linen of his shirt. There were tears in his eyes as he said, "You weren't the only one whose heart was broken."

"I know."

"I tried to do the right thing."

"You did. For her. I do understand that, forgive that. What I can't . . . get past is that you lied to me."

"Jesus, I was twenty-one."

"Not in Los Angeles."

His head sagged and he inhaled deeply. "No, not then."

"Every day we were together in Los Angeles was a lie."

He was silent.

She shrugged slightly. "Why tell me all this now?"

"Because there's no way to have any future if we don't clear away our past." He went on hastily. "Not that there's any reason to suppose we have a future. I know that."

Jeanne shook her head. "What happened after the telegram?"

"I sailed for Paris that day and I found an apartment for Liliane and me. She followed a month later and we were married in a little church outside of Paris near Chartres Cathedral. Our son, Salam, was born the following February."

"So when we were in Los Angeles and you told me you had a stepson—"

He smiled slightly. "Another lie, I guess. If I had told you he was mine, you would have guessed the rest."

He looked down, then back at her. "Salam grew up in Europe, but he wanted to go to school in the States. He's an American after all. He was accepted at Princeton. We moved Liliane to Manhattan at the same time. We thought it was best for her. By the time I was transferred to LA, we hadn't lived together for years." He looked at her expectantly.

As if playing a part, she asked, "Why didn't you stay together?"

"She got sick again—her mind. Those blank spells were happening more frequently and lasting longer. When she had them, she could hurt herself or others without even knowing it. It was more than we could handle, especially with the travel for my job. We found a good place in New York. The doctors told us it was progressive dementia. In a few months, she didn't even know us."

"That's awful."

"It was harder on Sal than me because he was there all the time."

"You call him Sal?"

He smiled briefly and nodded. "Yeah. Liliane said it was improper, but I liked it. Anyway, he's in his fifties now, married, has kids—my grandkids. He and his family are coming to visit in a few days. Maybe you'll meet them. Anyway, I visited Liliane as much as I could. To be with her and to make sure they were taking good care of her. Weekends sometimes, all my vacations. She could still hold my hand even though she didn't know who I was. I kept that up until she passed away."

"That was why you took all those trips when we were together in Los Angeles?"

"Yes. I guess I could have told you all this back then, but I felt so guilty about seeing you, cheating on her. Somehow, telling her secrets to you, a woman I loved, would have made the betrayal even worse. That's why I couldn't divorce her. How could I abandon her when she was so helpless?"

She nodded slightly.

"And I was so ashamed of how I treated you, of what I did. But, Jeanne—"

"What?"

He took a deep breath. "I never got over you."

It sounded almost like a proposal, but she was saved from responding by the sound of a car approaching the house, its tires crunching the hard crust of the dirt road.

John's eyes narrowed and squinted. "It's Ricci, my construction manager."

Even at a distance, they could hear Ricci's voice. There was another figure in the passenger seat. After a minute, Ricci pushed open the driver's door violently and got out. His face was red and sweating. He stumbled and his hand slipped as he pushed the door shut. It took him two tries to get it closed.

"Is he drunk?" Jeanne said.

"Oh, yes."

The other man got out the passenger side. He was thin, dark complected, and dressed in a black suit. His hair was completely white, although he did not appear to be much past fifty.

"I need to talk to them," John said. "Stay here, okay? He can get nasty when he's been drinking."

"Who's the other man?"

"A friend of Ricci's," he said curtly. He walked to the drive. Ricci spoke loudly to John in Italian. He held on to the car with one hand to steady himself, pointed to his companion, and then shook the same finger at John.

John put up both hands and said, "*Aspetta, aspetta.*" He walked quickly back to the table. Jeanne stood up.

"I'm so sorry—this is going to take a while. Do you mind waiting?" His face was tense and his eyes were hard and determined.

"Is everything all right?"

"Sure, just a misunderstanding."

"I'll wait."

John spoke to Ricci and his companion. They murmured quietly for a moment before following John into the house.

It was five in the afternoon, eight in the morning in Los Angeles. She decided to make the call she'd been putting off. She took out her phone, found the number, and dialed.

"Cardiology Associates," a young man's voice chirped.

"Dr. Dahlberg, please."

"One moment, please."

"Jeanne? I thought you were in Italy?" He sounded older on the telephone. "What's the matter?"

"I feel worse."

"Hmm. Worse how?"

"Well, my feet and ankles are still swollen. I don't think the water pills are working."

"Okay, what else?"

"I get dizzy if I bend down. I get my stomach cramps when I exert myself even a little and sometimes I can hardly breathe. I thought the medicine was supposed to help, all those pills you have me taking."

"Sometimes they do. In your case, I'd say they aren't slowing the progression of the constrictive pericarditis."

"Are there other medicines I can try?"

"Nope."

"So what now? Surgery?"

"It's the only way," he said, his voice low and sympathetic. Her eyes began to water.

"If I don't?"

"Jeanne, we talked about this. You'll get sicker."

"How soon?"

"No way to know. Maybe a year."

"Okay. Thanks. Sorry." She forced herself to sound calm. "Where would I do it?"

"Cleveland. Number one cardiac hospital in the world. But first, enjoy the rest of your vacation. You'll have days you feel well, days you'll feel bad. We'll make the arrangements when you get back."

"Thank you, Doctor. Goodbye."

The sun was lower in the sky now. The scent of the flowers and trees was overwhelmingly sweet. She didn't want to leave Casale Leonardo. Someone opened the front door of the house and angry voices pierced the peaceful atmosphere. The dark thin man strode to the passenger side of the car. John was close behind him, talking and gesticulating. The man ignored him. He opened the car door. He turned back and said one word to John, who stopped talking immediately. The man got into the car and closed the door.

She pretended she was looking at her phone but kept her eye on them.

John glanced in her direction. She gave him a little wave. He waved back, then turned to the house where Ricci had emerged, still weaving and stumbling. Instead of heading to the car, he swayed toward the table.

"Eugene?" he slurred, coming closer to her.

"What?"

"You Jeanne?" he asked again.

"Yes."

He nodded and smiled as though everything about her added up exactly. John came up quickly and put a hand on Ricci's shoulder. "Your friend is waiting, you should get going," he said in English.

Ricci twisted clumsily away. He said to John while still looking at her, "You make a pretty big mistake in there, Jack."

"My mistake to make," John said, his voice cool.

Ricci shrugged, trying to focus his eyes. He was weaving now as though he were standing on the rolling deck of a ship. "This her, huh?"

John took a step toward Ricci. "Don't be disrespectful or I'll knock your teeth in."

Ricci started laughing. "You and who else, old man?"

"Get out of here," John said, coloring with embarrassment. "Get out. Now!"

His words seemed to penetrate the haze of drink. Ricci put his hands up. "Sure, boss, sure." He was still chuckling as he moved toward the car. As he did, he muttered, "*La ricca vedova. Lo pagherà tutto.*" He laughed louder as if he had told a very funny joke.

As he neared the car, he made a little song of the words, singing them over and over. He stabbed at the chrome handle of the car door. After several tries, he managed to open it and poured himself inside. The car coughed and started. It whirled rapidly around in a circle and sped away.

She was shaken. "What was all the arguing about?"

"Money."

"Are you in some kind of trouble?"

"No, no. I had to take out a loan to finish the place. Ricci helped me get the loan."

"Are you behind?"

"No, nothing like that. Signor Barone, the man with Ricci, represents the lender and came to discuss terms. The first payment is due next month and I asked for an extension because of the delayed opening. I'll make the payment or get another loan if I have to. When I get the advance from the publisher, it'll cover me the first couple of months till the place starts paying for itself."

He smiled convincingly. She almost believed him.

"What was that he was saying there at the end? Is that his last name, Vedova?"

"What?"

"As he was leaving, he kept saying, 'Ricci Vedova,' like he was telling a joke or something."

"No," he said, his face blank. "I've always known him as Ricci Capotosti. Which means, Ricky Hard Head." He changed the subject. "I'm sure you need to get back, but can I offer you something first? That was kind of an ordeal and I made you wait. Tea, maybe?"

She didn't want to leave. "I'd like that."

He pushed open the heavy door to the kitchen and they went in. Antonio was washing dishes. John bustled around, filling the kettle, setting it on the stove, and placing cookies on a blue glazed plate. He left the room. She moved to the window, looking out over the garden and the olive grove beyond.

"Good afternoon, signora. Did you enjoy the lunch?"

"Very much. Antonio, you must know Ricci."

"Sure. My uncle."

"Did you ever hear him called 'Ricci Vedova'?"

A puzzled look came over Antonio. "*Vedova*, signora?"

"Sì," she laughed, "yes."

"No, never heard that." He was washing pots now. Over his shoulder, he said, "*'Vedova' significa* . . . uh . . . *una donna.*"

"'Donna'—you mean a woman? It's a word for woman?"

"Yes, woman, no man—he *morta.*" He pulled a finger across his throat.

"Dead, you mean? Who's dead?"

"The man. Her husband dead. That's '*vedova.*'"

"A widow?"

His lips carefully formed the word. "Widow." He smiled brightly and nodded as he left.

Now she was even more confused. Why would he call himself Ricci Widow? Well, it wasn't much odder than Ricky Hard Head. She froze. He hadn't been saying "Ricci"; he had been saying "*ricca*"—rich. He had been laughing and calling her "the rich widow." The one who would pay *tutto*—everything.

He could only have heard that from one person. That was what this whole thing was about—why John had gone to all this trouble. It had nothing to do with writing a book. It was money he was looking for, not love—solving his present problems, not resolving their past. She was hot with anger, at him for trying to fool her and at herself for almost letting him.

John came back in the kitchen. The kettle was whistling. He scooped loose tea into the teapot and poured in the steaming water.

"John," she said stiffly. "Could you call me a taxi?"

"What's going on?"

"I need to meet Alice. I forgot we had plans. I should have been back an hour ago."

"I'll take you. What's wrong?"

"Nothing. I told you." She started to the door.

His eyes were puzzled. "Of course."

She forced a pleasant look on her face as they walked out of the house to his car. She would be sweet and gracious for every one of the hundred and however many curves it took them to drive back to her hotel. Let that be his last memory of her. That would be their coda; that would be their end.

35

Michael hadn't spoken to Kerry since they left Rome, although she had called him several times. He had been hiding in his hotel room except for a short conversation with his mother after her visit with John.

Alice banged on his door. He told her to go away, but she yelled through the door, "I'm not going away until you tell me what's going on."

"What do you mean?" he said, opening the door, scratching the three-day beard growth on his chin and adjusting his wrinkled pajamas.

"What do you mean what do I mean?" she shouted, advancing on him. "I'm not an idiot. You won't talk to us, you won't leave your room, you won't talk to Mom."

He retreated out the sliding door onto the terrace. She pursued him. He shuffled his bare feet on the hot tile and made an effort to throw off the inertia and lassitude that had straitjacketed him since Rome.

"Did your mom say something?" He squinted in the bright sun.

Alice shook her head. "Just you hadn't answered her messages. She wants us to see her rehearsal today."

"I don't think so."

"Why not?"

The weight of her attention pressed on him. "It's hard to explain."

"Try." She crossed her arms.

"You know, well, your mom and I are . . . well, aren't together."

"You're separated," she said.

"Kind of. It doesn't mean we're going to get divorced. But when you're separated, it's hard to know what . . . it can be difficult . . . There aren't any rules."

"Rules for what?" she asked.

"For how you're supposed to act."

She uncrossed her arms and eyed him skeptically. This was more difficult than he had imagined. "I guess I mean rules for what you're not supposed to do."

Her face relaxed into understanding. "Like flirting with your costar?"

"What? No," he said, although that was exactly what he meant.

"Yes, it is. It's so obvious. But do you really think Mom would fool around with such an obvious player? Sure, he's good-looking and talented and rich—"

He exhaled loudly.

"You know what I mean. And besides, she loves you."

Michael's hope spiked but faded quickly. It was a daughter's wishful thinking. Children always hope their parents are better than they appear to be, especially when they're at their worst. He'd been the same with his father.

"You're just being paranoid," she said. "Mom's not like that."

"This isn't just a suspicion. I know something's going on with them." He willed her to understand what he meant without saying the words.

"What do you mean?"

He looked down and shrugged. He put his arms around her tentatively. She didn't resist but didn't respond, either. They stood like that in the sun. "Let's go inside," he said. "Let me get you something to drink."

When they were inside, he gave her a chilled bottle of water. She asked, "What are you going to do, Dad?"

He was touched that his difficult daughter thought he had the answers. It gave him the courage to do the right thing. He made a decision. "I love your mom. This would be a lot easier if I didn't. Let's go to Spoleto for the rehearsal, like she wants. I'm through hiding out. Afterwards, she and I will have a talk."

Alice looked frightened.

"Just the two of us." He put his hands on her shoulders. "Whatever happens, honey, we love you, okay?"

She nodded.

"Okay." He tried to smile. "Wait outside. Meet you in the lobby in twenty minutes."

Later, as they drove to Spoleto, Michael asked casually, "Did your grandma tell you about the big date?"

Alice shook her head. "No, just she was glad to have seen him. Doesn't sound like she's going to see him again."

"No, I don't think so, either." His mother had told him all about her visit with John.

"And she talked to that professor guy yesterday," Alice said. "I think they're going to see Mom's opera Saturday."

An hour later, Michael sat beside his daughter on marble steps in the shade of the portico of the Teatro Nuovo in the ancient Roman city of Spoleto, Umbria. It was a sunny Thursday morning, June 26, a few days before the Festival dei Due Mondi, the Festival of Two Worlds, was to commence. The wooden doors of the building were closed and an ancient usher in a mulberry-colored uniform stood guard in the center of the three entrance archways. When they tried to enter earlier, he told them in a mix of Italian and English that they would not be permitted inside until the bell of the clock tower in the nearby Piazza del Mercato sounded the hour.

The clock in the square struck eleven. Without a glance in their direction, the superannuated usher did a slow *voltafaccia*, and marched into the colonnaded marble hall. They followed. Once inside, he handed them each a program, pointed at two red, thick-cushioned seats near the back of the orchestra section, and left the hall, his hard leather heels clicking on the highly polished wood floor.

The eight-hundred-seat theater was a gorgeous jewel box with four elaborately decorated tiers ringing the main floor. Several rows from the stage, the director and his various assistants sat at a long table piled with papers, electronic equipment, and computer monitors. The back of the conductor's head was just visible in the orchestra pit. Michael and Alice were the only ones in the audience. As they took their seats, the first notes of the overture sounded.

Michael had seen the opera before and was passingly familiar with the plot and characters. He glanced through a synopsis in the program and was struck anew by its naked cynicism. Two young soldiers in the Neapolitan army are in love with two sisters, Fiordiligi and Dorabella. The men are inveigled by an old roué into putting their love to the test. The three secretly wager that the girls can be persuaded to surrender their virtue to the other's lover. The soldiers part tearfully from the women, then return in what we must assume are very convincing disguises as wealthy Albanians to woo each other's intended. The women soon fall for their new boyfriends and make ready to wed them. At the last moment—a moment too late for Dorabella's virtue—they reveal the truth.

Michael tried to appreciate the irony of watching his wife perform with her lover in a musical celebration of endemic infidelity. He toughed out the love scenes between Kerry and Toljy in the first act. Things got easier later when Kerry was wooed by Toljy's counterpart, played by a portly baritone. Michael felt an illogical satisfaction in watching Kerry betray Toljy.

Kerry, costumed in a flowing re-creation of an eighteenth-century gown, was far more nervous than he had ever seen her. She had several stumbles in an early ensemble piece and the conductor stopped the rehearsal each time.

"Kerry," Nelson began.

"I know," she interrupted. "Early, right?"

"Yes. Sharp too. Try it again." He signaled the downbeat and they began, but he stopped them almost immediately.

"Listen to the other singers."

Kerry nodded and they began again.

Kerry's voice had a quality Michael had always loved. Despite the trained operatic tones, she somehow managed to sound warm, friendly even, as though she was simply talking to you. Whenever Kerry launched into a tricky solo, Michael found himself nervously hoping she would succeed as though he were a sports fan rooting for a favorite athlete. After her early mistakes, she seemed to relax and her voice grew fuller and stronger. Alice played with her phone during much of the performance but looked up whenever Kerry was singing.

When the rehearsal was over, Michael and Alice waited outside and Kerry emerged a short while later. She had scrubbed the stage makeup from her face and her hair was in a tight bun. "I'm so glad you came," she said.

Alice crossed her arms and said nothing.

"You looked great," Michael said, just to be saying something.

"Ah, but did I sound great?"

"Absolutely," he said automatically, knowing from experience that the last thing an artist needs from a family member is an objective critique.

"There's a café around the corner," she said. "Should we get a coffee or something?"

"Sure," Michael said. "If you have time."

"We have a vocal run-through in an hour, just to smooth out some of the rough spots—meaning me," she said glumly.

"I didn't hear any rough spots," Michael said.

She looked surprised. "You're sweet. Come on, it's this way." Kerry led them through the rising heat to a small café with outdoor tables. Alice trailed behind, her earbuds in.

Michael walked inside and ordered their drinks. He emerged several minutes later with a tray—coffee for him and Kerry, Orangina and a glass of ice for Alice. They sat in silence, sipping their drinks, each apparently waiting for the other to say something. Alice was the first to speak. "Since I have you both here, I wanted to tell you—ask you, I mean—something. Um, my friend Geoffrey and his sister Lydia, you know, from New York?"

"The boy you got arrested with?" Kerry said.

Alice rolled her eyes. "Yes, Mom, the master criminal who got busted with one whole joint."

Kerry reddened.

"Anyway, they're staying with their parents in a house near Florence. They invited me to go with them to Sienna to see the Palio—it's a kind of a horse race. Some of the kids I met in Rome are taking the train up. I really want to go."

"Where would you stay?" Michael said.

"I could share with Lydia. They have an apartment in Sienna."

Kerry looked at Michael, indicating with a glance it was up to him.

He nodded and said, "We'd need the details, the parents' phone numbers and such, addresses where you'll be staying, and you have to promise to respond to us when we text you, day or night, no matter how annoying we are."

Kerry shot him a look.

"Oh, right, and you have to be here for your mom's opening night on Saturday."

Alice was excited. "Really, I can go? Thank you, thank you, thank you." She didn't look at Kerry. "And I'll be here Saturday. I don't need to leave till Sunday." She gave Michael a long hug.

"It's so nice to see you two getting along so well," Kerry said.

"Why wouldn't we?" Alice asked, bristling.

"It's been a while since you spent time together."

"And whose fault is that?" Alice shot back.

"No one's fault," Kerry said, seemingly confused by Alice's hostility.

"Yes, it is. It's your fault. You're the one made us move away and stuck me in a shitty girls' school." She jumped to her feet and shouted, "And now you're hooking up with that asshole Russian." She knocked over her glass as she left, the watery orange contents of which spilled on Kerry.

"Alice!" Kerry said, surprised and angry.

Michael put his hand lightly on her arm.

"He's not Russian, he's Latvian," Kerry said.

"That's the least important part of what she just said. She won't go far. She needs time to cool off."

"I have to talk to her," Kerry said angrily and shook off his hand. They both stood up.

"Fine, go," he said.

She took one or two uncertain steps, then returned to stand by the table. She grabbed a napkin and tried to blot the liquid on her skirt.

"Did you tell her that, Michael?"

"What?" he said, his eyes sliding away.

"That I'm having an affair with Toljy."

He hated her saying his name. "Are you?"

"Come on!"

"That's not an answer."

She glared at him. "I can't believe you would even think that."

"Again, not exactly an answer."

"Oh, Michael. You have a couple of good days with your daughter and the first thing you do is turn her against me? You tell her I'm fooling around with that slick sleazeball."

"Just answer the damn question."

Her cheeks were crimson and her breath came rapidly. She took a step back and raised her voice. "If you think the way to get your daughter's affection is to make her hate me, you have bigger problems than I thought." She walked away.

"Kerry," he called.

Over her shoulder, she shouted, "You had no business bringing Alice into this."

Hopeless now, he let fly the hateful arrow he'd had notched since Rome, tipped with the sulfurous poison that had been brewing in his gut for days.

"I saw him leave your room at five in the morning. Don't make it worse by lying." He hated her for making him say it.

She turned and looked at him, her expression a mixture of surprise and pity.

"I don't understand you. Maybe I never did." She walked around the corner toward the theater.

36

Jack sat in the dark, cool office of the manager of the Banca Monte dei Paschi di Siena on the south end of the Todi's Piazza del Popolo, his hands folded in his lap. The bank manager, Signor Pelligrini, was a heavy-set man with thick cheeks and salt-and-pepper hair. A third man, an *avvocato*, was reading lengthy passages from a thick stack of documents spread on the manager's desk and explained their meaning in slow, polysyllabic Italian.

Once Antonio had explained to him what Ricci had said to Jeanne after their lunch, Jack had made the difficult decision to sell Casale Leonardo. Selling was the best way to convince her that he wanted to be with her and it had nothing to do with the house or her money. At the same time, it would settle his debt to Signor Barone, his lender, the man who had accompanied Ricci to the house.

"Can I interrupt, please?" Jack said to the lawyer who was from a firm of criminal defense attorneys in Milan that handled Barone's legal affairs. His face was angular, bisected by a dark slash of a mustache under a long, thin nose. He had tiny, wide-set eyes that peered through gold wire rim glasses.

The lawyer's flow of words ground to a reluctant halt. He raised his eyes. "Yes?" he responded, pained by the interruption.

"If I go through with this and sell my house to Signor Barone, it is understood that he releases me from the five hundred thousand euro loan. It will extinguish the debt, correct?"

The lawyer pushed his glasses up his nose. "Yes, that is so."

"And he'll pay me a quarter of a million in addition?"

The lawyer considered this carefully and said, "One hundred thousand euro in addition, no more."

"A total of six hundred thousand? That's less than half of what the house is worth. He must pay more."

The lawyer and the bank manager exchanged glances. The lawyer spoke.

"This is not a negotiation, signore. If it is not sufficient, don't sell."

"Maybe I won't," Jack said. But this was bluster. As much as he hated to lose his home, he was going to sell.

Neither of the other men responded.

"Fine," Jack went on, "let's complete the papers. But"—he waved a finger at the lawyer—"you tell Barone I get a week. We don't close the deal until next Saturday, the fifth of July. I won't sign the deed until then. I can still try to find someone who will pay me a fair price for the house."

Signor Pelligrini spread his large hands. "Yes, of course, I will ask, but, Signor Jack, to be realistic . . . it would have to be a buyer willing to cross Signor Barone." He shook his head.

"Right. Let's finish this." At least when this sale went through, he'd be free of debt, free of Ricci and Barone, would even have a hundred thousand euro in the bank. And Jeanne would know the house had nothing to do with the two of them.

Jack signed the papers except for the deed. Pelligrini, using a variety of wood-handled stamps and red, green, and black ink pads, stamped them in numerous places with such vigor his cheeks shook. When he was finished, Jack walked outside and stood on the gray stones of the piazza, just outside the brassbound door of the bank. He dug the toe of his boot into a crack in a paver stone. He had used stones just like it to finish one of the floors of his house.

He walked across the piazza to the steps of the cathedral a few hundred feet away and drifted inside. Its elaborate decoration was the antithesis of the plain stone church he attended with his family as a child in Chicago. They went mostly on Christmas and Easter, but sometimes, on hot, sticky summer days, he and his friends would duck inside to cool off. They would sit in the rear, sweat drying on their backs, watching old women in headscarves walk slowly to the confessionals, then emerge and say a rosary. He wondered if he should pray.

He went outside. After getting a sip of water from a continuously running fountain, he began the fifteen-minute walk to Jeanne's hotel. As he walked along the downward-curving street, past rows of tall cypress trees, he rehearsed what he would say—if she would see him. He wouldn't tell her about selling the house, not until it was final.

He entered the hotel's elaborate lobby and asked the clerk to ring her room.

"There is no answer," the clerk told him. "Any message?"

He shook his head and turned to leave but stopped when he saw a familiar man seated on a sofa. He was the only other person in the lobby. They looked at each other.

"You? You're the guy from the bar in Rome," Michael said.

Jack nodded. "Michael, right?"

"Yeah," Michael said. "You're Jack?"

Jack managed a smile. "That's me."

"What are you doing here?" Michael asked.

"I live near here. How about you?"

"Just part of our tour of Italy."

Jack walked to where Michael was sitting and stood over him.

"How did it go with you and your wife?" Jack asked.

Michael shook his head glumly. "Not good," he said softly. "I don't think she wants to be with me."

"That's rough," Jack said. "You giving up?"

Michael looked as though he was about to cry. He shook his head, his lips pressed together, then said, "No. I can't give her up."

Jack fished for something else to say. "So why Todi?"

"I'm traveling with my mom. She was supposed to meet a friend of hers she knew in the States, a guy who lives here."

Jack froze. "What guy?"

"Someone she knew years ago."

"His name, what's his name?"

"Uh, John McGrath."

"You're Michael. Jeanne's son."

"Yeah."

Jack laughed.

"What's funny?"

"*I'm* John McGrath."

Michael looked at him suspiciously. "Thought your name was Jack."

"That's what most people call me. But your mother still calls me John."

"This is unbelievable."

"I thought you looked familiar. You probably don't remember, but we met a long time ago. In LA," he said.

Michael stiffened. "I don't think so."

"No? Well, like I said, it was a long time ago."

There was an awkward silence.

"Can I buy you a drink or something? I seem to remember I owe you one," Jack finally said.

"No, thanks," Michael said coldly. "I'm just waiting for my daughter. She'll be here in a minute."

"Alice?"

"Right."

"Can I ask you a favor?" Jack said.

"No, you can't ask me for a favor," Michael burst out. He stood up. "You drag my mother here for some big romantic reunion and all along you just wanted her money? She was so hurt. So, fuck you, Jack, or whatever your name is. Fuck you." He said it loudly enough the clerk at reception looked up.

Jack was silent.

"I told her all along this trip was a mistake. I just knew you were full of shit," Michael continued. "She shouldn't be traveling anyway, and then all this . . . this disappointment."

"Michael, calm down."

"Who the hell are you to tell me to calm down."

"Listen, I want . . . I came here to talk to her."

"No way."

"I just need to talk to her."

"She won't now she knows what you're after."

"But she's wrong."

"What's that supposed to mean?"

"It was a misunderstanding. Please don't tell her, but I'm selling my house."

Michael eyed him carefully. "Yeah?"

Jack nodded.

Jack took a step toward Michael. "All I want is the chance to talk to her. Help me."

"Why should I?"

"I love her. You know better than most people love needs all the help it can get."

"Forget it," Michael said and started to walk off.

"Michael."

He stopped and turned.

"What did you mean when you said she shouldn't be traveling? Is she sick or something?"

"No, no, just . . . you know, it's not good for anybody," Michael said. "She's getting up there, you know." He was flustered. "I mean, you are, too, but . . ."

"Come on, I have to know."

"You're really selling that house? You're not after money?" Michael said.

"I just came from a meeting with the buyer's lawyer."

Michael considered, then said, "She went to Assisi, but she'll be in Spoleto Saturday afternoon, to see my wife . . . to see Kerry in her opera."

"Thanks."

"She's going to be with a guy, uh, Ernest."

"What's he like?"

"He's a history professor from England."

"What's he doing in Italy?"

"Co-teaching a summer class at the university in Perugia."

"Perugia? With who?"

"I don't know. He said the name at dinner, but . . . oh, wait, it was a woman, Benny something."

"Benedetta?'

"Maybe."

"Small world."

"So that's your competition," Michael said.

Jack shrugged.

Michael smiled a little. "Not worried?"

"Nope."

"I wish I was as confident as you."

"Michael, sometimes if you act like the man you want to be, there's a decent chance no one'll notice you're not."

Just then, a young woman came in the lobby, her hair still wet from the pool.

"Aren't you John McGrath?" she asked.

"I thought you went to Assisi with your grandma," Michael said.

Alice smiled. "No, I got out of that. She went with Ernest."

Michael exchanged a glance with Jack.

"You're Jeanne's granddaughter, Alice?" John said.

Her face brightened. "That's right, Alice."

"How did you know who I was?" Jack said.

"She had a picture."

"She did, huh?"

"Yes. She talks about you all the time."

"Does she?"

"Oh, sure."

"Good things?" he said.

"Lots. That trip to New York, meeting you later; I was so happy she was going to see you again."

"Really? Did she talk about our visit this week?" He gave Michael a sidelong glance.

Alice shook her head. "Not much. She said you took her to your house, that it's beautiful. It sounded like you had a nice time."

"I thought so. Did she say anything else?"

"Not really." Her forehead wrinkled. "When are you going to see her again?"

"I don't know."

"Why not?"

"Well, you could say we had kind of a fight, but it was really just a misunderstanding."

"A fight?" Alice looked as though she found it hard to believe that two people as old as they could fight about anything important.

"Yes." He looked at the pretty teenager. Why not be honest? "She seems to have gotten the idea that I asked her here to get her to invest in my project, you know, turning the farmhouse into an inn."

"Why would she think that?"

He looked embarrassed. "Just something someone said."

"But it's not true?"

"No."

"So tell her."

"I would, but she won't talk to me."

"That's silly."

"Well, I kind of have a history of disappointing her," he said. "Love gets more complicated when you're older."

"Yeah, I've been hearing that a lot lately." She glanced at her dad. "Are you gonna fix it?"

"I'm going to try. I'm selling the house."

"What?"

"I just came from arranging it at my bank," he said. "I need her to know that this isn't about money or about the house or what she can do for me. It's about us. And I'll go anywhere in the world to be with her."

"Wow."

"But do me a favor, don't say anything. Let me be the one to tell her once it's final."

Alice nodded as Michael interjected. "Honey, we better get going."

She said over her shoulder as they left, "I hope it works."

37

When Jeanne called Ernest the day after the disastrous conclusion of her visit with John, the first thing he asked was whether she planned to see John again.

"No, I really don't think so," she'd answered, trying to sound casual. "It was nice to catch up, but I'm not sure there's much more to say."

"Not much of a connection between a newly minted Italian *signor* and a rich American widow?"

She paused. "A what?"

"Sorry, just an expression."

"Well, I don't like it. That's what John's man Ricci said about me."

"Really? Oh, dear, I—" He rushed to change the subject. "So you took care of your unfinished business, then?"

"I told you there wasn't any unfinished business," she said lightly, though she was still disturbed by his comment.

"So you did."

"Didn't you believe me?"

"Let's just say I respected your right to tell me or not tell me as you thought fit. After all, you barely knew me."

"Then let me say, yes, there were some things I wanted to know and, yes, I found those out."

"And was it . . . I don't know, did it leave you feeling as you wished?"

"Yes. Much better than I'd hoped." She couldn't tell Ernest that John had wanted to see her only to persuade her to invest in his project. It was too humiliating.

"Good for you," Ernest had said without conviction. She wished she could see his face. "Then why not see him again?"

"I just don't think there would be much point," she had said. "Ernest, I know we said goodbye already, but I was thinking of taking a trip to Assisi on Thursday. I was wondering if you might like to come with me?"

"I feel like I'm being pursued," he said.

"I'm sorry."

"Don't be. It's quite pleasant."

"So?"

"I would be delighted." And so, they had gone. At the end of their day in the ancient Franciscan town, he had said, "There is something I'd like to tell you."

"Why not hold it and tell me when we see each other Saturday?" she had said.

"We're seeing each other Saturday?" Ernest said, surprised.

"I hope so."

• • •

On Saturday, they drove to Spoleto to see the premiere of Kerry's opera. They were early, so they took a short walking tour of the city's historic center ending at the twelfth-century Spoleto Cathedral.

"Remember, I did have something to tell you," he said.

"What is it?"

"Something about your friend I thought you should know." He said "your friend" as though there were quotation marks around it.

"About John?"

"I'd better explain. Should we sit?" he asked, indicating a wooden bench along a high stone wall in the Piazza Duomo.

"Do I need to?"

He gave an odd laugh and shook his head. "No, of course not, but, well, here goes."

They sat and for a moment watched the weekend crowd of people milling through the plaza.

"You might remember I'm co-teaching a class this summer at the university in Perugia," he continued.

"Yes, of course."

"My co-professor is a local *professoressa* named Benedetta Giambattisti. I just wanted to mention . . . Um, this is a bit difficult. Something I said. The other day on the telephone?"

"Yes?"

"You seemed upset, or, I don't know, put off when I used a certain phrase, describing you as a—"

"A 'rich widow'? I remember."

"Ah, yes, that's the one."

"So?"

"Yes, well, it's curious, but Benedetta reminded me, uh, that I myself used that phrase to describe you to her." His face was growing increasingly red and blotchy. "She told me that when she mentioned you to Ricci, Mr. McGrath's *geometra*, she repeated that phrase to him. She asked Ricci if that was why your friend had arranged your visit."

"What?"

"So, you see, I—" His face was completely red and damp now. "It was me. I said that. I didn't mean anything by it, you understand. Stupid, I'm so sorry."

"I see."

"But it seems that was why Ricci used those words when you were there at the house, not because, well, probably not because of anything Mr. McGrath would have told him about you."

"I see," she said again.

"I thought it only fair that you be in possession of all of the facts."

"Why?" She was curious.

"Jeanne, I haven't known you long, but I think well of you, very well indeed. In spite of, perhaps even because of, our *contretemps* in Rome."

"Because of?"

"The way you were after, your kindness. I wish you nothing but happiness, whether with Mr. McGrath, or . . . someone else, or on your own."

"Thank you."

"And I'm grateful to you." A smile creased his round face.

"Really?"

"Oh, yes. After my wife passed away, I was quite sure I would be alone for what remained of my life. But because of our brief time together, I

know that isn't true. I've been 'recalled to life,' as the writer says," he finished, looking at her pointedly.

"Thackeray, Professor?"

"Hardly."

"George Eliot, then."

"Now you're just playing," he said, though he managed to look superior.
She smiled enigmatically.

"Dickens, of course," he said finally.

"Ah, yes. *David Copperfield*." She didn't change her expression.

"You're teasing."

"You'll never know for sure."

"At any rate, I wanted you to know the truth about your friend."

"Oh, for goodness' sakes, stop calling him that!" she burst out.

Ernest drew back. "What?"

She looked off into the distance again. "I'm sorry. I know it's fashionable to say your lover is your best friend, but—"

His mouth tightened and he hunched his shoulders.

"We were in love, passionately. At least, I was. And there is a 'great
gulf fixed' between that kind of romantic love and 'friendship.'" Now
she was the one speaking with quote marks in her voice and making a
literary allusion.

He nodded knowingly. "I understand."

She looked at him, straight-faced but with raised eyebrows.

"Wordsworth?" he said finally.

She shook her head. "Nope."

His look became one of scholarly doubt. "Not Milton, I don't think."

"Warmer."

His face had a look of pedantic agony. "Well," he said, giving up for
the moment, "whatever the source, I suppose one has to decide what kind
of love one prefers, especially at our age."

She laughed. "You think we get to decide what kind of love comes to
us?" He didn't answer. "Nope. You get what you get and you should be
glad of it."

"Perhaps you're right."

She put a hand on his. "Let's walk a little more. There's still an hour until the opera begins. Perhaps if you buy me a gelato, I'll tell you the source of that quote."

He nodded his consent. They began a slow, comfortable stroll through the narrow streets whose multistoried buildings shaded them from the sun. She was breathing heavily when they arrived at the theater.

"Are you all right?" he asked.

"Sure," she said quickly. "Just haven't been getting enough exercise on this trip." She gave what she hoped was a convincing chuckle. "And I've been eating way too much."

"Jeanne," a voice said from the inner shadows of the theater's portico, "can we talk?" It was John. He stepped into the late afternoon sunlight.

She took a deep breath. "There's nothing you might say that I want to hear."

"Just give me a moment to explain."

"Sir—" Ernest began, but Jeanne stopped him.

"It's all right, Ernest. John, that's the third time I let you hurt me. Three times you've done it," she said. "You're out."

She took Ernest's arm and they walked past John through the door of the theater. She didn't look back.

38

Saturday evening had crept up on her and Kerry felt hopelessly unprepared. Nothing in her fifteen years of performing had readied her for the overwhelming anxiety that gripped her. Thirty minutes to curtain and her stomach burned, her hands shook, her throat was sore, and her nose was stuffed. She could barely make a musical sound.

She sat restlessly on a metal folding chair, staring into a cracked mirror in the bare dressing room she shared with the soprano who played Fiordiligi, and the Romanian girl who played the maid, Despina. She longed to test her voice but didn't want to reveal her dilemma to them. They were sure to run to Nelson with gleeful malice.

The fact that her family was in the audience—that she might fail in front of them—tortured her. Michael would probably think of it as karmic vengeance. She had to find out who Toljy had been with in her room. It was the only way to convince Michael it wasn't her. Her money was on the Romanian.

Half an hour remained before showtime. She made a quick decision. She was in wig and makeup but not yet in costume. She headed down the stairs and out of the building through a rear door. She went around the corner to the café where she, Michael, and Alice had gone. The tables outside were full, but no one else was inside. She ordered hot tea with lemon and honey. While she waited for it to steep, she opened her mouth and forced air through her larynx, just trying to make a clear tone. Her voice was fine only a few hours ago! How could it have gotten so bad so quickly? It had to be nerves. Well, tea was good for those, too. Maybe a glass of wine? No, she had to stay focused. She poured some tea, but it was still too hot. She added honey and lemon and began running quiet scales to warm her vocal cords.

There was no question of not performing. There were no "covers" as there would be in a major opera house, no one to substitute in at the last minute. She would have to sing. But should she inform the conductor of her condition so that an announcement could be made to the audience? It was a way of begging their indulgence should she hit a false note. It was commonly done and she had often suspected that some singers did it just to raise the tension—would the singer crack or wouldn't she?—and increase the audience's enthusiastic admiration when the plucky star made it through the performance perfectly, as they usually did.

She finished her tea and set the cup down. No announcement. She didn't want Nelson to think she couldn't stand the pressure. She tried a few phrases, finishing on a brief high note. The proprietor gave a sharp clap, but she was unsure if it was congratulatory or admonitory. It didn't matter. The short notes were easy—it was the solos that would be the real test. She stood up. Her voice was nowhere near ready, but it would have to do.

She left the café and made her way to the theater, slipping in through the rear entrance. Her roommates were already dressed and on their way out. They left without a word.

She crossed to the closet, pulled out her dress, and slipped it on. Having her family in the audience made her especially aware of how low the neckline was. The stage manager announced ten minutes to curtain. With a final look in the mirror, she walked out of the dressing room and made her way through the backstage shadows to her entrance. She stood there in the dark and emptied her mind of everything but the details of her performance. The burbling sounds of the audience vibrated the wood floor. Suddenly, two arms were around her waist. A body pressed hard against her from behind. Toljy!

"Let me go!" she said in a loud whisper. He kissed her neck while one of his hands lasciviously caressed her nearly uncovered breasts. Her nostrils filled with the unpleasant aroma of musky cologne and heavy stage makeup. She froze, cramped with fear and nausea, then stamped on his instep with her pointed heel.

He gave a high bark of surprise mixed with pain.

"Don't ever touch me again," she said, drawing out the words in a high, clear voice.

He nodded slowly, palms up in surrender, and gave a crooked smile. "It was a mistake," he said. "No more. My apologies."

"Five minutes," the stage manager called out.

"While you're feeling so sorry, tell me who you had in my room in Rome? My husband heard you and thought it was me. He's ready to file for divorce."

Toljy chuckled. "It was the woman from where we eat."

"What?"

"You remember. From the restaurant."

"The waitress? But you just met her."

He shrugged as though to say that was hardly an obstacle. "He must love you very much to be so jealous."

The ovation for the conductor sounded.

"I must go," he said. "They cannot begin without me." For once, this wasn't egoism. Toljy's character had the first line in the opera. He limped badly as he walked away, which brought a smile to her face.

•••

A half hour later, in the middle of a key ensemble, her voice cracked for the third time. Nelson looked at her with concern. If only she could rest for a while. But now she had to sing her goodbye duet with Toljy as she saw him off to "war." She and Toljy embraced. During rehearsals, he had usually taken the opportunity to grab her in inappropriate places, but not this time.

He whispered in her ear. "Your voice is all right?" She held him in the embrace and whispered back, "A little weak. Just nerves, I think."

"Never worry, I will cover you," he said. Throughout their parting duet, he sang louder than usual, occasionally singing the same melody as her rather than his harmony, which covered any imperfections in her pitch and tone. She gave Toljy a grateful glance as he waved goodbye and boarded the boat onstage and sailed away. People could surprise you. She didn't have time to dwell on Toljy, though. She launched into her ensemble with Fiordiligi, Don Alfonso, and Despina. She continued singing lightly despite Nelson's signals imploring her to turn up the volume. She had to preserve her voice for her solo in the next scene.

After a quick set change, it was time for her aria. She strode forward until she was at the edge of the pit, facing the audience. This was it. Nelson's eyes were big as the orchestra swung into the swirling undercurrent to Dorabella's song about her suicidal grief at parting from her love. The song lasted over three minutes and was a difficult test for her tender voice. The first time through the melody, singers were expected to sing it as written. The second time through, the singer was supposed to add ornamentation and embellishments. A singer who wasn't capable of those would simply sing the aria as written and could then look forward to a minor career.

Kerry sang through the song's first iteration exactly to the written tempo and melody. As she neared the end, she saw Nelson shake his head, signaling her not to try to add anything the second time through. *Don't risk it*, his eyes seemed to say. But this was her chance. She let her voice go full out and employed every ornament she knew to increase the beauty and thrill of the song.

Near the end, Dorabella sings that she may die from sorrow. Inspired to improvise, Kerry grabbed a large wooden spoon from a table on the set and held it to her chest like a dagger. As she sang the penultimate line, she mimed plunging it into her heart, stuck out her tongue, and crossed her eyes. She was rewarded with a respectable laugh. There was a pause in the music, which Nelson held until the laughs subsided. With raised eyebrows, he asked her if she were ready to continue. She nodded and sang her last line, building to, hitting, and holding her final high notes cleanly, clearly, perfectly. As she finished, she fell to her knees, still holding the spoon as though it were stuck in her chest, dropped on her back, stuck her legs in the air, then let them fall slowly as she held her last note. The applause and shouts of "brava" swept through the ornate hall before the orchestra stopped playing.

The string players were banging their instruments, a sure sign that those expert musicians approved of her performance. Even Nelson was clapping. He motioned her to rise, which she did slowly and gave a curtsy that only seemed to increase the audience's fervor. She bowed as far as she could without her breasts spilling out of her dress. Nelson raised his arms but was forced to hold them there a while longer until he was finally able to recommence the music.

At intermission, Toljy came to her side immediately. "I may hug you?"

"Like a brother," she said.

He gave her a quick hug and a peck on the cheek. "You were magnificent. Your colleagues are quite jealous." He walked off.

Nelson was right behind him. He took her hands. "You had me worried. Are you sick?"

"No, no. Just nerves."

"But your aria—I've never heard it sung better."

This was praise of high order from one of opera's most authoritative sources.

"Oh, Maestro, you don't know what that means to me."

"I think I do." His eyes were alight. "Do you ever get to Los Angeles?"

"What . . . ? Um, sure." She thought she detected the distant whiff of a job offer in the air, so she added, "Actually, that's my home. I'm just in New York for—" For what? Why had she uprooted her daughter and left her husband? "For work. I'm just there for the work."

His voice dropped. "Good. Keep this to yourself; I've been asked to be the next music director of the Los Angeles Opera in a couple of years."

She nodded eagerly.

"They're starting a young artists program. With your skills and experience, you could be a wonderful teacher. I can put in a word if you're interested."

A soft bell sounded the end of intermission as she nodded her thanks. The stage manager called places. Nelson smiled and patted her hand. "Let's show them something special."

PART VI

1947

39

It was one o'clock early Saturday morning when John finished dictating his story of Friday's events at the United Nations to the night stenographer in Chicago, just in time to make the morning edition of the *Sun*. Their bus from Flushing Meadows broke down halfway back to Manhattan and they didn't chug up to the Paramount Hotel until nearly ten. He grabbed Jeanne's notes and ran to his room and called from there. By combining her notes with his, he was able to construct a coherent description of the day's events. He had barely hung up when the telephone rang.

"McGrath?"

"Yes, Mr. Pilch."

"Just read your story. Hershon's not going to be happy."

"I know."

"We're way out on a limb here. No news on the girl?"

He hesitated a moment, then said, "No, nothing."

"Your source ready to go on record?"

"Nope, sorry."

"Don't apologize to me. Hershon ordered me to get his approval for your article, but I don't have the time. Why did you wait so late?"

"Our bus broke down on the way back from Queens."

"Uh-huh."

"Ask Father Bernard if you don't believe me."

"Hershon said to tell you if you don't deliver, you're off the crime beat. You'll be doing women's page stuff."

"Miss Photo Flash."

"Like that, yeah."

"I'd rather die."

"I think he'd be okay with that. Do better tomorrow, kid."

"I'll try, Mr. Pilch."

He had to see Liliane. He put on his overcoat and headed out. He skipped the slow elevator and instead trotted down eight flights of stairs. He strode through the empty lobby at the same time as a couple in evening dress were coming in, returning late from supper or early from a nightclub. The woman was laughing loudly at something her companion had said. The man had his hand on the small of her back as if to steady her after too much champagne.

John had a sudden stab of resentment—their flush of health, their easy humor, and their ignorance of the fact that, two miles away, a woman was fighting for her life.

Outside, he turned up his collar against the freezing night air. He crossed the empty street and walked toward Seventh Avenue past the Forty-Sixth Street Theater. There was a poster for the long-running musical *Finian's Rainbow* in the window. It featured a devilish leprechaun eying a dancing woman with long, dark hair. She reminded him of Liliane.

He hurried down the street and caught a cab near Times Square. Traffic had thinned considerably. In less than fifteen minutes, he walked into Bellevue Hospital. The click of his heels echoed as he walked along the tile floor in the empty entrance hall of the hospital. He followed the signs to the registration desk where a woman in her fifties sat. She wore a white cap over short gray hair and a nurse's uniform with a dark cape on her shoulders.

"Excuse me, I'm wondering if you can tell me where I can find a patient. She was brought in yesterday."

"Visiting hours were over at ten," she snapped.

"I didn't get off work until after midnight," he pleaded. "I came as fast as I could. I just have to see her. Please."

The woman shook her head but pulled down a loose-leaf binder from a shelf next to her desk.

"Her name?"

"Liliane al-Haffar."

"Relation?"

"Fiancé."

She ran her finger down a handwritten list of names. "She's on the fourth floor." She looked at him carefully. "There's a police officer waiting to question her. You can look in for a minute if it's all right with him. I'll let the nurse know you're coming."

John went to the staircase and trotted up the four flights of stairs. The nurse directed him to Liliane's room. The door was open and a uniformed officer sat nearby. John explained who he was and the officer patted him down and motioned he could go in.

He stood uncertainly in the entryway, afraid to approach the small, damaged figure lying under a white sheet and thin blue wool blanket. Moonlight from a small window cast an ashen glaze over her face. White bandages were wrapped around her head. Her chest moved slightly with shallow, uneven breaths. A bottle hung from a steel tree next to the bed. A tube ran from the bottle into her nose. Other tubes trailed from under the sheet.

"Why don't you go in? She won't wake," a quiet voice said behind him. Startled, he looked into the understanding eyes and concerned middle-aged face of the nurse.

"Poor dear. The doctor said she won't recover consciousness."

Hot tears shot from his eyes. "What?"

"Oh . . . I'm so sorry. Didn't anyone tell you?"

"No. Is the doctor sure?"

"Yes. She had a seizure two hours ago."

The nurse guided him to a chair near the bed and gestured for him to sit. She poured a glass of water from a carafe on the table by the bed and put the glass in his hand.

He drained the glass. He hadn't known he was so thirsty. She poured him another.

"I'll be right outside if you need anything."

He scooted his chair closer to the bed. He wanted to hold her hand, but her arms were under the covers and he was afraid to disturb her. He closed his eyes and tried to pray but came up empty. He sat with his head bowed and his eyes closed for a time.

He heard voices outside the door and a discussion between the policeman and someone else. The officer was frisking a man in Arab dress.

"May I come in?" the man said in a British-accented voice.

He had light brown skin and a beard and mustache of brown and white. He wore a round white cloth cap and a tan robe edged with gold. His hands were folded over his midsection.

"Who are you?"

"I am Imam Muhammad ibn Heshaam Jaabir. I was asked to pray for this unfortunate young woman."

"Do you know who she is?"

"I know her name. I know she is a child of God. What more is there to know?" Without a flicker of impatience, the imam said again, "May I come in?"

"Yes, sorry, I just . . . I was surprised. Not many people know she's here."

"God knows." The imam went to the other side of the bed. "The nurse said you and she are engaged to be married?" His warm brown eyes were seemingly ready to believe whatever John said.

"Not exactly. I'm John McGrath, just a friend. This is all my fault."

"That she is here is the will of God. Whether she will live, that too is according to the will of God. You would like to pray for her?"

"Yes," he answered, grateful for the chance to do something, even though he'd never understood prayer. What kind of God would decide whether a young woman lived or died depending on how many prayers He received?

The imam gently lowered the covers partway. He took Liliane's right hand and touched it gently to her forehead and prayed.

When he finished, John whispered, "Please, let her live. I promise I'll take care of her. Just please let her live."

The imam watched him. John waited for him to speak. When he didn't, he said, "Where are you from?"

"I was born in Yemen but lived in Palestine until just before the war, when I moved here."

"Palestine? You must know what is happening at the United Nations, then."

The imam nodded. "They are giving away our land to the Jews."

"Will your people fight?"

"Wouldn't you?"

"Me, well, I . . ."

"Where are you from, Mr. McGrath?" the imam interrupted.

Surprised, he answered, "Chicago, Illinois."

"You have friends and family there?"

"Sure."

"Didn't Chicago once belong to your Indian tribes?"

"Yes, the, uh . . ." He searched his mind. "Illinois confederacy."

"How many tribes in that confederacy?"

"Twelve, I think."

The imam smiled. It took John a moment to see the coincidence.

"And if tomorrow, the United Nations ordered Chicago returned to them, if they ordered your family to move to Oklahoma on pain of death, would you fight?"

"I guess I would."

"Really?" the imam said with mock outrage. "But this is justice, Mr. McGrath. The land belonged to those Indian tribes many years ago. Their God gave it to them. Still, you would fight them?"

"Yes."

"Oh, dear," the imam said, his dark eyebrows raised in a parody of surprise. "But please consider, they need your homeland very badly because evil Europeans have committed acts of genocide against these noble Indians. For shame. Where is your pity? Your humanity?"

John nodded in appreciation of the imam's hard logic. "You really think they'll kill your people?"

The imam smiled bitterly. "Oh, they will. They want our land and they will kill us like rats and drive us from our homes to achieve that end, just as they killed thousands of us and took our land in the time of their Torah. To them, we Palestinians are but obstacles to their God's divine plan."

"I hope that isn't true."

"You are right to hope. The Koran tells us never to lose hope in Allah's mercy." He moved to leave and they shook. His hand was unexpectedly strong.

When the imam was gone, John bent over and gently touched her cheek. The hospital smells of carbolic acid, soap, and bleach almost overwhelmed him, but through those smells, he imagined her floral scent still floated around her.

He stayed until the nurse entered the room an hour later. "Call anytime or come visit whenever you want," she said, "even if it's not visiting hours. I'm here every night this week."

"Thank you."

He walked slowly down the stairs, out the entry hall, and onto the street. It was three in the morning. He looked up and down First Avenue, but there wasn't a cab in sight, so he trudged the two miles back to the hotel, his gloved hands deep in his pockets against the bitter cold. By the time he reached the hotel, he knew what he had to do. He took the elevator to the tenth floor instead of his own and knocked on Jeanne's door. He waited for the sounds of movement. Hearing none, he knocked again. Jeanne answered, wrapped in her robe. She rubbed her eyes and blinked sleepily.

"John," she said.

"Sorry to wake you," he said. "I visited Liliane in the hospital."

Her eyes opened wide. "Give me a minute. I'll meet you downstairs."

He was pacing the empty lobby when she came out of the elevator. Her nightgown peeked out from the collar and the hem of her overcoat. He gestured to a low table nearby. "The desk clerk had a fresh pot of coffee—he poured us some."

"I don't want any coffee. How is she?"

He told her the details of his visit to the hospital—everything except his promise. "They don't think she's gonna make it."

She put her arms around him. He let her comfort him for a moment, then took a deep breath and said, "It was just such a shock."

When he started to break their embrace, she put her hands on his shoulders and looked him in the eye. She was fully awake now.

"John, you have to pull yourself together. You have a job to do, an important story to tell, and you can still help Grogan catch the man who did this."

"You're right. I thought Alfagari would have tried something at the General Assembly yesterday."

"Grogan said he never left the hotel."

"That can't be right," he said. "If you're trying to stop the vote, you can't do it from your hotel room. He had to be there."

"But the cops would have seen him," she said.

"Even if they did, the cops can't do anything without proof. We need to see Mr. Shertok." He was speaking faster now. "He has people that can help. He's at the Berkshire Hotel. That's on East Fifty-Second Street near Madison. Come on." He walked quickly to the door.

"Wait!" Jeanne cried.

"What?" he said, turning around.

"I'm still in my robe," she said.

"Who cares?" he said. After a moment's hesitation, she ran after him.

The snooty overdressed desk clerk at the Berkshire Hotel flatly refused to call Shertok's room. "Mr. Shertok left very clear instructions he is not to be disturbed."

"You don't have to disturb him, just tell us his room number. We'll disturb him," John said with what he hoped was a winning smile.

"Quite impossible." The clerk turned away and began busying himself sorting mail into the pigeonholes for the individual rooms. Each slot had a room number under it in gold lettering.

John grabbed a piece of hotel stationery and scribbled a note. He stuffed it in a hotel envelope. He wrote Shertok's name on the envelope in big block letters.

"Can you give him this message the moment he's available?"

The clerk half turned from shuffling papers and gave a curt nod.

"Thanks, we really appreciate it." He and Jeanne started for the door. He leaned to her and whispered, "I'm gonna pretend to make a call. Watch him, see where he puts the message, what the room number is."

John walked to a telephone booth and went inside. When he stepped out of the booth and started for the elevators, the clerk was still turned away from them.

"1210," Jeanne whispered when they were out of sight.

"Let's go disturb Mr. Shertok," he said, pushing the button for the elevator.

Room 1210 was the third door down the hall from the elevator. John knocked. The sound echoed in the quiet hallway. After waiting a few seconds, he knocked louder.

"What, what is it?" said a low, husky voice.

"John McGrath, Mr. Shertok."

"Who?"

"John McGrath, the reporter, *Chicago Sun*. We met earlier today."

"McGrath. The man with the mysterious plot. Why are you bothering me?"

"I need to talk to you."

"It's four in the morning, Mr. McGrath. I just got to bed. I don't need talk, I need sleep."

"It can't wait, sir."

The door opened a crack and Shertok peered out. He was in a navy blue robe and slippers.

"Not so loud, please. My wife and children are sleeping." He opened the door to the suite wider. "You brought the young lady, too. Soften me up, you thought?" He looked at Jeanne's pretty smile. "So, fine, it's working. Come in. Maybe I'll get some sleep next year." Shertok turned and padded away on the thick carpet of the room, leaving the door open.

John and Jeanne followed him. Shertok waved his hand to indicate they should sit. Jeanne perched on the edge of an overstuffed armchair in one corner of the room. John leaned against a desk. Shertok sat in the middle of a long sofa.

"So what's so important?"

"You have to help us, Mr. Shertok. You said you believed me, that there was an assassination plot by the Mufti to disrupt the vote."

"Yes."

"Mohammed Alfagari is the Mufti's assassin and he's going to be at the UN today."

"You know this?"

"I . . . *think* this. The Mufti sent him a telegram." He took the envelope out of his pocket and handed it to Shertok. "It says—"

"Let me read it," Shertok said, quickly scanning the document and nodding. "I think you're right." Shertok's brow creased. "The telegram is in Arabic except the French word for 'salve,' '*cérat*.' Did you notice? 'Eliminate *la cérat*.' What could that mean?"

"I don't know," John said, shaking his head, "but if he's going to do anything, it will be today."

"Why didn't he do something yesterday, then?" Shertok said. "The vote almost went forward."

"*Almost* went forward. But it didn't."

"But he couldn't have known that."

"Unless—"

"Unless he was there," Shertok said. "He shoots or throws a bomb. They stop the vote. In the fear, the confusion, I lose five or six votes." He nodded vigorously. "What do the police say?"

"They don't have any grounds to arrest him. They say he never left his hotel yesterday. I think he did and they missed him. He hid somewhere in the building where he could see everything going on. The police say they'll watch for him, but today it's like a needle in the haystack. Ten thousand people have requested visitor passes."

"Why come to me?"

"When we talked yesterday, you told me you have resources. Can you have someone keep an eye on him?"

"You think I call and the Haganah comes?"

"The what?" Jeanne asked.

"Jewish Defense Force," Shertok said.

"That's exactly what I think," John said.

"You're out of your mind." Shertok was silent for a while, thinking. He gave a tremendous yawn.

"We're sorry for waking you," Jeanne said.

Shertok eyed her robe, which peeked out from the sleeves and bottom of her overcoat. "He woke you, too?"

"Yes."

"Busy bee, this friend of yours." Shertok shook his head and moved to the room's darkened window and looked out. "I think I've got it."

"What's that, sir?" she asked.

"The votes—that's off the record, mister."

John nodded.

"I was with Liberia and Haiti until two. They finally said yes. We might even get the Philippines. I found their ambassador an hour ago, asked him for his vote. 'I'm thinking,' he tells me. 'What are you thinking about at three in the morning?' I say. 'Think about calling your president in the Philippines. It's time to cast the dice.' He said he would. They might change back to yes."

"All the more reason to protect the vote, sir," John said.

"Okay, enough." He looked at John intently. "I need to know everything about that man."

"Okay, this'll take a while," John said. He told him everything.

When he was finished, Shertok said, "I'll see what I can do."

John looked at Jeanne and they headed for the door.

"Shalom," Jeanne said brightly.

"Shalom," answered Shertok. "We'll need some luck today." As he closed the door, he muttered, "And for a long time to come."

• • •

It was five o'clock the next afternoon, Saturday, November 29, 1947. Voting would begin in thirty minutes. John was in the lobby of the General Assembly Hall looking for Grogan. It was jammed with people. Thousands who couldn't get in waited outside. His eyes burned from lack of sleep. He finally found Grogan near the entry doors, talking to one of the police officers he had recruited from the tiny Lake Success department.

"I don't care if you looked ten times. Look again," Grogan said to the officer.

The officer threw up his hands. "Fine, Detective, you want me to look again, I'll look again." He grumped off, shoving his way through the crowd.

"What do you want?" Grogan barked at John.

"Relax," he said, holding up his hand. "I'm just checking in."

"Would I be standing here if I had something?"

"Don't bite my head off. I heard you threw somebody out. Was he armed? Did he hurt anybody?"

"Nah, just a crazy crank, shouting at the Jews *and* the Arabs. Nobody could figure out whose side he was on."

John jerked his chin at the departing officer. "Where you sending him?"

"Second and third floor booths again." Those booths were for special visitors and for the press. "Most of the countries have their own press people, cameramen and such."

"I know," John said impatiently. "Did you check the booths assigned to the Muslim countries?"

"No, I'm a fucking idiot."

"Sorry."

"McGrath, I got twenty detectives and a dozen uniforms walking all over." He took a deep breath. "But thousands of people showed up here today, most of them without passes. There's no way to check them all out. The UN security can't do anything but crowd control."

"Sorry," John said again.

"Don't sweat it. I'm just pissed off. We're doing our best. Syria's got a booth, but the cameraman in it doesn't match Alfagari's description and his credentials check out. I just sent a cop to check again, make sure nobody new is up there, no one with a rifle."

"It has to be a rifle, right?" John asked, not for the first time. "Unless it's a suicide mission. Christ, it doesn't even have to be the Syrian booth."

Grogan shook his head. "Nope."

They had discussed this before. There was no way to stop a determined man with a pistol—or a bomb—hidden under a coat or in a pocket.

"How the hell do you get a rifle in here without someone seeing?"

The Lake Success officer returned, shaking his head at Grogan. "No change, nothing new."

Grogan said to John, "We've checked every square inch of this place ten times over. But I *know* he's here."

"What do you mean?"

"I can feel it."

40

lfagari sat on a chair in a large brightly lit booth on the second level, shielded from the view of anyone on the main floor below by the dozens of newsmen and cameramen crammed in front of him. His overcoat was pulled close and his hat set low. It was unnecessary—in the crush and excitement, no one paid him the least attention. Even so, he had seen the heavy police presence when he arrived and decided it would be safer not to enter the Syrian booth until just before the vote. From his position, he couldn't see anything, but he could hear what was said over the loudspeakers. He would arrive in his booth in plenty of time.

• • •

Jeanne was seated with Moshe Shertok near the rear of the floor of the General Assembly. The rest of the *Chicago Sun* students and chaperones were consigned to the mezzanine level. Men with long beards, wearing prayer shawls, black coats, and yarmulkes surrounded her and Shertok. A short, slender, bald man dressed in a dark suit sat immediately behind her on the aisle. Shertok spoke to him quietly several times during the afternoon but didn't introduce him to Jeanne. The man's hard, watchful eyes were in constant motion, looking everywhere and at everything. At irregular intervals, he would leave his seat for a while, then return and nod or shrug.

On the other side of Shertok, a tall, dark-haired man with horn-rimmed glasses was seated by a pretty young woman. When they first arrived, Shertok had handed him the envelope with the Mufti's telegram. The man read it, snorted, and handed it back. They had an urgent conversation and Shertok jumped up. "You're sure?"

"Of course, he told me himself," the man said. "Are we ready?"

Shertok had gestured to the slender, bald man. "As ready as we can be."

"Jeanne," Shertok said, "this is our liaison officer, Aubrey Eban. That blooming rose with him is his bride, Suzy. And next to her, my wife, Zipporah. May I present Miss Jeanne Cooper of Chicago."

"Abba Eban," the man said with an English accent.

Shertok shot him a look. "So now you're Abba, our 'father'?"

Eban smiled. "It is only right I have a Hebrew name now, don't you think? You should do the same."

"Aubrey, I mean, Abba," Shertok said to Jeanne, "is a key member of the brain trust that organized all this."

Shertok held a pair of mother-of-pearl opera glasses in his hand. He peered through them at the various delegations. "Can't see as far as I used to," he had said when she looked askance at him. "I like to see their faces."

"Can I try?" she said.

He nodded. "Sure, I'm going to check on something."

It was the fifth time that day he had used the same phrase. She asked him to explain.

"You and your friend asked me for a favor, no? So I made a call."

"You mean—" she said, looking at the little bald man behind them.

"I don't mean anything," he said irritably. "Just got some help." He stood and handed her the glasses. "They won't get started for a bit. Here, have a look."

"Thanks." The smooth surface was still warm from his hands. She put the glasses to her eyes, adjusted the magnification, and trained them on the huge UN symbol behind the speaker's rostrum. Guards stood at the front of each aisle facing the audience. Uniformed policemen walked continually through the auditorium. The aisles of the floor were filled with UN staff members crowding in from the offices throughout the building to witness the historic vote. If someone started a fire, no one would get out alive. She looked along the rows of clerks and stenographers in the well, taking the glasses from her eyes now and then to find a new target. She turned to check the time on the big clock on the face of the mezzanine. It was five fifteen.

A voice announced over the loudspeakers, "All delegates, please return to your seats for the vote." The phrase was repeated in French as hundreds of people streamed into the auditorium.

She scanned the booths encircling the main floor on the second tier. One on the second level on her left was brightly lit and crammed with people. She thought she saw Mrs. Roosevelt, but, by the time she had readjusted the focus of the glasses, the woman had turned away. Journalists and photographers occupied the smaller booths on the same side, farther away from the front of the auditorium. She glanced at each of them. The last one was completely dark inside. She was about to turn when a match flared and a man's face was illuminated while he lit a cigarette.

She jumped out of her seat. The opera glasses slipped from her hand and cracked as they hit the floor. She stepped into the aisle and pushed her way into the lobby, where she found John.

"I saw him!"

"Where?"

"Small booth at the far end," she said.

He grabbed her arms and looked in her eyes as people swarmed around them. "You're sure?"

Was she? She'd only seen him once, days ago in the club car. She swallowed. "Yes."

"Come on," he yelled as he ran back into the auditorium. They found Shertok and the little bald man at the rear of the auditorium speaking with one of the delegates. John told them what Jeanne had seen. They turned and pushed rudely through the crowd back to the lobby. The small man unbuttoned his jacket.

"Wait outside," John said to Jeanne.

"No, I want to—"

"There's going to be trouble."

She didn't move.

"Please, Jeanne! I can't let you get hurt too."

Like Liliane, he means. She shook her head. With a final backward glance, he ran through the lobby. She watched as John, Shertok, and the bald man went to the stairs. Grogan was standing nearby at the lobby door.

"Grogan," John shouted. "He's in the last booth upstairs!"

"He's going after Parodi!" Shertok shouted.

They ran up the stairs. Jeanne returned to the auditorium and took her seat by Abba Eban.

• • •

"Gentlemen, gentlemen, we will now call the vote," Dr. Oswaldo Aranha said as Jeanne twisted in her seat to look at the darkened booth where she'd seen Alfagari. Dr. Aranha, the tall, white-haired president of the Second Session of the United Nations General Assembly, was standing at his lectern, the UN symbol behind him. He was flanked by Trygve Lie, the rotund secretary-general, and by Andrew Cordier, his equally well-fed assistant. Aranha's dignified Portuguese-inflected English was transmitted on loudspeakers to every part of the auditorium and was being broadcast by radio all over the world. "You all know how to vote," he continued. "Those in favor will say yes. Those who are against will say no. And the abstainers, always they know what to say."

There was tense laughter from the crowd.

• • •

Alfagari stamped out his cigarette, picked up his weapon, and edged closer to the rail at the open side of the booth. There was a metallic slide and click as he ratcheted out the bolt and snapped it back into place. He raised the sniper rifle.

• • •

"We will start it now," Aranha said.

"Afghanistan?" said Assistant Secretary-General Cordier in a flat Midwestern accent.

"No," the Afghan delegate cried.

"No," Cordier repeated.

• • •

Alfagari inched forward on his chair, put the rifle to his shoulder, and sighted on Parodi. Satisfied he had a clear shot and adequate light, he pulled the rifle back.

• • •

"Argentina?" There was no response. "Abstention," Cordier said. "Australia?"

"Yes."

"Belgium?"

"Yes."

"Where did they go in such a hurry?" Eban asked Jeanne, but she was too frightened to answer.

His eyes narrowed. "The assassin?"

She nodded.

"There's going to be trouble in here," he said to his wife. "Suzy, take her outside."

Jeanne shook her head.

"This isn't your fight. Suzy, tell her."

Suzy Eban said, "Maybe she thinks this is everyone's fight, Aubrey."

"Please," Jeanne said. "I have to stay. I need to see what happens."

"All right." Eban took Jeanne's hand. "Stay close then."

Her foot touched something under her chair. It was the opera glasses. She picked them up with one hand, still holding Eban's with the other. One lens was cracked. She peered through them at the dark booth.

She remembered Benjamin Cohen's lecture the morning before about France being the key player and she could hear Moshe Shertok saying, "It will come down to France." That was it! If France changed its vote to yes, others would follow. Alfagari was waiting for them to call for France's vote. That was when he would fire.

"Bolivia?"

"Yes."

"Brazil?"

"Yes."

"Byelorussia?"

"Yes."

• • •

Alfagari moved his left foot slightly forward, his right a few inches back. He took a deep breath and let it out completely. How many more countries were there before they got to France? Six? There were already eleven yesses. In a few minutes, it wouldn't matter.

• • •

John and the bald man ran up the stairs to the second floor, Grogan and Shertok puffing behind. The bald man had a 9mm automatic pistol in his hand. It was dark and scarred and tipped with a long, thick suppressor. People in the narrow hall didn't see it or else didn't believe what they saw. He and John ran through the crowd, weaving like broken-field runners on a football field. The little man was fast, but John was faster. People yelled angrily at them as they bumped and elbowed their way through.

"Egypt?" Cordier called.

"No."

"El Salvador?"

"Abstention."

"Ethiopia?"

"Abstain."

• • •

France was next. Alfagari heard feet pounding and shouts. If they were coming for him, they would be too late. His chair creaked as he leaned forward, flexing his right forefinger. He lifted the rifle to his shoulder. He took a deep breath, then let it out halfway and held it as he had been trained to do at the Homs Military Academy in Syria many years before.

• • •

The booth was fifty feet away, thirty, ten, and then John was there. The heavy curtain was closed. Metal rings screeched on an iron rod as he tore it open.

Alfagari whirled around and pointed his rifle at him. John dove behind a chair and there was a sharp explosion. The bullet nicked his left hand and burned the air near his ear. Alfagari slammed back the bolt, ejecting the spent shell. The empty brass tinkled and danced on the floor as he rammed the bolt forward to chamber another round. A dark pistol appeared over John's right shoulder and fired twice, the sound no louder than a cap gun. A single dark hole the size of a dime appeared at the bridge of Alfagari's nose. He dropped the rifle with a racketing clatter, swayed, and fell backward. His skull cracked as it hit the floor.

• • •

A single flash illuminated the booth like the flashbulbs that kept explod-ing in the auditorium. Only because she was listening for it, Jeanne heard something like a shot through the ambient noise. No one else noticed. Two more flashes that were almost one quickly followed, but they made no sound. She squeezed Abba Eban's arm and pointed at the booth. "Something happened!"

She tried to stand, but Eban clamped his hand on her arm. "Moshe and his friend will take care of it. And the policemen."

"But they could be hurt. John might be hurt. Please."

"We'll check on them when we know it's safe."

She stared through the glasses, desperately trying to identify the shadowy figures now lit from behind.

• • •

John was on the floor wrapping a handkerchief around his injured finger. Grogan and Shertok studied the body for a minute, and then Grogan pulled the curtain shut to shield the mayhem from passing eyes. The bald man had disappeared.

John slowly stood, his heart beating rapidly and his legs shaking.

"You hit, McGrath?"

"Just nicked."

Grogan moved to the body. There was a fusty odor from the wet wool of his suit, pierced by the sharp smell of cordite. His knees cracked as he crouched. He looked at the open eyes and the small hole between them.

"Where'd he go?" John said.

"Who?" said Grogan.

"Mr. Shertok's friend. He shot him." The two men glanced at each other but didn't answer.

John was still trying to breathe normally. Grogan stood by the rail and looked out over the hundreds of people on the floor, in the mezzanine, and on the second and third tiers, shifting and moving and talking in the smoky yellow air. The vote was still going on. He turned as Shertok started to speak.

"NYPD's got this, Moshe."

"Will you need the gun?" Shertok asked.

There was a long pause.

"Nope," he said finally. "Guy died of a heart attack. Or a stroke. I haven't decided which. He'll get a proper Muslim burial tomorrow, nobody knows where, courtesy of the City of New York."

"I can't—" John began.

"I've got to go, the vote's still going," Shertok said, turning to leave.

"Hold on," John said. "How did you know it would be the Frenchman?"

Shertok shook his head. "I didn't. It was Aubrey. Parodi once told him that *La Cérat* was his code name when he fought with the Resistance during the war. It means—"

"'Salve,'" John finished. Shertok nodded.

"Peru?" Cordier's disembodied voice said over the loudspeaker.

"Yes."

"Philippines?"

Shertok held his breath.

"Yes."

"Thank God," he said. "Roxas came through." He put his hand on the curtain. "We okay, then, Detective?"

Grogan nodded. "Go on with you."

Shertok slipped through the curtain and Grogan turned to John. "You get out of here too. Have someone look at that hand. We'll talk soon, okay?"

"Grogan, if you think you can—"

"I said we'll talk later," Grogan snapped.

John took a last look at Alfagari's body. "I'm gonna call my paper." He yanked the curtain open and walked out.

John made his way back into the auditorium. He had just reached Jeanne when President Aranha declared that the resolution had been approved, thirty-three in favor, thirteen against, with ten abstentions and one absent. The noise in the auditorium swelled with cheers and shouts, some angry and many more joyful. Most of the onlookers began to leave. They all stood and Jeanne threw her arms around him.

"I was so worried!" she said. "Is everyone—?"

"They're okay."

"Alfagari?"

"Except him."

"What happened to your hand?"

"Nothing, just scratched it. Come on, let's go."

They held hands and threaded their way through the celebrating crowd. John pointed her into the pressroom and they went inside. The walls were masonry block painted white, decorated with black-and-white photographs of diplomats and buildings. Small tables with typewriters and telephones filled the space. An ocean of loose paper was scattered everywhere. The room was crammed with reporters shouting into telephones and the crackling hammer of dozens of typewriters and telex machines.

John took a seat at an empty desk and, using a pencil and a yellow legal pad, quickly sketched an outline of the story he would dictate over the telephone. Jeanne perched on the side of the desk, reading over his shoulder, and supplying him details he'd missed. Tomorrow his name would be in every paper in the country, the world even. He smiled at Thomas Hamilton of the *New York Times* working a couple of desks away, cigarette holder clamped in his mouth. "You look happy," Hamilton said. "Got something good?"

"You bet and you can read it tomorrow in the *Sun*. Who's that?" John said, nodding at a gray-haired man next to Hamilton. "You bring your dad to work with you?"

"Very funny. Who's this?" he asked, his eyes squinting from his cigarette smoke as he looked Jeanne over carefully. "Girl Friday?"

"Jeanne Cooper, editor in chief of her high school paper in Chicago. Tom Hamilton, with the *Times*."

"Pleased to meet you, Mr. Hamilton."

His eyebrows went up. "High school girl, huh?"

"Watch it, Hamilton."

As he picked up the telephone to call his paper, Grogan appeared and plucked the phone from his hand, and hung it up. He grabbed the yellow pad.

"Hey!" John said.

"We need to talk. And not here." He jerked his head. "Outside."

John angrily followed him, Jeanne trailing behind. They stopped a few yards away from where Moshe Shertok and Abba Eban, their wives by their sides, were holding court in the high-ceilinged lobby, accepting congratulations, receiving embraces from supporters, many of them in tears, and speaking to reporters.

"Gentlemen," Shertok said, "I am gratified beyond words at the results of the vote today. A year ago, I was in a Latrun jail because I fought for a Jewish homeland. Because of what happened today, soon I will be a citizen of that homeland. The entire world heard the voice of the great trumpet proclaiming our nation's redemption and has given us its blessing."

"Gimme that." John grabbed his yellow pad from Grogan's hand. "If you think you can keep me quiet, you're crazy."

Grogan signaled to Shertok, who walked over to them.

"Congratulations!" Jeanne said.

"Thank you, my dear, thank you. I can't believe we did it. I found the delegate from Venezuela hiding in the men's room. I recognized his shoes under the stall door. He was going to abstain. I pounded on the door until he came out and voted yes."

Jeanne laughed as a round woman wearing a tiny, black hat, a wide-meshed veil, and pearls pulled Shertok away for an embrace.

"Moshe," Grogan called out. "Please, a minute."

Shertok finished his hug and rejoined them. They walked away from the crowd into a small anteroom off the lobby. Abba and Suzy Eban and Zipporah Shertok drifted along behind them. The noise of the crowd faded.

Shertok dabbed away a crimson smear from his cheek.

"All of you are invited tonight! There's a big celebration at the St. Nicholas Arena on the Upper West Side. Everyone's coming, Weizmann, Silver, everyone. Jeanne, I want my daughter to meet you. She'll be so jealous you were here."

"Moshe, calm down for a minute," Grogan said.

Shertok, still glowing, tried to focus.

When he had his attention, Grogan went on. "Ernie Pyle here wants to report what happened upstairs. I thought maybe you could explain why that's not such a great idea."

Shertok looked at John soberly. "You want to report about Alfagari's death?"

"Of course," John said. "It's exactly what I said would happen and I'm the only reporter who knows about it. My editor thinks I'm making it all up. Wants to fire me. This will be the story of the year."

"Yes," Shertok said. "It's a big story. Can I tell you why publishing it might not be the right thing to do?"

John crossed his arms.

"The real story of the year, my friend, isn't another attempted murder. In Palestine, that happens every day."

"Same in New York," Grogan said.

"The real story is the creation of Israel. You remember me saying we had to do this properly? No violence, everything legal? If you tell your tale, what happens? Outraged Jews and outraged Arabs. And more fighting." He looked at Abba Eban. "What we are trying to do is change things in Palestine, to stop the killings, the endless retaliation. We do not want to live by the sword forever. I don't want the story to be about the Haganah or the Mufti." His passion quietly vibrated in his voice. "I want the story to be that we played by the world's rules and its good and courageous people gave us our home."

"Listen, kid, the NYPD says Alfagari died of a heart attack," Grogan said. "He's going in the ground tomorrow. What do you say?"

What John wanted to say was that this story would make his career and he wouldn't help them bury it. Instead, he turned to Jeanne. "What do you think?"

She looked surprised to be asked, but she didn't hesitate. "I think a good reporter picks a side." She put her hand on his arm and said softly, "Like you did in the war, like at Buchenwald."

"You were there?" Shertok said softly.

John's mouth firmed into a grim line and he was suddenly thousands of miles away and two and a half years in the past. The sickening smell had filled the air the whole morning. His unit was marching through grass and frozen mud with American tanks as they steamrollered layer after layer of barbed wire fence, and then chugged up a gentle hill toward a concentration of buildings. No one fired at them from the watchtowers. Group after ragged group of human beings, dressed only in remnants of striped pajamas, came crawling out to greet them. They didn't believe their suffering was over until they heard the magic word "American." Impossibly weak, they somehow found the strength to toss soldiers in the air in celebration.

Emaciated, naked, dirty, gray-green bodies were everywhere, stacked like lumber, a few of them still alive. Black, filthy smoke was pouring out of a massive chimney until they were told what was being burned and someone figured out how to turn off the ovens. His stomach was rolling and vomiting. Patton was gleaming and raging and ordering mountains of supplies. The prisoners captured a guard, made him tie a noose with thirteen coils, string it up, and hang himself. None of the American soldiers interfered while the guard's face turned blue, then black as he strangled to death. In the days that followed, Patton forced group after group of citizens from the ancient and cultured city of Weimar, only five miles away, to tour the camp. Yes, they had seen trains full of prisoners going to the camp. No, they said, shrugging, they hadn't asked why prisoners never left. A citizen must permit the government to go about its business. They were shocked at what they saw. Above it all hung the smell—the viscous, evil smell that was in his nostrils even now.

He took Jeanne's hand. Her touch warmed away the cold of a time when, for a while, he had lost his belief that there was good anywhere in the world.

"Thank you," Shertok said, offering his hand to John. "I didn't know. Thank you for what you did for us. Then. And today. We are in your debt."

Abba Eban stepped forward and shook John's hand, too, then held it in both of his large ones. "Let your story be about life, not death."

Suzy Eban added, "Tell the world about the hope that was born today, not the commonplace evil that died."

Shertok added, "Let your conscience be your compass, Mr. McGrath. That's what must guide you."

They all watched him, their faces tense and anxious. Except Jeanne. She seemed calm and certain, as though she already knew what he would do. It was her certainty, as much as anything, that decided him. His dream of glory drained away and as it did, he felt a stab of shame at his regret.

"Okay," he said, looking only at her. "I'll write just about the vote. But no one else better get the Alfagari story. Here." He ripped the page containing his outline from the yellow pad and thrust it at Grogan.

"May I keep that?" Eban asked. John handed it to him, and he folded the paper carefully and put it in a leather pocketbook.

"You're doing the right thing, son," Grogan said, putting a hand on his shoulder. "You're a credit—"

"I know," John muttered in despair. "I'm a credit to the Irish people."

"No, Mr. McGrath," Suzy Eban said. "You are a credit to the human race." She and her husband rejoined the celebrating crowd.

Shertok turned to John. "Please come see me tomorrow at my hotel. There's something I'd like to discuss. Three o'clock?"

"Our train leaves at four thirty-five," Jeanne said.

"We won't be long, trust me," Shertok said.

"Let's get some air," Grogan said.

They walked to the glass entry doors of the lobby. John held a door open and Jeanne and Grogan passed through. A crowd of reporters, including Hamilton, was gathered, facing away from the building toward the broad, asphalt-covered drive, busy writing on their notepads.

A group of men in Arab dress stood near a row of long, black limousines with whitewall tires. They faced the group of reporters and cameramen. John recognized Prince Faisal al Saud of Saudi Arabia, wearing a headdress and a gold-trimmed robe.

"We walked out before the end of the session to demonstrate to you and to the world that we will have nothing to do with this decision," the prince said. "In our eyes, gentlemen, the United Nations died today. Today's resolution has destroyed its charter and all covenants preceding it."

"It didn't die," said Faris al-Khoury, the representative of Syria. "It was murdered."

Houman al-Hafiz stood next to Khoury, his face strained and full of hate. Did he know Alfagari was dead?

"Some of you may be aware that the very land we stand on here, the land this building was constructed upon, was once a great pile of ash and garbage," al-Khoury continued. "I find that most appropriate since this organization has now consigned itself to the trash heap of history. We will not be bound by this vote. We will have absolutely nothing to do with the UN Commission for Palestine, nothing to do with the transition, and nothing to do with this partition. It was forced through by heavy pressure from the Jews. Let the Jews defend themselves."

Prince Faisal raised his fist. "There will be bloodshed! The partition line shall be nothing but a line of fire and blood. The blood will flow like rivers in the Middle East. We will smash them with our guns and obliterate every place the Jews seek shelter in. And the responsibility will not be ours but will rest on the shoulders of each of the countries that voted for partition. The war has begun!"

The Arab men scattered into their fleet of rented limousines and sped toward the flaring lights of Manhattan.

41

John worked swiftly to write his article about the vote when they returned to the Paramount Hotel. He kept his promise and omitted any mention of the assassination attempt and Alfagari's death. He cringed in anticipation of the excoriation Hershon would surely deliver, not to mention what would be said in other newspapers. Jeanne sat with him in the crowded lobby and helped him finish the article, using her seemingly eidetic memory to provide exact quotes from the various players. As soon as he had dictated the article to the *Sun*'s night stenographer from the lobby pay phone, Hershon got on the line and cursed him for his many failings as a reporter, as a man, and as an American. After they hung up, John called the hospital to ask about Liliane. The kindly night nurse told him there had been no change in her condition. Depressed and exhausted, he walked back to Jeanne who was perched on the edge of one of the overstuffed lobby chairs.

"What should we do to celebrate?" she said, smiling and excited.

"I'm going to have a couple of drinks," he said. "Then hit the hay. You have a good time tonight." The student group was headed to Radio City to watch an audience participation radio show.

"Are you kidding me?" Jeanne shrieked. "My last night in New York, who knows when I'll be back, and you think I'm going to some boring radio show?"

"You know," he said wearily, "you're starting to sound like Caroline."

Didn't she know what it cost him to quash the biggest story he was ever likely to get?

"I should be more like her. At least she knows how to enjoy herself."

"Well, excuse me. I'm tired."

She was incredulous. "Really? I feel great. I don't think I've ever felt so alive."

He had seen this same manic energy in soldiers during the war after a close shave. Jeanne would be like a toddler on a sugar high. She wouldn't rest until the accumulated physical exhaustion of the last few days stopped and dropped her.

"Don't be such a fuddy-duddy," she teased. "Hey, I know. Let's see a show, a real live Broadway musical."

"A show?"

"And then I want to go dancing."

"I think you're loopy from all the excitement."

"I might sound a little crazy, but I know exactly what I want to do and you're the one I want to do it with. Please?"

"All right, since you said please." He glanced at his watch. It was seven forty-five. "There's just time if we hurry."

She popped up and stood close to him. The light from the lobby chandeliers glowed in her blue-green eyes. Her scent, still impossibly fresh after the long day, floated to him. "Thank you," she said.

They found the concierge in the lobby, a little man in a forest-green jacket, seated at a desk littered with paper.

"Can you find us a couple of seats to a musical tonight?" he asked.

"Which one?" the concierge had asked.

Jeanne shook her head and smiled. "You decide."

The concierge rolled his eyes. "Well, there's lots to choose from." He recited from memory, not glancing at the framed posters around the lobby. "*Annie Get Your Gun*, that's with Ethel Merman, *Brigadoon*, *Oklahoma!*—the ads say it's still fresh as a daisy, though it's been running four years. Too bad you can't wait till next week when the new Tennessee Williams opens, *Streetcar Named Desire*. They say it's a hot one. You might—"

"Just pick one," John interrupted. "I mean"—he peered through a lobby window—"there's a show playing right across the street." He squinted at the marquee but couldn't quite make out the name. "*Finnegan's Wake* or something."

"You mean *Finian's Rainbow*," the little man said in a persnickety tone.

"Fine, that's the one." John pulled Jeanne along by the arm. "We're gonna get a quick bite," he yelled over his shoulder, pointing to the coffee shop. "Send the tickets there."

"Hey, you're talking six-sixty or eight-eighty—each!" the concierge yelled.

John dashed back, fumbling in his pocket. "Here's a double sawbuck," he said, slapping a twenty on the desk. "Keep the change."

They ate a quick dinner in the crowded hotel coffee shop. As a ravenous Jeanne gobbled an ice cream sundae, a uniformed page delivered two tickets for *Finian's Rainbow*.

"We've got to go," John said. "That is if you can be parted from your dessert. Jeez, who mixes pistachio and strawberry?"

"Me, that's who." She smiled and licked her spoon, unconsciously provoking a thrill of desire in him. He called for the check. When it came, he signed it, although Hershon had threatened not to honor his expenses.

They tugged on their coats and went out through the restaurant door that led directly to the street. Jeanne took his arm as they crossed to the theater and held it tightly while they stood in line under its arcade. She didn't stop talking, even inside the theater. He tried to shush her when the show started. She nodded but kept whispering in his ear during the overture. She finally quieted down, then took his hand and wouldn't relinquish it for the entire two and a half hours of the show.

When it was over, she smiled, kissed him on the cheek, and said, "That was wonderful. Now, dancing."

"I saw an ad for a midnight show with the King Cole Trio. I figure I owe you music you'd like after The 3 Deuces."

"That sounds dreamy," she replied, for once sounding like a teenager.

They held hands as they walked the few blocks to the Paramount Theater on Forty-Third Street. Jeanne sang snatches of "Old Devil Moon" and "How Are Things in Glocca Morra?"

Once inside, they were shown to a table and John ordered a bottle of champagne. There was a dance floor near the front and they danced to every song. He held her close while young Nat King Cole's warm, rich voice sang songs like "I Love You for Sentimental Reasons," "Sweet Lorraine," and "Smile." It was nearly three when the show ended. Jeanne looked like she could go another twenty-four hours as they walked out of the theater, their arms around each other's waists. The freezing night air bit into their faces.

"The cold feels wonderful after being inside," Jeanne exclaimed. She took a deep inhale and immediately began to sway. Her knees buckled and he helped her to a bus bench.

"Oooh, I don't feel so good." Her eyes fluttered as she sat.

"You're exhausted. I should have had you home hours ago."

He hailed a cab and half carried her into its overheated interior.

"Paramount Hotel," he told the driver. He turned back to Jeanne. She'd fallen asleep. When they arrived at the hotel, the doorman helped get her into the elevator. John held her around the waist with one arm and poked the button for the tenth floor with his free hand. He picked her up and carried her down the hall toward her room. She sleepily curled an arm around his neck and nestled closer.

A wave of tenderness overwhelmed him. He kissed her forehead softly, then put his cheek against hers, and closed his eyes. When she grew heavy in his arms, he thumped softly on the door with his elbow.

Caroline opened the door a crack. She was fully dressed and wearing her leopard print coat.

"Oh, god, is she okay?" Caroline asked, swinging the door open. Tony stood at the other side of the room and smiled sheepishly.

"Exhausted, I think," John whispered.

"Just lay her down. I'll take care of her."

"Thanks," he said, laying her gently on one of the beds.

"Have a good time?" she asked.

"Yeah, how about you two?"

Caroline gave a sly smile. "Tony and I kind of ditched the group and went to a nightclub near the park. What the heck—it's too late for them to do anything. I mean, we're going home tomorrow. Tony was just saying good night."

"Well, thanks for taking care of her. Guess I'll see you tomorrow."

He walked into the hall, but she followed him out, stopping the door with a foot shod in a red high heel.

"Can I talk to you?" Her usually carefree face was serious.

"Sure."

"Not to sound too high school, but do you like her? I mean, really like her?"

"Yes. I really do, Caroline."

"That other girl, the Arabian princess, you like her, too, though, right?" Is that how Jeanne referred to Liliane? Did girls talk about everything?

"She's not a princess, Caroline. And Jeanne must have told you the doctors say she's not expected to live, so"—he shrugged—"okay?"

"No, I didn't know. I'm sorry," she said, but didn't look satisfied at this evasion. "Just see you treat her right."

"I will. I promise."

42

John walked through the doors of the Berkshire Hotel at three o'clock on Sunday afternoon. Moshe Shertok was sitting in the lobby, reading through a mound of Sunday newspapers scattered on a low table—the *Times*, the *Tribune*, the *Post*, and, John was pleased to see, the *Chicago Sun*—all headlined with news of Saturday's vote. John had read through them anxiously and was relieved to see that no one had the story of Alfagari's assassination attempt and his death. However, as he had feared, there were several snide references to his earlier "unfounded" stories about an assassination plot.

Shertok stood and they shook hands. He motioned John to a sofa while he sank back onto a brocaded wingback chair. Shertok wore a gray suit, white shirt, and a dark tie. He seemed relaxed, even jovial, but there was still the undercurrent of watchful tension John had observed the first time they met, the air of at once engaging with the person in front of him while keeping the entire room under observation. The partition vote was only one battle in a war that would continue.

"You look like you finally got some sleep," John said.

"First night in months, even though we were up till all hours celebrating. You really should have come." Shertok smiled, his salt-and-pepper mustache lifting. "You?"

"We had a little celebration too."

Shertok took his watch from his trouser pocket and began winding it. "I read your article." He nodded at the front page of the *Sun*. "Thank you," he added.

"No thanks necessary—it was the right thing to do."

"Still, it must have pained you not to tell the world about Alfagari and his death. You have taken some abuse from your fellow journalists." He gestured to the pile of newspapers.

John shrugged. "Gives me something to put in my memoirs one day."

"From what I can tell, you already have a number of fascinating stories to tell."

"I suppose. Do you think the Arabs will follow through with their threats?"

Shertok heaved a deep sigh and said softly, "They already have. They ambushed a bus today and killed seven Jews."

"So it will be war?"

Shertok nodded. "Yes." He took a sip of tea and changed the subject. "And Miss Cooper? How is that brave and charming girl?"

"She's well," he said. "You wouldn't know anything had happened."

"The young have amazing recuperative powers," Shertok observed. "And you, Mr. McGrath, you are recovered from your exertions?"

"I'm fine." It was time to move this along. "So, Mr. Shertok, I have a train to catch."

"I'll get to the point, then." He set his watch on the table where he could see it. "You have been to some trouble on our behalf. You have even shed blood," he said, nodding at the small bandage on John's hand where Alfagari's bullet had creased it. "I do not like to think what could have happened without your intervention. Not"—he raised a hand to ward off any comment—"that you didn't have your own reasons to do what you did. But to say we are grateful would be a grave understatement."

"Like you said, I had my own reasons."

Shertok nodded in polite acknowledgment. "From what you told me, it seems you may suffer some adverse consequence with your employer because of acceding to our request, is that not so?"

"You can say that again. It looks like the beauty contest beat for me."

"I think we can do better than that. I understand you would like to work in the sphere of international journalism."

"I would, but there's no way the *Sun* lets me do that now."

"That may be true, but we have friends here. Do you know Whitelaw Reid?"

"He took over the *New York Herald Tribune* from his father a few months ago," John said. "They have the best international reporting of any paper in the country."

"Precisely. I told Mr. Reid about you. He was impressed by your writing, your war record, and everything you've done here. Mr. Reid has offered you a job in the *Herald*'s international section. If things go well, you could be assigned to one of their bureaus overseas."

"You and your friends seem to have a lot of pull."

Shertok pursed his lips. "No, no. The offer is entirely due to your own very substantial merits, Mr. McGrath. All we . . . all I did was bring those merits to Mr. Reid's attention. He was quite free to reject you. It is to your credit only he did not."

"You're not doing me a favor, then?"

Shertok looked surprised. "Not at all, or at least, it is one limited to a simple phone call to a friend. Indeed, one might argue that the only favor here is one we have done for Mr. Reid by bringing a valuable potential employee to his attention."

"That's good, because I have a big favor to ask of you."

Shertok, a veteran of a thousand tough negotiations, settled back in his chair. His eyes took on a look of calculation. "I see."

"There's a woman who needs help. Her name is Liliane. She's a Syrian. She was traveling with their delegation. She gave me the information on Alfagari. When . . . when he found out what she'd done, he shot her in the head." He blinked. "She's alive, but just barely."

"I didn't know. I am very sorry."

"I was thinking that maybe if she had a better doctor, a specialist, they might be able to help her. Even if it's a long shot, I have to do everything I can for her."

"Of course."

"So, specialists are expensive and—"

"You want us to find a specialist and pay for the necessary treatment?"

"If it wasn't for her—"

Shertok waved his hand. "There might not have been a vote, in which case there might not—"

"Be an Israel."

Shertok nodded appraisingly as if to say that was perhaps an over-statement, but he was not prepared to argue the point. "Where is she hospitalized?"

"Bellevue."

"We will do what you ask. Everything that can be done for this poor woman will be done. That leaves us with the offer of employment."

"Thank you. I'd have to move here right away?"

"Obviously."

What would Jeanne say? She'd be sorry that he wasn't coming back to Chicago, but she would hide her disappointment and tell him to take the job. He'd only known her for a few days, but he knew that much about her. And he would be here in New York. He would be able to keep his promise to see that Liliane was cared for.

"You don't strike me as someone concerned principally with money, but, of course, money is important," Shertok said, perhaps thinking that was the reason for his hesitation. "Mr. Reid tells me he would start you at triple what you're making at the *Sun*. And, of course, pay your expenses moving to New York."

"That's quite a raise," he said. But with the talk of money, he suddenly knew why he hadn't said yes. The job offer felt like a bribe for quashing the story about Alfagari. Did Shertok and his compatriots think he could be bought?

"My father had a saying. Would you care to hear it?" Shertok said.

"Sure."

"When God smiles at you, smile back."

"Meaning?"

"Meaning you should accept your good fortune, Mr. McGrath, with-out excessive philosophizing. When someone offers you what you desire, say yes." Shertok leaned forward in his chair. "Come, sir, what is the issue? There are no strings here, no hidden wires, no trapdoor. You wish to take the job? Fine. You decide you don't like it? You go back to your beauty queens. Also fine." He glanced at his watch and sat back. "So, Mr. McGrath, you mentioned you had a train to catch and I, too, have certain demands on my time."

Shertok was right. Who cared what they thought? "I'll wire my resignation to the *Sun* tonight." John wished he could see Hershon's face when the wire came in.

Shertok smiled. "In that case, I have your first story for the *Herald*. It seems the British diplomat Mr. McNeil, who was reported lost at sea, is alive and well in London."

"What? How do you know?"

"I had a transatlantic call with him this morning."

"But how?"

"When he learned he was targeted by the Mufti, he arranged to board the *Queen Mary* last Wednesday."

"Yes, I saw him."

"It was a feint. He slipped off before the ship left port and took a plane to London. But it seems his plane developed mechanical issues and he was in Shannon the last two days while repairs were effected. The rumor of his demise was started by his own Foreign Office to protect him. Now that the vote is over, he is eager to announce to the world that reports of his death—"

"Were greatly exaggerated," John finished.

"Precisely. I told Mr. Reid you would have a good story for him. Here is Mr. McNeil's telephone number." He handed John a card.

John stood. "In that case, I guess I'll be going."

Shertok stood too.

"I'll call Mr. Reid first thing tomorrow morning," John said. "Thank you, sir. For everything. I hope we meet again."

"I do too. Truly."

They shook hands and John walked out of the hotel. On impulse, he wandered uptown into the park and stopped at the pond. Ice partially covered its dark water and a half dozen ducks were swimming in widening circles. Why hadn't they left for the winter? As if on an unseen signal, they flapped into the air, slowly at first, then climbing quickly. He watched until they were tiny dots in the darkening Manhattan sky.

There was only a half hour until their train left. He walked to Columbus Circle, took the A train to Penn Station, and trotted to the railroad level.

Father Bernard and the two nuns, Sister Mary and Sister Rose, were walking back and forth on the platform like sentries in front of the four cars of the Pennsylvania "General" reserved for the students. Some of the windows were open and excited voices bubbled inside.

"Mr. McGrath," said Father Bernard, "we've been looking for you. Your luggage is already on board."

"Well, that's very nice, but as it turns out, I'm not going back to Chicago. I've been offered a new job with a paper here in New York and I have to start right away. I need to get my bag before the train leaves." He climbed the steps onto one of the cars and retrieved his suitcase. As he returned the way he came, Jeanne was standing a dozen feet away from him, a stricken look on her face. Caroline was next to her. She looked angry.

"So, Mr. Big Shot. You picked the princess," Caroline said.

He ignored her. "Jeanne, I have something to tell you."

"No need," Caroline said in a steely tone. "We heard." She gestured at the open train window. "You're in the big leagues, now."

He had known this would be difficult. Caroline was making it worse. "Can I talk to you?" he said to Jeanne.

"I don't think she needs to hear anything you have to say," Caroline said. She plucked at Jeanne's sleeve. "Come on, let's go to our room."

"Just let me talk to you," he said.

"Okay," she said softly.

"Jeanne," Caroline said, still pulling on her arm.

"No, Caroline," Jeanne said, gently disengaging her arm. "I want to . . . to say goodbye."

"Two minutes," yelled the conductor from the other end of the car.

"All aboard," a voice shouted outside the train.

"Come on!" John motioned her to the vestibule, picked up his bag, and they walked down the steps onto the platform. The smell of diesel fouled the damp, chill air. He set his suitcase down and stood close to her so he could be heard over the noise of the engine.

"Mr. Shertok got me a job on the international desk at the *New York Herald*. I want to start tomorrow because I already have a story."

"The *Herald*? John, that's wonderful!"

He was relieved.

"So, you understand why I can't go back with you?"

She bit her lip, then smiled. "Yes. And I know where I'm going to apply to college."

"Here?"

"Yes."

"Perfect."

"All aboard," a voice shouted again.

"I want to tell you all about it," he continued. "I'll call and I'll come home for Christmas, okay? That's just three weeks away."

She nodded again, then climbed onto the first rung of the stairs to the car. It put their heads at the same height. "I wish—" she said.

"We had more time," he said.

"We have enough for this," she said and flung her arms around him and kissed him hard on the lips. He put his arms around her and returned her kiss, lifting her off the step. The train began to move slowly. John kept pace awkwardly. They finally broke their kiss and he set her down on the moving step, still holding her hand and trotting along.

"I'll call you tomorrow," he said.

The train's speed increased. He let go of her hand and they stood looking and waving until a slight bend of the track took them out of each other's sight.

He turned and walked to the stairs, suitcase in hand, still alive with the scent and warmth of Jeanne's embrace. He needed to find a place to stay tonight, but, remembering his promise to Liliane, he put his suitcase in a locker and took the subway to Thirty-Fourth Street and First Avenue and walked to Bellevue. She didn't have anyone else to visit her. An hour of his time was little enough after what she had done for him, what she had sacrificed. He owed his new job—his new life—to her. Shertok was right. Heaven had smiled on him and for once he had thought to smile back.

PART VII

2003

43

Michael stared at his phone, the latest Palm Trēo, trying to decide whether to read the email from his lawyer, Lloyd Dowling, Esq., or pretend he never received it. It was dated today, July 3. The subject line said, "Poverstein, et al." Emily Poverstein was a disgruntled investor who'd been hounding him for months. Whatever the message said, it wouldn't be good news. He tossed the phone carelessly onto the smooth wood table where it spun on its curved back like a tiny break-dancer.

One of his developer friends had insisted he dump his perfectly serviceable flip phone and "join the twenty-first century." He hated his new phone's stumpy little antenna and raised keyboard. Most of all, he hated the fact that it delivered emails to him from six thousand miles away with the same speed and annoying alert tone he received in the office. His flip phone, for all its antiquated deficiencies, never did that to him.

He was on vacation. He longed for the days when he could go away for a couple of weeks and not be bothered. His secretary would have strict instructions not to call unless a death was involved. Now, people had no qualms about disturbing him with any trivial problem, day or night, and expected him to respond immediately. Here he was, sitting poolside at his hotel looking out over the—whatever the hell valley it was—and he was supposed to answer his emails as though he were sitting in his office? He glanced around. His mother and a dozen other hotel guests were stretched out on lounge chairs around the pool hiding from the midsummer heat under huge, green umbrellas. His mother was reading a book, a tall glass and large bottle of San Pellegrino perched in an ice bucket within easy reach.

The phone chirped and vibrated, skittering slowly on the table like a large, gray insect, gently bumping his second glass of beer. With a sigh, he picked up the telephone.

"Michael? Lloyd Dowling here. You have a minute?"

"Well, um, sure. I'm in Italy, you know, but go ahead."

"Bad news, I'm afraid. You read my email?"

"Haven't seen it yet."

"Hmm, I sent it over an hour ago. Anyway, it's the Poverstein claim. I'm afraid they filed suit. Their lawyer faxed me a copy." Michael didn't say anything. "They're suing for a half mil, Michael. They're saying you cheated them."

"Her investment was fifty thousand; how can she sue for half a million?"

"It's not just her. It's all of your investors. They're asking for punitive damages, too. Five million dollars."

"What?"

"But that's nonsense, of course," Dowling hurried on. "Just throwing up a big number to scare you."

They had succeeded—he was terrified. His marriage in the dumper and now this. He'd be broke, divorced, and homeless. He glanced again at his mother, a look of amusement on her face as she flipped a page of her book. She would have to save him now. She couldn't let her son drown in bankruptcy and scandal.

"Jeanne's there with you, right? As she's probably told you, her insurance company finally paid off, so she's, well, in a position to help." Dowling was her lawyer, too.

"Did she get it all, Lloyd?"

"Afraid I can't give you the details," Dowling said primly, as though he hadn't just committed a major breach of ethics. "I'm sure she'll be happy to tell you everything, now that the bastards caved. Imagine, a life insurance company holding a widow to ransom over some minor technicalities in the policy. Unbelievable."

It didn't sound unbelievable. It sounded exactly like most insurance companies he knew. "So, what do we do?"

"You must try to settle. Can you raise any money by selling the property?"

Michael shook his head, then realized Dowling couldn't see him. "It's mortgaged. We're upside down."

"By how much?"

"Does it matter?"

They were upside down by a lot. A longtime friend who specialized in subprime lending had secured a loan for him that far exceeded the value of the property, using an inflated appraisal. The situation worsened every month because the loan rolled the astronomical monthly interest payments into the principal during the first two years. "Don't worry, property values always go up on the Westside," the friend had told Michael.

"There's not a lot we can do in terms of defending this," Dowling continued. "Oh, we can put one of our nasty litigators on the case to drive them to distraction. It'll take them a couple of years to get it to trial. But, at the end of the day, it's their money and the court is going to give it to them. Not to mention what you'll pay us. It'd be best if you could make a substantial offer right away—maybe they'll see it's better to get some of their money back rather than risk spending years in bankruptcy court."

"But, I can't. I don't have—"

"I know."

They were silent for a moment.

"You have to ask her."

"I will," Michael said, sounding more decisive than he felt. "I'll ask her right now."

"You do that. I'm sure she'll help," Dowling said heartily. "Hey, how's It-ly?" He pronounced it without the middle syllable.

He snorted a laugh. "Enlightening."

"Great." Dowling didn't ask what he meant.

"Sure, we'll talk soon," Michael said and ended the call. He took a deep breath and a long swallow of his beer and walked to his mother.

"Hey," he said. He pulled out a chair and turned it so he could face her. It scraped on the stone tile. "How's the book?"

"Terrible and I can't stop reading it."

"Told you."

She took off her reading glasses and pushed up her hat to see him better.

She was wearing a burgundy one-piece bathing suit. There were red broken capillaries and crepey skin on her slender thighs. Her knees, though, were smooth and white. Spidery varicose veins lined her calves. Her ankles were swollen and doughy. Her eyes followed his.

"Why aren't you wearing a bathing suit?" she asked as though anxious to change the unspoken subject of her health. Michael wore a long-sleeved blue cotton dress shirt with his monogram on the left cuff, its tails untucked, tan shorts with no belt in the loops, and dark, wide-stitched leather sandals he bought in Rome.

He gave a brief smile. "Never been much of a swimmer."

"I think they're better," she said, nervously gesturing at her ankles.

He nodded. "Maybe. You seem like you're feeling well these last few days."

She smiled. "I am—really." She paused and then said, "You look serious. Work?"

"'Fraid so." His shoulders slumped and he looked at the ground. "That was the lawyer, Dowling, on the phone. I'm being sued."

"Oh, no. The condo project?"

He nodded.

"What did he say?"

"What do lawyers always say?"

"You must try to settle," she answered, mimicking Dowling's slow, pompous voice.

"You have him exactly. That what he told you with your insurance thing?"

"Yes. But I told him forget it. If what's-their-name, um, Megabillions Life Insurance Company or whatever wants to screw someone, they picked the wrong widow. Let's go to trial, I said, get 'em in front of a jury. You should have seen Dowling squirm." She laughed. "Lawyers hate going to trial. They much prefer a nice, peaceful settlement."

"He said they finally paid up."

"Did he? What else did my lawyer tell you about my business?"

"They gave you the full million, huh?"

The disappointment in her eyes reminded him of other times when he had fallen short of the mark. She registered her unhappiness not with words, but with a look.

"Not at first," she finally said. "We had a settlement conference with a retired judge. He asked what my settlement demand was. I said a million. He said, 'No, no, that's your claim. What is your demand?' He kept telling me I had to make a lower offer—'something less than a million.' He spoke loudly as though I were hard of hearing. I heard one of their lawyers whisper, 'She's so old, she'll never even be able to spend it all.'"

"You're kidding," Michael said.

"No. I told the judge I was insulted and I didn't think he was trying very hard."

"You didn't."

"I did. I got up and walked out. Just before we left on this trip, Dowling called me and said they were—get this—offering nine hundred ninety thousand. Can you believe it? I wanted the million, but Dowling said I had to take it. He was right, of course," she conceded.

He gave her a look of admiration, all the while thinking that she must know he was going to ask for money. She wouldn't be so cruel as to flaunt her wealth unless she were willing to help. This was just her way of telling him he had to fight to make the best deal he could, spend as little in settlement as possible.

"I said they could donate the ten thousand difference to the American Cancer Society in Jim's name. I think that shamed them, if that's even possible with insurance companies. Anyway, I got their check." She leaned back in satisfaction.

"That's a great story," he said. "I only hope my investors don't have your stick-to-itiveness." He looked out across the valley but didn't see its beauty. Waiting wasn't going to make it any easier. "Mom, I do want to settle this. Get those people some money and make a fresh start."

Her expression darkened for a moment, then went blank.

"So," he said, trying to smile.

"So," she said evenly.

"Come on," he said with a short laugh. "You're not going to make me beg, are you?"

She took a deep breath and sat up on the chaise. She put her feet on the tiled deck, faced him in his chair, and put her hands out to him. "Michael."

"I mean, it's not like you don't have the money."

She put her hands in her lap. "I can't—I'm not going to help you with this."

"It doesn't have to be everything. Just something, a chunk of money, two fifty or three even, something meaningful I can put on the table. Please?"

She crossed her arms.

"You have to help me."

She shook her head slowly. "No, Michael, I don't."

He fought back tears. "Mom, this is serious. I'll be bankrupt."

"I know," she said in a low voice.

"Shit, I'll be homeless."

"You know I'd never let that happen."

"I don't believe it," he said angrily, twisting in his chair. "If you won't do it for me, think of Alice, think of Kerry."

"I promise you, Michael, your wife and your daughter aren't going to suffer."

"Oh, fine, great. You'll help them, but you won't help me. You want us to be a happy little family? How's that going to happen if I can't support them?" He shifted in his chair. He wanted to get up, walk away, slam a door, or something. He was aware this was difficult for her but didn't care. "Don't bother trying to explain. I don't want to hear your reasons."

"I'm going to tell you anyway." He turned away from her. "Michael!" He turned back but didn't look at her.

"This is my money. I'm never going to get a sum of money like this again. I want to do special things with it, things for myself. If you think that's selfish, so be it. Helping Alice through school, helping Kerry in her career, taking you all on a trip like this, maybe buying something I really want—those things make me happy. Paying off your debts from a bad business deal will not."

He stared at the ground, baffled and furious.

"Look at me," she said sharply.

He looked up. She took his hands in hers.

"I loved you from the moment I knew I was pregnant. You have been far and away the greatest joy in my life and I know I've been a good mother to you."

His eyes watered. "You have, of course, you have." He heaved a sigh and relented. "I know it's my fault I'm in this predicament. But I can't help it. You've always been there for me—like when someone was mean to me, or I got a bad grade, if I broke somebody's window. Even stuff with Dad, the bad stuff, you always managed to make it better." He gave a reluctant smile. "Inside me, there's still a little kid that figures you'll fix whatever's wrong. So if you think about it, it's actually your fault I'm like this."

"I guess so." She didn't smile but gripped his hands tighter.

He looked off in the distance, blinked, then changed the subject. "You know Kerry's fooling around with that Toljy, don't you?"

"What?" She dropped his hands and sat back. "I don't believe it. Why would you say that? That's just cruel."

For the briefest of moments, he felt a shameful pleasure at puncturing her high opinion of her daughter-in-law. "I saw him coming out of her hotel room at five in the morning. I don't think they were rehearsing."

"But when?" There was real pain in her voice and he had a twinge of regret.

"What does it matter, when? But if you really need to know, it was the last night we were in Rome."

She looked confused and squinted. "The night I went to the opera with her?"

"Right."

She began to laugh.

"Mom!"

She panted a little, gave a cough, and finally did stop. There was still a smile of relief on her face. She took a sip of Pellegrino.

He crossed his arms and stiffly waited for her to explain.

"Michael, I know for a fact where Kerry was the last night we were in Rome and she was nowhere near Toljy. I'm sorry for laughing, honey, but you'll understand why in a second. Kerry and I went to the opera together, remember?"

He nodded once.

"When we got back to the hotel, Toljy was in the lobby, sulking, saying he couldn't find a room anywhere, trying to get her to let him stay in her room. Sister Teresa . . . you remember the old nun at the desk?"

He nodded again.

"Well, Sister Teresa heard him going on and on and told him that, if it was okay with Kerry, he could use her room and she could sleep in one of the sisters' beds in the convent."

"What?"

"So that's what she did. She stayed in the convent." She started to laugh again, but quickly stopped.

"But I heard them in her room."

"You sure it was her voice?"

He wrinkled his forehead. "No, actually, I mean . . . it was a woman's voice. I guess I assumed it was hers since it was her room."

"Well, son, I don't know who was in there with him, but from what I've heard, it could have been just about anyone. When you saw him coming out of her room in the wee hours, Kerry was chastely abed in a locked convent."

A weight of anger, hurt, and sadness sloughed off him like snow slipping from a roof warmed by the sun. She looked at him as though trying to decipher his reaction. "That's why I was laughing. It's just the idea—"

"That she was fooling around when she was literally in a convent." He shrugged and managed a smile. "It *is* funny."

She leaned forward and took both his hands in hers again. "I don't know what's going on with the two of you, but Kerry's not like that. I understand why you might have thought that. I mean—"

"I know," he said ruefully. "He's something."

"So are you, Michael. I know a little bit about women—maybe not quite as much about men." She snorted and looked off, then quickly shrugged. "If Kerry ever decides it's over between you, she'll tell you. She won't run off with someone or embarrass you in front of your family." She held his eyes with hers. "You should know that, too."

He pulled his hands away from her. "You think she's going to want to be with a guy who's broke?"

"I don't think that matters as much to her as it does to you. And you know you'll never be homeless. You and Kerry and Alice can always stay with me. There's plenty of room."

"I know, I know. I was being dramatic." A thought popped into his head, born no doubt of his mother's comparison of Kerry to herself.

"So you'll never guess who I ran into the other day here at the hotel," he said.

"The Pope?"

"Not quite that grand. Guess again."

"Berlusconi?"

"Taller."

"I give up."

"John McGrath. Your friend."

Her lips tightened. "You didn't mention it."

"I know, slipped my mind with everything else going on. The weird thing," he continued, "is I ran into him in Rome too. I didn't know who he was then."

"When was that?"

"Our now-famous last night in Rome. We both ended up in that restaurant at four in the morning. He was drinking pretty heavy. I think he might have known you went out with that professor."

"Oh my god. He never said a word about it." She thought for a moment. "When I told him where we stayed in Rome, he said he stayed nearby."

"Not nearby. The same hotel. He was supposed to be on the same floor but changed his room at the last minute. That's why there was an open room on our floor."

"You're kidding."

"Nope."

"And you saw him again?"

"Just a few days ago. Not such a coincidence, since he lives here and we came so you could visit him. I was waiting for Alice in the lobby and he came to see you the day you went to Assisi. We recognized each other, but then we talked a little more, put two and two together, and figured out who we both were."

"How did he seem?"

"I yelled at him for how he treated you."

"You did?" There was a flash of her warm smile.

"Of course—told him just what I thought of that. He was pretty apologetic."

"He was?"

"He asked me to help him get in touch with you," he continued. "He knows you were upset about what that guy Ricci said. He wanted a chance to explain."

She appeared to draw into herself. "I don't want to hear anything more from him."

"I don't think he's after money, Mom."

"Oh, really? Now you're an expert on John McGrath?"

"No, but I believed him."

She shrugged.

"So, maybe you'll give him a call?"

She shook her head. "I don't think so."

Michael pulled the bottle of Pellegrino from the ice bucket. Most of the ice had melted, but the glass was still cold to the touch. He poured some into his mother's glass. He hefted the bottle and asked, "Do you mind?"

"No, honey, finish it."

He tipped the bottle and let the cool, sparkling water fill his mouth and bathe his dry tongue and throat. He set the empty bottle upside down in the bucket, focused his gaze on his mother, and said diffidently, "I remember him, you know."

She went still and silent. There was a young couple dunking each other in the pool, laughing and splashing. He watched them for a moment.

"He asked if I did. I told him no, but I do," he continued. "When I was ten and we lived in the little apartment on Twelfth?"

"I wondered if you would," she said quietly. "What do you remember?"

"He came with us to the movies, I think?"

She nodded. "A few times."

"And by the beach to ride bikes. And I remember going to the pier, the old one where Pacific Ocean Park used to be."

"Mm-hmm. I wanted you to know each other, but I tried to keep it to a minimum. I didn't want you to get attached until I was sure he'd be around."

"And one Sunday he came over for dinner. You had to leave for a while, so it was just the two of us."

She nodded, remembering. "A friend of mine was sick. I had to run her over to St. John's. What did you do?"

A slow smile moved across his face, then disappeared. "Just watched the Rams on TV while he read the Sunday paper."

"Was that all?"

He swallowed. "Well, we talked some, sports, school, things like that. He was easy to talk to."

"Still is."

"He told me about the stories he was covering. I asked him to explain things and he was very patient. I liked him. By then, Dad wasn't coming much and it wasn't great when he did. I remember wishing John was my father instead. I felt like I could trust him." He looked at her, slowly coming out of his reverie. "I wondered if you'd get married. I was sad when you told me he was gone."

"I was so hurt and angry."

"Are you still?"

"In a different way. Not about what he did, but that he lied to me all these years. When I saw him the other day, he told me the whole story, why he acted as he did."

"What did he say?"

She told Michael about Liliane, about her pregnancy and her illness, their marriage, and about John's son.

"Does all that make a difference?" he asked.

"I think I would have done the same thing. I can't really fault him for marrying the mother of his child, taking care of them . . . not deserting her when she got sick. But why didn't he tell me the truth?"

"Right."

They were silent for a while.

"I am sorry for your trouble. Your business, I mean," she said. "I know it'll be hard on you."

"Sorry for putting you on the spot."

"You didn't. I knew it was why you let me browbeat you into making this trip."

"Right." He toyed with the empty bottle. "Oh, hell, I don't know what's going to happen. There's still a chance I can finish the project and sell the units—if the bank will let me. It's a long shot, but it's a chance. Then everyone will get some of their money back. It depends on the market. With the war, who knows."

He flipped the bottle upright and floated it on the water in the ice bucket. "I guess it's better this way. If I took your money, I don't know when I'd be able to pay you back." He paused. "I don't know how Kerry will take it."

"She's a good person, you know."

"You don't have to convince me. She's my wife."

"She said something similar to me about you."

"Really? When?"

"When she was still in London. I was trying to talk you up—"

"God, you never stop."

She ignored him. "And she said, 'He's my husband, Mom. You don't have to sell me on him.'"

Mist was now drifting throughout the valley. "I miss her. I miss Alice."

She smiled. "Did I tell you about when Alice was here at the pool the other day?"

He shook his head.

"She was like Penelope with the swarm of suitors. There must have been half a dozen young men vying for her attention."

"My Alice?"

"Have you seen her in a bikini lately?"

"Mom, jeez!"

"Don't 'mom' me. She's a looker."

"I didn't think she was that interested in boys."

"Well, she's interested and they are very interested in her."

He squinted at the sun, which was now peeking under the umbrella.

"What's that line Bette Davis said about old age?" he asked. "It's not for sissies?"

They both smiled at the word.

"Right," he said. "Well, being a parent isn't either."

"No matter how old your kid is," she said. "Alice needs you. I was a teenage girl once and I can tell you, she needs her father now more than ever."

"I want her to come home to LA."

She patted his hand. "I think the three of you will work it out. I think your time together on this trip has helped."

He chuckled. "Which was your plan all along."

"What?" She struggled to look innocent.

"Oh, drop it, Mrs. Carpenter. This was all part of your Machiavellian scheme to save our family."

She put her hands in the air. "So I went a little Machiavelli. Where better than Italy?" She lay back on her chaise and looked at him under lowered lids. "You mad?"

"When we first met them in the airport in London and I realized what you were up to, yeah, I was pretty pissed. It felt like you were trying to manage my life."

"Which of course you took to mean—"

"Which of course I took to mean you don't think I can manage it on my own."

"I know I do that."

"I can," he said. She looked at him, then glanced away. "I know, I know," he said, thinking of the lawsuit and of his troubled marriage. "All evidence to the contrary."

"Do you think you ever stop hoping for your child's happiness?"

"Hoping for it is one thing, manipulating is another."

"Well," she laughed, "I don't call it manipulation; I call it applied hope."

"How about applying some of that hope to my lawsuit?" he said. It came out more like a rebuke and less like the joke he had intended.

"Michael—"

"Sorry. It's just . . . it's not going to be easy to make it right," he said bleakly.

"I know. If getting life right was easy, everybody would do it."

44

Jack patrolled the perimeter of Todi's Piazza del Popolo, hoping to see Jeanne. Although she had refused to speak with him in Spoleto or in the week that followed, he still hoped she would respond to his most recent message. The sun had moved below the western rooflines and the piazza was cooler after the day's heat.

It was the Fourth of July and, although this was Italy, many of the buildings were draped with red, white, and blue bunting. John and some other members of the local expatriate American community had arranged for a concert by a local brass band, followed by fireworks, normally prohibited due to the danger of fire in the ancient city center. In the piazza, a low wooden stage opposite the cathedral had several hundred red plastic chairs arranged in a broad fan around it.

He had tried one last email that morning.

Dear Jeanne,

I understand that my actions have created a barrier between us that probably can't be broken. But before you leave, there's something I'd like to show you and something I need to tell you. I hope you'll give me the chance. Meet me in the piazza tonight before the concert?

Ciao,
John

She hadn't replied.

There was still an hour until the concert. Jack walked through the crowd on the steps in front of the cathedral and ran into Signor Barone. He was dressed, as usual, entirely in black. A much older woman with a thin face and an imperious expression stood with him.

"Signor Barone," he said and nodded.

Barone returned his nod. "Signor McGrath. *Felice quattro di luglio.*"

"Thanks. You are here for the concert?"

Barone shrugged and smiled. "Of course. May I present my mother, Signora Barone." Jack nodded. Signora Barone looked down her nose at him and inclined her head a fraction of an inch. "My son is a member of the *banda*—an excellent trombonist. They have been rehearsing for days, a selection of patriotic American standards, as arranged by the great Italian conductor, Creatore."

"How exciting for you," Jack said, bemused at the display of filial pride and duty from a man who had never shown him a softer side.

Barone's thin, dark face relaxed quickly to its usual deadpan look as though exhausted by the strain of smiling. "You will sign the deed to me tomorrow morning at the office of Signor Pelligrini." It wasn't a question.

Jack took a deep breath and let it out slowly, trying to keep his face impassive. "I was hoping you might give me a few days? I, too, have a son. He will be here tomorrow with my grandchildren and we hoped to have a small party for them on Sunday. So, if you could allow us a few days, I would be most appreciative."

"No, that's not possible," Barone said curtly. His mother shot Barone a look of disapproval. They spoke and gestured to each other as they moved to their seats.

A rush of anger shot through Jack. There was nothing right about his house ending up in that man's hands.

• • •

Jeanne was watching the crowd from a corner of the piazza that looked out over the valley. At the opposite end of the square, Alice sat with her friends on the cathedral steps. John was nearby talking to the man, Barone, she had seen with Ricci at John's house.

John looked in her direction and waved. She moved to the stone balustrade at the edge of the terrace and tensed her body, willing him to stay away.

"Jeanne."

She turned.

It was Ernest. A middle-aged woman with flowing dark hair and heavy makeup was with him. She was several inches taller.

"Good to see you, Jeanne. May I introduce Benedetta Giambattisti, my co-professor at the university?"

Benedetta gave a cold smile. "*Piacere.*"

"Pleased to meet you," Jeanne said, turning to Ernest, ignoring the woman's condescension. "What in the world are you doing here?"

"Some of our students told us of the celebration and we thought it might be fun. I understand your friend has arranged a firework display as well?"

"My friend?" Jeanne said. Why did that word grate so?

"Oh, yes, Benedetta tells me he somehow persuaded the town council to make an exception and allow a fireworks display."

"It would not be the first time he has bent the rules," said Benedetta, shaking her head. "Those people he works with."

Jeanne straightened her shoulders. "Meaning what?"

"*I ladri,*" Benedetta said, raising her eyebrows in question at Ernest.

"They're thieves, um, criminals, she means," he said. "You're not here alone, I trust."

"No. I'm meeting my son and granddaughter."

"Ah, well, then, we'll leave you to it. Cheerio."

Benedetta turned and walked away, her heels click-clacking on the gray stones of the piazza. Ernest didn't move. Instead, he asked, "Can I have a quick word?"

Jeanne looked around nervously for John.

"Jeanne," he said, catching her wandering attention. "I just wanted to say goodbye to you."

"I'm so glad. And thank you for what you told me about John. Not that it matters now."

"Your break is irremediable, then?"

"I think so."

"I am truly sorry."

"I am, too. But at least I won't blame him for something he didn't do."

"Ernesto!" Benedetta called.

He turned and waved to her. "I have to go."

"Of course, Ernesto. Are the two of you—?"

"Oh, no, nothing like that. I don't think." A moment of scholarly doubt seemed to intrude. "She's too young for me."

Jeanne thought of the deep crow's feet under her heavy makeup. "Don't be so sure. And don't underrate yourself, Professor." She held out her slender hand and he clasped it in both of his meaty ones. "You know, Ernest, I felt bad about what I said the other day about friendship. I didn't mean friendship's not important to me. Having a good friend is like owning a home. It makes you feel safe."

"And you and I, are we good friends?"

She smiled. "I think so. I hope so."

"I do as well," he said. He gave her hand a final squeeze and then let go.

"Uh, there was one other thing. Very minor, of course." He looked embarrassed.

"Yes?"

She knew what he meant but feigned ignorance. He looked at her beseechingly.

"You did promise."

"Oh, all right, Professor. The Book of Luke."

"Of course, the Bible!" He smacked his forehead. "Serves me right for neglecting my religious studies. A 'great gulf fixed,' the distance between heaven and hell?"

"Exactly. Goodbye, Ernest."

"Farewell, my dear."

He rejoined Benedetta, now sitting close to the stage, with her oversized purse on the seat next to her. Jeanne returned to the balustrade and stood watching the peaceful green valley below. Was that the direction of Casale Leonardo?

"Jeanne?" It was John. He was dressed in khaki-colored pants, a white linen shirt, and a light jacket. Her stomach quickly retied the knots that had loosened while she talked to Ernest.

"Got me at last," she said lightly.

"I wanted to talk to you."

"So you said." She put her hands on the stone balustrade but didn't turn.

"Look at me?" he said softly, coming closer.

She shook her head slowly. "Say what you have to say." Her voice cracked. She wouldn't see Casale Leonardo again and the thought saddened her.

"Okay. Well, I need you to know I didn't say anything to Ricci about you. It never crossed my mind to ask you for money. I don't know where he got that 'rich widow' stuff."

"I believe you."

"You do?"

"You said you had something to show me?" she said, turning toward him, hoping to hurry things along.

"Could we sit? Just for a minute?"

She exhaled deeply. "All right." They sat side by side on a stone bench. He took a document from the inside pocket of his jacket and handed it to her. "What is it?"

"Read it. Careful—it's kind of old."

She opened and smoothed the paper on her thigh. It was a single page of ruled yellow paper, most of its lines filled with writing in pencil.

"Oh, my goodness! This is the article outline you wrote in the pressroom. Right after the vote. It has the quotes I gave you."

"Did you read the note at the bottom?"

It was written in blue ink in the round and graceful *écriture* cursive script taught in French Catholic schools a hundred years ago.

Dear Mr. McGrath,

I found this page in one of Aubrey's notebooks a few months before he passed away. I will never forget that day, of course, or your courage nor the righteous decision you made without regard for your career.

I showed it to Aubrey. He could no longer speak but he wrote, "Send it to him. He and his dear young friend should tell their story to the world." I truly hope you—both of you—do so if you're able.

With great esteem,
Suzy Eban

"Amazing he kept this all these years," Jeanne said, handing it back to him.

"Probably kept everything—he trained as an historian, remember."

"I don't know what to say," she said.

He smiled and said, "Well, you could say you'll help me tell the story."

She got up and stepped toward the balustrade. "You don't need me."

"I do, but not just for the book. For me."

"Meaning I'm what you want, now I'm all that's left?"

"That's not fair, Jeanne."

"I don't care about fair!" she burst out, rounding on him. "I'm not a judge! Why would I come here, uproot my life, leave the people I love? For what?"

Her vehemence seemed to scare him silent.

"You say you want me," she went on, "but there was always something else you wanted more—your career, Liliane and your family, now your house, this book."

"I wanted you. I still do."

"To *go along* with your house, to *help* you write your book."

"No, that's not it. Sure, I love my house, but I'm—" He stopped and they were silent. Finally, he said, "There's something else."

She didn't respond.

"The offer from my publisher is contingent on you agreeing to be my co-author. No Jeanne, no book."

"What? Why?"

"He said so from the beginning, especially after I told him about Mrs. Eban's note."

"You never said."

"Because I didn't want you to feel obligated to do it."

"So why tell me now?"

"Maybe I don't care so much about being fair, either." He looked down, then back at her. "The book wouldn't be about me—it would really be about you." He stood and took a step toward her, but she turned away and returned to the balustrade. "Even if we can't share anything else, we could share this."

She took a deep breath and, when she was sure her voice wouldn't tremble, said, "You should go."

"Jeanne—" he started, and then stopped.

Her voice broke. "Be happy in your house, John. Write your book with my blessing. But leave me out of it." Jeanne tensed her shoulders, afraid he would touch her to try to bridge their unbridgeable past. After a minute, she said, "John?"

He didn't answer.

She turned. He was gone.

•••

Jeanne walked slowly up the steps of the cathedral where Alice, Geoffrey, and a half dozen other teenagers were sitting, waiting for the concert to start. Alice wore dark shorts and a sky-blue top. She leaned forward, resting her arms on her smooth, tanned legs that were crossed in front of her. Geoffrey was drinking a Peroni—it was obvious he was doing his best not to stare at the spot where the vee of her top slightly exposed her breasts.

"Hi, Alice," Jeanne said. "This must be Geoffrey." She was out of breath from her climb.

"You look tired," Alice said, standing up.

"I'm fine."

"Geoffrey, this is my grandma, Jeanne Carpenter."

Geoffrey set down his bottle of beer and wiped his mouth with the back of his hand. He stood up and reached out his other hand. "I've heard a lot about you, Mrs. Carpenter."

She took his hand. "I've heard about you too, Geoffrey. I hear you want to be an artist."

He looked at her suspiciously, as though trying to decide if she was making fun of him. "My parents want me to be a banker or a lawyer, but I've been drawing and painting since I was little and I feel like I have to give it a try."

"You've been visiting the museums here?"

"Yeah, it's been great."

"You want to paint?"

"Yes and no. I don't think you just do one thing anymore. The lines aren't so clear, you know—painting, sculpture, digital, whatever."

"Down, boy," Alice said.

"Sorry," he said with a grin. "I get kind of stirred up about art."

"Good for you."

Alice pointed to John standing on the terrace above the crowded piazza. "Did you talk to him?"

Jeanne tensed. "I did."

"How did that go?"

"Like you'd think."

"The 'rich widow' comment?"

"Uh, no. That wasn't him. It was Ernest."

"The professor?"

"Right. I guess he made sort of a joke to his friend Benedetta; then she passed it on to Ricci, who said it to me."

"What else did he say?"

"He still wants to write that book together. And he insists I'm what's most important to him."

"That's pretty romantic," Geoffrey said.

"What did you say?" Alice said.

"I told him that it was clear his house is what matters most to him."

"What did he say to that?"

"That was pretty much it."

"That's all?" Alice was shifting from one foot to the other.

"Mm-hmm. Why?"

"He didn't tell you?"

"Tell me what?"

"He's selling his house!"

A flutter of excitement laced with panic ran through her. "What?"

"He is! He told me. And Dad too. He asked us not to tell you, but I had to. He said you were what mattered to him most, and he wanted to be sure you knew that."

"Why didn't he tell me?" Jeanne said.

"He didn't want it to be just words. He wanted it to be—"

"*A fait accompli*," Geoffrey said.

Alice rolled her eyes. "—a done deal."

Jeanne shook her head. "I–I don't understand. He's going to sell the house? Or he already has?"

"He's going to!" Alice said. "To that scary guy over there, Mr. Barone. He loaned John some money for the renovation or something. But it's not final until tomorrow, Saturday."

"How in the world do you know who Mr. Barone is?"

"Jeez, everyone knows him. He's like the local godfather," Geoffrey said.

"Is it okay that I told you?" Alice said.

"Yes, yes, of course."

"So? You gonna talk to him about it?"

"To John? I don't know, maybe." Jeanne was suddenly full of impulsive energy. "I'll see you later," she said over her shoulder as she walked down the steps. "Nice meeting you, Geoffrey."

•••

Kerry walked away from the ticket office at the bottom of the hill and approached the tiny platform at the end of the stairs, where one boarded the Todi *ascensore* for the minute-and-a-half ride from the parking lot up to the historic center of the city. She was hypnotized by the sight of a car climbing away against the trees until it looked like a tiny toy and then, as it returned, becoming larger until it swung and rattled to a stop at the platform.

She stepped up to the car and checked her reflection in its glass door. She straightened the square-cut neckline of the midlength, mint green linen dress she wore. The door suddenly whooshed open and she jumped in surprise.

Kerry was afraid of heights. Planes and elevators didn't bother her, but standing near the window of a tall building or a cliff or riding up a steep hill in a glassed-in railcar paralyzed her with fear. She considered walking the half mile up the hill, but she had agreed to meet Alice at seven thirty and it was already a quarter past. She took a breath. *It'll be okay, just close your eyes.* Her breath was coming quickly. As though tiptoeing toward the edge of a precipice, she stepped into the car. The door snapped closed and she was trapped.

The car lurched and began to climb with a loud, uneven clanking. How old was the thing? Each clank sounded like it might be its last. She pictured it slipping and sliding down the aged cables and crashing into the massive concrete wall at the bottom, leaving it a smoking wreck and her body a mangled mess. She gripped the handrail and closed her eyes.

The car finally shuddered to a stop. She opened her eyes. A man with a lined, brown face gestured to her with a cupped hand. "*Venga, signorina, venga.*" When she didn't move, he reached out a hand and guided her over the yawning, four-inch gap between the car and the platform. She stepped onto the solid stone of the walkway near the street.

"*Dov'è la piazza?*" she said.

He answered in Italian and pointed to a sign with an arrow directing her toward the center of town. Standing a safe distance from the edge of a stone wall that separated the street from the cliff, she exhaled with relief. Plenty of time to meet Alice. She walked up the street toward the piazza. Just as the road veered to the right, she saw Michael emerging from a tiny shop with a small red door. They hadn't spoken in days. He had a small package in one hand. A wooden sign over the door said, "Gioielleria di Todi."

He was neatly dressed in pressed jeans and a light-colored blazer. He didn't seem to be able to look at her. She smiled and waited for him to realize she was glad to see him.

Paradoxically, her triumph in Spoleto and the encomiums of her fellow artists—accompanied by Nelson's mention of a teaching job—had injected a healthy note of realism into her dreams of success rather than putting more stars in her eyes. While it wasn't impossible that she might achieve fame, she knew that one successful engagement wouldn't move the needle enough to do so. Her loneliness since moving to New York, coupled with watching Jeanne navigate challenging relationships with erstwhile boyfriends at seventy-three years old, made her long for the stability and companionship of her family and her husband.

"Michael," she said with more warmth in her voice than there had been for months.

He finally looked up.

"Um, hi," he said. "Alice asked me to meet her on the cathedral steps."

"Me too."

"Funny she didn't mention you were coming."

"Same."

He looked at his watch. "The concert doesn't start for another half hour. Can we, um, would you mind talking for a few minutes?"

"I'd like that."

"There's a little pizzeria just up the road. We could sit?"

"That sounds nice."

"It's this way," he said, gesturing. They walked side by side along a narrow street until they reached a stone staircase that went down to the restaurant. They entered the dining room, which had a wide terrace with a view of the valley. Michael waved to a man behind a bar and pointed. The man nodded and continued his work. Michael led her to a small table at the rim of the terrace. There was a straight drop down the hill.

"Uh-oh, too close for you. Maybe this one?" he said, pointing to a table farther from the edge. "Hey, how'd you do coming up the funicular?" he said as they took their seats.

"I closed my eyes and thought of England." They laughed together for the first time since she had moved to New York. A waiter approached.

"A glass of wine, slice of pizza?"

"Wine," they said in unison.

The waiter ran through the options and they ordered a half bottle.

"I wanted to—" they said in unison.

"You first," she said.

"I don't know why I'm so nervous."

"I am too."

They sat in silence until the waiter returned with their wine. He seemed to take forever to open the bottle. They drank eagerly.

"I wanted to say how sorry I am for that business about Toljy," Michael began. "I should never have said any of that."

"No, you shouldn't have."

"Mom told me about that night, you staying in the convent."

"Michael, that doesn't—"

"I know. I should have believed you without that."

"Yeah." She looked at him shyly. "I don't—I mean, I haven't done anything since we've been apart."

"Me neither."

"And I get it," she said. "You saw him come out of my room. It wasn't weird that you wanted an explanation, but—"

"I didn't give you a chance to explain."

"Right."

He looked off in the distance. "That's as close to crazy as I've ever been. But why didn't you just tell me?"

"I'm not like that. It made me so mad you could think I was."

"Aren't all women like that?" He smiled to show he was joking.

"Mozart on women, Michael? Really?"

"He wasn't such an expert?"

"Hardly."

"Kerry, I'm so proud of you. You got this chance and you're a hit."

"Thanks. I'm kind of proud of me too."

"Where to next? Paris, Vienna, London?"

She paused a moment, then said, "I kind of like the idea of Los Angeles."

"What?"

She touched his hand. "I want to come home, if that's okay. I miss you. So does Alice."

"I miss you guys, too." He held her hand for a moment, gingerly, tentatively, and then removed it. "What about your career?"

"Don't tell anybody, but Maestro Nelson is coming to LA. He said he'll put in a word for me."

"Really?"

"They have a teaching position opening up in their young artists program."

"A teacher, huh?"

She assumed a stern expression, daring him to comment further.

He put both palms up. "I didn't say a word."

"Very wise."

"Have you said anything to Alice?"

"No, I hoped we could tell her together."

He took her hand. "I have to tell you something. The condo project—"

"You're being sued. Mom told me. I'm so sorry."

"I'll be starting from scratch."

She shook her head. "I don't care."

"Really?"

"Really. We'll be a family, living in a regular-size apartment instead of that home for hobbits Alice and I are in."

He nodded. "Right, in fact we can stay with Mom until we get things going again."

She remembered him coming out of the store. "Hey, what's in the package?" It was on a chair beside him.

"It's for you."

He took a heart-shaped wooden box out of the bag and handed it to her. It smelled like cedar. Inside the box, there was a velvet bag and inside the bag there was a large diamond solitaire on a thin chain.

"Oh, Michael, it's so beautiful!" Unlike some women, jewelry had never been the way to her heart. But in this case, he had found exactly the right thing. She was overwhelmed. "Silver?"

He shook his head. "Platinum. I know it's early—platinum is for the twentieth anniversary—but I thought I'd take a leap of faith."

"I'm glad you did."

He unclasped the catch and helped her put it on. She touched the jewel and chain where it now lay on her skin as he put his hands on her shoulders and they kissed.

"We should get moving," she said softly.

"Okay." Michael put some euros on the table and, hand in hand, they walked the short distance to the piazza.

"Oh, look—there's Mom," Kerry said. "Who's that she's talking to?" She waved with her free hand. "Jeanne!"

Jeanne was speaking with a slender elderly woman with a forbidding expression, standing with a man in an unseasonable black suit. She waved when Kerry called her name but continued talking. When she was finished, the woman slowly nodded and shook Jeanne's hand. The man shrugged and then nodded, too. Jeanne walked over to where Kerry stood with Michael.

"Who was that you were talking with?" Kerry said.

"Another new boyfriend?" Michael said, looking at Kerry with a goofy smile.

"What's with you two?" she said distractedly.

"I don't know what you mean," Kerry said.

They were holding hands and swinging them back and forth. Jeanne looked at their faces. "Oh." She hugged them both. She held them for a moment, then released her grip and said briskly, "I've got to go."

"What?" Kerry said.

"I'll explain later. Bye."

•••

From his perch on top of the exterior stone steps of the Palazzo del Popolo, Jack looked out over the crowd seated for the concert. Jeanne sat with Alice and a teenage boy on one side and Michael and Kerry on the other. Michael and Kerry were holding hands. *He must have decided to forgive her.* Signor Barone was with his mother in the front row, opposite the trombone section. Benedetta and Ernest were a few rows back. One of her hands was on his shoulder. None of them looked in his direction.

The conductor, a tall, thin man in his seventies, took the stage. He gestured to the band to rise, then turned to acknowledge the crowd's applause.

His hair and mustache were dyed a brilliant black. The band members were dressed in white uniforms and caps, trimmed with gold braid. They launched into a lengthy medley of operatic marches from *Norma*, *Aida*, and *Carmen* to the delight of the Italians in the audience. The conductor led with quick, jerky movements of his arms, his body bending back and forth as he coaxed every nuance of sound from the musicians.

The band segued into a series of songs one might hear at any Fourth of July celebration—"You're a Grand Old Flag," "This Land Is Your Land," and "Anchors Aweigh," followed by a slow, haunting rendition of "America the Beautiful," which the brass band played as softly and sweetly as a string ensemble. When they were finished, the conductor turned to the applauding crowd and signaled for silence. His face was damp with sweat in the twilight warmth and he dabbed at his high forehead with a snow-white handkerchief. The sky behind him was pearl gray, streaked with dying pink-and-red embers of sunlight. Jack started down the steps and moved through the crowd toward the stage.

"*Signore e signori, ospiti onorevoli,*" the conductor began and then switched to English. "I try English, you know, for the holiday. Ladies and gentlemen, honorable guests"—here he bobbed his head at the mayor and members of the town council who were sitting near Signor Barone—"thank you for attending our concert this night. Before we finish and all the fireworks, our *sindaco* ask a local American man give us some words to the honor of the holiday. Ladies and gentlemen, *il nostro amico*, Jack McGrath."

Jack bounded up the few steps to the platform and walked to the center of the stage. There was some polite applause.

Jack nodded to the conductor. "Thank you, Maestro. We are grateful to you and to your wonderful musicians for a spectacular concert," he said, turning sideways and gestured.

There was more applause, louder and longer this time.

"To my Italian friends," he said in their language, "thank you for permitting this celebration on a day that is full of meaning for every American, a day—" Jeanne was staring at him intently. He faltered. "A day, that is, on which our ancestors declared not just their independence, but created a country where people were free to pursue those things in life that will make them happy."

He switched back to English and gave a brief translation of what he had said, then continued. "There are those who might say that the pursuit of happiness is a vain one—"

Jeanne was whispering in Alice's ear. Alice nodded and gave her a hug. They both had the same look of pleasure.

"—but we Americans believe it is our birthright. For the last few years, I've tried to pursue happiness here, and although I have failed at some of my pursuits—"

Alice bounced in her seat. Jeanne grabbed her arm. What was going on?

"—I will always cherish the friends I've made in this town. I'll be leaving soon and returning to my country."

There were a few demurring rumbles from the crowd. Alice and Michael and Kerry all shot looks at Jeanne. She smiled.

"I will never forget the happiness I have known here with you. Thank you from the bottom of my heart. *Addio a tutti.*"

There were shouts, cheers, and some applause. The conductor stepped forward and the band burst into "Stars and Stripes Forever." Fireworks flashed over the dark piazza. Jack retreated to its edge, but he didn't watch the fireworks. He watched the faces in the crowd as they were illuminated by the gold and red and blue of the rockets' flares. Some of them he knew well. Some he had just met.

One he loved.

He walked out of the piazza and headed to the *ascensore*. A dark mass loomed before him in the twilight. It was Signor Pelligrini.

"Signor Jack?"

"Yes?"

"That was a nice speech. I do need to remind you—"

"I know. We have the deed to sign in the morning."

"I'm sorry." Pelligrini seemed upset.

"Me too. I'll see you at nine."

"Yes, and remember that Sunday—"

"No chance, I suppose, I can still have the party?" He grinned to show he didn't really expect a yes.

"No, *dispiace*, Signor Jack. I am sorry. The new owner was quite clear."

Evidently, even he didn't like to say Barone's name.

Jack nodded. "It's okay. I moved to a hotel. I'll come out Sunday around noon to get the rest of my stuff."

"Again, I'm sorry, Signor Jack."

"Not your fault."

"Still." Pelligrini raised his eyebrows in sympathy.

"Yeah."

Sal was arriving in Todi tomorrow with his wife and children, one bright spot in this dismal situation. He hadn't told them yet about the house, but they knew something was up.

He climbed into a funicular car and headed down to the parking lot. The first cold stars glistened in the heavy black sky. Regret rippled through his body and curdled inside. What a waste. What a damnable waste.

45

On Sunday, Jack drove slowly down the hill from Todi, as though the longer he took to get to Casale Leonardo, the longer it would remain his. The aging Alfa Romeo spit and coughed black exhaust as he downshifted to spare the worn brakes. From long habit, he subconsciously counted each curve in the narrow road.

Thirty-three.

Thirty-four.

He had signed the deed to Barone at the bank yesterday. Casale Leonardo was his no longer. But it wouldn't be real until he saw for himself it was in the hands of others and removed his things.

"He's stealing it, you know. It's worth twice what he paid," Jack said glumly when he met Pellegrini in his office.

Pelligrini had shrugged but said nothing. He handed Jack a gold pen and gestured to the documents before them. There were yellow highlights at the places he needed to sign or initial. "Signor Jack, please?"

He studied the banker carefully. Was Pelligrini suppressing a smile at his misfortune? *Bastard!* No, he must be mistaken. It was his imagination—he'd been so sympathetic the other day.

He turned to the first page, raised the pen, and began signing and initialing the documents. He handed them to Pelligrini who stamped them in several places with a decisive thwack. "Addio, Casale Leonardo," he murmured.

"Very good, Signor," Pelligrini said, seemingly relieved at his acquiescence. "But let us be hopeful and say only *arrivederci*."

"No," he said. "This is final."

"Only death is final," Pelligrini said.

"Death seems very near today." It sounded melodramatic, especially in Italian.

Pelligrini was chagrined. "No, do not say that!" He crossed himself. "You are sad. That is understandable. But this is not the end. Fortunes can change in an instant, is it not so?"

"You are right. Anything can happen, even at my age. Farewell."

They stood and shook hands.

"And I will just say ciao," Pelligrini said and escorted him through the door.

Seventy-eight.

Seventy-nine.

He was driving through brown fields on a flat stretch of road. It was almost noon and the interior of the car, its air-conditioning still broken, was sweltering. He should get it fixed. No, what was he thinking? He was going to sell the car and buy another in America—one suited to Chicago winters.

He'd asked Sal to accompany him on this dismal task of picking up his few remaining belongings and saying goodbye to his dream. Sal had said he'd promised his twin teenage boys a shopping trip to Perugia for their birthday and would be gone most of the day.

"You can shop anytime, and their birthday isn't till Monday," he had protested, hurt at Sal's refusal.

"You try explaining that to them," Sal responded. "Come on, Dad. You'll be there and back in no time and we'll all meet at the hotel for dinner. We have three more days before I have to go to Rome—plenty of time to hang out. Try to have a good day," Sal said, rushing off the phone.

"Jeez, Jack, stop feeling sorry for yourself," said a clear voice in his head that sounded like Jeanne. He swayed and jounced around another unbanked curve. "Perhaps Signor Pelligrini is correct. It isn't goodbye, it's just ciao."

He could imagine the laugh in her voice and her lips curved in a smile at their old joke.

The hell with that. I'm entitled to feel sorry for myself.

"No, you're not, you stupid bastard," said a harsher voice he couldn't identify. "You're pretty fucking lucky."

It was his old boss, his editor at the *Sun*, what was his name? He struggled to remember. *Herelick? Hirschtik? Hershey? Like the chocolate? No, I'd remember that. Hershon. That's it.*

Jeanne's voice chimed in again, less astringent this time. "John, you have a son and grandchildren who love you. You can still work if you want, write your book. Count your blessings."

The car's worn tires rattled on the bumps and ruts on the road's next curve. For once, he'd lost track of the number.

Jeanne. Oh, Christ. How had he managed to screw that up? Again. Despite everything, she still loved him. He was willing to bet on that, although she had denied it. So make another try, Jack. Maybe after she gets back home. Surprise her at the house in Santa Monica Canyon he hadn't seen since the two of them had toured it thirty years ago. He better hurry. That guy Ernest was probably out of the picture, but who knew who else might make a play for her, seventy-three or no seventy-three?

He was close now, climbing through the last hills before the house. The highway narrowed and there was a sheer drop-off at its right edge. He hunched forward and watched the road carefully.

No, the idea of rekindling what they had was ridiculous. He had lost her. They were finished.

A horn blasted. His head jerked up.

Jesus!

A huge flatbed truck almost as wide as the narrow road stacked high with wooden wine barrels was heading straight for him. The horn screamed again, but the driver didn't slow down.

He was seized with a desperate calm. *Fine, then. I've had a good, long life. If this is it, this is it.*

He steeled himself for the impact. The truck was approaching fast, its horn sounding continuously. A thin dirt and gravel verge lay ahead, if only he could reach it. He downshifted, stomped on the accelerator, and shot forward, trying to skirt around the fast-approaching truck. His right tires spun on the edge, but the other two held the road. He made it to the dirt strip, slammed on the brakes, and came to a sliding, dusty halt, the truck blasting by, only inches away.

He was covered in sweat, panting with fear, his heart bouncing in his chest. He shifted into first gear and lurched back onto the road, and arrived at the house minutes later.

It seemed more desirable than ever, like a beautiful girlfriend who had moved on to another man. It was hot and quiet. The house felt deserted.

If Ricci or Barone are here, just be polite. Go in, smile, get your stuff, and leave. No long last looks. Cut the cord and rip the thing out of your heart.

He stopped the car on the rise, gripping the wheel so tightly his hands hurt. He fought and struggled but, at last, his chest heaved.

• • •

"It's him," Alice called to Jeanne.

"Shush. He'll hear you," Jeanne said quietly to Alice from her perch on the huge bed in the master bedroom. She and some others were gathered in the master bedroom on the second floor of the house. Alice was on the landing at the top of the exterior stairs peering around the corner of the outside door.

"What's he doing now?" Jeanne said. Her feet didn't quite touch the floor and she was swinging them in her excitement.

"Um, he stopped on that little hill at the entrance to the driveway."

"Let me see," said Geoffrey, tilting his head around the corner, his hand resting on Alice's shoulder. "He's just sitting in his car. Sal, come see."

"Go look," Jeanne suggested.

Sal McGrath, Jack's son, went out of the bedroom. He was tall, though not quite so tall as Jack. His black hair was sprinkled with gray, but his face was unlined. His skin was light olive. He had his father's blue eyes, firm mouth, and, she had already observed, his sense of humor. Although they'd only met twenty-four hours ago, she was already fond of him. Sal's shy, dark-eyed wife sat nearby in a leather armchair. Their twin fourteen-year-olds were not there, having been banished to one of the rear bedrooms because they could not be relied upon to stay quiet. They had protested mightily, arguing that this was supposed to be their birthday party, but their continued squabbling was muted as Sal closed the door on them.

Pelligrini, the banker, had told Jeanne where Sal and his family were staying and she had called him yesterday afternoon. She told him who she was and that she wanted to buy John's house from Barone.

"Wow! Are you sure this Barone guy will go for it? My dad says he's a real tough customer."

"I think so, but I don't want to tell your dad unless it's really done and everything's signed. I don't trust that man."

"Why are you doing this?"

It was the question she'd asked herself since she found out John was selling the house and had decided to intervene. There were reasons she could point to, but, in the end, it was simply because she wanted to.

"Because it makes me happy."

"That I understand," Sal said.

"Anyway," she said, "he's going out there at noon to pick up his things and say goodbye. If we can get Barone to sign off by then, I hope instead we'll be there to meet him, maybe have a little surprise party to celebrate. I spoke to Signor Pelligrini and to Antonio. They said they'll help."

Sal had laughed. "If you can pull it off, that's going to be the nicest surprise anyone ever got. Listen, I'm on my own this afternoon. Dad took the kids and my wife sightseeing. Would you like to meet for coffee?"

"That'd be nice. I have to see Mr. Pelligrini at the bank anyway."

"Good. It'll be nice to finally meet the famous Jeanne."

"It will be nice to meet you too, Sal."

Sal returned to the bedroom. "He's crying."

"What?" Jeanne said.

"His head's down. I think he's crying."

"Oh, shoot, I didn't think this through," she said. "I feel terrible."

"Me too," Sal said. "I'll go tell him."

"Too late, he's coming," Alice and Geoffrey called out as they dashed into the bedroom.

"Leave the door ajar," Jeanne said in a loud whisper.

"Hey, boss." It was Antonio, his voice filtering up from the first floor.

"Not your boss anymore," Jack said, his voice low but strong.

"Maybe not," Antonio responded.

"Anybody around?" Jack asked. The tone of his voice said he was hoping the answer was no.

Antonio didn't answer immediately.

"He's going to give it away," Alice whispered loudly.

"Shh!" Kerry said. She was standing behind Alice with Michael. He put a hand on his daughter's shoulder.

"No, boss, just us," Antonio said.

"I guess I better get my stuff. It's all upstairs?"

"Yes, boss." Antonio stifled a sound.

"Are you laughing?" Jack asked, hurt in his voice.

"Me, boss? Never. I'm sad. *Molto triste.*"

"Okay, thanks," Jack said, his voice full of suspicion.

There were footsteps on the stairway. A moment passed; then the door to the master bedroom swung open. Jack was there, Antonio a step behind him. Jeanne bounced off the bed onto her feet. Everyone in the room stood, with the kind of silly half smiles you see at surprise parties. Jack looked at Jeanne and she looked at him. The grim expression on his face eased and changed to one of puzzlement.

"I thought you were gone," he said, his voice shaking a little.

"I thought so, too."

"And never wanted to see me again."

She shrugged very slightly. "I guess I changed my mind."

• • •

An hour later, the house was full of people and Jeanne had still not had a moment alone with Jack to tell him the full story. In addition to Jack's family and Jeanne's, there were guests summoned by Signor Pelligrini from Todi and the surrounding homes. Antonio and his *nonna*, a bustling woman in black, had prepared enough food for a wedding feast. They were everywhere at once, bringing out more food and drink and keeping everything clean.

Jack had visibly relaxed after getting over the shock of discovering his house had not gone to Barone. Now standing in the living room, mellowed by a couple of glasses of chilled prosecco, he said, "Antonio, let 'em make a mess. We'll clean up tomorrow."

"No, boss," Antonio responded somberly, "we have guests coming tomorrow, paying guests. Or did you forget?"

"Guests tomorrow?" Jack said.

"He's right, we do," Jeanne said. She had not left his side since he had arrived in the bedroom upstairs.

"What do you mean 'we'?"

"Um, can we talk outside?"

Jack nodded and gestured to the door.

Her heart thumped. What if he didn't approve of what she'd done? What if, despite, everything he'd said, he didn't want to be with her? She walked outside, turned right, and went past a crowd of people sitting under the pergola laughing and drinking. No one noticed her as she walked down the path. She remembered running there when she had first found out about John and Liliane. Was that only a week ago?

She slowed her pace after passing the pool and came to a stop under the oak tree that looked out over the valley. Jack stopped beside her.

"So maybe you should tell me what's this all about," he said. "You bought my house from Barone?"

She nodded. "For the same amount he paid you."

He looked incredulous. "How in the world did you talk him into that?"

Jeanne smiled. "I didn't, I talked his mother into it. Remember, she was with him at the concert? She made him do it. Even shady Italian men love their mothers."

"Incredible," he said, shaking his head. "So now you own it?" He struggled to control his expression, but she could tell he was shocked. "I guess that's better than Barone."

"Yes, but . . ."

"But?"

She took a deep breath. "I want it to be ours, together."

"What?"

The hopeful expression on his face was almost reward enough for what she had done. She forced herself to speak slowly and evenly. "I want to put it in both our names. It's worth twice what I paid Barone. Mr. Pelligrini said so and he told me you thought so, too. And most of its value is because of all the time and money and hard work you put into it over the last two years."

"So?"

"So I . . . I thought we could be partners."

His expression was neutral, matching her dispassionate tone. She wished she could tell what he was thinking. "But if you don't want me, at least as a partner," she continued nervously, "just say so and I'll sign it over to you. Mr. Pelligrini promised his bank would loan you the money to pay me back—a legitimate mortgage, not like the loan from Mr. Barone."

He put his hands lightly on her slender shoulders. "What else?"

"What?"

"You said 'at least as a partner.' What else besides?"

She was silent. He would have to figure that out for himself.

"Oh," he finally whispered.

She nodded and removed his hands from her shoulders and held them with her own.

"You're sure?" he asked.

"I'm sure. But, Jack—"

"What's with this 'Jack'? I thought I'd always be John to you."

She laughed. "I thought so, too. But somehow Jack suits you better in Italy." She looked away, past the olive groves, toward the valley and the mountains beyond. She nodded to herself. "Maybe you'll be John when we visit the States."

We.

"Reminds me of that Oscar Wilde play," he said.

She laughed again. "Right, Jack in the country, Ernest in town."

"Maybe not Ernest," he said with a grimace. "But seriously, Jeanne, I know you love Italy, but you really want to stay here? With me?"

"I think you'll have to ask another question first to get the answer to that one," she said primly.

"Ah," he said, drawing out the syllable. "Well, I guess at our age a long engagement wouldn't make much sense. I should have done this a long time ago." He began to take a knee. His joints gave a series of almost musical cracks.

"Whoa, whoa, whoa, old man! Get up." She pulled at his hands.

He rose slowly, his knees still clicking.

"Did I misunderstand?"

"No." She kept his hands in hers. "But there's something I need to tell you first."

"What is it?"

"It's . . . I've been seeing a doctor."

"Good god, you're pregnant."

He laughed and she did too. A little too hard. "I wish that were it."

"Now I'm worried."

She grew serious. "I'm sick, John."

His face filled with fear. "Cancer?"

"It's my heart."

She told him everything. It didn't take long. He listened intently, ignoring several shouts of greeting from their guests. When she was finished, he hugged her close and then let her go.

"So, you'll have to have the surgery?"

"Yes." She nodded. "I like to pretend I won't, but that's just fooling myself. The best place to have it is Cleveland. The clinic there."

He shook his head. "There's somewhere else just as good."

She was dubious. "I don't think so."

"Sure, there is, and it's right here in Italy. It's called the Ospedale San Raffaele. In Milan."

"How would you know?"

"I lived in Milan for years before I moved here."

"But is it really that good?"

"Yes. All the best crooks go there, even Berlusconi—and he could afford to go anywhere. And this way, you'll be in beautiful Milan, not Cleveland. I'll be with you the whole time and when you get out, we'll bring you down to Casale Leonardo. You'll stay here."

"For penance? You need absolution?"

"Nobody can give you absolution. It's something you earn. But it isn't that. I want to be with you, Jeanne; I want to take care of you."

She walked a few feet away from him. "You were always looking past me, past whatever you had in front of you, looking for something more, something better."

He stepped forward and turned her gently toward him. "I've stopped looking."

"So I'm your consolation prize?" She tensed with doubt.

He shook his head. "You're what I always wanted most."

"You put on a pretty good show of wanting other things and other people."

"Not anymore."

"Because you're older?"

"Because I'm wiser." He gestured at the house and the surrounding grounds. "Will this be enough for you? Can you be happy here?"

"I want to be here with you. It will be enough."

"Well," he said, "in that case, where was I?" He began to bend his crackling knees again.

"Stop! I don't need you on your knees."

She put her arms around his waist and he wrapped her in his. The familiar scent and feel transported her back to the day they met and all that followed. For a moment, she was alive outside of time and deep in memory—at a table in Union Station with its war-blackened skylights, kissing inside a Pullman car, holding hands in the crowded streets of midcentury Manhattan, sliding through a Chicago covered in Christmas snow, and witnessing the creation of a new world. Then the afternoon shadows shifted and she saw him as he was now—like her—deeply marked by the past but as passionately alive as ever.

"I want you on your feet beside me," she said, "for as long as we both can stand."

They kissed. It felt new and very familiar.

"So I'm a little confused," he said. "You don't want to get married?"

"I didn't say that. Do you think they'd let a couple of lapsed Catholics get married in that church where we met last week?" she asked.

He snorted. "Sure they'll let us. That's why I was there the day we met."

"No!"

"Yep, I wanted to speak to the priest about us getting married there. That's where we'll do it?"

"Yes, let's."

They kissed again. "We probably need to get back to our guests," he murmured. He shook his head in wonder. "I can't believe this is happening."

She took his hand and they started to walk. "Me, neither. I guess we should tell everyone?"

He smiled. "In a while. Let's keep it to ourselves for just a little longer."

• • •

By late afternoon, most of the guests had gone; only family remained. The sun was lower in the sky and, in a short while, it would dip behind the western hills and Casale Leonardo would be in shadow. Antonio and his grandmother were busy cleaning and readying the house for the first paying guests due to arrive the next day.

Those remaining gravitated to the table under the pergola to enjoy the sunset and sweet smell of the evening air. Antonio set out trays of cakes, pastries, and fruit, along with chilled bottles of sparkling water and white wine. The tinkle of silver and crystal accompanied the hum of conversation. Jeanne and John were standing in their *soggiorno*, looking out the window at their families and the setting sun. He walked to the heavy door and opened it. Latticed strips of light and shade swarmed into the room and cast a glow over the ancient wooden beams, yellow walls, and rust-red tiles.

"Scared?" he said.

"Of telling them?" She smiled. "No. They'll be happy for us."

"I know. I meant scared of the future."

She shook her head. "Not a bit. You?"

He paused a moment, then cocked his head and smiled in puzzled wonder.

"Not anymore."

ACKNOWLEDGMENTS

One of the great pleasures of writing *Come November* was meeting and working with the many skilled and knowledgeable specialists at the New York Historical Society, the New York Public Library, the United Nations Headquarters, and the University of California, Los Angeles Library. I want especially to thank Victoria Steele, PhD, UCLA's former Curator of Humanities' Centers, Programs, & Collections, for her kind reception and help researching the United Nations in the 1940s, as well as the intricacies of Leonardo da Vinci's notebooks and his cathedral and residential designs. Thanks also to Bob Roe for his lengthy and incredibly detailed edit of an early version of my manuscript and his myriad helpful suggestions. Special thanks to Yael Medini for reading the portions of the manuscript relating to her father, Moshe Shertok (Sharett) and her recollections of November 29, 1947. Her kind notes greatly assisted in rendering a more accurate portrait of him. Many thanks also to the team at Greenleaf Book Group for their assistance in substantially improving the manuscript and shepherding it to publication.

Finally, I am endlessly grateful to my mother, Gloria Jeanne Fiorda Tidstrand Munger, for the carefully constructed and preserved scrapbook of her trip to the United Nations in November 1947, which inspired this book.

ABOUT THE AUTHOR

SCOTT LORD is a longtime Los Angeles trial lawyer, as well as a writer and librettist. He graduated with honors from the University of California at Santa Cruz and from the Santa Clara University School of Law where he was a member of the Law Review. He and his wife, Susan, are the parents of six children and live in Santa Monica, California. His previous novel, *The Logic Bomb*, a legal thriller, was published in 2015.

ABOUT THE AUTHOR

SCOTT LORD is a longtime Los Angeles trial lawyer, as well as a writer and librettist. He graduated with honors from the University of California at Santa Cruz and from the Santa Clara University School of Law where he was a member of the Law Review. He and his wife, Susan, are the parents of six children and live in Santa Monica, California. His previous novel, *The Logic Bomb*, a legal thriller, was published in 2015.